VENOM OF THE
MOUNTAIN MAN

VENOM OF THE MOUNTAIN MAN

WILLIAM W. JOHNSTONE
with J. A. Johnstone

PINNACLE BOOKS
Kensington Publishing Corp.
www.kensingtonbooks.com

PINNACLE BOOKS are published by

Kensington Publishing Corp.
119 West 40th Street
New York, NY 10018

PUBLISHER'S NOTE
Following the death of William W. Johnstone, the Johnstone family is working with a carefully selected writer to organize and complete Mr. Johnstone's outlines and many unfinished manuscripts to create additional novels in all of his series like The Last Gunfighter, Mountain Man, and Eagles, among others. This novel was inspired by Mr. Johnstone's superb storytelling.

All Kensington titles, imprints, and distributed lines are available at special quantity discounts for bulk purchases for sales promotions, premiums, fund-raising, educational, or institutional use. Special book excerpts or customized printings can also be created to fit specific needs. For details, write or phone the office of the Kensington sales manager: Kensington Publishing Corp., 119 West 40th Street, New York, NY 10018, attn: Sales Department; phone 1-800-221-2647.

ISBN-13: 978-0-7860-3364-5
ISBN-10: 0-7860-3364-9

First printing: December 2017

10 9 8 7 6 5 4 3 2 1

Printed in the United States of America

First electronic edition: December 2017

ISBN-13: 978-0-7860-3365-2
ISBN-10: 0-7860-3365-7

THE JENSEN FAMILY
FIRST FAMILY OF THE AMERICAN FRONTIER

Smoke Jensen—*The Mountain Man*
The youngest of three children and orphaned as a young boy, Smoke Jensen is considered one of the fastest draws in the West. His quest to tame the lawless West has become the stuff of legend. Smoke owns the Sugarloaf Ranch in Colorado. Married to Sally Jensen, father to Denise ("Denny") and Louis.

Preacher—*The First Mountain Man*
Though not a blood relative, grizzled frontiersman Preacher became a father figure to the young Smoke Jensen, teaching him how to survive in the brutal, often deadly Rocky Mountains. Fought the battles that forged his destiny. Armed with a long gun, Preacher is as fierce as the land itself.

Matt Jensen—*The Last Mountain Man*
Orphaned but taken in by Smoke Jensen, Matt Jensen has become like a younger brother to Smoke and even took the Jensen name. And like Smoke, Matt has carved out his destiny on the American frontier. He lives by the gun and surrenders to no man.

Luke Jensen—*Bounty Hunter*
Mountain Man Smoke Jensen's long-lost brother Luke Jensen is scarred by war and a dead shot—the right qualities to be a bounty hunter. And he's cunning, and fierce enough, to bring down the deadliest outlaws of his day.

Ace Jensen and Chance Jensen—*Those Jensen Boys!*
Smoke Jensen's long-lost nephews, Ace and Chance, are a pair of young-gun twins as reckless and wild as the frontier itself . . . Their father is Luke Jensen, thought killed in the Civil War. Their uncle Smoke Jensen is one of the fiercest gunfighters the West has ever known. It's no surprise that the inseparable Ace and Chance Jensen have a knack for taking risks—even if they have to blast their way out of them.

CHAPTER ONE

Salcedo, Wyoming Territory

The hooves of Smoke Jensen's horse Seven made a dry clatter on the rocks as Smoke made a rather steep descent down from a seldom-used trail. Seeing the road below, he felt a sense of relief. "There it is, Seven, there's the road. Taking the cutoff wasn't all that good an idea. I was beginning to think we never would see that road again."

Seven whickered.

"No, I wasn't lost. You know I don't get lost. I just get a little disoriented every now and then."

Seven whickered again.

"Ah, so now you're making fun of me, are you?"

On long rides, Smoke often talked to his horse because he wanted to hear a voice, even if it was his own. Talking to his horse seemed a step above talking to himself.

Smoke dismounted and reached up to squeeze Seven's ear. Seven dipped his head in appreciation of the gesture.

"Yeah, I know you like this. Tell you what. Why don't I walk the rest of the way down this hill? That way you won't have to be working as hard. And when we get on the road, we'll have a little breather."

Before they reached the road, Seven suddenly let out an anxious whinny, and using his head, pushed Smoke aside so violently that he fell painfully onto the rocks.

"What was that all about?" Smoke said angrily.

Seven whinnied again and began backing away, lifting his forelegs high and bobbing his head up and down.

Smoke saw the rattler, coiled and bobbing its head, ready to strike. He drew his pistol and fired. There was a mist of blood where the snake's head had been, the head now at least five feet away from the reptile's still coiled and decapitated body.

"Are you all right?" Smoke asked anxiously as he began examining Seven's forelegs and feet. He found no indication that the snake had bitten him. He wrapped his arms around Seven's neck. "Good boy. Oh, wait. I know what you really want."

Again, he began squeezing Seven's ear. "Well, as much as you like this, we can't hang around here all day. We need to get going."

Smoke led Seven on down the rocky incline, then just before he reached the road, his foot slipped off a rock, and he felt the heel of his boot break off. "Damn," he said, picking up the heel. "Don't worry. I'm not going to remount right away, but probably a little earlier than I previously intended."

He limped along for at least two more miles. When he was certain Seven was well rested, he swung back into the saddle. "All right, boy. Let's go." He started Seven forward at a trot that was comfortable for both of them.

"We'll be coming into Salcedo soon. Tell me, Seven, do you think this bustling community will have a shoe store?"

Seven dipped his head.

"Oh, yeah, you would say that. You always are the optimist."

Salcedo was the result of what had once been a trading post, then a saloon, then a couple houses and a general store until, gradually, it became a town along the banks of the Platte River. The river was not navigable for steamboats, and even flatboats had a difficult time because of the shallowness of the water and the many sandbars and rocks along the route.

A sign at the town limits, exaggerting somewhat, stated

SALCEDO
POP 210

Smoke had been to Rawlins and was on his way back to his Sugarloaf ranch when he broke the heel. He found a boot and shoe store on Main Street, and the cobbler said that he could fix the boot. As Smoke stood at the window of the shoe repair shop, his attention was drawn to a stagecoach parked at the depot just across the street.

"Swan, Mule Gap, and Douglas!" the driver shouted. "If you're goin' to Swan, Mule Gap, or Douglas, get aboard now!"

Five passengers responded to the driver's call—two men, and a woman with two children. The coach had a shotgun guard, and as soon as he was in position, the driver popped his whip, the six horses strained in their harness, and the coach pulled away.

"Your boot is ready," George Friegh, the shoemaker, said as he stepped up beside Smoke watching the coach leave. "It's carryin' five thousand dollars in cash money."

"You mean that's common knowledge?" Smoke replied. "I thought stagecoach companies didn't want it known when they were carrying a sizeable cash shipment."

"Yeah, most of the time they do try 'n keep it quiet. But you can't do that with Emile Taylor."

"Who is Emile Taylor?" Smoke asked.

"Taylor's the shotgun guard. He's an old soldier, and like a lot of old soldiers, he's a drinkin' man. I heard him carryin' on last night while he was getting' hisself snockered at the Trail's End."

The Trail's End was the only saloon in Salcedo.

"He started talkin' about the money shipment they're takin' down to Douglas. Five thousand dollars he said it was."

"He told you that?"

"Not just me. Hell, mister, he was talkin' loud enough that ever'one in the saloon heard him."

Smoke examined the boot, then paid for the work. "You did a good job," he said, slipping the boot back on. "I'd better be getting back on the road."

Five miles south of Salcedo on the Douglas Pike

Four men were waiting on the side of the road, their horses ground hobbled behind them.

"You're sure it's carryin' five thousand dollars?" one of them asked.

"Yeah, I'm sure. I heard the shotgun guard braggin' about it."

"The reason I ask if you're sure is the last time we held up a stage we didn't get nothin' but thirty-seven dollars, 'n that's what we got from the passengers. Hell, you could get shot holdin' up a stage, and thirty-seven dollars ain't worth it."

"This here stagecoach has five thousand dollars. You can trust me on this."

"Here it comes," one of the other men said as the coach crested the hill and came into view.

"All right. You three get mounted and get your guns out. Gabe, you hold my horse. I'll have 'em throw the money bag down to me. Get your hoods on," he added as he pulled a hood down over his own head.

Smoke heard the unmistakable sound of a gunshot in the distance before him. There was only one shot, and it could have been a hunter, but he didn't think so. There was a sharp flatness to the sound—more like that of a pistol rather than a rifle. He wondered about it, but there was only one shot, and it could have been anything, so he didn't give it that much of a thought.

When he reached the top of the hill he saw the

stagecoach stopped on the road in front of him. It was the same stagecoach he had watched leave Salcedo, and the passengers, including the woman and children, were standing outside the coach with their hands up. The driver had his hands up as well. For just a second he wondered about the shotgun guard, then he saw a body lying in the road beside the front wheel of the coach.

Four armed men, all but one mounted, were all wearing hoods that covered their faces. There was no doubt that Smoke had come upon a robbery.

Pulling his pistol, he urged Seven into a gallop and quickly closed the distance between himself and the stagecoach robbers. "Drop your guns!" he shouted.

"What the hell?" one of the robbers yelled, and all four of them shot at Smoke.

Smoke shot back, and the dismounted robber went down. There was another exchange of gunfire, and one of the mounted robbers went down as well.

"Let's get out of here!" one of the two remaining robbers shouted, and they galloped off.

Smoke reached the coach then dismounted to check on the two fallen robbers to make certain they presented no further danger to the coach. They didn't. Both were dead.

A quick examination of the shotgun guard determined that he, too, was dead.

"Mister, I don't know who you are," the driver said, "but you sure come along in time to save our bacon."

"The name is Jensen. Smoke Jensen. Are all of you all right? Was anyone hurt?"

"We're fine, Mr. Jensen, thanks to you," the woman passenger said.

From the *Douglas Budget:*

> Smoke Jensen is best known as the owner of Sugarloaf, a successful ranch near Big Rock, Colorado. He is also well-known as a paladin, a man whose skillful employment of a pistol has, on many occasions, defended the endangered from harm being visited upon them by evil-doers.
>
> Such was the case a few days ago when fate, in the form of the fortuitous arrival of Mr. Jensen, foiled an attempted stagecoach robbery, and perhaps saved the lives of the driver and passengers. The incident occurred on Douglas Pike Road, some five miles south of Salcedo, and five miles north of Mule Gap.
>
> Although Mr. Jensen called out to the road agents, offering them the opportunity to drop their guns, the four outlaws refused to do so, choosing instead to engage Jensen in a gunfight. This was a fatal decision for Lucas Monroe and Asa Briggs, both of whom were killed in the ensuing gunplay. Two of the men, already mounted, were able to escape.
>
> Although the bandits were wearing hoods during the entire exchange, it is widely believed that one of the men who got away was Gabe Briggs, as he and his brother, Asa, like the James and Dalton brothers, rode the outlaw trail together.

Wiregrass Ranch, adjacent to Sugarloaf

Wiregrass Ranch had once belonged to Ned and Molly Condon. When they were murdered, Sam Condon, Ned's brother, came west from St. Louis. Sam had been a successful lawyer in that city, and everyone had thought he was coming to arrange for the sale of the ranch. Instead, he'd decided to stay, and he brought his wife, Sara Sue, and their then twelve-year-old son Thad with him. Both adjusted to their new surroundings quickly and easily. Thad not only adjusted, he thrived in the new environment.

Sam had made the conscious decision to sell off all the cattle Ned had owned and replaced them with two highly regarded registered Hereford bulls and ten registered Hereford cows. Within two years he had a herd of fifty, composed of ten bulls and forty cows.

Keeping his herd small, he was able to keep down expenses by having no permanent cowboys. Although not yet fourteen, Thad had become a very good hand.

Sam Condon's approach to ranching paid off well, and he earned a rather substantial income by selling registered cattle, both bulls and cows, to ranchers who wanted to improve their stock.

Sam and Sara Sue were celebrating their seventeenth wedding anniversary, and they had invited Smoke and Sally, their neighbors from the adjacent ranch, to have a celebratory dinner with them.

"Chicken and dumplin's, Missouri style," Sara Sue said.

"Oh, you don't have to educate me, Sara Sue," Smoke said as his hostess spooned the pastry onto his plate. "It's been a while, but I'm a Missouri boy, too."

"Well, I'm from the Northeast, but I've learned to

enjoy chicken and dumplings as well," Sally said. "Smoke loves them so, that I had to learn how to make the flat dumplings."

"She learned how to make them all right," Smoke said. "She just hasn't learned how to say *dumplin's*, without adding that last *g*," he teased.

The others laughed.

"Mr. Jensen, I read about you in the paper," Thad said.

"Oh?"

"Yes, sir. I read how you stopped a stagecoach holdup, 'n how you kilt two men."

"Thad," Sam said. "That's hardly a subject fit for discussion over the dinner table."

"But that is what you done, ain't it? You kilt two men?"

"That's what you did, isn't it?" Sara Sue said, correcting Thad's grammar.

"See, Pa, even Ma is talking about it," Thad said.

The others at the table laughed.

"I'll tell you what," Sam said. "We'll talk about it after dinner. That is, if Smoke is amenable to it."

"*Amenable*. Oh, a good lawyer's word," Sally said with a smile.

After dinner, Smoke, Sam, and Thad sat out on the front porch while Sally helped Sara Sue clean up from the meal. In the west, Red Table Mountain was living up to its name by glowing red in the setting sun.

"The newspaper said that one of the men who got away was Gabe Briggs," Sam said.

"He probably was, but they never removed their masks, so there is no way of knowing," Smoke replied.

"Would you have recognized him if he hadn't been wearing a mask?"

Smoke shook his head. "No, I don't think I would have. I've heard of the Briggs Brothers, but then, who in this part of the country hasn't? But I've never seen either of them before that little fracas on the road."

"But he did see you," Sam said.

"Yes."

"Doesn't that worry you a little? I mean, he knows what you look like, but you don't know what he looks like. If he is bent upon revenging his brother you could be in serious danger."

"I appreciate your concern," Smoke said, "but my life has been such that I have made as many enemies as I have friends. I never know when some unknown enemy is going to call me out or, even worse, try and shoot me from ambush. I've lived with that for many years. Gabe Briggs will be just one more."

"How many men have you kilt, Mr. Jensen?" Thad asked.

"Thad! That's not a question you should ever ask anyone!" Sam scolded.

"I'm sorry," Thad said contritely. "I didn't mean it in a bad way. I think Mr. Jensen is a hero."

Smoke chuckled softly. "I'm not a hero, Thad, but I have always tried to do the right thing. I'm not proud of the number of men I've killed. No one should ever kill someone as a matter of pride. But I will tell you this. I've never killed anyone who wasn't trying to kill me."

CHAPTER TWO

New York, New York

In operations such as gambling, prostitution, protection, and robbery, the Irish Assembly and the Five Points Gang had been competitors for the last three years. For a while they had been able to establish individual territories, and thus avoid any direct confrontation, but over the last couple months, the Irish Assembly had been expanding the area of their franchise and they and the Five Points Gang had renewed their hostilities.

It had come to a head two days ago when a member of the Five Points Gang was killed by the Irish Assembly.

Both gangs were currently gathered under the Second Street El. They had started their confrontation by shouting insults at each other, but the insults had grown sharper until a shot was fired.

For fifteen minutes guns blazed and bullets flew as merchants and citizens along Second Street stayed inside to avoid being shot. When it was over, the Five

Points gang hauled away their dead and wounded, and the Irish Assembly did the same.

"Three killed," Gallagher said. "We lost three good men!"

"So did the Five Points Gang," Kelly said.

"Aye, well, they can afford it, for 'tis a lot more people they have than we do. Would someone be for tellin' me what good did it do?"

"Here now, Ian, you wouldn't be for lettin' them be runnin' over us, would you?" Kelly asked.

"Gallagher's right. I think the time has come for us to change," one of the others said.

"And give up ever'thing we've built up?" Ian asked.

"We've built nothing 'n if we don't change, we'll be for losin' it all."

"In what way would you be for changing? I'm asking that," Gallagher said.

"I'd say come to an accommodation with the Five Points gang," Kelly said.

"You'd be for givin' up to 'em?"

"Aye. Let's face facts. 'Tis time to realize that we can't beat them. The only thing we can do is find some way to work with them."

Sugarloaf Ranch

"You're sure you want to do this now?" Pearlie asked.

"Yes," Thad said.

"Maybe we ought to ask your mama before you do something like this."

"No, Pearlie, don't do that. She would just say no."

Smoke had recently bought five new, unbroken horses. Pearlie and Cal always broke the new horses, and so far Cal had broken two, and Pearlie two. There was one horse remaining, and Thad, who had come over to Sugarloaf Ranch with his parents, had left them visiting with Smoke and Sally while he went out to watch. It was just before Pearlie was about to mount the horse that Thad had asked to be allowed to do it.

"I'm thirteen years old. I'm not a baby."

"All right," Pearlie said. "I guess this is as good a time as any to learn."

"What do I do?"

"Keep a hard seat and keep your heels down. Watch his ears. That'll help tell you when it's coming. Keep his head up. As long as his head is up, he can't do all that much."

Pearlie pointed to a loop. "Put your right hand in here and grab a fistful of mane with your left hand. And don't be afraid to haul back on the mane. That'll let 'im know who is in control."

"All right," Thad said somewhat tentatively.

"You gettin' a little nervous? You want to back out? Nobody is goin' to say anything to you if you do back out. Ridin' a buckin' horse is not an easy thing to do." Pearlie chuckled. "And there's most that'll tell you, it's not exactly a smart thing to do, either."

"I'm a little scared," Thad said. "But I want to do it anyway."

A broad smile spread across Pearlie's mouth. "Good for you. If you weren't scared, I would say that you are too dumb to ride. If you admit that you are scared, but you are still willing to do it, then you may have just enough sense and courage to have what it takes to do this. Climb up here, and let's get it done."

Thad climbed up onto the side of the stall where, a few minutes earlier, Cal had brought the already-saddled horse. Thad paused for a moment, then he dropped down into the saddle just as Cal opened the gate.

The horse exploded out of the stall, leaping up, then coming down on four stiffened legs. The first leap almost threw Thad from the saddle.

"Pull back on his mane!" Pearlie shouted.

"Hang on tight!" Cal added.

The horse kicked its hind legs into the air, but Thad hung on. It tried to lower its head, but following Pearlie's instructions, Thad pulled back on the mane and prevented the horse from doing so. It began whirling around, but it was unable to throw its rider.

"Yahoo!" Cal shouted.

"Thata boy, Thad! Hang on!" Pearlie called.

"THAD!" Sara Sue screamed, coming out with the others to see what was going on.

"Watch, Ma! Watch!" Thad shouted excitedly.

The horse tried for another several seconds then, unable to rid itself of its rider, began trotting around the corral under Thad's complete control.

"What are you doing?"

"Well, Sara Sue, it looks to me like he's just broken a horse," Sam said with a big smile.

"And you approve of that? He could have broken his neck."

"He didn't break his neck, but he did break the horse. I not only approve of it, I'm proud of him. In fact, Smoke, if you would be willing to sell him, I would like to buy that horse from you. Seems to me that any boy who can break a horse ought to own the horse that he broke."

"I'm sorry, Sam, but that horse isn't for sale," Smoke said.

"Oh? Well, I'm disappointed, but I understand."

"He isn't for sale because I'm giving him to Thad," Smoke said with a big smile.

"Really? This horse is mine?" Thad said while still in the saddle of the now docile horse.

"He's yours."

"Oh, thank you!" Thad shouted.

"Yes, Smoke, thank you very much. That's very nice of you," Sam said.

"What are you going to name him?" Pearlie asked.

Thad bent forward to pat the horse on his neck. "I'm going to name him Fire, because I got him from Mr. Smoke Jensen. Smoke and fire. Do you get it?"

"I get it. And I think it's a great name," Pearlie said, "because this horse also has fire in his belly."

"Open the gate to the corral so I can ride him around," Thad said.

"Cal, open the gate," Pearlie called.

Cal opened the gate.

"Now, watch us run!" Thad slapped his legs against Fire's sides, and the horse burst forth like a cannon-ball. Thad leaned forward but an inch above Fire's neck. He galloped to the far end of the lane, about a quarter of a mile away, then turning on a dime, raced back before he dismounted.

"Ma, when we go home, can I sleep in the stable with Fire tonight?"

"You most certainly cannot."

Sam laughed. "I guess we're lucky he doesn't want to bring Fire in to sleep in bed with him tonight."

Sara Sue laughed as well, then ran her hand through her son's hair. "Come on in. Mrs. Jensen has supper on the table."

"What are we havin'?" Thad asked.

"Thad! We are guests! A guest never asks the hostess what is being served," Sara Sue scolded.

"I just wanted to make sure she wasn't serving cauliflower. I hate cauliflower."

Smoke laughed. "Then you are safe, young man. Sally never serves cauliflower, because I don't like it, either."

New York City

"Mule Gap? And is it serious that you be, Warren Kennedy, that you would be going to a place called Mule Gap?"

"Aye, Clooney, 'tis serious I am," Kennedy replied.

The two men were in Grand Central Depot, awaiting the departure of the next transcontinental train. Clooney had come to see Kennedy off.

"And would you be for tellin' me, why you would pick a place with the name of Mule Fart, Wyoming?"

Kennedy laughed. "Mule Gap, not Mule Fart. And the why of it is because there is nothing left for me here in New York. Our last adventure was too costly. I have studied Mule Gap, 'n 'tis my thinking that such a wee place can provide opportunity for someone with an adventurous spirit 'n a willingness to apply himself to the possibilities offered."

"I've read about the West," Clooney said. "There

are crazy men who walk around out there with guns strapped around their waists. They say that such men would as soon shoot you as look at you."

"'N are you for tellin' me, Ryan Clooney, that in this very city the people who lived along Second Street weren't dodging the bullets that were flying through the street? Aye, 'n we as well."

"That was different. There was a war bein' fought between the Five Points Gang and the Irish Assembly, 'n we just happened to be caught up in it," Clooney insisted.

"Aye, that may be true. But I'd just as soon not be caught up in such a thing again. 'N before someone decides to start another war, 'tis my intention to be well out of here."

"I can't believe you would leave New York 'n all your friends 'n family behind."

"I have no family but m' father, 'n he has said he wants nothing to do with me. I can make new friends."

"Still, it'll be strange havin' you gone."

"All aboard for the Western Flyer!" someone shouted through a megaphone. "Track number nine. All aboard."

"That's my train," Kennedy said, starting to the door that led to the tracks. "If you think you'd like to come out, let me know, and I'll find a place for you."

"Find a place for me? Find a place doin' what?"

"Same as before. Doin' whatever I tell you to do," Kennedy said with a little chuckle.

He boarded the train, then settled back into his seat. Born in Ireland, he had lived in New York from the time he was four years old. He knew nothing but New York, yet he was leaving it all behind him.

And he didn't feel so much as one twinge of regret.

Walcott, Wyoming

Seven days later, after just under two thousand miles of cities and small towns, farmland and ranches, rich cropland and bare plains, desert and mountain, the train pulled into the small town of Walcott, Wyoming. When the train rolled away, continuing its journey on to the coast, Kennedy had a moment of indecision. He was used to big buildings, sidewalks crowded with people, all of whom were in a hurry, streets filled with carriages, trolley cars, and elevated trains. The entire town of Walcott could be fitted into one city block.

He went into the depot to claim his luggage.

"This here luggage says it was checked in at New York City," the baggage master said. "Are you from New York?"

"Aye, that I am," Kennedy replied.

"I've never been to New York, but I've read about it. Is it true what they say as to how big it is?"

"Two million people."

"Two million people? I can hardly think about such a number. Tell me, are you just visitin' or are you plannin' on settlin' down here?"

"Neither. I'm headed for Mule Gap. I plan to make that my residence."

To Kennedy's surprise, the baggage master laughed.

"What is it? What's so funny?"

"I can't imagine a New York feller like you wantin'

to live in a little ol' place like Mule Gap. Walcott, maybe, I mean, bein' as we're a pretty big town our ownselves, but a little ol' place like Mule Gap? Now that, I've got to see."

Kennedy was beginning to have even more reservations about the wisdom of moving to Mule Gap. If a resident of Walcott thought it was small, it must be miniscule indeed.

"In for a penny, in for a pound," he said.

"Now, mister, I don't have the slightest idea what it is you just said, but here's your luggage."

Carrying his luggage with him, Kennedy walked to the stagecoach depot, which was just next door. There, he bought a ticket for Mule Gap.

Warm Springs, Wyoming

"These are good-looking horses," Dooley Lewis said. "They'll make a fine addition to my string. But I thought you said you had five horses you were going to sell me."

"One of them got waylaid by a thirteen-year-old boy," Smoke replied with a smile.

"Well, never let it be said that I would step in between a boy and his horse. I'll take these and be proud to have 'em." Lewis owned DL Ranch, just outside Warm Springs.

"How'd you fare the winter?" Lewis asked.

"We got through it just fine," Smoke said. "You?"

"We had a pretty severe storm, but we was fortunate. None of the ranchers lost many cows. I did lose a couple horses, though, which is why I'm grateful to you for selling me these four. By the way, you wouldn't want to sell that horse you're ridin', would you?"

With a chuckle, Smoke reached up and grabbed one of Seven's ears and began squeezing it gently. "Don't you listen to him, Seven. You know I would never sell you."

Seven dipped his head, then pressed his forehead against Smoke's chest.

"Set much a store by that horse, do you?" Lewis asked.

"He's more than just a horse," Smoke said. "He's same as flesh and blood."

Lewis nodded. "I reckon I can see that. I've had a few critters I've felt about like that, myself.

"Glad you understand. I'll be getting on, then." Smoke swung into the saddle and started the long ride back to Sugarloaf Ranch.

CHAPTER THREE

Mule Gap

By stagecoach from Walcott, one didn't approach Mule Gap as much as one descended into it. Kennedy's first sight of the town was from the road several hundred feet high that hugged the edge of the Rattlesnake Mountain range. From there, he could see the entire town, each and every building, both commercial properties and private homes. The town consisted of probably no more than forty structures laid out along four roads that formed a cross with two legs and two arms. The tallest structure in town was a church steeple, and the largest building appeared to be the livery stable.

"Hold on back there, folks!" the driver called to his three passengers. "We're about to go into Mule Gap and the road down is a little steep, so sometimes the teams get to runnin' 'n its hard to hold 'em back!"

True to the driver's warning, the coach began going faster and jerking back and forth, which had the effect of tossing the passengers around.

Kennedy couldn't help but notice the stoicism with which the other two passengers, a drummer and a middle-aged woman, accepted the rapid and dangerous run down from Rattlesnake Mountain. He held on tightly and attempted, to the degree possible, to exhibit an equal amount of stoicism.

Smoke looped Seven's reins around the hitching rail in front of Rafferty's General Store. Seeing the stagecoach coming rapidly down the long grade from the mountain ridge road, he smiled as he thought of the passengers inside. Some enjoyed the thrill of the rapid descent, some were terrified of it, but all would be treated to a very rough ride.

He entered the store and quickly made his selections. It had been three months since the last time Smoke was in Wyoming. Having completed his business with Dooley Lewis, he'd decided to stop in Mule Gap. The small town had been built on the promise of a railroad that never materialized.

Being on the North Platte River meant an ample supply of water, good grazing land nearby, and daily stagecoach service, which provided transportation up to Walcott, the nearest access to the railroad, and south to Douglas. It was those assets that allowed the town to survive.

Gil Rafferty was putting Smoke's purchases in a bag when the little bell on the door signaled the entrance of another customer. "Emma, we have another customer," he called out to his wife.

"I'll be right with you, sir," a woman called from the back of the store.

"'Tis no hurry I'm in, ma'am. Take your time," the customer replied.

Smoke glanced toward him and saw a man of average height and build, whose most distinguishing feature was his piercing hazel eyes. Unlike the denim trousers and cotton shirts worn by most Westerners, this man was wearing a blue suit, a white shirt covered by a red vest, and a black bowtie. As Smoke examined him more closely, he saw that the clothing was of the finest cut and most expensive material. The quality of the material and the cut of the suit, however, did nothing to deter the dust. His suit was covered with it. Smoke noticed that he was not wearing a pistol belt.

"Hello, friend," the man said to Smoke. Smiling, he extended his hand. "Kennedy is the name. Warren Kennedy."

"Smoke Jensen," Smoke replied, accepting the proffered hand. He smiled. "How did you like the last half mile of your ride on the stagecoach?"

"Ha. And 'tis thinkin' I am, that you would be talkin' about the rapid descent down the road."

"Yes."

"And how would you be for knowin' that I was on the coach?" Kennedy asked.

Smoke chuckled. "It's not hard, Mr. Kennedy."

With a laugh, Kennedy patted his hands against the jacket he was wearing. That action was answered by a cloud of dust. "No, I don't suppose it would be hard to tell. As to the answer for your question, 'twas exciting, I'll say that. But sure 'n what better way could I ask to arrive in what will be my new hometown?"

"Mr. Kennedy, I'm Emma Rafferty," an attractive

middle-aged woman said. "My husband and I own this store. Mule Gap is to be your new hometown?"

"Aye, for 'tis my intention to settle here."

"Then let me be the first to welcome you. Now, what can I do for you?"

"I'll be for buying a house as soon as I can, 'n I've made out a list of things I think I'll be needin'." He handed Emma a piece of paper. "I would like for to be making the purchases now, 'n payin' you for them, but I'll be wantin' you to be for holding them for me till I have a house where I can put them."

"We'll be glad to do that for you, Mr. Kennedy. And for now you can just look around the store to see if there's anything you may have forgotten," Emma said.

"I thank you for your service, Mrs. Rafferty." In accordance with Emma's suggestion, Kennedy began drifting around the store.

A moment later, three men came into the store. All three men had hoods pulled down over their faces.

"This is a holdup!" one of the men shouted, then he pointed to Smoke. "That's the son of a bitch that kilt my brother! Kill 'im!"

As soon the order was given, the man carrying a double-barreled shotgun swung it toward Smoke.

Smoke drew his own gun, but even as he was drawing, a shot rang out and the man wielding the scattergun went down.

Two more shots were fired, only one of them coming from Smoke's pistol, and the remaining two men went down.

When Smoke looked around to see who had saved his life, he saw a smiling Warren Kennedy standing near one of the display tables. A thin wisp of gun smoke curled up from the barrel of a gun Kennedy was holding.

Because he wasn't wearing a pistol belt, Smoke wondered where the gun had come from.

"Well, that was a bit of excitement, wasn't it? 'Tis a foine welcome I received," Kennedy said with a broad smile. He returned the pistol to a shoulder holster that had been hidden by his jacket, and the mystery of where the gun had come from was solved.

"Mister Kennedy, I'm glad you came around when you did," Rafferty said. "You sure saved our bacon."

"Yeah, I guess I could say that as well." Smoke pulled the hoods from their faces.

"Do you know any of them, Mr. Jensen?" Rafferty asked.

"I've never actually seen this man," Smoke said, standing over the one who had recognized him. "But from what he yelled out just before the shooting started, I would make a guess that this would be Gabe Briggs."

"Briggs?" Rafferty said. "Yes, I remember the story from the newspaper. A man named Briggs was one of the ones who'd tried to hold up the stagecoach. You stopped the holdup, as I recall."

"Yes, Asa Briggs was the man's name." Smoke turned toward the well-dressed man who, having just arrived on the stagecoach, had also taken part in stopping this robbery. "Mr. Kennedy—"

"It's Warren, please. I'd like to be for considering you the first new friend I've made in my new hometown."

"Well, I have to say Mist . . . Warren . . . that saving my life is a way to get on my good side really fast."

Kennedy laughed. "Aye, 'twould be a way of makin' a new friend, I would think."

"Warren, why don't you come down to the saloon with me and let me buy you a drink? Mr. Rafferty, you can hold my groceries here until I come back for them, can't you?"

"I sure can."

"Thanks for the offer of a drink," Kennedy said. "'Twould be good to get a bit o' the dust out of my mouth, I'm thinking."

By the time they reached the saloon, word of the would-be robbery and shoot-out had already spread. Both men were greeted with accolades, and though Smoke had offered to buy Kennedy's drinks, he wasn't allowed to pay for them, as the saloon keeper said they were "on the house."

The two men took a table in the back of the Silver Dollar Saloon.

"Those three robbers knew you," Kennedy said. "But when their hoods were removed, you said you didn't know them."

"No, I'd never seen any of them before."

"Sure now, and 'tis not that rather odd? 'Twas knowin' you they did, but you weren't for knowin' them."

"Where are you from, Warren?"

"I'm from New York."

Smoke smiled. "Well then, that explains it. I've been out here for quite a while now, and over the years I've made a few enemies. As a matter of fact I've made a lot of enemies . . . but I'm glad to say that I have made more friends than enemies."

"Aye, 'n a new one today."

"A new one today," Smoke repeated, holding his glass of beer up to Kennedy's Irish whiskey.

During the ensuing conversation Kennedy learned that Smoke owned a rather large ranch down in Colorado.

"What do you do, Warren? And what has brought you to a place like Mule Gap?"

"I've made my living for many years being involved in various business ventures," Kennedy said. "Some have been profitable, some have been costly. I recently ran into some business difficulty in New York and decided it would be a good idea to leave the city 'n start somewhere else, so I decided to take what funds I had left and come West in search of new opportunity." He laughed. "And the reason I chose Mule Gap was because I was intrigued by the name."

Smoke laughed. "Are you telling me that you would invest in something because you like the name?"

"Aye," Kennedy replied with a sheepish grin. "Maybe that's the mistake I made in New York . . . investing in something because of its name."

"I think you're pulling my leg a bit," Smoke said.

"Perhaps just a bit," Kennedy replied, his smile growing broader. "I have studied Mule Gap. I think it is bound to grow, and I intend to grow with it."

"Well, I wish you luck, Warren," Smoke said, once more lifting his drink in an informal toast. "Here's mud in your eye."

Warren made a toast of his own. "'N I'll be replyin' with an old Irish toast, taught to me by m' sainted mither, may she rest in peace." He held his glass up.

"May we get what we want, may we get what we need, but may we never get what we deserve."

With a chuckle, Smoke joined him in the drink.

Two months later, the *Mule Gap Ledger* carried a story about Kennedy.

Warren Kennedy to Start Bank

Mule Gap to Become a Commercial City

Our readers will no doubt recognize Warren Kennedy, Mule Gap's newest citizen, as a hero for stopping a robbery and saving the lives of Mr. and Mrs. Gilbert Rafferty. What many may not know is Mr. Kennedy's entrepreneurial spirit. He has announced his intention to build a much-needed bank in our fair community and to that end has begun construction in the empty lot next to McGee's Boot and Shoe store.

With the addition of a bank, Mule Gap will be able to take its rightful place among the more progressive cities and towns of Wyoming. All citizens of Mule Gap should be thankful that this fine man has chosen our community as his new home.

A full year passed before Smoke made another visit to Mule Gap. As he approached the little town from the south, he heard gunfire and, slapping his legs against Seven's sides, pulled his pistol and proceeded toward the sound of shooting at a full gallop. He eased up, though, when he heard more shots fired, this time followed by shouts of excitement, not fear.

"Yahoo!" someone shouted, and again there were gunshots. "Yahoo!"

As Smoke came into town he saw that many of the buildings of the town were festooned with colorful streamers. He saw, also, that at least three of the businesses he had known before were now partnerships. The grocery store was now Rafferty and Kennedy. The boot store was sporting the sign McGEE AND KENNEDY, and Warren Kennedy had built a new saloon to compete with the Silver Dollar.

Smoke saw, then, the source of the shouting and gunshots, for a rider was galloping down the middle of First Street, shooting into the air, and yelling at the top of his voice.

"Yahoo! Three cheers for his honor the mayor, Warren Kennedy! Yahoo!"

Smoke dismounted in front of Kennedy's Saloon, and looped the reins around the hitching rail, knowing full well that Seven would make no effort to leave even if he had just dropped the reins on the ground in front of the horse.

When he stepped into the saloon it was crowded with cheering men and laughing bar girls. A sign was stretched out across the wall behind the bar. *To CELEBRATE HIS ELECTION, DRINKS ARE ON THE HOUSE TODAY!*

"I remember you," Warren Kennedy called. "'N I know you to be Smoke Jensen if memory serves."

"Smoke Jensen it is. You have a good memory."

"Well, Smoke Jensen, 'n would you be for havin' a drink with the new mayor of Mule Gap?"

Smoke smiled and walked over to take Kennedy's extended hand. "I'd be glad to have a drink with you. And, congratulations, Mayor. I knew you were an ambitious fellow, but I never thought you would get involved with politics."

"Believe me, 'twas never my intention," Kennedy said. "But the damndest thing . . . people kept after me and kept after me to run until I felt it wouldn't be fair to just keep saying no all the time. So, I broke down and said aye, and now here I am . . . the new mayor."

"I wish you luck."

"I've already been lucky. I ran against Gil Rafferty, and, as you know, he is as fine a man as you would hope to meet. Gil and I are business partners now."

"Yes, I saw the sign on his store."

"Even though many were asking me to run, 'tis surprised I am that I, being a citizen of Mule Gap for barely over a year, would have prevailed over someone like m' friend Gil Rafferty, who has been here for as long as the town has been in existence. But tell me, Smoke, what brings you to town?"

"Your bank," Smoke said. "I do a lot of business in Wyoming, so I thought it might be a good idea to have a local account."

"Well, I'll be very happy to have your business. After we have a drink together, come on down to the bank and I'll personally open your account."

Half an hour later, Smoke was sitting across the desk from Kennedy. "Warren, looking around town, I can't help but notice that you have expanded your business interests considerably beyond just banking."

"That's true," he said. "As Mule Gap began to grow, many of the businessmen and -women wanted their businesses to expand with it. They came to me for investment money, and if it seemed propitious for me to do so, I made the investment." Kennedy chuckled. "It seems that I now own almost half the town. That wasn't my intention. My intention was just to help the town grow. But, as they say, good things come from good deeds."

"Yes," Smoke said. "You came to Mule Gap to do good, and you have done very well."

Kennedy laughed out loud. "That is one way of putting it, my friend. But don't be fooled by what you see."

"Not sure I understand."

"I've made loans, 'n I've made investments to the degree that I've found myself overextended. I think the investments have been wise, 'n I think there is a great future in Mule Gap. But I'll have to be limiting any future investments until I'm able to accumulate a little more money."

"Warren, are you . . . ?" Smoke started to ask, but Kennedy held out his hand to interrupt the question.

"Smoke, if it was a loan of money you were about to offer, I thank you for that. But I'll not be for needing a loan. I've recently gone into a business venture with some new acquaintances, 'n 'tis thinking I am that it is one that will be very lucrative. And there is no competition in the endeavor."

"Oh? What is it?"

Kennedy held up his finger and wagged it back and forth gently. "Please don't ask me to tell you. Bein' Irish, as I am, I have many superstitions, 'n I fear that if I tell too many people of my plans, it'll bring me bad luck."

Smoke chuckled. "Far be it from me to want to bring you bad luck. So . . . if it isn't bad luck to wish you good luck, I'll do just that."

"I'll take yer good wishes, 'n then some," Kennedy replied.

CHAPTER FOUR

Stinking Water, Wyoming

The man dressed all in black dismounted in front of the Nippy Jones Saloon. Before he reached the step, he was confronted by a big man with a prominent scar on his face. The man was holding a pistol.

"Where do you think you're agoin'?" the scar-faced man asked.

"Not that it is any of your business, sir, but it is my intention to drink a beer, have dinner, then get a hotel room so I can spend the night."

"You're the one they call The Professor, ain't you? I've heard of you. Always dressed in black, they say."

"My name is Frank Bodine."

"But you're called The Professor?"

"Actually, I would be more properly called Professor Bodine, but yes, there are some who call me The Professor."

"Well, you ain't comin' in here, Professor."

"And just why wouldn't I be entering that establishment?"

"Because I said you ain't."

"Tell me, sir, do you have any particular grievance with me? I am unaware of our paths ever having crossed in the past."

"I've heard of you."

"Evidently you have, as a moment ago you used the sobriquet that is so often attached to me."

"I done what?" the scar-faced man replied.

"You have heard of me," The Professor said.

"Yeah, that's what I said. I've heard of you," Scarface repeated.

"Merely having heard of me, does not, in itself, give you a reason to behave in such a contemptible fashion," The Professor said. "Now, please, sir, if you would, step aside."

Scarface shook his head. "Uh-uh. Come this time tomorrow, ever'one is goin' to know that The Professor has been kilt, 'n they're goin' to know who done it."

"I think you are making a big mistake, sir. Now, I'm going to ask you very politely to step aside and allow me to enter this saloon so that I can have myself dinner and a beer."

"You ain't goin' nowhere, you fancy-talkin' son of a bitch!" Scarface made his move, bringing the pistol up as quickly as a striking rattlesnake.

Even though Scarface had the advantage, the reaction of The Professor was not what he thought it would be. Instead of seeing fear in his eyes, Scarface saw complete confidence. Even worse, Scarface saw the faintest suggestion of a smile on The Professor's face.

Scarface was very good with a gun, and in most of his encounters, he had the advantage because his very reputation instilled fear in his adversaries. But there was no fear in the face of the man facing him, and it was Scarface who suddenly felt fear.

He wasn't frightened for very long. The Professor's draw was smooth and instantaneous, and his practiced thumb came back on the hammer in one fluid motion. He put the slightest pressure on the hair trigger of his Colt, causing a blossom of flame, followed by a booming thunderclap as the gun jumped in his hand.

Scarface tried to shoot the pistol he was holding, but the .44 slug from The Professor's pistol caught him in the middle of his chest. He dropped his own pistol unfired, then staggered backwards, crashing through the batwing doors and backpedaling into a table before coming down onto it with a crash that turned the table into firewood. He landed flat on his back on the floor, his mouth open and a little sliver of blood oozing down his chin. His body was still jerking a bit, but his eyes were open and unseeing. He was already dead, the muscles continuing to respond as if waiting for signals that could no longer be sent.

The Professor holstered his pistol then pushed through the batwing doors, following the lawman's body inside. Without so much as a second glance at the man he had just killed, he stepped calmly up to the bar. "Beer," he said, aware that everyone in the saloon was shifting their gaze from the lawman's body to the man dressed in black standing at the bar. Most had been caught by surprise at the sudden turn of events. They stood there, staring awestruck at the lawman lying in the *V* of the broken table.

"Mister, do you know who you just shot?" one of the men in the saloon asked.

"I'm afraid we didn't have time to get acquainted," The Professor replied.

"His name is Barton. Billy Barton. I never figured anyone would be good enough to beat him. What do they call you?"

"I'll tell you what they call him," another man said. "They call him The Professor."

Upon hearing the name, there was a collective gasp in the room. The Professor drank his beer without looking around.

Mule Gap

It was the first time The Professor had ever been in Mule Gap, but his reputation had preceded him. Several citizens saw the man sitting tall in the saddle and dressed all in black. They knew who he was, and they were aware of his deadly skill with a handgun.

As he rode through the center of town, heading for Kennedy's Saloon, he passed by a large white house that, at first glance, could be taken as the residence of one of the town's wealthier citizens. A second glance toward the establishment disclosed a square brown sign with the name of the establishment in gold script. *The Delilah House.* It billed itself as a "Sporting House for Gentlemen."

Like several other businesses in town, the Delilah House was half owned by Warren Kennedy, though this was one business that did not sport his name on the front of the building as its co-owner. In fact, his participation in the house of ill repute was kept secret for political purposes. As far as anyone knew, the business was owned and run by Delilah Dupree, a beautiful woman who had arrived two years earlier from New Orleans. She had no reservations about the avocation she followed. She believed that, because of the overall shortage of women in Carbon County, she was actually providing a service. And to that end, she proudly promoted her services by advertising in the local newspaper, *The Mule Gap Ledger.*

~ The Delilah House ~
A Sporting House for Gentlemen
WHERE
BEAUTIFUL *and* CULTURED
LADIES
will provide you with every
PLEASURE.

"Why should I be ashamed of it?" she would reply to anyone who questioned her. "I give my girls a clean place to stay, and I insist that the gentlemen callers be on their best behavior. If they are not well behaved, I don't let them return."

Three men who had come into her establishment a short while earlier were behaving in any way but gentlemanly. At the moment, the three visitors were in the parlor, where they were being loud and obnoxious. One of the men was sitting on the silk-covered sofa, with his boots up on a carved table. He had a droopy eyelid and a broken and misshapen nose. He was watching the other two men who had come with him. One was large and clean-shaven, the other was of medium build and had a sweeping handlebar mustache.

Delilah kept her staff small, believing that four girls specifically chosen for their beauty and charm would be preferable to a larger staff of women who had less to offer. Three of the young women, Fancy Bliss, Joy Love, and Candy Sweet, had welcomed the three visitors with practiced smiles when they first arrived. However, as the behavior of the men became more and more disturbing, the women became apprehensive, and their interaction with the men was cautious.

"Hey, Turley," one of the two men said to the other. "Which one of 'em are you goin' to choose?"

"I can't make up my mind. What about you, Gibbons?"

"I ain't made up my mind, neither," Gibbons responded. "Hey, I know what. Why don't you whores show us your goodies? How are we s'posed to know which one of you we want to take up to your room, lessen we can see 'em and decide?"

"Why no, we couldn't do that," one of the women said.

"What do you mean, you can't do that? Iffen we choose one of you, why, you'll have to get nekkid when we take you to bed, won't you? So what's the difference 'bout us seein' you nekkid then, or a-lookin' at your titties now?"

Because Delilah was in her office at the moment, she was unaware of the boorish behavior of the three men, but Fancy Bliss had managed to slip away.

When she went into the office there was an agitated expression on her face. "Miss Dupree?"

"Yes, Fancy, what is it?"

"There are three gentlemen in the parlor that . . . well, they are not being very gentlemanly."

"Thank you, Fancy. I'll take care of it."

"Yes, ma'am."

Delilah stepped up front to the parlor and saw immediately what Fancy was talking about. "Ladies, please withdraw to your rooms now."

"Yes, ma'am," they all replied, and quickly left.

"Hey, what did you do that for?" Gibbons asked. "What good is a whorehouse without whores? I was just fixin' to pick one of 'em out."

"Please leave," Delilah said. "This house is closed."

"What do you mean, *closed*?" Turley asked. "I know they's someone upstairs with one of your whores now, on account of I seen 'em go up."

"I will soon be sending him on his way, as well. This house is now closed. Please leave."

"The hell I will. I ain't goin' nowhere till . . ."

"Please do what Miss Dupree asked you to do." Fancy had stepped back into Delilah's office and had come out holding a sawed-off shotgun."

"Let's go, Turley," the man sitting on the sofa said. "We don't want to be where we aren't wanted, now, do we?"

"Come on. We ain't even—" Turley started to say, but again his comment was interrupted by Gibbons.

"I said let's go."

"All right, all right, I'm a-goin'."

The man who had issued the order turned toward Delilah, and she took a quick intake of breath when she saw the scar. She had heard of this man, and she realized that she was walking on thin ice, ordering them around as she did.

"We'll be goin' now," he said.

"Thank you. You are welcome back anytime your . . . friends . . . can exhibit less boorish behavior."

The scar-faced man chuckled. "You hear that

Gibbons, Turley? We're boring. I been called lots of things, but I ain't never been accused of borin' nobody.

"Boorish, not boring," Delilah said, but even as she made the correction, she realized that none of the three had the slightest understanding of the word. She made no further effort to enlighten them, remaining silent, except for the sigh of relief when they left her establishment.

"Joy?" Delilah said.

"Yes, ma'am?"

"As unobtrusively as you can, go upstairs and try to determine how long it will be before Jasmine is finished with her gentleman visitor."

"Yes, ma'am."

Jasmine Delight was a beautiful octoroon with golden-hued skin and emerald eyes. She had come from New Orleans with Delilah.

Joy didn't have to check on Jasmine. Even as she started to, they could hear Jasmine's voice as she came downstairs with her client, Abner Wilson. A frequent visitor from Rawlins, he was a member of the territorial legislature.

"I do hope your visit with us was a pleasant one, Mr. Wilson," Delilah said as the distinguished-looking middle-aged man stepped out into the lobby."

"How can it not be a pleasant visit when one can spend company with a young lady as delightful as Jasmine?" Wilson replied. "And may I also say that I appreciate your discretion? If word of my visits were to reach the wrong ears, it would, I fear, be the end of my political career."

"You are always the perfect gentleman, sir, and

you are always welcome at the Delilah House, where discretion is as important to us as any pleasure we can provide."

Just down the street from the Delilah House, a recent arrival in town was playing poker in Kennedy's Saloon. "I'll take three," said the man dressed in all black.

The dealer gave the man in black three cards, then looked over at the next player.

"What about you, Maloney?" the dealer asked. "How many cards?"

"One," Win said.

"Drawing to an inside straight, are you?" the dealer joked, slapping a new card down in front of Maloney.

Maloney was actually trying to fill a heart flush, but when he saw that the card was a spade, he folded.

"Well, mister, it's going to cost you five bucks to see what I've got," one of the other players said to the man in black.

The man in black looked at his cards, thought about it for a moment, then, with a shrug, folded.

One of the other players who had bet heavily on the hand lost, then pushed his chair back from the table. "Boys, I'd better give this game up while I still got enough to buy myself a beer."

Just as he was leaving the game, three men were coming into the saloon. One of them, seeing an open chair, came over to the table and, without being asked, sat down.

"A person with manners would have asked if he could join," the man in black said.

"Mister, you got 'ny idea who you're talkin' to?" the new man asked.

"Obviously, I'm talking to someone who is sans manners," the man in black replied.

"Sans manners? What does that mean?"

"It means your demeanor is boorish."

"Damn, that's the second time today, I've been called a bore."

The man in black smiled patronizingly.

"You really don't know who I am, do you?" asked the man with the drooping eyelid and misshapen nose.

"So far there's nothing about your personality that would lead me to *want* to know who you are."

"Well, I damn sure know you. You're the one folks call The Professor. My name is Puckett. Billy Bob Puckett. Does that name mean anything to you?"

The Professor recognized the name but gave no indication he did. "No, I don't think I've ever heard of you. Are you someone I should know?"

The other players around the table readily recognized the name, and realizing that a showdown between two well-known gunfighters was about to occur, they reacted in apprehension.

"Mister, Professor," the player who had just won the hand said. "Maybe you ain't never heard of him, but Billy Bob Puckett is . . . uh—" he stopped in mid-sentence, not wanting to agitate Puckett in any way.

"You can say it," Puckett said. "You can tell The Professor here that I ain't the kind of man a feller is goin' to want to rile. That is, not if he wants to live any longer."

"Well then, Mr. Puckett, I don't want to rile you because I certainly do plan to live longer . . . so please, do join us," The Professor said. "I have to admit that I have been admiring your hat. Perhaps, if there is a fortuitous fall of the pasteboards, I might just win it tonight."

Puckett took off his hat, a low-crowned black hat surrounded by a band of silver conchas. "You ain't gettin' my hat." He pulled a stack of bills from his pocket and put them on the table in front of him. "On the other hand, after I take all your money, I might just buy me a fancy brocaded vest to go with my hat."

The Professor chuckled. "We'll see, Mr. Puckett. We'll just see."

CHAPTER FIVE

The Professor won the first hand, and the next hand as well, and with that hand was a few dollars ahead.

"You're a pretty lucky fella, ain't you?" Puckett said.

"Sometimes it happens," The Professor replied as he raked in his winnings. "But luck is only effective when one has the skill to best employ it."

"Yeah, like what happened last week. Was you lucky or skillful?"

"Last week?"

"Yeah, last week in Stinking Water. Are you tryin' to tell me that you don't know what I'm talkin' about? You are the one they call The Professor, ain't you?"

"I am."

"You kilt Billy Barton."

"I did."

"Well, Mr. Professor, Billy Barton was a good friend of mine. And me 'n you is goin' to have an accountin' over that."

"Wait a minute," one of the other card players

said, recognizing immediately that this raw-edged conversation might well lead to gunplay. "Are you sure you two want—"

"Stay out of this, friend," Puckett said.

First that player, then the others got up and walked away, leaving only Puckett and The Professor. They were facing each other across a table upon which lay a spread of cards, some faceup, some facedown. There also remained on the table little personal banks of money in front of where each of the players had been sitting.

"Now you've done it," The Professor said. "Your ill-mannered behavior has ruined a perfectly good card game."

"Yeah? Well, they can always find another card game, but Barton can't, can he? He can't never play cards again, and he can't never have no women again, he can't never do nothin' again, on account of he's dead. I guess maybe you didn't know at the time that he was a good friend of mine, did you?" Puckett asked.

"No, but even if I had known, it wouldn't have made any difference. By the way, your grammar is atrocious," The Professor said.

"My gran'ma is what? Look here, you ain't got no business talkin' 'bout my gran'ma! She was a fine woman!"

"I'm sure she was."

"Now that you can think back on it, I'll just bet you wish you hadn'ta shot my friend, don't you?"

"No, I would've killed him anyway," The Professor said. "He was clearly a man who needed killing."

"You see them two fellas standin' over at the bar?" Puckett asked.

When The Professor looked in the direction pointed out by Puckett, he saw two men; one large and clean-shaven, the other of medium build, with a handlebar mustache. Both were looking toward the table.

"Them two boys is Gibbons and Turley. It turns out that Billy Barton was a friend of theirs, too. Me 'n them is just all broke up over losin' a good friend like we done."

"Yes, I could tell just how upset you gentlemen must have been over the demise of your friend by the grief you expressed at his funeral," The Professor said. "Oh, wait. That's right. There was no funeral, was there?"

"We was plannin' one," Puckett said.

"Really? Apparently, you didn't mention that little detail to the undertaker. Mr. Barton was laid out in a plain pine box, then buried on the far side of Boot Hill without even a marker."

"How do you know?"

"Because I was there," The Professor answered. "And I was the only one, except for the two grave diggers."

"You always go to the buryin' of men you kill?" Puckett asked.

The Professor flashed a cold look at Puckett. "When I can," he answered pointedly. "Sometimes I bury them myself."

"Just how many men have you killed?" Puckett asked.

"As many as I needed to."

"Is that right? Well, you won't be killin' no more."

"And why would you say that?"

"Because I'm about to kill you."

"And would that be just you, Mr. Puckett? Or do

your two friends intend to cut themselves in to the dance?"

"Well now, that don't really matter none, does it? I mean, as long as you'll be dead."

Puckett started to draw his pistol, unaware that The Professor had already drawn his gun and was holding it under the table. The Professor fired, and Puckett's eyes opened in surprise as the bullet plowed into him before he could even clear leather.

The Professor turned his gun toward the two men at the bar . . . and though the odds had been three to one, he had the advantage. He already had his gun out, and Gibbons and Turley had been given no advance warning as to when Puckett intended to make his move. The Professor shot two more times. Gibbons, who was able to draw and point his gun toward The Professor, managed to take two steps before he fell. Turley had gone down in place.

"Son of a bitch! Did you all see that?" someone said. "The Professor took on three of 'em 'n kilt all three! 'N one of 'em he kilt was Billy Bob Puckett!"

Warren Kennedy poured cognac from a cut-glass decanter into two crystal snifters. "This is vintage 1858. I think you will find it more than adequate."

The Professor lifted the glass to his nose and took a whiff. "It has a very good nose."

The Professor and Kennedy held their glasses toward each other, though they didn't actually clink them together.

"Your real name is Frank Bodine?" Kennedy asked.

"Yes."

"Tell me, Mr. Bodine. Why do they call you the Professor?"

"I am called that because I actually am a professor. I have a PhD in English and taught that subject at the College of William and Mary."

Kennedy looked surprised. "Begorra! And are you for telling me you really were a professor? I thought perhaps they called you that because—"

"Of my skill with a pistol?" The Professor interrupted the observation with his reply. I suppose there is some justification for having that opinion."

"Yes. How did you . . . that is . . . a college professor as a professional gunman? You have to admit that 'tis a strange combination. How is that you be here in the West, following your . . . uh . . . particular line of work, rather than bein' a professor back at William and Mary?"

"I should have been promoted to head of the department," The Professor said. "I had the most seniority and I had the best record. But I was passed over in favor of the dean's nephew."

"That explains why you are no longer teaching, but not your skill with a pistol."

"The art of the fast draw and pistol marksmanship had always been a hobby of mine. I practiced until I was quite proficient, then I began to give demonstrations. I know there could be nothing more contrary to expectation than someone in the staid profession of academia being extraordinarily skilled in the use of a pistol, but I think that was, at least in part, what drew me to the practice. When I gave up my professorship, I decided to see if I could convert my hobby into a profession, and I realized that the best place to do that would be in the West. And that is what I have done for the last few years."

"Converting your hobby into a profession? That is an interesting choice of words," Kennedy said. "What you mean is you have been selling your gun to the highest bidder."

"Yes. Except, of course, when I am challenged by someone for a real or manufactured reason, such as the incident involving Billy Barton. I must confess that in contemplating my new profession, I had not considered the idea that there would be people wanting to kill me for the simple reason of enhancing their own reputation. I am quite certain that is what Billy Barton had in mind when he forced the encounter with me back in Stinking Water. And, despite Puckett's claim of revenge over the loss of his friend, I have no doubt but that his challenge was inspired by the same desire to enhance his reputation by killing The Professor."

"How would you like to get out of that business and use your gun only for legitimate purposes?"

"You mean become a lawman?"

"Aye."

The Professor shook his head. "I got five hundred dollars for killing Billy Barton. I'll be getting a like amount for killing Billy Bob Puckett. I don't know yet if there was any reward on either Gibbons or Turley, but I expect there is."

"There is. One hundred and fifty dollars on each of them," Kennedy said.

"Well then, there's thirteen hundred dollars I have earned legitimately just in the last two weeks. When I say that I have been selling my guns, that is true . . . but so far I have employed them only in the pursuit of wanted men for which bounties have been posted. No law position can pay that much."

"It can, if you combine the salary of being the city marshal for Mule Gap and my personal bodyguard," Kennedy said. "I can pay you a thousand dollars per month, and you won't have to be riding all over the territory, looking for elusive wanted men. However should you, in the pursuit of your duty, happen to kill a wanted man, we can put a caveat in your employment contract that would authorize you to keep any reward offered."

"Why would you need a bodyguard?"

"I have gotten involved in several business operations since arriving in Mule Gap," Kennedy said. "And in so doing, I have also made some enemies. I am quite proficient myself in the use of a pistol, though I'm sure I'm not as good as you are. 'Tis thinkin' I am that with my own efficacy, augmented by your even more formidable skill, my position as mayor and as a businessman would be practically unassailable."

"A thousand dollars per month?"

"Yes."

"Are your businesses doing that well that you can afford to pay me a thousand dollars a month?"

"Oh, I won't be paying you from my own pocket. I'll impose a special protection tax that will cover your salary." Kennedy laughed. "Like you, Professor Bodine, I also had a life before I came west, and in New York one of my particular specialties was in collecting a protection tax from businessmen, even if they didn't particularly want to buy the insurance."

The Professor extended his hand. "In that case, I think that from now on, *Marshal Bodine* would be a more appropriate sobriquet than *The Professor*. I accept your most generous offer."

"Thank you, Marshal Bodine. Go ahead and set up your office. Please feel free to come to me with anything that you might need."

"Deputies?"

"Yes, I'm glad you brought that up. I think you should have at least ten deputies. Pick out ten men who are particularly good with guns."

"Ten? For a town this small, why would I need any deputies at all?"

"I have plans," Kennedy said without being more specific. "Do you think you can find ten good men?"

"It depends on what you mean by *good*. 'Good' and 'good with guns' are not always compatible concepts. If you are talking about good with guns, I don't think they would be particularly interested in being deputy city marshals."

"You can offer them two hundred dollars a month and promise them extra sources of income that would pay even more than their salaries."

"What sources of income would those be?"

Kennedy finished his cognac before he replied. "As I told you, I'm a businessman, Marshal Bodine. And as it so happens, I'm a very good businessman. You let me worry about the additional sources of income."

"Just so that you understand, the deputies I hire will be of somewhat unsavory character."

"In the pursuit of peace, I am prepared to close my eyes to any such iniquities as your deputies might bring with them."

The Professor smiled. "Then I shall assemble my police force."

Sugarloaf Ranch

"Guess who I got a letter from today?" Sally said when Smoke came into the house.

"The Queen of England?"

"No, that was yesterday," Sally said, laughing. "Today I got a letter from Rosanna MacCallister. She and Andrew are opening a new play next week, and she's invited you and me."

"Sally, you know I can't go. I'm going up to Mule Gap."

"For two days," Sally said. "You would be back in plenty of time. I know you very well, Kirby Jensen. It isn't that you can't go, it's that you don't *want* to go."

"You're right. I don't want to go. I've been to New York. It's too crowded. But that doesn't mean you can't go."

"I don't want to go without you. I wouldn't enjoy it without you."

"You would enjoy it even more, and you know it. I would just be complaining and finding fault with everything."

Sally chuckled. "Yes, you would be doing that. You don't mind if I go by myself, do you?"

"No, I don't mind. Go, enjoy yourself, and give my excuses to Andrew and Rosanna."

"What excuse will I give?"

"You're the smartest person I know, Sally. You'll be able to come up with something."

"How about, Smoke sends his regrets, but he is auditioning for the ballet in San Francisco?"

Smoke laughed. "Yes, that ought to work."

Big Rock, Colorado

The ticket agent began stamping his authorization block, first on the inkpad, then on one of the ticket stubs, doing it several times so quickly that it sounded almost like beating a drum. When he was finished, he attached the tickets into two bundles with a couple spring clamps, smiled, and handed them to Sally. "There you are, Mrs. Jensen. This first batch of tickets will allow you to change trains in Denver, Kansas City, St. Louis, Chicago, Cleveland, and New York. Well, of course you won't change trains in New York until you start back home again. Then you use the second batch of tickets to change trains in—"

"Let me guess," Sally said. "Cleveland, Chicago, St. Louis, Kansas City, and Denver."

"Yes, that's it exactly."

"Thank you, Mr. Peabody. I'll try and remember that."

"You might want to make a note," Peabody suggested.

"Thank you," Sally said again.

CHAPTER SIX

Sally had come to town, not only to buy tickets for her upcoming trip to New York, but also to shop for some new clothes. She had come with Smoke and they had taken the surrey rather than riding into town. Before they left, Smoke had apologized to Seven for leaving him behind.

"Smoke, for heaven's sake, Seven isn't a dog who misses his master," Sally had told him. "He's a horse."

"Yes, but he isn't just any horse, and you know it."

Sally laughed. "You're right. He is a magnificent horse, but the surrey is best for bringing my purchases back home."

Once they'd reached town, Smoke had announced that he would get a haircut, then wait for her at Longmont's Saloon.

He was in Earl's Barbershop when Sam Condon came in.

"Hello, neighbor," Smoke said.

"Hi, Smoke. I was just down to the bank and heard that you would be going up to Mule Gap tomorrow."

"That's right."

"Do you know a rancher there named Jim Harris? He owns Cross Trail, a ranch that's just outside Mule Gap."

"Yes, I know Jim. He's a good man."

"I just sold him Yankee Star."

"Yankee Star, huh? That's a damn fine bull," Smoke said.

"He is indeed, and I sort of hate to see him go, but Mr. Harris made a very generous offer, and I don't feel I can turn him down. But, here's the thing. There's no bank in Mule Gap, and Harris is holding twenty-five hundred dollars in cash for me, the rest to be paid when the bull is delivered. I was going to go up and get it myself, but I heard you were going up, and if you could pick the money up for me, it would save me a trip, seeing as I will have to go up again when Thad and I deliver the bull."

"I'd be glad to, Sam, but there is a bank in Mule Gap. I do a lot of business in the Wyoming Territory, and I thought it would be good to have an account there. As a matter of fact, that's why I'm going up."

"Hmm. Well, maybe I misunderstood him. Anyway he's holding the money for me in cash, and I'd be pleased if you would pick it up for me."

"All right. If he wants to do a cash business, I'll pick up the money for you."

Earl chuckled.

"What are you laughing about?" Smoke asked.

"Well, think about it, Smoke. How many men would trust another man to bring him two thousand five hundred dollars in cash money?"

"Anyone who has a good friend who is also an

honest man," Sam replied, answering the question even though it had been posed to Smoke.

Earl nodded. "I reckon you're right, at that."

"So, Thad's going to help you deliver the bull?" Smoke asked.

"Yes, he's looking forward to riding Fire up there. It will be the longest he's ever ridden him. You have no idea how much he and Fire have taken to each other. That was quite a wonderful thing you did when you gave him that horse."

"Thad's become quite a good hand for you, hasn't he?"

"Yes, he has, for all that he is only fourteen years old. He's a good enough worker that I have no need for any hired hands."

"You do pay him, don't you?" Earl asked.

"Oh yes, he insists upon it, and I do pay him. But I'm making him put one half of it in a special savings account so that he'll have enough money to go to college when he comes of age. I have to admit he complains about that a little."

"That's a good idea to make him save like that. He may complain now, but he'll thank you someday," Earl said.

Sam chuckled. "Yeah, I'll tell him that."

"Sam, I'll need a letter from you to Jim, authorizing me to pick up the money," Smoke said.

"If you'll stop by Longmont's after you're finished here, I'll write the letter out for you," Sam promised.

"By coincidence, that's just where I planned to go next. I'll be down soon as Earl finishes up with me."

With a parting wave, Sam left the barbershop.

"Mr. Condon seems like a good man," Earl said. "When he came here after Ned and Molly were murdered, most of us thought he would just sell Wiregrass 'n go back to St. Louis. I mean, him bein' a lawyer 'n all. Who would have thought that a lawyer would want to run a ranch?"

"He's a good businessman, and even though Wiregrass is a small ranch, Sam has found a way to make it very successful," Smoke said. "He doesn't need hired hands because he's never had more than twenty to fifty head at any given time. He has specialized in raising only purebred Herefords, and he gets good money for them. Well, you heard him. He wants me to pick up twenty-five hundred dollars from Jim Harris for Yankee Star, and that's only half the money."

"I've had ranchers in here feeling good when their cows bring forty dollars a head." Earl pulled the barber's cape from Smoke, then turned the chair around so Smoke could examine himself in the mirror. "All finished, young man. What do you think?"

"Considering what you started with, I'd say you did a good job." Smoke gave the barber forty cents, a sum that included a fifteen-cent tip. "I guess I'll go have my beer now."

Louis Longmont was a Frenchman from New Orleans, and he was quick to point out that he was truly French, not Cajun. The difference, he explained, was that his parents moved to Louisiana directly from France, and not from Acadia. Louis owned Longmont's, which was one of two saloons in Big

Rock, the other saloon being the Brown Dirt Cowboy Saloon

The Brown Dirt tended to cater to cowboys and workingmen, and it provided not only alcoholic beverages and a limited menu, but also bar girls who did more than just provide drinks. Longmont's, on the other hand, was more like a club in which ladies not only felt welcome, but were assured there would be no stigma to their frequenting the establishment.

When Smoke stepped into the saloon he saw Sam sitting at Louis Longmont's private table. Access to Louis's private table was limited to those people he invited or those who he classified as personal friends. Smoke had been in the latter category for a number of years now, and Sam had been included shortly after he arrived.

"Stop by the bar and grab your beer," Sam said. "It's already paid for."

A moment later, with beer in hand, Smoke joined Sam and Louis at Louis's table.

"Sam was telling me all about Yankee Star," Louis said. "I offered to draw high card for him, but he said he wasn't interested."

"I don't blame him," Smoke said. "Who would gamble a bull like Yankee Star on one card?"

"But think of it this way. If he won, he'd have the price of the bull and he'd still have the bull."

"You and I both know he wouldn't have won," Smoke said.

"Wait a minute. It's too big a gamble for me to take, but how do you know I wouldn't have won? The odds would be fifty-fifty that I would win."

"No, the odds would be one hundred percent that you wouldn't win. Let me show you why you were smart not to take him up on his offer," Smoke said. Smoke put a gold double eagle on the table. "All right, Louis. Let's cut."

"You first," Louis replied.

Smoke smiled. "He always has his sucker go first so he knows what card he will draw to win."

"You don't mean what he *will* draw to win. You mean what he *has* to draw to win, don't you?" Sam replied.

"No, I mean what he *will* draw to win. Watch."

Smoke drew a nine. Louis drew a jack.

"Double or nothing?" Louis asked with a smile.

Smoke drew a five. Louis drew a seven.

"Wait. That's just dumb luck, isn't it?" Sam asked.

With a laugh, Louis slid the gold coin back toward Smoke, then put the deck down in front of Sam. "Draw a card, Sam," he invited. "No bet."

Sam drew a king, then smiled. "Beat that."

Louis drew an ace.

"What the hell? How are you doing that? And you wanted to draw high card for Yankee Star?"

"I would have given him back," Louis said.

"You mean if you had won. What am I talking about? Of course you would have won."

"I was just teaching you an object lesson," Louis said. "Never gamble when all the odds are against you."

"I've got a feeling that if anyone gambles with you, the odds are always against them."

"That's why I never gamble," Louis said. He paused for a moment. "At least, not anymore."

"May I join you? Or is this a gentlemen-only club?"

All three men stood when Sally approached the table, and Smoke pulled out a chair for her.

"Did you get everything done?" Smoke asked.

"Yes, train tickets and a new dress to wear to the opening of the play."

"Madam Jensen, as beautiful as you will be in a new dress, all eyes in the audience will be on you, and I fear the poor players will strut and fret their hour upon the stage and be heard no more," Longmont said.

Sally laughed and clapped her hands. "Louis, you are wonderful the way compliments roll trippingly from the tongue."

"Are you two just going to trade Shakespeare with each other, or are we going to eat dinner?" Smoke said.

"Lunch, not dinner," Sally replied.

"All right, lunch. And, Louis no disrespect for the meals you serve, but I'm in the mood for a big thick, steak, so we'll be taking our dinner—"

"Lunch," Sally corrected again.

"Lunch at Lamberts."

"Just don't get hit by a throwed roll," Sam said.

"Thrown," Sally said. "And, yes, I know what the sign on the false front of the building says, but I just refuse to see it."

"Perhaps I should throw bottles of wine to my customers," Louis suggested. He laughed. "Every now and then I'm tempted to do just that, only I wouldn't be throwing a bottle *to* them, as much as it would be *at* them."

Moniel, Wyoming

When Duly Plappert dismounted in front of the Ace High Saloon, he pulled his pistol, rotated the cylinder so that a loaded chamber was under the firing pin, then pushed in through the batwing doors. Plappert was a bounty hunter, and the man he was looking for, Don Ingles, was standing at the far end of the bar.

"All you folks standing at the bar, step away," Plappert called.

"Who the hell are you to tell us to step—" Recognizing Plappert, the man who spoke swallowed the rest of his question, grabbed his drink, and left the bar. The others did the same, but when Ingles started to leave the bar, Plappert called out to him.

"Not you, Ingles. Me 'n you got business to settle."

"I ain't goin' to fight you, Plappert," Ingles said. "If you want to take me in, go ahead. But I ain't goin' to fight you."

"You got no choice," Plappert said. "You're worth two hunnert 'n fifty dollars to me, dead or alive. So if you don't draw on me, I'll just kill you anyway, then step down to the marshal's office to collect my reward."

"I ain't goin' to draw ag'in you. I told you that."

Plappert smiled a slow, evil smile. "And I told you, I don't care whether you draw on me or not. I can kill you, 'n it'll all be legal."

With a shout of fear, Ingles made a frantic grab for his pistol. Plappert's smile grew broader. He was actually enjoying the moment. He drew his pistol in a quick, smooth draw, then fired, his bullet catching

Ingles in the chest. Then, even as Ingles lay dying on the floor, Plappert walked down to City Marshal Coleman's office to claim his prize.

Plappert waited in the office while Marshal Coleman walked down to the saloon to make certain that the man Plappert shot really was Don Ingles. As Plappert waited, he started looking through the marshal's wanted posters for his next job. That was when he saw a recruiting poster from Mule Gap.

—WANTED—

Men to Serve as
SPECIAL DEPUTIES

HIGH SALARY ! *and* ADDITIONAL REWARDS !

☞ *See* The Professor
MULE GAP, WYOMING

Plappert was intrigued by the offer of "high salary and additional rewards." He was also intrigued by the fact that the person offering the job was the man known as The Professor. Plappert knew The Professor, and he knew that he wouldn't be involved in anything like this unless the pay was very good.

Coleman came back into the office.

"You satisfied that it's Ingles?" Plappert asked.

"He ain't dead yet," Coleman said.

"But you seen that it's Ingles, right?"

"He's dyin' hard."

"Marshal, I don't give damn how hard he's dyin' or how long it takes for the son of a bitch to die. All I need from you is to say that the man lying on the floor back in the saloon is Don Ingles, 'n that they's people in the saloon will tell you that I'm the one that shot 'im."

"It's Ingles," Marshal Coleman said.

"Now I'll need you to authorize payment of the two hunnert 'n fifty dollars."

"Two hundred fifty dollars seems an awfully small amount of money for a man's life," Coleman said.

"Hell, it ain't my fault that it's no higher, Marshal. I don't set the rewards," Plappert said.

One hour later and two hundred and fifty dollars richer, Plappert rode out of town. Folded up in his pocket was the recruiting poster he had seen in the marshal's office. He was heading toward Mule Gap.

CHAPTER SEVEN

Mule Gap

Smoke was visiting Warren Kennedy in the mayor's office.

"None of my people gave you any trouble in making your deposit, did they?" Kennedy asked.

Smoke chuckled. "Warren, have you ever heard of a bank that *didn't* want to take your money?"

Kennedy laughed as well. "I guess you have a point there. I'm disappointed you didn't bring Sally with you. I would have enjoyed taking the two of you out to dinner."

"In your restaurant," Smoke said.

"I only own half of it," Kennedy replied

"Which means what? That you would have only had to pay for half the meal?"

Kennedy laughed again.

"Sally is at home, getting ready for her trip."

"Her trip? What trip?"

"Three days from now she'll be boarding the train to go to New York."

"Do you mean to tell me that she's going to New York, and you aren't going with her?"

"There's nothing in New York that I need to see," Smoke said.

"I agree with you there. I see no need for me to return to New York."

"Well," Smoke said, standing. "I'd better be going. I have to stop by Cross Trail before I start back."

"Harris's ranch? What are you doing out there?"

"A friend of mine sold a very expensive bull to Harris. I'm picking up twenty-five hundred dollars in cash, which is the first half of the purchase price. The other half is to be paid when the bull is delivered. To be honest, it seems a little strange to me. I don't know why Harris wants to deal in cash, when he has a bank here."

"I don't understand that, either," Kennedy said. "Who is your friend that sold the bull?"

"His name is Sam Condon. He runs Wiregrass, a small ranch next to mine."

Kennedy laughed. "He owns a *small* ranch next to yours? Smoke, from what I've heard about Sugarloaf, by comparison, just about *every* ranch is small."

Smoke nodded. "I do have a lot of acres. But in this case, Wiregrass really is small. Sam raises only pure-bred cattle, and the only help he has is his son."

"Can he make a living, raising just purebred cattle?"

"Are you kidding?" Smoke asked. "Do you really have no idea how much money purebred bulls can bring in? Sam Conrad is doing exceptionally well. He lives modestly, no hired hands, just him, his wife, and their boy. But he is a very wealthy man."

"How old is the boy?"

"If you would have asked me that a week ago, I wouldn't have been able to tell you. But he's fourteen. I know, because Sam just told me the other day."

"Well, I'm happy for anyone who is successful," Kennedy replied. "Come. I'll walk you to the door."

"No need to do that." Smoke laughed. "I'm sure that someone who owns half a town, as well as being the mayor, can find more things to keep him busy than to walk a visitor to the door."

"Ah, but you aren't just any visitor," Kennedy said. "You're a special visitor, and someday I'll find a way to get you to transfer all your money from the Bank of Big Rock to my bank."

"I don't think you'll be able to do that unless you move your bank at least twenty miles closer to Sugarloaf."

"Well, you've got me there," Kennedy said. "Next time you come to Mule Gap, be sure and bring Sally with you. I'll take both of you out to dinner."

"Maybe, when she gets back from New York, we'll do just that."

Fort Laramie, Wyoming

Clem Bates, Dan Cooper, Henry Barnes, and Slim Gibson were civilian scouts riding with the Second Cavalry. The great battles with the Northern Plains Indians had mostly passed, but there were still isolated raids against neighboring ranches, freight wagons, remote stores, and trading posts. One recent raid, led by Stone Eagle, had looted a store, then burned the building down.

Captain Neil Lewis of D Troop, 2nd Cavalry, led his troop in pursuit, and they caught up with three of the warriors on Horseshoe Creek, just north of the Laramie Peaks.

"Bates—you, Cooper, Barnes, and Gibson take these three back to the fort," Captain Lewis said. "I'm sure Stone Eagle is in one of the canyons in Laramie Peaks, and I think I know which one. We're going after him, and the ones with him."

Bates waited until the soldiers were out of sight, then he turned to the others. "I'm all for goin' back to the fort and havin' a beer, but I see no reason to take these heathen bastards along with us."

"What do you have in mind?" Barnes asked.

Bates looked at the three Indians who were standing with their hands tied in front of them. The Indians were staring sullenly at the four white men who had been left in charge.

"You are not Long Knives?" one of the Indians asked, referring to the term used by the Indians when speaking of soldiers.

"Nah," Barnes said. "We are civilians. We work for the army, but we ain't army."

"You will take us to the fort?"

Barnes shook his head. "We ain't takin' you to the fort. We're goin' to let you go."

The Indian translated for the other two, and all three smiled. The English-speaking Indian held out his hands. "You untie, and give us our guns?"

"No, I ain't goin' that far with you. I'm lettin' you go. Ain't that enough?"

"Yes, that is enough."

The Indians started toward their ponies, but Barnes called out to them.

"Uh-uh. You walk. If I give you your horses, like as not you'd join back up with Stone Eagle. You walk."

With a nod of understanding, the Indians turned and started to walk away.

Barnes drew his pistol and signaled for the others to do the same. He fired the first shot, shots from the other three coming quickly behind his shot. For the next few seconds the valley ran with gunshots as all three Indians went down.

Gibson was the first to get to them.

"Are they dead?" Barnes called out.

"Deader 'n a doornail," Gibson replied.

It was three days later when Colonel Roxbury called the four scouts into his office. "You say that the Indians were trying to run away, and I can't prove that they weren't, but there were a total of eighteen bullet holes in those three men, every one of them in the back."

"Yes, sir, well, when someone is running from you, their back is all you see," Barnes said.

Roxbury stroked his chin. "I'm lettin' you boys go. Every one of you. We have a hard enough time maintaining peace with the Indians as it is. It is people like you that make things even harder. I want you off this fort within the next fifteen minutes."

It was in the North Pass Saloon in Millersburg, later that afternoon, that they learned that a marshal they called The Professor was looking for men to be his deputies. The unusual aspect of the call was that he was willing to pay well and offered additional inducements.

"Come on, boys," Barnes said. "We're goin' to be deputies."

The Blackwell residence, Mule Gap

Lorena Coy was sitting in the swing on the front porch, keeping an eye on seven-year-old Eddie Blackwell, who, because he was small even for a seven-year-old, was called "Wee." His father Richard owned the Blackwell Emporium and was the wealthiest man in Mule Gap, even wealthier than Warren Kennedy. His store was successful enough that, unlike several other business owners in town, he was able to resist offers of partnership with Kennedy. And because he had loaned a few of his friends and fellow businessmen money when they needed it, he helped them stave off Kennedy's offer of partnership as well.

As a result not only of Blackwell's independence but also of his role in helping other businesses maintain their autonomy, he and Kennedy became business competitors, though they treated their adversarial relationship in a gentlemanly manner.

Richard Blackwell owned a brick house just outside the city limits, saying that he preferred country living to city living.

"City? What city? Surely you aren't calling Mule Gap a city, are you?" one of his friends had teased.

"Any place that has houses no more than fifty feet apart is a city," Richard had insisted.

Lorena was a fourteen-year-old-girl who lived

with her mother. Since her father had died two years earlier, it had been difficult for the Coy family. Lorena's mother Sandra had to give up the house and move her and Lorena into a three-room apartment in Welsh's Boarding House. She then went to work as a clerk in the Blackwell Emporium, while Lorena took on the job of watching out for Wee, as both Richard and Edna Blackwell worked in the emporium.

At the moment, Wee was sitting on the ground under a tree.

"Wee, stay in the grass," Lorena called out to him. "Don't get in the mud and get all dirty. If you do, your mama would be really upset with you."

"She'd be upset with you, too, for letting me get all dirty," Wee said.

Lorena chuckled. "Yes, she would. And you don't want me getting in trouble, do you?"

"I'll stay out of the dirt," Wee promised.

Lorena turned her attention back to reading the book, only to be interrupted a few minutes later by a buckboard being driven into the front yard. There were two men in the buckboard, and both of them climbed down.

"If you've come to see Mr. Blackwell, he isn't here," Lorena said.

"That's good, because we didn't come to see either one of them," one of the men said.

"Oh? Then, what can I do for you?"

"You can come get into the buckboard," one of the men said.

"What? Why on earth would I want to do that?"

One of the men pointed his pistol at Wee. "Because you are going with us."

"What do you mean, go with you? Go where?"

"You'll go where we take you, and quit asking so damn many questions. Because if you don't come, we're goin' to kill this kid."

"Lorena, don't let them kill me!" Wee called out.

"All right, all right. I'll go with you," Lorena said. "Please, don't hurt him."

Lorena walked out to the buckboard, then she hesitated. "I can't go with you. There's no one to look after Wee. I can't leave him by himself."

"Oh, you don't have to worry none about that, girly. He'll be comin' with us, as well."

One of the two men walked up to the front porch and, using a knife, pinned a note to the front door of the house.

We have your boy and the girl. You will be contacted with instructions as to how much money it will cost you and where to leave it. If you ever want to see your boy again, you will do as you are told.

A few miles north of the Blackwell residence, and unaware of the drama that was being played out there, Smoke Jensen was enjoying an after-lunch cup of coffee at Cross Trail Ranch. "Mrs. Harris, that was a great dinner."

"There's plenty left," Mrs. Harris said.

"Thank you, but I don't think I could eat another bite."

"Well, then, I shall leave you men to your business," she said.

Jim poured another cup of coffee, then slid it across the table to Smoke. "If you'll just sit there, I'll go get the money, then come back and count out the twenty-five hundred dollars. I had the bank in Douglas give it to me, all in twenty-dollar bills."

"All right," Smoke agreed, taking a swallow of his coffee as Jim left the room. He returned a moment later, holding a bundle of money. He began counting it out, making five stacks of twenty-dollar bills, twenty-five of them in each stack.

"Have you seen Yankee Star?" Jim asked as he counted out the money.

"Yes, I have. He's a fine bull, and you are getting your money's worth. But then, any bull Sam sells is worth the money. He is one smart man, finding a way to make such a small spread as profitable as he has."

"Yes, from my dealings with him I figured out long ago that he was a smart man."

"Jim, I'm curious. Why are you dealing in cash? The bank in Big Rock will certainly recognize drafts drawn on the bank of Mule Gap."

Jim chuckled. "They won't honor my draft if I have no money in Kennedy's bank to back it up."

"You said you had the bank in Douglas issue the money in twenty-dollar bills. But you are a lot closer to Mule Gap than Douglas. Why not use the bank in Mule Gap?"

"You've seen how things are in town, haven't you? Hell, Kennedy has his finger in just about every business in Mule Gap. I don't want to wind up with him owning half of Cross Trail."

"There's no way he could do that unless you sell half of it to him, or borrow against the ranch and are unable to pay it back."

"You don't have to worry any about that. I have no intention of selling any of my ranch to him, nor do I ever intend to borrow money from him. I just don't trust him."

"I think you have him all wrong. Don't confuse being an astute and opportunistic businessman with dishonesty."

"As far as I know, cash is still negotiable, is it not?" Harris replied.

"Indeed it is."

"Then, as long as I don't need to borrow any money, I have no need for a bank."

"I suppose not." Smoke replied with a chuckle. He picked up the first of the five stacks of bills, all of which were bound by ribbons Mrs. Harris had provided for that purpose. He had brought his saddle bags into the house and put the stacks into the bag. "I'd better get started. I've a long ride ahead of me."

"Take care, Smoke, and thank you for doing this for us."

"No problem," Smoke said, tossing a wave over his shoulder as he started toward Seven, who had been waiting patiently for him.

CHAPTER EIGHT

On the road to Mule Gap

"Hey Beamus. You see anythin' yet?"

The man named Beamus was lying on a rock, look-ing north toward Mule Gap. "No, I ain't seen nothin' yet. Listen, Quince, are you sure this fella is goin' to have twenty-five hunnert dollars on 'im?"

"Yeah, I'm sure. Twenty-five hunnert dollars in cash money."

Though at the moment only Beamus and Quince were talking, there were actually three men waiting at North Gate Canyon, which was just south of the line that separated Wyoming from Colorado. The third man was taking a leak.

"Hey, Parker, how long does it take you to piss, anyway?" Quince asked. "You want to be standin' there with your pecker in your hand when Jensen shows up?"

"You heard what Beamus said. He said he ain't seen nothin' yet," Parker replied, buttoning up his pants. "Hey, you're good at cipherin', Beamus. Oncet we get a-holt of this money, how much will that be for each of us?"

"Five hunnert dollars apiece."

"Five hunnert? Hell, they's only three of us. Even I know that a third of twenty-five hunnert dollars is more 'n five hunnert."

"A thousand dollars goes to the feller that set this up for us," Beamus said.

"Wait. He gets a thousand dollars, 'n he don't take no risk a-tall? That ain't right," Parker said.

"We wouldn'ta even knowed about it iffen he hadn't told us. Besides, when was the last time you had five hunnert dollars that was all your'n?"

"That's a easy question to answer, on account of I ain't never had five hunnert dollars all at the same time."

"Well then, what's your complaint?"

"It just don't seem right, is all. Hey, I've got a idea. Why don't we keep all the money for our ownself, 'n just ride outta here?"

Beamus shook his head. "You ever hear tell of killin' the golden goose?"

"What golden goose?"

"Never mind. The reason we ain't goin' to just keep the money 'n ride outta here, is on account of cause he'll be comin' up with a lot of other jobs for us, just like this. We can make a lot of money if we just stick with him."

"Someone's a-comin'," Quince called down to the two men.

"All right. Let's get ready for 'im," Beamus ordered.

* * *

Smoke had been riding for a little over two hours. Behind him, like a line drawn down through the middle of the road, the darker color of hoof-churned earth stood out against the lighter, sunbaked ground. The way before him stretched out in motionless waves, one right after another. As each wave was crested, another was exposed and beyond that another still. The ride was a symphony of sound—the jangle of the horse's bit and harness, the squeaking leather as he shifted his weight upon the saddle, and the dull thud of hoofbeats.

Seven knew the way back home, and Smoke, who had had a long day, was so relaxed in the saddle that he was taking quick, short naps. The lack of attention to detail meant a man was able to leap out in front of him.

"Stop right there, mister!" the man shouted. He held a double-barreled shotgun leveled at Smoke

"Now, why do I get the idea you didn't stop me to ask for directions?" Smoke asked.

"Ha-ha. Did you hear that, Quince? Parker? We've got the drop on him, 'n he's makin' jokes."

The two other men walked out from behind an outcropping of rocks adjacent to the road. Neither of them had drawn their pistols, depending on the shotgun to be all the cover they needed.

"Yeah, Beamus," Quince said. "He's just real funny."

"Get down off that horse," Beamus ordered.

Smoke could barely contain the smile as he slid out of the saddle. His chances against the three men were greatly improved by being dismounted.

"Now, mister, if you want to live, you'll hand over the money," Beamus said.

"What money?"

"Don't give us none o' that," Beamus said. "The twenty-five hunnert dollars in cash that you're a-carryin'."

"How do you know I'm carrying exactly two thousand five hundred dollars? To know the specific amount requires previous knowledge."

"It don't matter how we know. The point is you're about to hand that money over to us."

"I'm afraid I can't do that. If you know about the money, you also know that the money doesn't belong to me."

"Well, hell. If it ain't your money, then it ought not to bother you none to give it over to us," Quince said.

"Besides which, if you don't give us the money we'll just kill you and take it anyway," Parker added.

"Speaking of killing . . . isn't it funny how people will wake up in the morning with no idea that they won't be alive to see nightfall?" Smoke said.

"Well, hell, mister, you can still be alive come nightfall. All you have to do is hand over the money like we told you to."

"Oh, I wasn't talking about me not being alive," Smoke said. "I was talking about the three of you. I'll bet that when you three woke up this morning, you had no idea this would be the day you'd die."

"Are you crazy, mister? There's three of us," Parker said.

"That's all right. I've got three bullets."

"Damn, Beamus, shoot the son of a bitch!" Quince

shouted as first he and then Parker sent their hands darting toward their pistols.

Beamus put his thumb on the hammers of the shotgun, but before he could pull them back, Smoke drew and fired. His second shot and third shots were so close upon the heels of the first that it sounded as if only one shot had been fired. Quince and Parker had barely cleared their holsters and were already collapsing before Beamus hit the ground.

Smoke checked the three men, ascertaining what he already knew . . . that they were dead. It took him but a few minutes to find the horses they had staked out. He didn't know which horse belonged to whom, but under the circumstances, he didn't think it mattered. He draped a body across each horse, then tying the reins of the two trailing horses to the saddle horn before them, he took the reins of the first horse and led them three miles until he reached the next town, Walden. He was acquainted with the sheriff there.

A single rider leading three horses, each containing a body thrown across the saddle, attracted a lot of attention. Though the townspeople didn't follow him down the street, the boardwalks on each side of Main Street quickly filled with the morbidly curious.

Smoke stopped and called out to one of the men, "Where's the undertaker?"

"He's on this street down at the corner of Fifth 'n Main. He's got his place in the back of the Adam's Feed 'n Seed store."

"Thanks. Would you mind stopping at the sheriff's office and asking him to come down?"

"You *want* the sheriff?" the man asked, surprised by the request.

For a moment, Smoke wondered why there was such a tone of surprise in the man's response, then he realized that the man might think he had murdered the three men.

"Yes, tell Sheriff Rand that Smoke Jensen would like to see him down at the mortuary."

That seemed to assuage the man's concern, and with a nod, he hurried to his task.

"Yeah, I know all three of these boys," Sheriff Rand said a few minutes later after he had examined the bodies. "They've been hopping back and forth across the Wyoming and Colorado line for the last five years, causin' trouble in both places."

"I'm transporting twenty-five hundred dollars in cash," Smoke said, "and these three knew the exact amount I was carrying."

"Well now, how would they know that?" the sheriff asked.

"That's a very good question," Smoke replied. "Just how did they know not only that I was carrying money, but the exact amount I was carrying?"

"Someone had to tell them," the sheriff said. "Who knew about it?"

"I don't know. The people in the bank at Douglas. Maybe someone who just happened to be in the bank when Mr. Harris got the money. Could be some of the hands who worked on Cross Trail knew about it," Smoke said.

"Yes, well, thanks to you, the money is still there.

By the way, I think there's a couple hundred dollars reward on each of these boys."

"Collect the reward and give it to the county," Smoke said.

"That's real generous of you, Smoke. The county appreciates that."

"You can do the same thing with their horses."

"All three of the horses is more 'n likely stoled," the sheriff said, "but if we don't find the owners, we'll do just that."

With the sheriff informed and the bodies taken care of, Smoke left the mortuary and walked out to Seven.

"What about Pearlie and Cal?" Sheriff Rand asked. "Those two boys stayin' out of trouble?"

"About the only trouble they ever get into is with Sally," Smoke replied with a little laugh, "and almost all of it starts and ends in her kitchen."

"Ha!" Sheriff Rand replied. "I'll bet it doesn't take much for her to whip them into shape, either, does it."

"Not much," Smoke agreed.

"Yes well, I'm glad you stopped by. Just between us, I'm glad you put those three ne'er-do-wells out of business."

Smoke swung into the saddle. Lifting his hand, he turned Seven back into the street and continued his ride south.

Cheyenne, Wyoming

Everything had gone wrong when Chubb Slago, Lute Cruthis, Boots Zimmerman, and two others had attempted a bank robbery in Hutchinson County, Texas, a month ago. Right from the very beginning the would-be bank robbery had turned into a shoot-out. It began in the bank when the teller with more courage than sense produced a gun and began shooting. His act got him killed, but it also kept the robbers from getting any money. The shooting had alerted the rest of the town, and when the unsuccessful robbers left the bank, it seemed that everyone in Windom had a gun of some sort—pistol, rifle, or shotgun.

The five riders rode through the gauntlet of fire, losing two of their number.

Cruthis, Slago, and Zimmerman left Texas. One month and two small robberies later, they found themselves in Cheyenne, Wyoming, with very little money and no prospects, having escaped the Texas authorities. Boots had gone into the post office to see if they were on any wanted posters in Wyoming—they weren't—and he discovered the flyer from Mule Gap looking for deputies.

"Are you out of your mind?" Cruthis asked. "We run *from* deputies, not to them."

"Wait, Cruthis," Slago said. "Boots may have a good idea here."

"I'd like to know what would be so good about being a deputy city marshal," Cruthis said.

"Well for one thing, if any paper ever showed up with our names on it, it would be kinda good to be able to get to it first and get rid of it, wouldn't it?"

"Yeah." Cruthis smiled. "Yeah! That would be damn good."

"And it says well paying and other rewards," Slago said. "I don't know what it means by well paid, and I don't know what other rewards it is talking about, but no matter what it is, you have to admit that it is better than we've got now."

"Hey Boots, how do you think I'd look with a star?" Cruthis asked.

Zimmerman laughed. "I think you'd look damn fine."

Mule Gap

Clem Bates, Dan Cooper, Henry Barnes, and Slim Gibson were standing around in various poses in Marshal Bodine's office. Duly Plappert, whom Bodine had made his chief deputy, was sitting at the only other desk in the room. Chubb Slago, Lute Cruthis, and Boots Zimmerman were there as well, and so was Angus Delmer. They were watching Bodine swear in Boney Walls, the tenth and last deputy that Bodine intended to hire.

"All right, gentlemen, our little constabulary is complete," Bodine said, addressing the others. "From now on you will begin earning the generous stipend that is being offered for services rendered, so it is time you begin rendering said services."

"What the hell did he just say?" Zimmerman asked Slago.

"I'm not sure, but I think he said it was time we started working."

From that point forward, the deputies became a ubiquitous presence in Mule Gap. They patrolled the streets, strictly enforcing draconian laws against being drunk, being disorderly, spitting, tossing away a cigar butt, and anything else a deputy decided should be enforced. Each infraction of the laws, even if it was against a law no one had heard of, resulted in fines. In addition, every business in town saw additional taxes applied.

"I lived through reconstruction," said Albert Kirkland, who owned the gun shop. "And I swear, this is just as bad."

"Well, they have to police the entire county," Bud Coleman said. He owned the wagon freighting service. "And seeing as my wagons are out there, I don't mind tellin' you that I appreciate having that protection."

"Then why aren't they out there policing?" another asked.

"And while they're at it, they might also try and find some of them kids that have been took," still another added.

"You're talking about the Blackwell boy and the Coy girl, are you?" Kirkland asked.

"My drivers tell me there's at least three more missing," Coleman said. "A couple boys from Warm Springs 'n another girl."

"I thought they was let go."

"No, that was an earlier group they had. Their folks paid the ransom on them, 'n they was sent home."

"Hell, couldn't they tell the law where they was bein' held?"

"They did, but when Bodine sent a couple of his deputies out there to check up on 'em, they said there warn't nobody there."

"I'm surprised he even let the deputies go check it out," Kirkland said. "Seems to me like all he has them doin' is collecting money."

CHAPTER NINE

Wiregrass

Sam Condon had invited Smoke and Sally to dinner as sort of a repayment for Smoke having brought him the twenty-five hundred dollars that was the down payment on the bull, Yankee Star.

"Do you want another piece of pie, Mrs. Jensen? I'll get it for you," Thad offered.

"Thank you, Thad, but I think I'll pass this time," Sally said.

"You sure you don't want another piece? I'll be glad to get it."

"Thad, Mrs. Jensen said no," Sara Sue said to her son.

Sam chuckled. "Thad is just trying to wrangle a second piece of pie for himself."

"Well, he didn't ask me," Smoke said. "I'll take another piece as long as it is very small."

A wide smile spread across Thad's face. "I'll get it!" he said, standing up from the table. He returned a moment later with a small piece of pie for Smoke, and a much larger piece for himself.

"Thad," Sara Sue scolded.

"Well, Ma, you always tell me I should be polite, and it wouldn't be polite for Mr. Jensen to have to take seconds all by himself, would it? And he said he only wanted a small piece."

Sam laughed. "He's got you there, Sara Sue."

"Sally, is it true that you are going to New York?" Sara Sue asked.

"Yes. Andrew and Rosanna MacCallister have a new play in New York, and they sent me an invitation."

"Andrew and Rosanna MacCallister? Why, they are famous," Sara Sue said. "They personally sent you an invitation? Do you know them?"

"It is more a case of me knowing their brother, Falcon MacCallister. He is a very good friend of ours," Sally said. "I met Rosanna and Andrew through him. I must say that for all their fame and success, they are exceptionally nice people."

"Will you be going as well, Smoke?" Sam asked.

"No. Sally has an old college friend that she wants to visit as well, and that's an *opportunity* I can afford to miss."

The others laughed at his emphasis on the word *opportunity*.

"Cal is going with me," Sally said.

"Cal Wood?" Sara Sue asked. "Isn't he one of your hired hands?"

"I suppose you could say that," Sally said, "though he is much more than a hired hand."

Smoke chuckled. "We've practically adopted him . . . ever since he tried to rob Sally at gunpoint."

"What?" Sara Sue gasped.

"He was very young and very desperate," Sally said.

"I knew then that he had no real intention of hurting me. I brought him home, gave him his first good meal in no telling how long, then talked Smoke into hiring him."

"He and Pearlie are more like a part of our family than hired hands," Smoke said.

"I can believe that," Sam said. "I've seen the way you are when you're together. It's not like they're hired hands at all. Don't get me wrong, they respect you, but it is more like you're family."

"Is Pearlie going to New York, as well?" Sara Sue asked.

"No. Pearlie has been there before, but Cal has never seen New York, and I would like to broaden his experience at least once."

"Sounds to me like that young man was dealt four aces when he ran into you two," Sam said.

"I expect he was." Smoke reached over, took Sally's hand, and smiled at her. "But then, I can say that as well, because I was dealt the same hand when I ran into Sally."

They continued their visit after dinner, going into the parlor to listen to music on the Symphonion disc player, and enjoying three-dimensional photographs of the wonders of the world on the stereopticon. By the time they were finished with their visit, it had grown dark.

"Oh my, look at the time," Sally said. "We didn't intend to impose upon your hospitality for so long."

"Nonsense, it was no imposition at all," Sara Sue replied. "We have greatly enjoyed your company."

"Thad, go outside and light the lanterns on the

surrey for them so they can see to drive home," Sam directed.

"All right, Pa," Thad said, eager to help.

"Thad is a fine young man," Smoke said after Thad left. "I can see where he is such a help to you in running your operation here."

"Yes, he is." Sam chuckled. "But I'm glad you waited until he was out of the house before you said that. He has a big enough head as it is."

Smoke laughed.

"I'll tell you this—he has taken to Fire the way you have to Seven," Sam said. "He and that horse are as close as any boy would be with a dog."

"A good horse is like that," Smoke replied.

"I can't tell you how appreciative we are for that gift, and as far as Thad is concerned, you've made a friend for life."

"A good investment, I would say."

When Smoke and Sally went out to the surrey, both running lanterns were lit and the polished mirror behind the flames cast twin beams of light that joined a few feet in front of them to light their way.

"Thank you, Thad," Smoke said as he helped Sally in, then climbed up behind her. "Sam, Sara Sue, it was a wonderful evening, and we thank you for the invitation."

"It was great having you. Sally, do have a safe and most enjoyable trip," Sara Sue said.

With waves of good-bye, Smoke snapped the reins, and the team started out for the six-mile trip back to the Sugarloaf.

"I didn't know Cal had agreed to go with you," Smoke said as the surrey moved swiftly down the road.

"He hasn't yet, but the only reason he hasn't is because he thinks it wouldn't be fair to Pearlie for him to go and Pearlie to stay behind."

"I'm pretty sure Pearlie doesn't want to go."

"Are you kidding? He told me, and I quote, 'Miss Sally, the only way you're going to ever get me to go to someplace like New York is if you hog-tie me and drag me there.' I took that to mean that he didn't want to go."

Smoke laughed. "Yes, I'd say that is a pretty good indication of his lack of interest."

Though they didn't always do so, Pearlie and Cal had breakfast with Smoke and Sally the next morning. She had invited the two, sweetening the invitation with the promise of a freshly made batch of bear sign.

"I'll tell you what, Miss Sally, if God ever made anything on earth that was any better than your bear sign, He sure did keep them for Himself," Pearlie said.

"You got that right," Cal added. "I'll bet you can't get anything like that in New York."

"No, but you can get a *tarte aux pommes* that will make your mouth water," Sally said.

"What's that?" Cal asked.

"Think about a flaky piecrust covered with a coat of sugar-glazed cake. Inside are honey-sweetened apples baked so soft that you can eat them with a spoon."

"When do we leave?" Cal asked.

"You mean you are no longer worried about leaving Pearlie behind?"

"Let him get his own trip to New York, and his own

torty poms," Cal said with a broad smile. "I'm going with you."

French Creek Canyon in the
Medicine Bow Mountains, Wyoming

It had been eight days since Lorena Coy and Eddie "Wee" Blackwell were taken in the back of a buckboard. When they'd arrived they saw that three other children were already there, and now all five shared the same cabin. Lorena, at fourteen, was the oldest. There was one other girl and two other boys. Except for Lorena and Eddie Blackwell, none of the others had ever met one another until they were together in the cabin. Circumstances had made them brothers and sisters. Marilyn Grant, who was twelve, was the other girl. The other boys were Burt Rowe, also twelve, and Travis Calhoun, who was thirteen.

"I want to go home," Wee said.

"We all want to go home, sweetheart," Lorena said, trying to comfort the boy. "And someday, we will."

"Why won't they let me go home?"

"Because they are mean men," Lorena said.

"They'll let us go home as soon as our folks pay the ransom," Travis said. "The problem is, I don't think my pa has as much money as they are asking for."

"My mother lives all alone and has no money at all," Lorena said.

"Why did they kidnap you?" Burt asked.

"Because I was looking after Wee when they kidnapped him. I don't know how this is all going to work out. If Mr. Blackwell pays for Wee, then perhaps they will let me go as well."

"Here comes Weasel," Burt said. He had been looking through the window.

"Is he bringing food?" Travis asked.

"Yeah, it looks like it. That is, if you can call that soup they been servin' us *food*," Burt said.

The door opened and Andy Whitman, called Weasel by everyone, stepped inside carrying a pot by its handle. He set the pot down on the table. The clear, hot broth in the pot had little substance to it.

"All right, boys and girls, get your bowls out. It's time for breakfast."

"I don't want any," Marilyn said.

"Yes, you do," Lorena insisted.

"It's not soup. It's nothing but hot water."

"It's a broth. It isn't very good, I admit, but you have to eat, Marilyn, even if you don't want to," Lorena said. "Please at least try."

"All right," Marilyn said reluctantly. She picked up her bowl. "I'll try."

"Mr. Weasel, have you heard anything from my pa?" Burt asked. "Has he got the money yet?"

"I ain't heard," Weasel said as he spooned the broth into the bowls. "Somebody else will be handlin' that. All I'm s'posed to do is keep an eye on you 'n feed you."

"Where's everyone else?" Lorena asked.

"They're gone," Weasel said without further explanation.

"You mean you're the only one here that's guardin' us right now?" Travis asked.

"Yeah. Why do you ask? Do you think you can get away from me?"

"Maybe," Travis said.

"Why don't you try it?" Weasel asked.

"Where are the others?" Marilyn asked.

"Who knows where they are? Perhaps they've gone to get you another brother," Weasel said with an evil laugh.

Red and White Mountain, Eagle County, Colorado

Fred Keefer, Elmer Reece, and Clyde Sanders had spent the night camped out just below the Red and White Mountain. Although it was light, the sun had not yet climbed above Bald Mountain silhouetted against a brightening dawn to the east.

"How far is it from here?" Reece asked.

"Not far. Only about another couple miles," Keefer said. "We'll be there before they finish their breakfast."

"Who are we pickin' up? A boy or a girl?"

"It's a boy. The chief said this one will pay well."

"He says that about all of 'em," Sanders said, "but we still got a cabin full of brats that we ain't yet got us so much as one dollar from."

"We made good money from that first batch," Sanders said.

"Except for one," Reece said.

"They prob'ly woulda paid for her, too, if she hadn't tried to escape 'n got herself kilt," Sanders said.

"Yeah well, it ain't our job to be a-worryin' none about things like that," Keefer said. "It's our job to grab 'em, 'n it's the chief's job to get the money for 'em. He says that the ones we've already got is the same as havin' money in the bank."

"Yeah well, it wouldn't be so bad them bein' there if the chief wasn't such a damn fuddy-duddy 'bout the girls that's there. I mean, we could at least be havin' a little fun with 'em," Reece said. "Now you take the one that escaped 'n got herself kilt? She was a looker. Almost as good lookin' as the two we got now."

"What do you mean, have fun with 'em?" Keefer asked. "They ain't nothin' but girls."

"Yeah? Well, one of 'em, Lorena, is tittied up just real good, 'n I wouldn't mind at all showin' her what it's all about."

"Then we would have damaged goods," Keefer said. "And you can't get much money for damaged goods. Besides, we got a little money now. You can always go to that whorehouse in Mule Gap. Them whores is all good lookin', 'n whores is much better anyway, on account of they don't need no teachin'."

"The whores there is all right, except they're kinda hoity-toity about things."

"Yeah well, that's 'cause Delilah is all hoity-toity her ownself," Keefer replied.

"I don't see how we're goin' to get any money for Lorena at all, on account of her mama don't hardly have no money. I don't even know why we're keepin' her," Sanders said.

"She come with that little one, 'n his pa has got lots of money. The chief says that the little one's pa will pay for both of 'em."

"Yeah well, I still can't see why we can't have a little fun with 'er before we turn 'er loose. That is, if we ever turn 'em loose," Reece said.

CHAPTER TEN

Wiregrass

Sara Sue had been the first to rise this morning and she was in the kitchen preparing breakfast when her son came in. He was still yawning and stretching, and his hair looked like a haystack. She had long ago given up trying to make Thad comb his hair before breakfast.

"Thad, you'd better get out there and milk Ada. I can hear her bawling."

"All right, Ma." He grabbed a couple biscuits that his mother had just removed from the oven and took a bite from one. "You goin' to make gravy this mornin', Ma?"

"Yes. So you'd better leave enough biscuits."

"Good!" Thad said enthusiastically. He put one of the biscuits back.

Sara Sue laughed. "Thaddeus Condon, you and your father are two peas in the same pod . . . except he will at least comb his hair when he gets out of bed." She ran her hand through Thad's disheveled hair.

With the pail in one hand and the biscuit in the other, Thad started toward the barn.

Sara Sue watched him through the kitchen window. "My goodness, you are growing so fast I can't keep you in clothes," she said quietly.

"Talking to yourself are you, woman?" Sam teased, coming into the kitchen at that moment.

"I was just noticing how big Thad is getting," she replied, making no effort to apologize for talking aloud.

"He's a fine boy, and he's going to be a big help in taking Yankee Star up to Cross Trail. We'll get started right after breakfast."

"How long do you think you'll be gone?"

"Oh, no more than a couple days, I wouldn't think. Smoke said that Pearlie will come over at least once a day to keep an eye on the rest of the cattle."

"That's good of him to do so. Oh, I'm going to need some water to clean up after breakfast. Would you get some, please?"

"Sure," Sam replied as he grabbed the water bucket. "Someday I'm going to connect a pipe from the wind-mill pump to the kitchen. Then we'll have running water without having to go outside."

Sara Sue laughed. "You've been saying that ever since we got here."

"I'm going to do it someday. You'll see." Sam snatched a biscuit.

"Sam, can't you wait for breakfast? I swear, you are as bad as your son," Sara Sue scolded, though she was smiling as she chastised him.

As Sam began pumping water, he could hear Thad singing from the barn while he was milking the cow.

"Oh, the years creep slowly by, Lorena,
the snow is on the ground again."

"Lorena" was a song Sam had learned while he was a soldier during the war. He had taught it to Thad, who actually had a pretty good voice.

With the bucket full, Sam returned to the kitchen. "He's singing to Ada again," he said with a little chuckle.

"He says Ada gives more milk when he sings to her," Sara Sue replied.

"Maybe he's right. They say that music has charms to soothe a savage beast."

"Sam, are you calling Ada a savage beast?"

"And are you telling me you've never seen Ada mad?" Sam replied with a laugh.

"Pa! Pa, help!"

Thad's call came from outside the house and both Sara Sue and Sam could hear the panic in his voice. They rushed out onto the back porch just in time to see that there were three horsemen surrounding their son. Thad was struggling to free himself from the rope that was looped around him, and the pail he had been carrying was turned over beside him with the milk spilled out on the ground.

A second rope was thrown over Thad, and one of the three horsemen dismounted and started toward him.

"Let him go, you son of a bitch!" Sam shouted, running toward the man who was closest to Thad.

One of the riders raised his pistol and fired, and Sam went down.

"Sam!" Sara Sue called hurrying toward him.

The same gunman who had shot Sam aimed at Sara Sue.

"No, don't shoot her!" another shouted. "Don't shoot her. If we kill both of 'em, who'll pay the ransom?"

Knowing she could do nothing for Thad right now, Sara Sue knelt by Sam, who was still alive and taking labored breaths.

"Thad," Sam said.

Sara Sue looked toward her son and saw that the rope was wrapped around him many times so that his arms were bound to his side. Two men lifted him up onto a horse ridden by the third man.

"They're taking him, Sam. Oh, they are taking him."

"Read this!" one of the men shouted, dropping a piece of paper on the ground just before the three men, with Thad as their prisoner, galloped away.

"Thad! We'll come for you!" Sara Sue shouted at the galloping horses. "We'll come for you!"

"Did they . . . did they take him?" Sam asked, barely able to speak."

"Yes. Oh, Sam, they took our son."

He sat up. "Help me saddle a horse."

"You're in no condition to ride. I've got to get you in town to the doctor. If I hitch up the buckboard, do you think you can help me get you into it?"

"Yeah," Sam replied. "I can do that."

Sara Sue started toward the barn.

"Sara Sue," Sam called. "Don't try and connect a team. Just use Harry. He's all we'll need."

Big Rock Railroad Depot

Smoke, Sally, Cal, and Pearlie were standing on the depot platform alongside the train that had already pulled into the station. The engine relief valve was opening and closing, venting steam in great gasping breaths. The overheated wheel bearings and journals were snapping and popping as they cooled.

"I'll bring you a souvenir from New York," Cal promised Pearlie.

"Yeah? Tell you what. Bring me a picture of you 'n Miz Sally standin' in Central Park."

"Oh, I think we can do better than that," Sally said. "We'll come up with something."

"All aboard!" the conductor shouted as he checked his watch.

Sally gave Smoke a kiss, and Pearlie a hug. Cal started toward Pearlie.

"Now, hold on there," Pearlie said, holding his hands out in front of him. "You aren't fixin' to give me a hug, too, are you?"

Cal chuckled. "Well, I was just going to shake your hand, but if you want a hug . . ." he teased.

"A handshake will be fine, thank you," Pearlie replied.

Cal shook Smoke's hand as well, then he followed Sally onto the train. A moment later, Sally's face appeared in the window, then almost as soon as she was seated, the engineer blew the whistle and there was a huge puff of steam as he opened the throttle. That was followed by a chain reaction of creaks and rattles as the slack was taken up from the connectors between the cars and the train started forward. Smoke walked along, keeping pace with Sally until he reached the end of the platform. By that time the train had picked up so much speed that even if the platform had gone on farther, he would not have been able to stay with it.

Smoke and Pearlie stood at the end of the platform as the remaining cars passed. Not until the final car sped by them did they turn away.

"Hey Smoke, you think maybe we could get something to eat before we go back out to the ranch?" Pearlie asked. "I'd hate to come into town and waste the opportunity."

"I was just thinking the same thing," Smoke said.

Delmonico's Fine Dining was only four buildings down from the depot, and Smoke and Pearlie stepped inside just before Sara Sue reached town, urging the horse into a rapid trot as she drove the buckboard east on Front Street. She was going so fast that the buckboard skidded a little as she turned right onto Sikes Street then pulled Harry to a stop in front of the single-story, unimposing building between the Big Rock Theater and the Brown Dirt Cowboy that was Dr. Urban's office.

"Doc! Dr. Urban, come quick!" Sara Sue called. Hopping down from the buckboard, she ran into the office repeating her call. "Come quick, please. Come quick!"

Dr. Urban was an exceptionally skinny man with a protruding Adam's apple. He pushed his glasses up his nose as he came into the front in response to Sara Sue's call. "Mrs. Condon! What is it? What's wrong?"

"It's Sam, Doctor. I've got him in the buckboard out front. He's been shot!"

"You say he's been shot?"

"Yes. Please, come quick!"

Delmonico's restaurant

"Ha!" Pearlie said. "I'd like to see the expression on Cal's face the first time he sees all those people in New York. He thinks Denver is a big city."

"It'll be a good experience for him," Smoke said.

"He'll be a babe in the woods."

"Sally knows New York well. She'll look out for him."

A few minutes later, Dick DeWeese, owner of Delmonico's restaurant, came out of the kitchen pushing a wheeled cart toward Smoke and Pearlie's table. The meal they had ordered was on a large round tray and covered by a silver dome. Ignoring a squeaking wheel, Dick reached the table and lifted the cover, releasing the delicious aroma.

"Here are your lamb chops, Mr. Jensen, cooked to absolute perfection. I know that because I cooked them myself, and I'm delivering them personally to avoid any embarrassment."

"Embarrassment?" Smoke replied. "What embarrassment are you talking about?"

"Why, the embarrassment of one of the top ranchers in the entire state eating lamb. If someone like Tim Murchison or Ed Gillespie, or even Sheriff Carson, got wind of the fact that you are actually eating lamb, they would never let you live it down."

"Yeah well, you notice I ain't eatin' lamb," Pearlie said. "I ordered beefsteak 'n I hope that's what you brought me."

"Indeed I did. My remarks were addressed to Mr. Jensen."

Smoke laughed. "You can blame Sally for that. I had never tasted lamb in my life until she and I were married. Turns out this is what they eat where she came from." Smoke carved a piece of meat off, put it in his mouth, and smiled. "And it also turns out that I love it."

Having just finished a piece of chocolate cake, Smoke and Pearlie were enjoying a cup of coffee when a woman came into the restaurant and started toward their table.

"That's Mrs. Condon, isn't it?" Pearlie asked.

Smoke looked over toward the woman approaching the table. "Yes, it is." As she got closer, Smoke was shocked to see that tears were streaming down her face. He and Pearlie stood. "Sara Sue, what is it? What's wrong?"

"They've got Thad," Sara Sue sobbed. "They shot Sam, and they've got my child! Dr. Urban is with Sam now. Oh, Smoke, Sam might die!"

"Who has Thad?" Smoke asked. "And who shot Sam?"

"After they rode away, they left this note." She handed Smoke the piece of paper the riders had left behind.

If you want to see your boy alive again, come to the
Del Rey Hotel in Mule Gap, Wyoming, with fifteen
thousand dollars. You have one week from today to
raise the money. You will be contacted at the hotel
and told where to deliver the money and pick up
your boy. Come alone.

Leaving the restaurant, Smoke and Pearlie accompanied Sara Sue back to Dr. Urban's office. Sam
Condon was lying on the bed, naked from the waist
up. His trousers were pulled as low as they could go,
while still preserving some modesty. A large bandage
covered the lower right side of his abdomen.

"How is he doing?" Smoke asked.

"He hasn't awakened yet from the anesthetic, but
right now that is the best thing for him. The less he
moves around, the better off he will be," Dr. Urban
said. "The bullet was low . . . too low to hit anything
vital. I got it out. Now all we have to worry about is
infection."

"Do you think that will be a problem?" Smoke
asked.

"Mrs. Condon did a good job of getting him here
quickly. We've got a really good start on it, so I think
we'll be able to hold it back."

Sara Sue told Smoke and Pearlie about the three
men who'd ridden in and snatched Thad. "I can get
the fifteen thousand dollars, but to tell the truth, I'm
a little frightened to go meet them by myself. When I
found out you were in town at the restaurant, I came
to see you to ask if—"

Smoke held out his hand. "There is no need for you

to ask anything, Sara Sue. You know I will go with you."

"I am a little worried, though. The note said tell nobody. If they saw us together, I wouldn't want to take any chances on them doing anything to harm Thad."

"You don't need to worry about that. Thad is worth money to them only as long as he is alive and well."

"I pray that you are right. That he is still alive and unhurt," Sara Sue said.

"Prayer is always good," Smoke replied.

CHAPTER ELEVEN

French Creek Canyon

"Get down, boy,"

"Tied up like this, you'll have to help me down," Thad replied.

"Help 'im down, Sanders."

Sanders, the rider with whom Thad had ridden double for the entire morning, dismounted first then reached up to help Thad down from the horse. The boy examined his surroundings. Two cabins were backed up against French Creek. The larger of the two looked fairly well-kept and appeared to have been recently painted. The smaller one was constructed of wide weather-grayed planking.

A fourth man came out of the larger house.

"Any trouble while we were gone, Whitman?" Keefer asked.

"No, they have been calm as a passel of puppies. This is the one you was talkin' about?" Whitman asked, staring at Thad. "The one whose papa raises registered bulls?"

"Yeah."

"He's bigger 'n the others," Whitman said. "Hope he don't give us no trouble."

"He ain't goin' to give us no trouble, are you, boy?" Keefer asked as one of the men loosened the rope that was wrapped around Thad.

"Now I know Keefer, Sanders, and Whitman," Thad said. He looked at the fourth man. "What's your name?"

"What's it to you, what my name is?"

"I want to know your name because you're the one that shot Pa. And if he dies, I plan to kill you."

Sanders laughed. "Damn, Reece! How does it feel to have a fourteen-year-old after you?"

"Yeah, I'm only fourteen," Thad said. "But how old do you have to be to kill someone? I'll remember your name, Reece."

Reece walked up to Thad and slapped him hard. Thad retaliated by kicking Reece in the groin. Reece doubled over with pain as the others laughed.

"Why, you little shit!' Reece said when he straightened up again. He pulled his pistol then brought it down hard on Thad's head.

Thad went down.

"Here, Reece! Don't be damagin' the merchandise!" Keefer said, dismounting and hurrying over as Sanders knelt down to examine Thad. "If you've killed this boy you've just pissed away fifteen thousand dollars, and the chief ain't goin' to like that. He ain't goin' to like it at all."

"I ain't puttin' up with no mouthin'-off from a

kid. He needs to learn how to respect his elders," Reece said.

"He's alive. He's just knocked out, is all," Sanders said, rising up from his quick examination.

"It's a good thing for you, Reece, that he is alive," Keefer said. "Get 'im inside with the others."

Whitman and Sanders picked Thad up then carried him into the smaller of the two cabins where they dropped him on the floor. Thad had regained consciousness, but barely, and was aware only of the sensation of being moved. When he was dropped on the floor, his head spun so that the only thing he could do, for the moment, was lie there.

"Are you all right?"

Thad opened his eyes and saw the face of a young girl hovering over him. He wasn't sure if he was actually seeing her or if it was some sort of an illusion brought on by the blow to his head.

"Are you all right?" the girl asked again.

Thad reached up to put his hand on her face, and she pulled away from his touch.

"You're real," he said.

"What?" the girl responded. "Yes, of course I'm real."

Thad sat up and his head began to spin so that he wasn't sure he could even sit there. He put his hand to his head, then winced in pain when his hand found the lump. "Wow, they must have hit me a lick."

"Yes, we were watching through the window. We saw Reece hit you."

"We?"

"There are five of us here," the girl said.

Looking around, Thad saw not only the young girl who was talking to him, but four others—another girl and three boys. A quick appraisal of them suggested that he might be the oldest one in the room. He wasn't sure about the girl who had just questioned him, though. She might be older than he was.

"How old are you?" Thad asked.

"What?" the girl responded, surprised by the question. She laughed. "You are hit on the head, dropped in here nearly as much dead as you are alive, but do you ask my name or where or what this place is? No, you ask me how old I am. Lord have mercy, that blow to your head must have made you daft."

"How old are you?" he asked again.

"I'm fourteen. Why?"

"When will you be fifteen?"

"Not until November."

Thad smiled. "I'll be fifteen in August. That makes me older."

Despite the seriousness of the situation, the girl laughed. "You are a strange boy. We are all prisoners, and the only thing you are worried about is who is the oldest."

"Someone has to make plans," Thad said. "And it is obvious that the best person to make the plans would be the one who is the oldest."

"Make plans for what?" the girl asked.

"Escape," Thad replied in a single clipped word.

"Escape?"

"Yeah, I don't plan to stay here, and I'll take anyone with me who wants to go. You're right. I didn't ask you your name. What is it?"

"My name is Lorena."

"Lorena?" Thad said. "Really? Your name is Lorena?"

"Yes. Is there something wrong with my name?" the girl asked, a little piqued by his response to her name.

"No, nothing at all. I think it's great!" He began to sing. "'The sun's low down the sky, Lorena, the frost gleams where the flowers have been.'"

"Yes!" Lorena said, laughing. "Mama said that is how I got my name. She used to listen to people singing that song and—" She stopped in midsentence. Her eyes welled with tears and they began sliding down her cheeks. "I'm afraid I may never see Mama again."

"Yes, you will," Thad said. "We all will." He looked at the other girl and three boys. Not one of them had spoken since he arrived. "My name is Thad. I've met Lorena. What are your names?"

"My name is Marilyn Grant," the other girl said.

"How old are you, Marilyn?"

"I'm twelve."

Two boys were Travis Calhoun, who was thirteen, and Burt Rowe, who was eleven.

"And who are you?" Thad asked the smallest, who had not yet spoken.

"Wee."

"We? No, just you. The others have told me their names."

Lorena laughed. "Wee is his name. Actually, it's Eddie, but his mama and daddy started calling him Wee because he is so small."

Thad smiled and stuck out his hand. "It's nice to meet you, Wee."

Smiling back at Thad, Wee took his hand.

"We are sort of like brothers and sisters here," Lorena said. "That's how it has to be since we are all in the same boat."

"How long have you been here?" Thad asked.

Burt Rowe had been there the longest—six weeks. Next came Travis, then Marilyn Grant, then Lorena and Wee.

"Wee and I were taken together," Lorena said. "I was watching over him for his parents." She grew quiet, then her eyes welled with tears again. "I certainly wasn't doing a very good job of it, though, or those men wouldn't have taken us."

"Why do you say that?" Thad asked. "Was there really anything you could have done to prevent it?"

"No, but—"

"There are no buts to it. I wasn't able to keep them from getting me. How were you supposed to be able to stop them from getting you and Wee?"

"There wasn't any way," Lorena admitted.

"Then don't say you weren't doing a very good job."

"I want to go home," Wee said. "I want my mama." Tears slid down his cheeks, but he wasn't weeping aloud.

"You'll go home again, Wee. Marilyn, Travis, Burt, you will, too. I'll tell the four of you the same thing I told Lorena. You will see your ma and pa again."

"How?" Travis asked. "I know that the men who took us are asking for a whole lot of money. I don't think Pop even has that much money."

"If we all stick together and pay attention to what's going on around us, we'll find some way to get out of here, and it won't cost any of our folks anything. I promise you," Thad said.

He had thought they were only dealing with four men, but he learned from Lorena that there were more.

"How many are there?"

"I don't know. I've never seen anyone but the four who stay here all the time. Keefer is the leader of the ones here, but I know there's someone else who is in charge of all of them because I've heard them talk about him. But I've never heard the name," Lorena said.

"Why did Reece hit you in the head with a pistol?" Travis asked. "I don't think any of the rest of us were hit."

"It may be because I kicked him in the—" Because he didn't want to say the word in front of the two girls, Thad altered his sentence. "Uh, it was because I told him I was going to kill him."

Marilyn gasped. "You don't really mean that, do you?"

"Reece shot my pa. If I find out that Pa is dead, then, yes, I do mean it. I'll kill Reece."

"How are you going to do that?" Travis asked. "He's got a gun. All of them have guns. We don't."

"I haven't figured out yet how I'll do it." A determined expression showed on Thad's face as he responded to the question Travis had put to him. "But I will find a way."

"Here comes Sanders." Burt had been looking through the window.

"What do you suppose he wants?" Travis asked.

"It looks like he's bringin' us our dinner," Burt answered.

"Good. All I had for breakfast was a biscuit, and I'm hungry," Thad said.

"After you eat, you'll still be hungry," Travis said. "Believe me."

Travis was right. The "meal" consisted of a bowl of soup, though the soup was little more than hot water with a few globules of fat from the meat that had been its base but was missing from what was being served. There were also a few vegetables, small pieces of potato, and some cabbage.

"Is this what they serve every meal?" Thad asked, looking at his bowl in dismay.

"No," Travis said. "Sometimes it's worse."

"Do you really plan to try and escape?" Marilyn asked as the six ate their lunch.

"Yes, but not just me," Thad said. "Like I said, I plan for all of us to escape."

"How are we going to do that?" Travis asked.

"Simple. We'll just slip out the door in the middle of the night. They can't keep an eye on us twenty-four hours a day."

Travis shook his head. "There's only one door to this cabin, and they keep it locked, day and night. And as you can see, the window is too little for anyone but Wee to get through. Even with him, it would be a tight squeeze."

"I'll find some way," Thad said determinedly.

"We can't all of us escape. Even if we managed to get out of the house some way, Wee is too young. He wouldn't be able to keep up with the rest of us."

"Yes, I would," Wee insisted. "I can run fast."

"It probably wouldn't be running as much as it would be staying out of sight," Thad said.

Wee smiled. "I'm real good at playing hide-'n-seek. Sometimes me 'n Lorena used to play hide-'n-seek, 'n I can hide real good, can't I, Lorena?"

"Yes, honey, you are very good at hide-'n-seek," Lorena said, smiling at the boy.

"Can you keep real quiet when you have to?" Thad asked.

"Uh-huh. All I have to do is put a lock on my lips," Wee said, and the two girls chuckled.

"Don't worry," Thad said to the others. "When we go, Wee goes with us, and he won't be a problem."

"When are we going to go?" Burt asked.

"I don't know yet. I'll have to study things for a while until I can figure out the best thing to do. Do they ever let us out of the house?"

"Only to use the privy," Travis said. "They come unlock the door in the middle of the morning and in the middle of the afternoon so we can use the privy, but they only let us out one at a time."

"Except for the girls," Lorena said. "We always go together so one of us can be outside to let the others know it's being used."

"And all the time we're using the privy, whoever it was that unlocked the door for us is standing on the front porch, waiting for us to all get back in the cabin," Burt said.

"It's sort of creepy," Lorena said.

"Yes, it is," Marilyn agreed. "I don't like the way Reece looks at us."

"Me, neither," Lorena said. "The way he looks at us makes my skin crawl."

"You won't have to worry about how he looks at you much longer," Thad promised.

"Why do you say that? Are you coming up with a plan?" Lorena asked.

"Not yet. But I will."

CHAPTER TWELVE

Big Rock

Five days after Sara Sue took Sam to the doctor, Dr. Urban declared that the immediate danger was over and Sam could go home.

"I intend to do more than just go home," Sam said. "I want you to wrap me up good and tight. I'm going after my son."

"You do, and you'll more than likely be dead within a week," Dr. Urban replied. "You need rest, and you need to drink a lot of beef broth to restore your blood."

Smoke had come to town with Sara Sue to help her take Sam back home. Smoke actually had a fine, well-sprung carriage which he very rarely used, but it was perfect for giving Sam a gentle ride back to Wiregrass Ranch. Once there, with Pearlie on one side and Smoke on the other, they were able to help Sam walk into his house.

"You rest easy, Sam. I'll go after Thad," Smoke promised.

"I appreciate that, but I want you to deliver the bull to Mr. Harris."

"I intend to do both," Smoke said. "The note said for Sara Sue to come alone. I'll be with her, but I'll have the cover of delivering the bull."

"Yes," Sam said. "Yes, I hadn't thought of that. That might work. Smoke, please, bring my son back."

"Don't worry. I'll get him safely home to you."

"Thank you, Smoke. From the bottom of my heart, thank you."

"Is Mr. Condon actually going to pay those bastards?" Pearlie asked as they drove back to Sugarloaf. "I hate to see him have to do that."

"I feel the same way," Smoke replied. "But right now the most important thing to Sam and Sara Sue is the safe return of their son, and I agree with them. Thad's safety is the number one priority. So the first thing I intend to do is to get young Thad back alive and unharmed. If that means paying the ransom, we'll do that. After that, will be time to deal with the kidnappers."

"When do we start?" Pearlie asked.

"We'll start in a few days by delivering the bull to Jim Harris."

Three days later Smoke and Pearlie returned to Wiregrass. They were glad to see that Sam was able to move around on his own, though he had to do so very slowly and be careful not to open up the wound.

"When will you be going up to Mule Gap, Sara Sue?" Smoke asked.

"I'll ride into town tomorrow morning and take the coach up," she replied.

"All right. We'll see you there."

Smoke and Pearlie went out into the corral to get Yankee Star.

"That's him, Seven," Smoke said to his horse. "Go get him and bring him to me."

Smoke and Pearlie leaned against the corral fence and watched as Seven moved through the half-dozen cows until he reached the bull. Moving first to one side of the bull, then the other, Seven herded Yankee Star back to the corral gate and held him there as Smoke dropped the lead rope over the cow's head.

"Heck, Smoke, why do we even have to go?" Pearlie teased. "Just tell Seven to take him up there."

Smoke laughed. "I don't doubt but that he could do it."

"Is this your favorite Seven? I know he is number three."

"Oh, I don't know that he is my favorite," Smoke replied. "They have all had their own unique personality, and I've been really close to every one of them. But I do think this Seven may be the smartest of all of them. I can talk to him like a person, and I swear he can follow the conversation."

"He's one fine horse, all right," Pearlie agreed.

Chicago, Illinois

It was nine o'clock in the evening when the train from St. Louis carrying Sally and Cal rolled into the Central Depot located in the middle of Chicago. They would change trains for the last time before continuing on to New York.

Leaving the train, they walked up a long concrete walkway that separated the tracks, as well as the trains already sitting in the station. As they walked by a sitting train, Cal glanced into the window and saw a very beautiful young woman. They made eye contact, and she smiled shyly, but held his gaze as long as she could.

"Ships in the night," Sally said.

"Ma'am?" Cal replied.

Sally chuckled. "I saw you and the young lady exchange long glances. It was a sweet moment, but poignant as well, for that train will be going to Atlanta, and we're going on to New York . . . like ships passing in the night. It's from a poem by Longfellow."

Sally recited the poem.

> *"Ships that pass in the night, and speak each other in*
> *   passing,*
> *Only a signal shown and a distant voice in the*
> *   darkness;*
> *So on the ocean of life we pass and speak one another,*
> *Only a look and a voice, then darkness again and a*
> *   silence."*

"Wow. You know what?" Cal said. "I think I actually understand that. It means that the girl I looked at on the train and I will never see each other again, doesn't it?"

Sally chuckled "Very astute, Cal."

Inside the depot they found a curious mix of architectural styles with several restaurants and spacious waiting rooms.

"I wish we could stay here long enough for me to

see Chicago," Cal said. "I've heard about it a lot, and I would really like to see it."

"Maybe we can see it on the way back home," Sally suggested. "Now, we have to get to New York in time for the play, but on the way back home, there will be no time constraints imposed upon us."

As they waited for the train, Cal saw a copy of the *New York Evening World* and bought it to read.

WILLIAM DOOLIN FREED TODAY

William Doolin, one-time member of the Irish Assembly, a gang of ruffians who ply their trade in the Bridgetown section of the city, has been released. Sometimes using the alias Brockway, he served six years for armed robbery. He has been cautioned not to return to his old pursuits, but he seems most likely to do so.

"Cal," Sally said, returning to the bench where he was seated, reading the newspaper. "The Hummer will depart on track nine at six o'clock tomorrow morning. We'll be in New York by two o'clock the following day." She smiled broadly. "Are you getting excited?"

"A little, I guess," Cal said.

"Do you think you can rest on the benches here in the waiting room? If we got a hotel room it would be at least an hour and a half before we got in bed, and I would be so frightened that we would miss the train, that I would want us up by three o'clock in the morning. We would wind up with no more than four hours in the hotel."

"This will be fine, Miz Sally." Cal laughed. "Maybe

you're forgettin' how many times I've had to throw my blanket out on the ground, sometimes in the snow, even. I don't think we'll be getting any snow in here."

Sally laughed. "It isn't very likely."

Cal wasn't sure what awakened him, but he woke in the middle of the night and lay there with his eyes open, staring at the vaulted ceiling far above. The room was illuminated by dozens of hanging chandeliers, as well of scores of sconce lanterns attached either to the wall or to the many supporting columns. He lifted his head to check on Sally, and that's when he saw a man reaching carefully, ever so carefully, for Sally's purse that lay between her and the seat back.

The man was startled midreach by the clicking sound of a hammer being pulled back and a cylinder rotating to bring a bullet in alignment, both with the barrel and the firing pin. The would-be purse snatcher looked in the direction from which the sound had come.

"Yeah, you heard right," Cal said, smiling broadly over the .44 Colt he was holding, pointed directly at the intruder. "That was the sound of me cocking the pistol. And if you don't pull your hand away from that purse, the next and last sound you hear will be when I pull the trigger and blow your head half off." He spoke the words calmly and with a cool detachment that frightened the thief, even more than if the words had been spit out in anger.

"Go away," Cal said. "Stay away."

"Y-yes sir!" the would-be thief said, making a hasty departure.

"Cal?" Sally mumbled in a sleepy voice. "Is everything all right? I thought I heard you talking."

"Yes, ma'am, everything is just fine," Cal said.

CHAPTER THIRTEEN

New York City

Even though the Irish Assembly was no more, Ian Gallagher was still very active, controlling all the action in the Bay Ridge neighborhood of Brooklyn. Prostitution, gambling, and protection all came under his purview, and nobody dared to begin operating without his permission and without giving him his cut.

At the moment, Gallagher was ensconced at "his" table in the back of Paddy's Pub, playing the game of Brandubh with Paddy Boyle, who owned the pub. Reaching down to the board, he moved one of his pieces.

"That's the third time you've made that same move, Gallagher," Boyle said. "Repetitive moves mean you lose."

"I haven't made the move yet, Paddy, I was just studyin' where to move next," Gallagher replied, returning the piece to its original position.

If Boyle had been playing anyone else, he would have insisted that the game had just been forfeited to him. But this wasn't anyone else. This was Ian Gallagher, and people didn't argue with Ian Gallagher. That is, not if they wanted to stay alive.

"All right. I was just warnin' you in case you did decide to make that move."

"Mr. Gallagher? Is Mr. Gallagher in here?" The questioner was a young boy wearing a cap sporting the words WESTERN UNION.

"I'm back here, boy," Gallagher called out.

"I have a telegram for you, sir." The boy hurried back to the table and presented the telegram. "The telegrapher said there wasn't no name on who sent it." He waited for the expected tip.

"All right, you've delivered the telegram 'n told me there wasn't no name, so what is it that you're waiting on?" Gallagher asked the boy as he tore open the envelope.

"Most usually whenever someone gets a telegram, what they do is give the one what brung it to 'em a tip, sir."

"You get paid by Western Union, don't you?"

"Yes, sir."

"And they pay you to deliver telegrams?"

"Yes sir, but—"

"There ain't no buts," Gallagher said with a dismissive wave of his hand. "So be gone with you, now."

"Yes, sir," the boy replied, intimidated by the gruff voice of someone the boy knew was not to be crossed.

MRS KIRBY JENSEN ARRIVING
GRAND CENTRAL DEPOT ON BOARD
TRANSCONTINENTAL TRAIN HUMMER
TWO PM THIS DAY STOP ARRANGE
FOR HER TO BE YOUR GUEST UNTIL
FURTHER NOTICE STOP YOU WILL BE
WELL COMPENSATED FOR HER STAY
WITH YOU STOP

Gallagher folded the telegram over and stuck it in his pocket.

"Now, that don't make any sense at all. There ain't no name on the telegram." Doolin, recently released from prison, had been kibitzing the game. "The boy said there wouldn't be a name. Do you know who sent it?"

"Yeah," Gallagher replied without giving any further information.

"Anythin' serious?" Boyle asked.

"No, nothing serious. It's my move, I believe."

"Aye," Boyle said, overlooking the disqualifying move Gallagher had made just before the arrival of the telegram. "It's your move, that's for sure and certain."

Half an hour later, Gallagher and Brockway were meeting with Kelly and O'Leary, two of the men in his gang, for that is truly what men who worked with him could be called.

"What do we do with her when we snatch her?" Kelly asked.

"Hold her until someone pays us to let her go," Gallagher said.

"How will we recognize who she is?"

"You know she won't be coming here without baggage," Gallagher said. "We've got people in the depot. When she claims her baggage, we'll know who she is."

On board the Hummer

Six days and five trains after leaving the Big Rock Depot, the transcontinental train called the Hummer rolled into New York. From the moment the train crossed the Hudson River, Cal had been glued to the window, beholding sights like nothing he had ever seen before. Then the train stopped.

"Why did we stop?" he asked.

"We've reached Grand Central Depot," Sally answered.

"Where? I don't see a depot."

Sally chuckled. "You will. Just wait."

The train began backing up and Cal, who was more confused now than he had been before, studied the sights outside. He saw that they were backing toward a huge, sprawling, five-story building. Projecting out from the building was a network of tracks, most of which were occupied by trains. He continued to watch as they backed into the station, and a moment later, saw that they were slipping in between two trains that were already in place. This train and the one closest to it were separated by a long, narrow, brick path. He realized then, that they had also passed under an overhead roof of some sort. He stared at the windows of the adjacent train, realizing he couldn't possibly see again the young woman he had seen in the train window in Chicago, but thinking it might be nice to have another 'ships that pass in the night' moment . . . but no such moment occurred.

"All right, folks. This is Grand Central Depot," the conductor said, coming through the car. "Please watch your step as you leave the train."

Cal followed Sally and the other passengers through the aisle of the car, then down the steps, and onto the brick platform. Other trains were arriving and departing, and the roof high overhead seemed to capture the sounds. Chugging engines, vented steam, rolling wheels, clattering connectors, squeaking brakes, clanging bells, and hundreds of voices cast the cacophonous clamor back down.

"I'm sure it'll be a few minutes before we'll be able to claim our luggage, so we may as well get something to eat," Sally said once they stepped into the depot.

"Yes, ma'am," Cal replied with a broad smile. "You know me, Miss Sally. I'm always ready to eat."

Gallagher and Brockway were waiting in the baggage claim area of the depot. Gallagher was leaning up against the wall with his arms folded across his chest. A few minutes earlier he had given Guido Sarducci a five-dollar bill, and all Sarducci had to do was identify the luggage belonging to Mrs. Kirby Jensen.

"It's that piece there," Sarducci told Gallagher as he pointed to a large, maroon leather case.

"Set it aside from the other pieces of luggage so I can see who comes for it," Gallagher ordered.

"Yes, sir."

Gallagher watched as men and women came to

claim their luggage, but the maroon piece Sarducci had pointed out remained unclaimed until an attractive woman and a man considerably younger step up to the open window.

"Yes, ma'am, Mrs. Jensen. I have your luggage right here," Sarducci said, speaking loudly enough for Gallagher to hear the exchange.

Gallagher watched as first Mrs. Jensen claimed her luggage, then the young man with her.

"Cal Wood," the young man said to Sarducci.

There had been no mention of a Cal Wood in the telegram, so Gallagher didn't know if they were traveling together or if they just happened to arrive at the baggage claim at the same time. When he saw a redcap take both pieces, though, he realized that they must be together.

Gallagher and Brockway followed them outside, heard the Jensen woman tell the cabdriver that they wished to go to the Fifth Avenue Hotel, and got into the cab behind the one that she and Cal had taken.

"Fifth Avenue Hotel," Gallagher said.

Reaching their destination, he paid the driver, then he and Brockway followed Sally and Cal into the hotel. Brockway stayed in the lobby as Gallagher stepped up to the front desk and stood to one side as if waiting to register. His intention was to find out what room they would be staying in.

"Mrs. Jensen, yes," the desk clerk said with a smile. "I believe I would be holding two tickets for you, for opening night of the play *Bold Lady* at the Rex Theater."

"Yes, thank you."

"Enjoy the play, the clerk said. "If Andrew and

Rosanna MacCallister are going to be in it, I know it will be great."

As first Sally and then Cal signed the registration book, Gallagher's plans changed. It no longer mattered what room she was staying in. She would be going to a play the next night. That was all the information he needed.

He turned and gave a brief nod to Brockway, and they left the hotel.

CHAPTER FOURTEEN

Cross Trails Ranch

"Oh now, that is a fine-looking bull," Jim Harris said as he examined Yankee Star.

Smoke and Pearlie had arrived with the bull a few minutes earlier, and he was turned out in the reinforced cattle pen that Harris had constructed just for him.

"He is a good-looking bull, and he comes from a champion sire and dam," Smoke said.

"I'm curious. Why didn't Sam Condon deliver the bull himself?"

"Haven't you heard? Sam was shot last week," Smoke said.

"No, I hadn't heard! Was he killed?"

"No. He's recovering now."

"Thank God for that. What happened?"

Smoke described what had taken place at Wiregrass Ranch, ending with the fact that Sam's son, Thad, had been abducted. "It looks like Sam is going to pull through being shot all right, but he and Sara Sue are both very worried about their son."

"Oh, Lord, I didn't know that was going on down in Colorado, as well," Harris replied.

"What do you mean, going on in Colorado *as well*?" Smoke asked, surprised by the comment.

"We've had a rash of abductions around here," Harris said. "There have been at least ten that I know of."

"Ten children are missing?"

"No, only five of them are still missing. Four have been returned, but it cost their folks a lot of money to get them back."

"You said you knew of ten, five still missing and four returned. What about the tenth one?"

"Oh, that was Lucy Blair." Harris shook his head. "Sadly, she was found dead on the banks of Savery Creek."

"How was she killed?" Pearlie asked.

"Somebody had cut her throat. Some folks say it was because she was too much for the outlaws to handle. Sixteen, she was, and a real pretty thing, too."

"What about the sheriff?" Smoke asked.

"The sheriff's up in Rawlins. He's over sixty years old and has no deputies. His office is pretty much just a political position. Nobody ever really depends on him for any real law."

"Where do you get your law support?"

"There's a marshal in town, 'n there's some talk of comin' up with a way for him to be able to operate out of town. I don't know if that's happened yet, but I hope they can get it done."

* * *

After delivering the bull to Jim Harris, Smoke and Pearlie rode on into Mule Gap. This was one full day before Sara Sue was supposed to meet with someone representing the kidnappers of her son. They had come a day earlier so that it would not appear as if they were with her. The early arrival also allowed them to have a look around the town to determine whether or not any danger faced the woman when she came to keep her appointment.

The meeting was to take place in the Del Rey Hotel on the next day, but Smoke and Pearlie planned to spend this night camping out just south of town on the Pinkhampton Pike. Sara Sue would be coming in by stagecoach, the next day, and the coach would have to come by way of that road.

The two men stopped in front of Kennedy's Saloon, looped the reins around the hitching rail, then stepped inside.

"Smoke!" a friendly voice called.

Looking toward the sound of the voice, Smoke saw Warren Kennedy. A man dressed all in black was sitting at the table with Kennedy.

"Ethan," Kennedy called out to the bartender, "Smoke Jensen's money is no good in my saloon. Find out what he and the gentleman with him want, then have one of the girls bring it to our table."

"Yes, gentlemen, what will it be?" Ethan asked as Smoke and Pearlie reached the bar.

"I'll have a beer," Smoke said.

"And I'll have the same," Pearlie added.

"Who's with you?" Kennedy asked as Smoke and Pearlie joined the two men at the table.

"This is my ranch foreman," Smoke said. "Pearlie."

"Pearlie . . ." Kennedy repeated, dragging it out, obviously looking for a last name.

"Pearlie," he replied without giving a last name. That finished the inquisition.

"Pearlie, this is Warren Kennedy," Smoke said. "Or perhaps I should say, His Honor, since Mr. Kennedy is also the mayor of Mule Gap."

"Pleased to meet you, Mayor," Pearlie said.

Smoke turned his attention to the man dressed in black, who, unlike Kennedy, had not stood at their approach. He was staring at Smoke with eyes that could best be described as flat and featureless.

"And this fearsome-looking gentleman is City Marshal Frank Bodine," Smoke said, continuing the introductions.

"County Marshal Bodine," Kennedy said.

"County Marshal?" Smoke replied, unfamiliar with the term.

"We have a sheriff, but he never leaves his office in Rawlins, and he has no deputies. The result of the sheriff's inactivity is that the residents of Carbon County are left without any type of law enforcement."

"Yes, come to think of it, that's exactly what Jim Harris said," Smoke replied. "He said you were trying to come up with a way to extend the town marshal's jurisdiction."

"And I have done so. I didn't want to make Marshal Bodine a deputy sheriff and thus subservient to the sheriff up in Rawlins, so I made him the county marshal."

"How were you able to do that? Legally, I mean."

"I have filed with the territorial capital in Cheyenne our intention to incorporate the entire county, except for the towns of Rawlins, Douglas, and Warm Springs, into the town of Mule Gap."

"And they have approved that?"

"It hasn't been disapproved," Kennedy replied with a smile.

Smoke laughed. "I have to give you credit, Warren, you do seem to have a way of getting things done. And I agree that the citizens of the county do need some protection by the law. But this is an awfully large area for one man to handle."

"That's why Marshal Bodine has recruited so many deputies," Kennedy replied. "I have—that is, the town of Mule Gap has—authorized a strength of ten deputy marshals."

"That's quite a sizeable police force."

"Yes, but as you say, Carbon County is a large area to cover."

Smoke turned his attention to the man in black. "So tell me, Marshal Bodine. Are you working on finding the kidnapped children and getting them returned to their families?"

"You know about the kidnappings?" Kennedy asked.

"Yes. A few days ago a boy was taken from a neighboring ranch. In trying to defend him, his father was shot."

"Oh," Kennedy replied. "Was he killed?"

"No, he survived the shooting."

"That is good to hear. What is he doing about

recovering his son?" Kennedy asked. "I mean, I hope he is going to pay the ransom."

"Why would you say that?"

"We have been experiencing a rash of these kidnappings. The ransom has been paid on four of the children, and they have been returned safely to their families. That is a favorable outcome for all concerned."

"Except the families who may be out their life savings," Smoke said.

"Surely, Smoke, you aren't putting mere money above the life of the child, are you?" Kennedy challenged.

"No, of course I'm not doing that, but it does seem to me that the most favorable outcome would be to catch the men who are doing this, free the children, and put the men in prison."

"Yes, of course that would be the most favorable outcome, and I believe that, in time, Marshal Bodine will be able to do just that. But until then, don't you agree with me that the best thing for these families to do is pay the ransom?"

"Under the circumstances, yes," Smoke replied. "I do believe it is Sam Condon's intention to pay the ransom."

"Yes, well, if Mr. Condon can afford it, that is no doubt the best and safest way to have his son released without harm," Kennedy said. "But I am interested. What brings you to my town? Does it have anything to do with the kidnapping of the Condon boy?"

"No, our visit has nothing to do with that. Pearlie and I just delivered a bull to Jim Harris. Being here at the time of the boy's kidnapping is purely coincidental."

"I see. Harris, no doubt, paid you in cash again because he won't use my bank."

"You know him well," Smoke said.

"Evidently I don't know him well enough. I have been totally incapable of talking him into using my bank."

"Jim Harris is a stubborn man, all right."

"Will you be staying with us tonight?" Kennedy asked. "You know, I own half of the Del Rey Hotel, and I think I can promise you a comfortable stay."

"We have somewhere else we have to be tonight, but we'll be back tomorrow and will probably spend one or two nights," Smoke said.

"Oh? Why so long? Not that you aren't welcome," Kennedy added with a smile. "As you have no doubt learned by now, I am a businessman, and having a couple guests in my hotel for a few nights is always a good thing."

"Warren Kennedy looking for every way he can to make another dollar? You don't say," Smoke teased. "As you may know, Sally is in New York now, so I've no real reason to get back home so quickly. Pearlie and I thought we might take advantage of our time up here to get in a little hunting."

"For the kidnapped boy?" Bodine asked.

"No, that would be your job, so I'll leave that up to you," Smoke said. "I was thinking more along the lines of pronghorn deer."

CHAPTER FIFTEEN

Rosanna MacCallister as Dame Sara stood in the light at center stage, holding a dagger before her. "Oh noble sire, that you would have given your life in defense of my honor—honor which I do not have—has left me prostrate with grief and shame. Grief, because I cannot imagine a world without you, and shame because the honor for which you gave your life does not exist.

"Yes, Albert, it shames me to say that I have long hidden the truth from you. For you see, I am a woman debased. I am not, as you believe, the daughter of nobility. I was to a lowly servant woman born, my birth killing the very woman who had given me life. I was taken as their own by the nobles whom my mother served, Lord and Lady Montjoy. Would but the blood from the thrust of this dagger wash clean the stain on my soul." She raised the dagger above her breast.

Andrew MacCallister as Lord Albert Cairns rushed in from stage left. "Wait. Do not harm yourself because of foolish pride and wrong intelligence! The news that I was slain was inaccurately reported. I live yet, and I have long known of your humble origins. Do you not believe that your noble upbringing has made you as noble as one to the manor born? It is not who you were, but who you *are* that has earned my love."

Dame Sara dropped the dirk and the two embraced at center stage.

As the curtain closed, the theater erupted with applause and cheers. Sally and Cal had been given seats in the orchestra section of the theater, and they rose with the others to give the two actors upon the stage a standing ovation.

The curtains opened again, and all the secondary players rushed out to take their curtain call, their appearances on stage in inverse order of the significance of their roles. After taking their bows, the actors moved to either side of the stage and held their arms out toward the two principals of the show, Andrew and Rosanna MacCallister. The stage manager hurried onto the stage carrying a large bouquet of yellow roses, which he presented to Rosanna.

Again, the applause swelled.

Across the street from the theater, Gallagher, Brockway, Kelly, and O'Leary watched as the patrons left the theater. The theatergoers were talking about the play they had just seen.

"Isn't Rosanna MacCallister just the most beautiful woman you ever saw?"

"It is the skill of the stage makeup artist that causes her to look so beautiful."

"If she wasn't already beautiful, no makeup artistry could make her so."

"We're a-lookin' for the same woman we saw gettin' off the train, right?" Brockway asked.

"Yes."

"I don't see her."

"She was sitting down front. She will be one of the last to leave," Gallagher said as he handed a small brown bottle and a handkerchief to Brockway. "Do you know how to use this?"

"Yeah, I know," Brockway replied.

"I'm goin' on ahead," Gallagher said. "When she comes out, you three follow her."

"All right."

He left the other three and hurried on ahead, positioning himself between the Rex Theater and the Fifth Avenue Hotel.

"Mrs. Jensen?" one of the theater ushers asked, approaching Sally and Cal just as they were rising from their seats.

"Yes?" Sally replied.

"Mr. MacCallister has issued an invitation for you two to join the company backstage."

"Oh, how nice of him," Sally said.

"If you would come with me, please, madam."

Sally and Cal followed the usher through a small door just to the left of the stage, then wandered through the labyrinth of flats, props, ropes, and miscellaneous components that were necessary to stage a major play before a sophisticated New York audience.

"Ah!" Cal gasped, jumping back in shock when he saw a severed human head. "What's that?"

"Do not be concerned, sir," the usher replied. "That is the head of Yorick."

"Who? Well, what's his head doing here?"

Sally chuckled, then reached for the head and holding it in front of her, began reciting. "'Alas, poor Yorick! I knew him, Horatio; a fellow of infinite jest, of most excellent fancy; he hath borne me on his back a thousand times; and now, how abhorred in my imagination it is! My gorge rises at it. Here hung those lips that I have kissed I know not how oft. Where be your gibes now? Your gambols? Your songs? Your flashes of merriment, that were wont to set the table on a roar.'"

"Oh, most excellent, madam!" the theater usher said, clapping his hands. "You know your Shakespeare."

"Not really. A few lines from *Hamlet, Macbeth, Romeo and Juliet* is all. Just enough to allow me to show off from time to time."

As they were talking, Cal was making a closer examination of the head. "Oh," he said with an understanding smile. "This isn't real."

"They used to use real heads, but they didn't last long," Sally said.

"What?" Cal gasped.

Sally laughed out loud. "I'm teasing you, Cal."

As they continued to explore, they came to an area that was reserved for the players—a large common room with mirrors and dressing screens for the "bit actors" and dressing rooms for those with larger roles. The doors leading to the dressing rooms for Andrew and Rosanna each had a star and their name, but at the moment the two stars of the play were sharing the common room with the others.

Everyone was still keyed up from the performance, and they were laughing and talking excitedly. Andrew called for attention, and everyone grew quiet.

"I would like to congratulate each and every one of you," he said. "You did well as you strutted and fretted your hour upon the stage."

"But," Rosanna interrupted, holding up her finger, "unlike the next line in the bard's famous soliloquy, I predict that all of you *will* be heard again."

"Who could not do well when playing with the two best thespians in New York theater, Andrew and Rosanna MacCallister?" one of the supporting actors declared, holding his arm out toward the brother and sister.

The other actors applauded.

"Sally, how wonderful of you and your friend to come to our opening night," Rosanna said when she saw Sally and Cal.

"Are you kidding? Who could resist such an invitation?" Sally replied.

"Yes, if you are living in the city. But, my goodness, you came two thousand miles."

"It was a good excuse to visit New York again," Sally replied. "And to show the city to a young man that Smoke and I have come to regard as family."

"Yes, seeing the city through the eyes of someone who is seeing it for the first time can be quite exhilarating," Rosanna replied

"Sally, will you be taking dinner tonight with Rosanna, me, and some of the others?" Andrew asked.

"We would be most happy to," Sally said.

"We'll gather at Delmonico's at midnight," Andrew said. "The restaurant will be closed then to all except our private party. I will give the maître d' your names so that you may be assured entry."

"At midnight?"

"Yes. If that is too late for you, I understand."

"No, that'll be fine," Sally said. "It will give Cal and me time to stop by our rooms at the hotel."

"Good. We'll see you then."

"What the hell?" O'Leary asked. "How come she ain't come out yet? You think maybe there's a back door to that place?"

"I don't know, there might be but . . . wait. That's her comin' out right now," Brockway said.

"Who's that man with her?" O'Leary said."

"I don't know, but he was on the train with her," Brockway replied.

"So what?" Kelly asked.

"So, what are we going to do with him? I mean, he'll be in the way, won't he?"

"He won't be in the way."

"What do you mean, 'he won't be in the way'? He's there, ain't he?"

"He won't be in the way, 'cause we'll kill 'im."

"Your friends are good people," Cal said as he and Sally started the ten-block walk from the theater to the hotel. "They don't seem like New York people at all."

Sally laughed. "What do you mean, 'they don't

seem like New York people'? What are New York people like?"

"I've seen them in Denver before. They're just sort of very full of themselves."

"Well, Rosanna and Andrew may live in New York now, but they're from Colorado. Don't forget, they are Falcon MacCallister's brother and sister."

"Yeah, that's true, isn't it? I forgot."

"Did you enjoy the play?"

"Oh, yes, ma'am, I sure did. Why, that was about the most wonderful thing I've ever seen. I mean, the way ever'one was upon that stage, why, it was like we was"—Cal paused, then, with a smile, corrected his grammar—"like we *were* right there in the same room with them, just watching ever'thing that was going on."

"That's the illusion brilliant thespians can create," Sally replied. "And thank you for correcting your grammar."

"Yes, ma'am. Well, bein' that you"—he paused for a second—"*were* once a schoolteacher, I know what a store you put in proper English, so I try to use good grammar whenever I can."

"Very good, Cal, very good," Sally said.

"I think it's funny that we're goin' to be eatin' with them at the Delmonico restaurant," Cal said.

"Funny? Why do you say that? What's funny about having a late dinner at Delmonico's?"

"Well, think about it, Miz Sally. There's a Delmonico's in Big Rock 'n there's one here in New York. I mean, when we go back 'n tell Mr. DeWeese that there's a restaurant in New York that's got the same name as his, why, he'll more 'n likely be proud of that, don't you think?"

Sally laughed. "He more than likely will be."

As the two continued their walk back to the hotel, Cal happened to notice in the window of a closed store the reflection of three men following them. It seemed too late for any casual pedestrians, but there had been a full house for the play. Also there were other theaters nearby, and their audiences had turned out onto the street at about the same time, so it was possible that those men were part of the theater crowd.

Using that reasoning, Cal discounted the three men, but a little later he caught another glimpse of them and something in their actions alerted him. It looked to him as if the men might be trying to avoid being seen. Why would that be, unless they were up to no good?

"Miz Sally, I think maybe we ought to step it up a bit," Cal said.

"What do you mean?"

"There are some men on the street behind us."

Sally chuckled. "Cal, it isn't unusual that there would be people on the street. Over two million people live in New York."

"Yes, ma'am, but it's not the rest of the two million people I'm worryin' about. It's the three men that are behind us. They're actin' kind of funny."

"Funny how?"

"Like they don't want to be seen."

Sally looked back and as she did, the two men stepped into an alcove. It might have been a coincidence, but Cal might also be right. She got the same feeling of apprehension that he was experiencing. "All right. If it'll make you feel better . . ."

"I'd feel just a whole lot better if I had my gun with me," Cal said.

"So would I," Sally agreed.

As they approached the end of the block, a man suddenly stepped in front of them. He was holding a pistol, and Cal automatically went for his own gun. But there was no gun there. His gun was back in his suitcase in the hotel room.

"Just hold it right there." The man smiled, though it was a smile without humor.

"You don't really expect us to be carrying around a great deal of money, do you?" Sally asked. "If this is a holdup, I'm afraid you are going to be quite disappointed."

"Oh, this isn't a holdup. No ma'am, we have something else in mind for you, Mrs. Jensen."

"What?" Sally replied, shocked to be addressed by name.

Many people back in Colorado knew her, even in Denver. That could be expected as she was married to one of the biggest ranchers in the state. Smoke Jensen's fame went considerably further than the mere fact that he was a successful rancher. His skill with a gun was unmatched.

But she wasn't in Colorado. She was in New York. And what were the chances of someone in New York knowing her by name? "How is it that you know my name?"

"We have plans for you," the man said.

"The hell you do," Cal said. "If you hurt—" That was

as far as he got before he was hit just above his right ear by something hard and heavy. He went down.

"Cal!" Sally started to bend down to see to him when powerful arms were wrapped around her. She felt a cloth being pressed over her nose and mouth. She fought against it and couldn't help but take several deep breaths. She was aware of a cloying, sweet smell . . . then nothing.

CHAPTER SIXTEEN

Mule Gap

Lute Cruthis and Boots Zimmerman were patrolling First Street when they saw someone coming out of the Silver Dollar Saloon.

"Hey, Boots. Ain't that Melvin Varner?"

"I don't know," Zimmerman said. "I ain't never seen 'im before."

"I have. Me 'n him 'n some others done a job together back in Kansas a couple years ago. He got caught for it 'n when to jail, but I heard he escaped, 'n here he is."

"Think they's a reward on 'im?"

"Yeah, I know there is."

Varner had just rolled himself a cigarette and was lighting it. He was unaware of the two deputies approaching him.

"Hello, Varner," Cruthis said.

Varner looked up in surprise at being addressed by name. At first there was an expression of concern on his face until he recognized Cruthis. Then he smiled.

"Lute! I'll be damned. It's been a coon's age since I last seen you. What are you doing in these—" Varner paused in midsentence when he saw what was on front of Cruthis's shirt. "You're a star packer now?"

"That's right. 'N you're under arrest."

Varner held his hand out. "No, now, you don't want to do that to an old friend. What you might not know is I kilt me a guard when I broke outta jail back in Kansas. If I go back there I'll more 'n likely hang."

"I know. That's why they's a thousand-dollar reward out for you," Cruthis said.

"Reward? What would that mean to you? If you're the law, you can't collect."

"Yeah, we can. We got us a special deal," Cruthis said. "Draw, Varner."

Even as Cruthis said the word, he was already reaching for his gun.

"No!" Varner shouted, but seeing Cruthis start his draw, Varner had no choice. He went for his gun and though Cruthis beat him, he waited for a second to let Varner clear leather before he shot.

Varner went down with the gun in his hand.

At the sound of the shot, several people rushed out of the saloon, and a couple men on the other side of the street crossed over to the scene.

"What happened?" someone asked.

"This is Melvin Varner," Cruthis said, still holding the smoking gun in his hand. "He's wanted for murder. When I tried to arrest him, he drew his gun." Cruthis pointed to the gun in Varner's hand.

"Damn, Deputy, you was lucky you beat 'im," another said.

"I seen the whole thing," Zimmerman said. "It's just

like Lute said. He told Varner he was under arrest, 'n next thing you know, Varner was drawing on 'im."

On the Pinkhampton Pike, four miles south of Mule Gap

Smoke and Pearlie had camped alongside the South Platte River, about one hundred yards off the Pinkhampton Pike. The coffee had already been made, and as Smoke washed his face in water dipped from the river, Pearlie was looking after six pieces of bacon twitching in the pan over the fire. There were no eggs, but yesterday they had bought a loaf of bread and it would be fried up in the bacon grease to complete their breakfast meal.

"What time will the stage be comin' through?" Pearlie asked.

"The way station is halfway between here and Douglas, and I expect they got underway by seven this morning," Smoke said. "They should be coming by here at about eight.

"Mrs. Condon is carrying fifteen thousand dollars in cash, is she?"

"No, she's carrying a draft from the bank of Big Rock for that amount. It wouldn't do anyone else any good to steal it."

Pearlie nodded. "That's good."

Taking the bacon out, Smoke dropped some bread slices into the grease, then he laughed.

"What is it?"

"Can you imagine what Sally would say if she saw me eating something like this? She's convinced that bacon grease is bad for you."

"Now, how can anything that tastes that good be bad for you?" Pearlie asked.

They ate in silence for a moment.

"I hope Cal is havin' hisself a fine time up there in New York," Pearlie said.

"I expect he is. For someone like Cal, seeing the city for the first time, it has to be exciting for him."

New York City

"Get up!"

Cal felt someone kicking him in the side.

"Get up. I'll not be havin' it said that Mickey Muldoon has drunks sleepin' on the streets on his beat. Get up."

Cal was kicked again. "Ow! Stop kicking me! What are you kicking me for?" He raised up on his hands and knees and saw that it was daylight.

What was he doing on the sidewalk like this?

"Are you still drunk? Do you think you can for findin' your way home? Or do I need to put ye in jail?"

"What do you mean, put me in jail? Put me in jail for what?" Cal stood up and saw that the obnoxious man yelling at him was a police officer. He noticed a tenderness just above his ear, and putting his hand there, winced with pain from the contact. "I'm not drunk." He pulled his hand away and looked at it. Blood showed on the tips of his fingers.

"Here, let me take a look, lad," the policeman asked, his entire demeanor changing at the sight of the blood. "Aye, 'tis a good lick you have there. Who done it?"

"I don't know," Cal said. "They came up behind me an' . . . Mrs. Jensen! Where is Mrs. Jensen?"

"Who? Lad, when I came upon you a few minutes ago, you were layin' there all alone. 'Twas thinkin',

I was, that you be drunk. Who is the lady you be askin' about?"

"Mrs. Jensen. She was with me, and we were goin' back to the hotel when—" He stopped in mid-sentence. "The man with the gun knew her. How did he know her? And what did he mean when he said he had plans for her?"

"A man with a gun? Begorra, 'n you said nothing about a man with a gun. He knew the lady, you say? I think you said her name was Jensen?"

"Yes, sir. Mrs. Kirby Jensen. Her husband is one of the biggest ranchers in all of Colorado, is all," Cal said. "But we're in New York, so how did he know Miz Sally's name?"

"Mrs. Sally? Here now 'n 'twas the name *Jensen* you told me."

"Yes, Mrs. Jensen. But her first name is Sally, 'n that's what me 'n Pearlie call her. Only, to be respect-ful, we call her Miz Sally."

"If this Mrs. Jensen is a rich woman from Colorado, what is she doin' in New York?"

"She come here to see some old friends, 'n she brought me with her 'cause I had never been to New York before."

"So, where is this lady now?" Officer Muldoon asked. "How come it is that she left you lyin' on the sidewalk?"

"That's just it, Deputy. Miz Sally would never just leave me there, lessen somethin' happened to her."

The policeman shook his head. "What's your name?"

"Cal. Uh, Cal Wood."

"Sure 'n tell me now, Mr. Wood, would you be for havin any way of collaboratin' this story you're tellin' me?"

"Collaboratin'? What does that mean?"

"Is there any way you can prove to me what you're saying? My first thought is that you was drunk last night. All right. I can see that you was hit in the head, but how do I know you didn't just get drunk 'n get into a fight?"

"Because I'm tellin' you I wasn't drunk."

"Is there any way you can prove that story to me?"

"No, I told you, we aren't from here. We're from Colorado 'n I don't know anyone here who can—" Cal paused in midsentence again. "Wait a minute. Andrew MacCallister."

"Who?"

"Andrew MacCallister 'n his sister Rosanna. They're famous actors, and we went to see their play last night. They can tell you about Mrs. Jensen."

Officer Muldoon laughed. "Lad, are you tryin' to tell me now, that just because you was in the audience of a play they was in, that they can verify your story? Sure 'n there must've been two or three hundred people watchin' the play last night. How are they goin' to be able to pick you out like that?"

"Miz Sally 'n I went backstage after the play to see them."

"You went backstage to see them, did you? Well then, maybe they can and maybe they can't. I expect lots of people go backstage after a play," the policeman replied. He shook his head. "But 'tis tellin' you right now, I'll not be for botherin' those people."

"You've got to, Deputy! Don't you see? The men

who did this to me have captured Mrs. Jensen! I don't know what they have in mind for her, but it can't be good."

"All right. Come with me, then, 'n I'll be for lettin' you tell yer story to the desk sergeant. He'll be the one makin' the decision as to what should be done with you."

Still a little dizzy and with the knot above his ear still very painful, Cal followed the policeman back to the Midtown South Precinct.

"Sergeant, I'll be for turnin' this man over to you," the policeman who had awakened Cal said. "Passed out on the street, he was, when I found 'im, 'n I was thinkin' that he was drunk. Turns out he was hit on the head 'n knocked out."

"That may be, Muldoon, but why are you bringin' 'im to me? Are you plannin' on puttin' 'im in jail?"

"No, but he's got 'im a story I think maybe you ought to hear. Tell the sergeant your story, Mr. Wood."

Cal told the story of coming to New York for Mrs. Jensen to visit with some old friends and Cal to see the city for the first time.

"What is about New York that would make a man come all the way from Texas, just to pay us a visit?" the desk sergeant asked.

"Colorado," Cal corrected. "And I just wanted to see the big city."

"Well, last night 'twould appear that you saw more than you wanted."

"Lad, tell the sergeant about them famous actors," Muldoon said.

"Wait," the desk sergeant said. "'Tis thinkin' I am that we should get Lieutenant Kilpatrick to listen to the lad's story."

After a short wait, Lieutenant Kilpatrick joined the discussion. He was a big man with red hair and a red mustache.

"All right, Mr. Wood, go on with your story," the lieutenant said when he was told why he was summoned.

Cal told about seeing the play and going backstage to meet all the actors and actresses afterwards.

"And you're saying that if we talk to the MacCallisters, they'll collaborate everything you're telling us?" Lieutenant Kilpatrick asked.

There was that word again . . . *collaborate.* "Yeah," Cal said. "They will."

"Just because you happened to go backstage to see them after the play?"

"Yes, sir. Well, not just that. Andrew and Rosanna MacCallister are very good friends of Miz Sally's. They're the ones that gave us the tickets to see the play. We were supposed to have supper with 'em last night, only we got attacked by the four men before we could do it."

"Four men, you say?"

"Yes, sir. There was one man in front of us. He was holdin' a gun. And three who had been trailin' us."

"Lieutenant, if there were four men, I'd say it be a bit more than a mere street burglary," Muldoon said.

"I think you may be right, Muldoon"

"It must've been one of them that hit me. And when I came to this morning, Miz Sally was gone. They took her."

"Do you have any idea why they would take her?"

"No, sir, I don't. But I do remember that the man with the gun called her by name."

"Did this woman, Mrs. Sally . . ."

"Jensen," Cal corrected. "Miz Jensen."

"Yes. Did Mrs. Jensen know the man?"

"No, sir, she didn't."

Lieutenant Kilpatrick, who was the watch commander, stroked his chin. "Hmm, how would someone in New York know someone from Colorado?"

"She isn't from Colorado," Cal said. "I think she's originally from someplace like Boston or something. And she's even lived here in New York."

"I thought you said she was from Colorado," the desk sergeant said, confused by Cal's response.

"Yes, sir, she is. That is, she is now. She's married to Smoke Jensen, who is one of the biggest ranchers in the whole state."

"If her husband is a rich man, maybe somebody grabbed her to hold her for ransom," Muldoon suggested.

"And would you be for tellin' me, Mickey Muldoon, how 'tis that any of our brigands would be knowin' that?" the desk sergeant replied.

"The lad said that the man with the gun knew her name," Muldoon said. "If he was for knowin' her name, don't you think, Sergeant Keogh, that he might also know that her husband was rich?"

"Aye, that could be the case," Lieutenant Kilpatrick said. "But before we go any further with this, I want to hear from the actors if they verify the lad's story."

CHAPTER SEVENTEEN

When Sally awakened, she found herself on a bed with her arms stretched over her head and tied by her wrists to the headboard. She didn't know where she was, but she was fairly certain that she was in the middle of a business district. She could smell cabbage and corned beef and had been smelling it all day as if it was being cooked for a restaurant, rather than in someone's personal kitchen. She had also heard passing trains on elevated tracks, as well as the hollow clopping sound of hooves on the paver blocks of the street.

She had come to in the middle of the night, realizing then that she had been put out by chloroform being applied over her nose and mouth. She had not been hurt, but she was very uncomfortable and her back hurt because she couldn't change positions. Rags had been stuffed into her mouth in order to keep her from screaming.

She had no idea what time it was, but based on the way sunshine was streaming in through an incredibly dirty window, she believed it had to be midmorning.

She had not eaten since lunch the previous day, but being hungry was not her greatest concern at the moment.

The door opened, and someone came in. This, she knew, was Kelly, because he had been in to check on her before.

"How are you getting along, Mrs. Jensen?"

Sally made a few sounds, but because of the gag, she couldn't actually talk.

"Oh, well now, you can't be for answerin' me with the gag in your mouth, can you?" Kelly said. "Would you like me to take it out?"

She nodded.

"You won't be for doin' a lot of screamin' now, will you? 'Cause to tell you the truth, in this neighborhood screamin' won't do you no good, 'n it'll just piss off Gallagher. He ain't no one you want to be for pissin' off. Do you promise not to scream?"

Sally nodded again, and Kelly removed the gag then took the rag from her mouth. She took several gasping breaths, then tried to spit out the few pieces of cloth that had gotten into her mouth.

"Would you like a drink of water?" Kelly asked.

"Yes, please."

He held a cup of water to her lips, but she drank with some difficulty, unable to lift her head very far from the bed.

"'Tis thinkin' I am, that you might be a bit hungry. Would you be for wanting some cabbage, Mrs. Jensen?"

"How am I going to eat if I'm tied to the bed like this?"

"Aye now, 'tis a good question. I'll be for fetchin'

you some food 'n then I'll be right back to untie the ropes."

As Sally waited for Kelly to return, she heard an elevated train pass by outside. It seemed to be on the same relative level, and she realized that she was on one of the upper floors of the building. She had no idea what her captors wanted with her. They had not robbed her, nor had they mistreated her in any way, other than in keeping her as a prisoner. She was also worried about Cal. What had happened to him? Was he also a prisoner?

"Here you are, Mrs. Jensen," Kelly said, coming back into the room. He was carrying a plate. "Cabbage 'n boiled potatoes for you." He set the plate on a small table then leaned over the bed to untie the ropes.

"Thank you," Sally said. Sitting up on the edge of the bed, she began rubbing her wrists. "How do you know my name? And why am I here?"

"The reason we know your name is 'cause Gallagher told me 'n O'Leary 'n Brockway what it was. Only, I'm not for knowin' why 'tis that we're for holdin' you here."

"You mean you are holding me prisoner for no reason?"

"I wouldn't be for sayin' that now, Mrs. Jensen. 'Tis just that I'm not for knowin' what the reason may be."

"Where is Cal?"

"Where is who?"

"Cal is the young man who was with me. Where is he?"

"I don't know where he is. We just left him there."

"Is he dead?"

"If he is, we ain't the ones that done it. All we done is give 'im a good knock on the head so as to keep him out of the way when we took you."

"Poor Cal. He must be worried sick."

Kelly laughed. "Here you be a prisoner, 'n 'tis the lad you was with that you be worried about."

Rex Theater

"Oh, heavens!" Rosanna MacCallister gasped. "Someone has taken Sally?"

"Yes, ma'am." Cal had been brought to the Rex Theater by Lieutenant Kilpatrick, who wanted to hear for himself if Cal's story could be verified. And, truth to tell, he also wanted to meet the famous brother-and-sister acting duo.

"So you are willing to corroborate this man's story?" the lieutenant asked.

"I can't speak to what has happened to her, because I wasn't there," Rosanna said. "But I will say that Sally Jensen is a friend of mine . . . a very good friend. And Mr. Wood is correct in saying that she is one of the most prominent ladies in Colorado."

"And she and Mr. Wood were here last night?"

"Indeed they were," Rosanna said. "My brother and I had specifically provided them with tickets to the best seats in the house."

"And they were good seats, too. Me 'n Miz Sally . . . that is, Miz Sally and I," Cal corrected, "were just talkin' about it on the way back to the hotel. We were really lookin' forward to havin' supper with you at Delmonico's."

"Yes, we were wondering why you didn't show up.

We thought perhaps you were just too tired from the long trip."

"No, ma'am. We didn't show up on account of what happened to Miz Sally."

"Officer, you've got to get her back," Rosanna said.

"I promise you, ma'am, we'll do all we can," Lieutenant Kilpatrick replied.

"I want to help," Cal said.

"You can help best by staying out of the way," Lieutenant Kilpatrick said.

"You would be making a big mistake if you exclude Cal Wood," Andrew said. "I know him to be quite helpful in situations like this. I have seen him in action before."

"He's a civilian. I have no authority to let him be involved."

"I'm not exactly a civilian," Cal said.

"What do you mean?"

"I'm a deputy sheriff in Eagle County, Colorado."

Kilpatrick laughed. "You're a deputy sheriff in Eagle County, Colorado? Why, you wouldn't even have any authority outside that county, let alone outside of the state. I'm afraid you would be a sheep among wolves, here in New York."

"Lieutenant, I've been among wolves before," Cal said. "And grizzlies 'n mountain lions, bad outlaws, 'n even worse . . . Indians. I'm pretty sure I can handle myself among the worst you have here."

"Yeah? Then tell me, Wood, how did you wind up facedown on the sidewalk last night?"

"I . . . guess you've got me on that one," Cal replied timorously.

"You go back to the hotel. If we are able to find anything out, we'll let you know.

Mayor Grace's office, New York City

"Your Honor, you have a couple visitors waiting to see you, sir," the mayor's administrative aide said.

Mayor Grace looked confused. "Visitors? I thought the appointment book was completed."

"Yes, sir, well, these two aren't on the appointment book. It's Andrew and Rosanna MacCallister."

"Are you talking about the actors?"

"Yes, sir."

The mayor smiled broadly. "Well, by all means, show them in." He stood to greet them when they entered.

"Mr. and Mrs. MacCallister, what an honor to have you call. Oh, wait. You aren't husband and wife. You are brother and sister, I believe."

"That is correct, Your Honor," Andrew said.

"Well, what can I do for you?"

"We need some help for a friend of ours," Andrew said.

"What sort of help?"

"First, let me show you this." Andrew showed the mayor a dime novel—*Smoke Jensen and the Rocky Mountain Gang* by Ned Buntline. "Have you ever heard of this person?"

"Ned Buntline?"

"No, Smoke Jensen."

"You mean a character in a book?"

"No, I mean Smoke Jensen. He is a real person," Andrew said. "True, these are made-up stories about him, but his real adventures would make an even more exciting story."

"Why are you showing me this? Does your request have something to do with Smoke Jensen?"

"It has to do with his wife," Rosanna said. "Sally Jensen is here in New York now."

Mayor Grace smiled. "Ah, you mean she wants to meet me. Of course, bring her in. I would be glad to meet her."

"I'm sure she would like to meet you, Mr. Mayor," Andrew said. "Right now I think she would be happy to meet anyone, but she can't. She has been taken prisoner."

"Taken prisoner? What do you mean? Who has taken her prisoner?"

"Lieutenant Kilpatrick thinks it might be the Irish Assembly," Andrew said.

Mayor Grace shook his head. "Impossible. There is no Irish Assembly anymore."

"True, but Kilpatrick thinks it might be some of the same men who were once a part of the Irish Assembly."

"All right," Mayor Grace said. "That could be, but I'm sure the police are doing all they can to find her. What do you want me to do?"

"Sally came to New York to see our new play," Rosanna said. "And she brought Cal Wood with her. Cal is a young man who works for Smoke and Sally on their ranch, Sugarloaf. He wants to help look for Sally, but the police say that he has no authority to do so."

"Well, that's silly. If all he wants to do is look for her, he doesn't need any authority."

"But we want you to give him authority to do more

than just look," Andrew said. "We want him to have the same authority as a policeman."

"You want me to make him a policeman? All right. I can do that."

"No, we want him to work *with* the police, not be one. He is a deputy sheriff for Eagle County, Colorado, so it isn't as if he has no experience in working with the law. And he has been with Smoke for some time now, which means that many of the adventures Smoke is famous for have involved Cal."

"Suppose I make him a special New York deputy, answerable directly to me?" Mayor Grace suggested. "That will give him the authority to work with the police, but not limit him to being a beat policeman."

"Yes!" Andrew replied with a big smile. "That is exactly what we were hoping you would do!"

"If you would like to have coffee with me and tell me about your new play, I'll have the commission drawn up while we are waiting."

Cal, unaware that Andrew and Rosanna were arranging for his appointment as New York City deputy sheriff, was standing at the corner where the attack had taken place. Officer Mickey Muldoon was with him.

"'N you say that the brigand who attacked you came from here?" Muldoon pointed to the gap between the two buildings.

"Yes. No. That is, the fella with the gun come from there, but the three men who attacked Miz Sally and me came up from behind us."

"How is it that you know it was three men if they were behind you?"

"I saw them a couple times. At first I thought maybe they were just out on the street at the same time Miz Sally and I were, but then I saw that they were acting like they didn't want to be seen."

"And would you for be knowin' what time it was?"

"I'd say it was about ten o'clock," Cal said.

"Ten, was it?"

"Yes."

"Not many on the street at ten. 'Tis goin' to be hard findin' a witness, I'm afraid."

CHAPTER EIGHTEEN

Near Mule Gap

"Here comes the coach," Pearlie said, though his declaration wasn't necessary.

Even as Smoke was rolling up his blankets he could hear the coach approaching—the drum of hooves, the squeak and rattle of the coach, and the shouts of the driver.

Smoke and Pearlie stepped out to the side of the road and watched as the coach rolled by. Smoke was glad to see that Sara Sue was sitting next to the window, but though they made no overt acknowledgment, it was evident that they did see each other.

"What'll we do now? Are we goin' to follow the coach into town?" Pearlie asked.

"We won't exactly follow it, I mean, not to the degree that we can keep it in sight, but I think, after a few minutes, we will go on into town."

* * *

"Did you know them two cowboys, miss?" the man sitting on the seat across from her asked. He appeared to be in his late twenties or early thirties, and had a narrow face, a sharp nose, and a small mustache.

"What two cowboys?"

"The two men standing alongside the road. I saw you looking at them, and was wonderin' if, perhaps, you know'd 'em."

"No, why? Is there any reason I should?"

"No, ma'am, none that I can think of. It's just that they seemed to be payin' an awful lot of attention to you. 'Course, you bein' a seemly lookin' woman, I can see as how they mighta took a second look at you."

Before Sara Sue could respond, a sudden gust of wind came in through the open windows, carrying upon its breath a great and smothering billow of dust. For a moment the cloud of dust so filled the coach one couldn't see from one side to the other.

"Oh, heavens!" Sara Sue said, coughing and fanning herself.

"That's the trouble when you're a-travelin' on a real clear day," the narrow-faced passenger said. "But then, all things considered, I reckon I'd rather put up with a few clouds of dust, now 'n then, than a pourin' rain comin' in 'n gettin' ever' thing 'n ever'one soakin' wet."

"I suppose that's true."

"What's your business in comin' to Mule Gap?" the man asked.

"Sir! With all due respect, my business isn't any of your business," Sara Sue replied.

The other passenger chuckled. "No ma'am, I

guess you're right. Anyhow, we're comin' into Mule Gap now."

Sara Sue looked through the window and saw the buildings passing by—at first a scattering of houses, then business buildings, until, finally, the coach came to a halt.

She exited the coach and checked in to the Del Rey Hotel, requesting that a bathtub and water be brought to her room.

"I don't know if she's got the money with her or not, but she come alone," the thin-faced, mustachioed man said.

"Very good."

"You said I'd get paid for it."

"If she has the money, we'll all enjoy a payday soon."

"All right. Just so's you know I done my part, even if I wasn't one o' them what went down into Colorado and took the boy."

One hour after the stagecoach rolled into Mule Gap, Sara Sue Condon, feeling much cleaner, presented herself at the Bank of Mule Gap.

"Yes, ma'am," the teller said.

"I should like to speak with Mr. Kennedy," Sara Sue said.

"May I tell him what it's about?"

"Yes, I intend to make a rather sizeable deposit."

"Why, ma'am, you don't need to see Mr. Kennedy to do that. I can take care of it for you."

"I would prefer to see—"

"It's all right, Mr. May, I'll see the young lady," Kennedy said. "Madam, would you like to speak in my office?"

"Yes, thank you," Sara Sue said, following the banker into an office that opened off the back of the room.

"Now, you said something about a rather sizeable deposit, I believe?"

"Yes, but I think I should tell you, I don't expect it to be here for very long."

"Oh? You are about to make a purchase in our town, perhaps?"

"No, Mr. Kennedy. I'm about to pay the ransom for the release of my son."

"Oh. You must be Mrs. Condon," Kennedy said. "Yes, I heard about your unfortunate experience. You have my best wishes for the safe return of the boy."

"How did you know about it?" Sara Sue asked.

"Your neighbor, Mr. Jensen, told me."

"Oh, yes. He delivered a bull to Mr. Harris for us. And of course, he is aware of what happened."

"Are you disturbed that I know about it?" Kennedy asked solicitously.

"No, I suppose not. I guess it was only obvious that he might have said something about it. He wanted to offer his help in some way, but I told him no. In the first place, what, exactly could he do? And in the second place, the ransom note demanded that I be alone, and I've no doubt but that means I don't allow anyone else to get involved. My number one priority, Mr. Kennedy, and I'm sure you can understand, is to get my son back. I will do nothing to jeopardize that."

"I quite understand," Kennedy said. "So you will be depositing the full amount requested by the brigands who have taken your son?"

"Yes, I have a fifteen-thousand-dollar draft from the bank in Big Rock," Sara Sue said.

Kennedy nodded. "I will personally set up the account for you," he promised.

"We'd like two rooms, please," Smoke said to the desk clerk of the Del Rey Hotel.

"Yes, sir," the clerk replied, turning the registration book around to Smoke.

As Smoke signed in, he saw that the name just above his was *Mrs. Sam Condon.* He also took note of her room number, which was 207.

"How long will you gentlemen be staying with us?" the clerk asked, after Pearlie added his name to the book.

"I don't know for sure," Smoke replied. "It depends on how our business goes."

After he and Pearlie received their keys, they climbed the stairs to the second floor, then Smoke knocked on the door of Sara Sue's room.

"Yes, who is it?" a hesitant voice called from the other side of the door.

Smoke recognized the voice as belonging to Sara Sue. "Mrs. Smith?" he called. It was the signal that had been worked out between them.

"You have the wrong room," Sara Sue replied.

That, too, was a signal, and it told Smoke that she wasn't alone.

"I beg your pardon, ma'am." Smoke glanced at Pearlie, who was also aware of the meaning of the response.

Pearlie stepped down to one of the hall lights, a sconce lantern attached to the wall just by the head of the stairs. From that position he enjoyed a view of the door to Sara Sue's room, as well as the sofa in the lobby below. He removed the globe to the lantern as if working on it, and Smoke went down to the lobby and sat on the sofa. He picked up the newspaper and began to "read" it, though he kept an eye on the top of the stairs, ready to receive a signal from Pearlie.

Sara Sue was comforted to know that Smoke was there. She had responded in a way that let him know that she wasn't alone in her room. A man who had identified himself as Fred Keefer was in the room with her. He was the representative from the kidnappers.

"Who was that at the door?" Keefer asked.

"I don't know. You heard him. He was looking for someone named Smith."

"You didn't bring anyone with you, did you?"

"You were in the lobby of the hotel when I arrived," Sara Sue said. "I saw you sitting on the sofa. You know that I came alone."

"There could have been someone waiting outside."

"There could have been, but there wasn't."

"Did you bring the money?"

"Yes."

"Where is it?"

"It's in the bank."

"It ain't supposed to be in the bank. You're supposed to have the money with you," Keefer said, his tone of voice little more than a growl.

"My husband said that I shouldn't pay the money until I have proof that Thad is still alive and unharmed."

"I can tell you he is still alive, 'n he ain't been hurt none."

"I'm sorry, but your word isn't good enough," Sara Sue said. "I shall require more proof than that."

"What kind of proof? You want me to bring a piece of his shirt or somethin'?"

"No, I want a note from Thad written in his own hand, telling me that he is unharmed."

"I ain't got a note like that."

"When you can provide me with that note, I'll give you half the money," Sara Sue said.

"Half the money? What do you mean, '*half the money*'? If you want your boy back alive, you're goin' to have to come up with *all* the money."

"And I will," Sara Sue promised. "Half when I see a note from Thad, telling me he is all right, and the other half when my son is delivered safely to me."

"I don't think the chief is goin' to like that," Keefer said.

"I would think that it would depend upon how much he wants the money, wouldn't you?"

"Seems to me like you ain't in no position to be makin' any demands," Keefer said. "Especially since we have your boy."

"Do you know how much reward money Bob Ford was paid for killing Jesse James?" Sara Sue asked.

Keefer shook his head. "What? No, I don't have

no idea. Why would you ask such a fool question, anyway?"

"It was ten thousand dollars," Sara Sue said. "If we don't get my son back alive and unharmed, my husband and I will use this ransom money to establish a reward of five thousand dollars to be paid for each of you, Mr. Keefer—you and the other two men who took Thad. Oh, and this won't be a dead-or-alive reward. It will only be paid when we have proof that you are dead."

"Maybe there's somethin' you don't understand. The three of us ain't the only ones that's a part of this. Iffen we was to get kilt, your boy would still be a prisoner," Keefer said.

"What difference would that make to you?" Sara Sue challenged.

"What? What do you mean?"

"It's a simple question. If you are dead, then it won't make any difference to you whether my boy is still a prisoner or not, will it? And when you think about it, nothing in the entire world will make any difference to you, because you will be dead. On the other hand, if you deliver my son to me in as good health as he was when you took him, why, you and your friends will be fifteen thousand dollars richer. I would think it would be to your personal advantage to see that is done.

"Now, do you really want to pass up the seventy-five hundred dollars that I'll give you after I have proof that my son is alive and well, and the other seventy-five hundred dollars that will paid upon safe delivery of my son?"

"I'll . . . uh . . . see the others 'n see what they have to say," Keefer said.

"You do that."

"It might be a while before we get back to you."

"Don't be too long. As you know, I have a wounded husband that I want to get back to."

"I wasn't the one that shot 'im," Keefer said.

"But you did nothing to stop him from being shot," Sara Sue replied.

"If you remember, I kept you from bein' shot."

"I remember," Sara Sue said coolly.

"All right. Well, uh, I'll be goin' now," Keefer said. The meeting had not gone as planned, and he was unsure of what he should do next.

As he started down the stairs, he paid no attention to the man who seemed to be working on the hallway lantern. He did recognize the man who was reading a paper in the hotel lobby. It was Smoke Jensen. Keefer hadn't had any personal run-ins with Smoke Jensen, but he did know who he was. A few weeks ago, when he'd learned that Jensen would be carrying twenty-five hundred dollars in cash, he had given the information to Bemus, Parker, and Quince. He had thought it would be a quick way to earn a little money, and it seemed like a simple enough thing to do, especially with the odds of three men to one. But when they tried to hold up Jensen, the three of them wound up dead.

Keefer knew that Jensen and the Condons were friends. He didn't know why Smoke Jensen was there now, but he knew that he didn't like it.

* * *

Pearlie looked back toward Sara Sue's room and saw her step out into the hallway. "Are you all right, Miz Condon?"

"Yes," she answered. "I did just as Sam and Smoke suggested. I hope I didn't make a mistake."

"You didn't."

CHAPTER NINETEEN

French Creek Canyon

As Travis had pointed out, the door was securely locked all the time, keeping Thad and the others trapped inside. But every time Thad used the privy, he made as close an observation of their surroundings as he could. The little cabin where the captive children were staying was set considerably closer to the creek than the larger house that was being used by their guards. That meant that if they could escape through the back of the cabin, they couldn't be immediately seen from the house where the guards were staying. The task would be how to get out the back, as there was neither door nor window there.

A further examination of the cabin gave him an idea, and he smiled. The smaller of the two buildings was not only closer to the creek, it was also on uneven ground, with the back of the cabin on stilts that elevated it about two feet above the ground. The best way to escape would be through the floor.

"Travis," Thad said when he returned to the cabin.

"Keep a lookout through the window, will you? Tell me if you see anyone coming."

"Why? What are you going to do?"

"I'm going to figure out a way for us to escape," Thad said as he got down on his hands and knees to look at the floor near the back wall. He saw right away that the problem was going to be in removing the nails. But even if he had a way of extracting them, they were so deep into the wood that he couldn't get to them. Sighing, he stood up. "I don't know how we are going to get the nails out."

"Why do you want the nails out?" Marilyn asked.

"Because I want to pull up the boards."

"Maybe you could use a nail to scratch around those nails," Lorena suggested. "The wood is old and dry-rotted. It shouldn't take much to scrape it away."

"Yes, but I would need a loose nail and something to pry the nails up."

"Here's a nail," Burt said, pointing to a nail that stuck halfway out of a wall stud.

Thad walked over to grab the nail and try to pull it out, but he couldn't make it budge. "It's no use. I'll have to come up with some other way."

"Maybe not," Lorena said. Walking over to the door, she reached above it, then took down the horseshoe that was hanging there. "Try this," she suggested with a smile.

Using the horseshoe, Thad was able to extract the nail. Then, using the nail to scratch around those on the floor, he was finally able to get purchase, and after a few tries was rewarded by seeing the nail come up about a quarter of an inch. A short while later, he had the nail completely out. "Yes! Yes, this will work!"

"Why do you want to pull the nails out of the floor?" Burt asked.

"When we get all the nails pulled, we can take up the boards and crawl through the floor and out back. We'll do it in the middle of the night, but they probably couldn't see us anyway. They can't see the back of the cabin from the house."

"It's going to take a long time to get all the nails out," Marilyn said.

"What else have we got to do?" Thad replied.

"It won't work," Travis said.

"Why not?"

"One of them is always comin' in. What if he sees holes in the floor where the nails have been?"

"How's he going to notice that? He'd have to be looking right at the floor," Burt said.

"No, Travis has a point," Thad said. "I'm not sure how we'll handle that."

"How about every time one of us goes out, we pick up a handful of dirt?" Lorena suggested. "Then, we can just drop the dirt over the nail hole."

"Yes!" Thad said. "That's a good idea, Lorena!"

Lorena beamed proudly as Thad started working on the next nail.

Mule Gap

Keefer was in the Silver Dollar Saloon sitting at a table with two other men.

"You didn't get the money?" Clyde Sanders asked.

"No," Keefer replied. "She said she would give us half of the money when we showed her proof that her boy was still alive 'n the other half when we turned him over to her. That is, if she even has the money."

"She has the money," the third man said.

"How do you know?"

"She made a deposit of that amount in the bank."

"All right," Sander said with a big smile. "Once we get the money for the Condon kid, the others will pay as well."

"Yeah, well, there may be a problem," Keefer suggested.

"What problem is that?" Sanders asked.

"Smoke Jensen."

"Who is Smoke Jensen?"

"He owns a ranch next to the Condon Ranch," Keefer said. "You might remember what happened when Bemus, Parker, and Quince tried to rob him."

"Oh, yeah," Sanders said. "He kilt all three of 'em."

"Well, he's here in town. I seen 'im sittin' in the lobby of the hotel."

"You think he might cause us some trouble?" Sanders asked.

"I don't know. It could just be a coincidence, but it's better to be safe than sorry," Keefer said. "I think we need to take care of the situation."

"What do you think we should do about it?" Sanders asked.

"You two do nothing," the third man said. "Keefer, I want you and Sanders to get back out to the cabin and keep an eye on those kids. Thanks to Marshal Bodine, we now have a town full of deputy marshals—gunmen, every one. All we have to do is put out a reward on Mr. Jensen, and the deputies will take care of the situation for us."

"How much of a reward?" Keefer asked.

"Five thousand dollars should be enough."

"Damn, do we have that much money?"

"We've gotten ten thousand in ransom payments for the first group that we took."

"And you think it's a good idea to use up half the money just to get rid of one man?"

"You said yourself, Keefer, Smoke Jensen could be a problem. I would rather pay five thousand dollars to take care of the problem than let him take care of all of us."

"Yeah," Keefer said. "Yeah, I see what you are saying."

"How do you think is the best way to handle it?" Pearlie asked as he and Smoke had lunch at the Purity Café.

"He's going to have to go to wherever they are keeping the boy to get the note. When he leaves town, we'll follow him."

"How do we know he hasn't already left town?"

Smoke nodded toward the window. "When he left the hotel, he went into the Silver Dollar Saloon. That bay on the right end of the hitching rail is his horse. He hasn't left yet."

Finishing their lunch, the two men killed time by drinking coffee as they waited for Keefer to leave.

Then Pearlie saw him. "There he is."

"We'll give him time to ride off, then we'll follow him," Smoke said.

The four streets in Mule Gap were laid out in such a way as to form a three-by-three grid. Keefer rode north to First Street, then turned west. Smoke and Pearlie finished their coffee, then left the café.

"Hello, Seven," Smoke said, greeting his horse as

he unwrapped the reins from the hitching rail. "What do you say we go for a ride?"

Seven dipped his head.

"Yeah, I thought you might like—"

That was as far as he got before a shot rang out and Smoke saw a hole suddenly appear in Seven's neck. The horse went down.

"Seven!" Smoke shouted.

A second shot zipped by Smoke's ear so close that it popped as it went by.

Looking up from his downed horse, Smoke saw four men in the middle of the street, coming toward him and Pearlie. All four men had guns in their hands, and all four guns were blazing. Pearlie went down.

"Pearlie!"

"Get 'em, Smoke. Get 'em," Pearlie called out to him.

"You sons of bitches!" Smoke shouted. With pistol in hand, he moved to the middle of the street. The four men continued to fire, but not one of their bullets found Smoke. He fired only four times, and all four men went down. With the immediate danger over, he rushed back to check on Pearlie.

"Did you get the bastards?" Pearlie asked.

"Yeah. Where are you hit?"

"All over."

"You're hit all over?"

"Well, I hurt all over," Pearlie said.

Smoke made a quick examination and found the wound in Pearlie's hip, and he was bleeding profusely. Smoke tore off a piece of Pearlie's shirt, then stuffed it into the bullet hole to stop the bleeding. By then half the town had turned out to see what was going on. Very few had actually seen the gunfight—it had been over so fast—but the ones who had seen it were talking excitedly to the others about Smoke Jensen engaged in a gun battle with four men and shooting all four down.

Smoke looked up toward the people who were standing on the porch in front of the Purity Café. "Somebody get a doctor, please."

"He's out there lookin' at them four in the street," someone replied.

"There's no need for him to be looking at them," Smoke said. "They're all dead."

"How do you know they're dead, mister?"

"Because I didn't have time not to kill them."

"Smoke," Pearlie said. "You'd better see to Seven."

"When the doctor gets here, I'll see to Seven."

"Go ahead. See to him now," Pearlie said. "I'm not going anywhere."

Smoke nodded, then stepped over to his horse. The bullet that hit him in the neck had apparently cut his jugular vein. Seven's head was lying in an enormous pool of blood. His eyes were open, but they were already opaque with death.

Smoke closed his eyes and pinched the bridge of his nose. Not since his first wife Nicole and their son Art had been murdered had he come so close to crying. Though he felt like it, he fought against the tears and pushed the lump in his throat back down. He blinked a few times then reached out to put his hand on Seven's ear. He rubbed the ear as he so often had. Seven loved that, and even though Smoke knew Seven couldn't feel it . . . Smoke could. And he very much wanted . . . no, he very much *needed* to do it.

"I know horses go to heaven." His voice broke,

but as he was talking so quietly, nobody heard him. "Heaven is supposed to be a place of total happiness, and I won't be happy unless I see you there. Run free, Seven, you've done your duty here on earth. Wait for me, old friend. Someday we'll ride together again."

Smoke left Seven lying there then hurried back over to Pearlie, reaching him just as the doctor arrived.

"Let me take a look here," the doctor said. He saw the little piece of shirt that was jammed into the bullet hole. "How the blazes did this cloth get in here?"

"I put it there," Smoke said. "He was bleeding quite a bit, and I figured I should stop it."

"Well, you are right about that," the doctor said, "but I wish you could have found something a little cleaner than this to use."

"Come on, Doc, my shirt is clean enough," Pearlie said. "It hasn't been more 'n a week since I washed it last."

"Well, he was right to stop the bleeding," the doctor said.

"How bad is it?" Smoke asked.

"Doesn't look like it's too bad."

"Who killed these men?" someone shouted from the middle of the street.

Looking toward the sound of the angry voice, Smoke saw the one they called The Professor, Frank Bodine. The badge of a marshal was prominent on the black shirt he was wearing.

"I did," Smoke said, rising up from the squatting position he had been in beside Pearlie.

"Do you want to tell me why you killed them?"

"Because the sons of bitches killed my horse," Smoke said in an angry, clipped voice.

"You killed four men over a horse?"

"It ain't quite like that, Marshal," one of the towns-people said. "I seen the whole thing. These two men, that one"—he pointed to Smoke—"and the feller on the ground come out of the café there, 'n them four that's lyin' out in the street commenced firin' without so much as a fare-thee-well. This feller was just fixin' to get on his horse when it was hit 'n went down. And that feller was hit at the same time." He pointed toward Pearlie. "So this man—"

"His name is Jensen," Bodine said. "Smoke Jensen."

"Yes, sir. Well, Mr. Jensen, he stepped into the street 'n shot back. He musta shot four times 'cause all four o' them men went down, but if he did shoot four times, he done it so fast I couldn't tell."

"Harvey Long is tellin' the truth, Marshal, 'cause I seen it, too. 'N it was just like Harvey said it was. Them men in the street commenced shootin' just as soon as Jensen 'n that other man started to mount up. Why, there weren't even no words spoke a-fore the shootin' started."

"These four men were my deputies," Bodine said. "I'm pretty sure they thought they were doing their duty."

"Was it their duty to ambush my friend and me?" Smoke asked.

"No, of course not. I would theorize that they saw the two of you in violation of some city ordinance or county law, and it was their intention to bring you in for questioning."

"They wanted us for questioning? They why didn't they say so? Whatever possessed them to simply start shooting like that?" Smoke asked.

Bodine shook his head. "I don't know. Perhaps they were coming to question you when they perceived danger and reacted without thinking it through. At any rate, the county has lost four good men."

"Will you be needing me for anything, Marshal?" Smoke asked pointedly.

"No, I can't say that I do. You're free to go."

"Thank you."

"Mr. Jensen?" the doctor said.

"Yes?"

"We need to get your friend down to my office so I can cleanse his wound and get him wrapped up with a sterile bandage."

"Yeah," Smoke said. "I had better make some arrangements for Seven, as well."

CHAPTER TWENTY

French Creek Canyon

For two days Thad and the others had been pulling nails up from the floor. The work was painstaking. Enough of the wood had to be scraped away from each nail to get purchase on the nail head so it could be removed. Even then, it wasn't easy to pull the nail. The horseshoe could only catch one side of the nail head, and then not too securely. The horseshoe had to be worked around the nail a little on one side then a little on the other, lifting it about a quarter of an inch at a time with each effort.

Because it was so painstaking and time consuming, the effort was tiring and had to be spread out evenly among all of them except Wee. But even he did his part, often returning from his trips to the privy with a pocket full of dirt. Thad allowed Wee to cover the holes that had been opened as a result of the extracted nails.

To date, they had extracted thirty nails, which was enough to allow them to pull up three boards. Thad calculated that they would need at least three more boards in order to create an opening wide enough to enable them to slip down through the hole in the floor.

"Here comes Mr. Reece," Wee called from the window.

"Some of the newer holes can be seen," Thad said.

Lorena grabbed a broom and just as Reece came into the building, she began sweeping the dirt around over the area where they had been working.

"Well now, sweepin' are you? Can you cook, too? You're goin' to be a real looker soon," Reece said. "You could be a real man-pleaser one of these days. Especially if you would let me teach you a few things." His words dripped with sexual innuendo.

"You stay away from her, Reece," Thad said menacingly.

"Oh yes, you are the one who is goin' to kill me, ain't you?" Reece asked with a mocking laugh. "You her protector now? Boy, you pure-dee got me shakin' in my boots."

Thad glared at Reece, but didn't respond to his taunting challenge.

"How does it feel, girl, to know that you got someone that's goin' to protect you?" Reece asked.

"What do you want, Reece?" Thad asked.

"That would be Mr. Reece to you, boy."

"What do you want, Reece?" Thad repeated.

Reece grinned, though there was no humor in his smile. "I got good news for you, boy. It looks like your mama is goin' to pay the money for you to get out of here."

"That doesn't change anything," Thad replied.

"It doesn't change anything? Didn't you hear what I said? I said your mama is goin' to pay us to set you free."

"That doesn't change anything," Thad repeated.

"You mean you still plan to kill me?"

Thad glared at Reece, but he didn't respond.

"Well, I just come in to tell you the good news," Reece said. "Little lady, you just go back to sweepin'. From all the dirt on the floor in here, it looks like it needs it." He left, and the others turned to look at Thad.

"Are you going to go home?" Travis asked.

"Yeah, I'm going home," Thad replied. Then he smiled. "We are all going home. I'm not leaving here until we all leave here."

"I knew you wouldn't leave us!" Burt said with a happy smile.

"We need to do this a little faster," Thad said. "Let's all work on the nails at the same time. We've pulled enough nails we can use them to scrape around the nails we haven't pulled yet.

"Me too?" Wee asked.

"No, you keep doing just what you were doing," Thad said. "You did a good job, Wee, warning us about Reece. I'm proud of you."

A pleased smile spread across Wee's face, and he went back over to stand on the box that let him look through the window.

"Let's get to work," Thad said to the others.

Fancy Bliss, Joy Love, and Candy Sweet were riding in the buckboard being driven by Clyde Sanders when it arrived at the house and cabin located on the bank of French Creek. Delilah Dupree had agreed to let them make a client visit, at double the cost of what their services would have been at the House of Pleasure.

As they arrived, they saw a young girl standing in front of a privy.

"Oh," Fancy said. "There are children here?"

"Don't worry none about it," Sanders said. "They're all stayin' in that little cabin. They won't have nothin' to do with our business."

"What do you mean, *all* are staying in that little cabin? How many are there?"

"They's six of 'em now, but if it all works out, there'll only be five pretty soon. Maybe we can get rid of the others, too."

"Get rid of them? What are you talking about? Why are the children here?" Fancy asked.

"You ask too many questions," Sanders said. "We ain't payin' you women to come out here just so we would have someone to talk to. Now, get on into the big house 'n let's get down to business."

A second girl came out of the privy as Fancy and the other two ladies climbed down from the buckboard. The two girls looked at Fancy, and she tried to study the expression on their faces.

Keefer, Reece, and Whitman were smiling broadly when Sanders and the three women went into the house.

"Well, now, ladies, we're goin' to have us a real fine time here," Keefer said.

"Oh my. There are four of you. It looks as if one of us will be doing double duty," Joy said.

"We're payin' you to spend the whole night with us," Keefer said. "I expect all of you will be doin' double duty."

"We done drawed high cards," Whitman said. "Reece is goin' to have to wait his turn. I got high card so I get my pick," he added with a broad, salacious smile.

"Hey Keefer, you left town too soon," Sanders said. "You missed the killin' ."

Keefer smiled. "Jensen got kilt, did he?"

"No. Four of the deputies tried to kill him, but he wound up killin' all four of them, shootin' 'em down in the street. It was the damnedest thing I've ever seen."

"You talk like you're excited about it," Keefer scolded.

"Well, I don't like the way it turned out, that's for sure 'n certain," Sanders said. Inexplicably, a broad smile spread across his face. "But if that warn't the damndest thing I've ever seen, I don't know what else would be."

"Are you tellin' me that Jensen took on four of the deputies and kilt them all by hisself?" Keefer asked.

"He's right, honey," Candy said. "Why, the whole town is talking about it."

"Seein' as how Bates, Cooper, Barnes, and Gibson is all Bodine's deputies, how come he ain't put Jensen in jail?"

"On account of in the first place, it was self-defense 'n there was lots of people that seen it," Sanders said. "And in the second place, if you want to know the truth, I'm not just real sure that Bodine could handle Jensen."

"What are you talkin' about? Bodine is the best there is," Keefer insisted.

"Maybe not," Sanders said.

"I'll be damned," Keefer said. "We'd better keep an eye on Jensen. He's goin' to be trouble, you mark my words."

"Why are you so concerned about Smoke Jensen?" Fancy asked. "What do you mean there's going to be trouble? Is there bad blood between you?"

"No, I ain't never even met the man," Keefer replied.

"Does it have anything to do with the children who are staying out here?"

"What children?" Keefer asked, surprised by the question.

"I saw two little girls going from the privy to that little cabin. Mr. Sanders said there are six children staying in the cabin."

Keefer shot an angry glance toward Sanders before he looked back at Fancy, replacing the momentary flash of anger with a quick forced smile.

"Yeah, their parents are payin' us to keep 'em out here for a while. They thought it would be good for them to spend some time on the creek with friends. It's sort of a vacation for them."

"Oh, how wonderful! Maybe we can visit with them a while, later on," Joy suggested.

Keefer shook his head. "I don't think so. You're all whores. Do you really think these kids' mamas and papas are goin' to want their kids spending any time with a whore?"

Joy's smile faded, replaced by a momentary look of shame. She smiled again, and if it was a practiced smile, it at least had the effect of lightening the mood and changing the subject. "I believe you said something about a party?"

* * *

"Did you see the three ladies?" Wee asked when Lorena and Marilyn returned to the cabin.

"We saw them," Lorena said, "but I don't think you could exactly call them ladies."

"What do you call them?" Wee asked, confused by Lorena's response.

Lorena smiled. "Never mind. You can call them ladies."

"Did they go into the house?" Thad asked.

"Yes."

"Good."

"Why good?"

"That means they won't be paying too much attention to us for a while. We should be able get a lot of work done today."

Mule Gap

"I'll buy your horse from you," Boyd Evans, the manager of the livery stable, said to Smoke as they were standing over Seven's body.

"You want to buy Seven? Whatever for? Why would you pay for a dead horse?"

"Horses have a lot of collagen, and the glue factories pay well for that."

"No!" Smoke said. "Seven is not going to be used to make glue! This is my third horse named Seven. Number one is dead, but number two has been turned out to pasture."

"You've had three horses named Seven?" Evans asked.

"I'm about to have another horse named Seven,

and why not? If England can have eight kings named Henry I can have as many horses named Seven as I want."

"Wait. Are you telling me that England has eight kings, and all of them are named Henry?"

"No," Smoke replied in an exasperated tone of voice. "What I am telling you is that I want Seven to have a respectable burial."

"Where do you want him buried?"

"Where in Mule Gap are horses buried?"

"There's a place out behind the livery where some of 'em are buried. And some folks bury 'em on their own land."

"I can't take him back to Sugarloaf, so we'll have to bury him here."

Evans brought out a team of mules, connected a harness to Seven, and pulled his body to a place behind the livery stable. There, he hired four men to dig a hole big enough and deep enough to inter Seven.

Smoke watched until the grave was closed, then he went back into the livery to pay the bill. "And I want to rent a horse for the time I'm here."

"You want to rent one or buy one?" the stable owner said. "I have some fine horses for sale."

"No, my next horse is already back at my ranch. He's a two-year-old, the son of Seven, and he looks just like him."

"All right. You can pick out the one you want to rent."

Smoke chose a bay with four stockings and a blaze. He ran his hand over the horse, feeling for any abnormalities in its configuration, but found none. "All right. I'll take this one."

"For how long?"

"Until I bring him back."

"In that case, I'll take a hundred dollars to hold until you bring him back."

Smoke agreed.

He returned to the doctor's office a short while later and found Pearlie sitting up in a chair, fully dressed. "What are you doing up? I thought you would be in bed."

"I'm up, 'cause I wasn't really hurt."

"What do you mean you weren't hurt? You were shot. I saw the bullet wound."

"Well, yeah, I was shot, but like I said, I wasn't really hurt. The doctor himself said I wasn't hurt."

"I said no such thing," the doctor said, coming into the waiting room of his office. "I said that none of your vital organs were involved and that, if you are careful, this wound won't give you any trouble."

"You also said I could leave," Pearlie said.

"I did say that, but you may also recall that I said you couldn't leave until I saw Mr. Jensen and would be assured that he would take care of you."

"Well, he's here, 'n he's goin' to take me out of here. Aren't you, Smoke?"

Smoke laughed. "Yes, if you're up to leaving here, I'll take you with me."

"Let's go have supper," Pearlie suggested.

CHAPTER TWENTY-ONE

"Mrs. Condon, imagine seeing you here," Smoke said when he and Pearlie stepped into the restaurant at the Del Rey Hotel.

"Why, Mr. Jensen," Sara Sue said, "won't the two of you join me?"

"You aren't expecting anyone else?"

"No, I'm here alone," Sara Sue replied.

The exchange was loud enough for others in the dining room to hear, and it was specifically designed to make anyone who was paying particular attention to them think that the meeting was accidental. Not until Smoke and Pearlie joined her at the table, with Pearlie walking with a pronounced limp, did they speak quietly enough to be able to hold a private conversation.

"Have you heard anything yet?" Smoke asked.

"No, and I'm so worried."

"I wouldn't be worried yet. It's obvious that the man who visited you has no authority to make the decision himself. That has to come from someone else, and it is sure to be one or maybe two days before anyone contacts you."

"Oh, I just hate to think of Thad being held for two more days by those awful men," Sara Sue said.

"I know Thad," Smoke said. "He is a very tough and resourceful young man. I have a feeling that he is more than holding his own against them."

"Oh!" Sara Sue said. "You were in a shooting today. And Pearlie, I heard that you were shot. I'm glad to see you up and about, and forgive me for not inquiring sooner about you."

"I'm doing just fine, Mrs. Condon. I've got a little bit of a limp is all. You might call it a hitch in my get-about," he added with a chuckle.

"I'm worried about the shooting," Sara Sue said. "Do you think it's because they know you are helping me?"

"It could be," Smoke admitted. "But it could just as likely be someone trying to settle an old score with me."

"Heavens, you mean there is someone out there who might actually want to shoot you?"

"More than one, I'm afraid," Smoke said.

"I knew you were . . . uh . . . rather well-known for your skill with a gun, and I knew that you had helped many people, but I didn't know there would actually be men who would want to shoot you."

"This isn't the first time, and they haven't gotten the job done yet."

"The worst thing," Pearlie said, "worse than me getting shot, is that they killed his horse."

"Seven?" Sara Sue said. "Oh, Smoke, no! I didn't

hear about that. I'm so sorry. I know what store you set by that horse."

"It was tough to lose him, all right," Smoke said. "But I'm thankful I didn't lose Pearlie."

"Yes, as am I."

"What do you hear from Sam?"

"I got a telegram from him today. He says he's doing fine, he misses me, and he knows I will get—" Sara Sue paused in midsentence then, with a choke in her voice, she continued. "He said he knows I will get Thad back safely."

"*We* will get him back safely," Smoke said.

Sara Sue smiled through her tears. "I am so thankful to you for helping us."

"Smoke, you told a big one at the dinner table tonight, didn't you?" Pearlie said as the two men left the hotel.

"What was that?"

"You told Mrs. Condon that the shooting today coulda been someone tryin' to settle an old score. You know as well as I do that someone has figured out we're helpin' Mrs. Condon, and they was just tryin' to get us out of the way."

"You're right," Smoke said. "But she's worried enough as it is. If she thinks the kidnappers know we're helping her, she will be afraid they will follow through on their threat to harm Thad. I see no reason to give her anything more to worry about."

"Yeah, I guess you're right," Pearlie said. "She seemed real upset about Seven."

"Yes, she always had a few lumps of sugar for Seven anytime she saw him."

"I'm real sorry about Seven, Smoke. He was as good a horse as I've ever known."

"He was a good one, all right. I'm going to hate to have to tell Sally about it. She loved him as much as I did."

"She's going to take it hard, that's for sure," Pearlie said.

"We've obviously lost the trail on Keefer," Smoke. "I think our best bet now is just to wait until they contact Mrs. Condon again. They'll do that because, so far, she hasn't paid them one red cent."

"Say, as long as we're going to wait until they contact Miz Condon again, you don't mind if we wait in the saloon, do you?" Pearlie asked as they walked by Kennedy's Saloon.

Smoke chuckled. "As a matter of fact, a saloon is a perfect place to wait. You can sometimes pick up some good information in a saloon."

Kennedy wasn't in the saloon, but the bartender recognized Smoke and greeted him with a smile. Then he turned his attention to Pearlie.

"And how are you doin', young fella? The last time I seen you, you was lyin' in the dirt, bleedin' like a stuck pig."

"You saw that, did you?"

"Oh, I think most of the town saw it."

"Well, thanks to Smoke stoppin' the bleeding, and the doc cleaning out the wound, I'm getting along pretty well," Pearlie replied.

"Well, I must say, Smoke Jensen has certainly made

our town famous. How many towns can say that Smoke Jensen faced down four men in the street?"

"Smoke Jensen?" another man said. He had been standing at the far end of the bar, nursing his drink. "Are you the . . . *great* . . . Smoke Jensen?" He set the word *great* apart in his question, twisting it in a way that indicated it was meant as a mockery and not as an accolade.

"Glen, give the gentleman at the other end of the bar a drink on me," Smoke said easily. He had recognized the taunting in the man's voice and was trying to defuse the situation.

"I'll buy my own drink," the man said.

"Good, I like a man who pays his own way," Smoke said, purposely turning a deaf ear to the man's taunts.

"I seen the fight you was in today," the man said. "Them four was fools. They wan't a damn one of 'em what coulda hit a bull in the ass if they was ten foot from it. Oh, wait, they did kill your horse, though, didn't they?" He laughed. "Did you cry when your horse got shot?"

"I got a lump in my throat, yes," Smoke said.

"Well now, ain't that just too bad?" The heckler laughed again.

"Mr. Allison, you got no call to act like that about a man losin' his horse," Glen, the bartender, said. "You know how most men feel about their horses."

"Allison?" Smoke said. "Would you be the one they call Blackjack Allison?"

"Heard of me, have you?"

"Yeah." The only reason Smoke had heard of Blackjack Allison was because Sheriff Carson, down in

Big Rock, had mentioned him no more than a week earlier. Smoke recalled what the sheriff had said.

"I just got another notice on someone named Blackjack Allison. He's been in seven or eight gunfights recently. But as they were all face-to-face gunfights, he hasn't been charged for any of them. From what I've heard, though, he's someone who is trying to build a reputation. On at least a few of the fights, it is said that he pushed the other man into drawing on him."

"Are you trying to push me into a gunfight, Allison?"

"I don't know," Allison said. "Are me 'n you, the *great* Smoke Jensen, about to have a gunfight?"

Most in the saloon, sensing there was about to be a gunfight, began moving out of the way. Only Pearlie, standing just behind Smoke and certainly in the line of fire if shooting began, didn't move. He continued to drink his beer with as much nonchalance as if he had been sitting alone at a table.

"There's no need for us to fight," Smoke said.

"Oh, yes, there is. You see, you're worth five thousand dollars to me. Dead."

"Five thousand dollars? Mr. Allison, are you out of your mind? I don't have any paper out on me anywhere. What in the world makes you think I'm worth five thousand dollars?"

"I didn't say they was paper out on you," Allison replied. "All I said was you was worth five thousand dollars to me iffen I was to kill you."

"Who has made that offer?"

"It ain't none of your concern who has made that offer, seein' as you won't be around to do nothin' about it." Alison called to Pearlie, "Hey you, the one drinkin' the beer."

"The name is Pearlie." He spoke as calmly as if introducing himself at a friendly encounter.

"Yeah? Well, Pearlie, you done got shot oncet today. Iffen you don't want to get shot again, you'd better move out of the way."

"What do you mean, if I don't want to get shot?" Pearlie replied. "I thought Smoke is the one you're getting paid to shoot. Just how is it that I'm going to get shot?"

"What's the matter with you? Are you crazy? Me 'n Smoke Jensen here is about to have ourselves a little dance. And you bein' where you are could likely get shot."

"Oh, I see what you're saying, but there's no problem," Pearlie said. "Besides, I haven't finished my drink."

"Jensen, you'd better tell your friend here to get out of the way," Allison said.

"Oh, I think he's quite safe," Smoke replied.

Allison smiled. "Because you don't think I'll miss?"

"No, the truth is, Allison, you won't even get a shot off."

"The hell I won't!" Allison yelled as he started toward his gun.

In a lightning draw, Smoke had his pistol in his hand.

"No! Wait!" Allison shouted, letting his gun drop back into its holster and raising both arms over his head. "How? How the hell did you do that?"

The saloon patrons observing the unfolding scene from their vantage points within the room were as shocked as Allison, and the same question he had asked was on many of their lips. *How did he get his gun out so fast?*

"Look, I was just funnin' with you," Allison said. "I didn't have no real idea of drawin' ag'in you. What . . . what are you goin' to do?"

"Yes, Smoke, what *are* you going to do?" Warren Kennedy asked, having just stepped into the saloon that bore his name.

"I'm not sure what I'm going to do," Smoke said. "I think I'll just shoot him."

"You ain't goin' to shoot me," Allison said. "It would be murder."

"I'll leave it up to you, Warren," Smoke said easily. "This is your saloon. Do you want me to kill him? Or should I let him live?"

"I'm tempted to tell you to go ahead and shoot him." Kennedy smiled. "You're quite a well-known figure, Mr. Jensen. Why, if I put a sign on the wall behind the bar that said Smoke Jensen killed Blackjack Allison here, why, I've no doubt it would be good for business."

"You wouldn't do that," Allison said nervously. "Not after we—"

"Get out of here, Allison," Kennedy said with a contemptuous nod of his head toward the door. "And don't come back into my saloon picking a fight you can't handle."

"Can I put my hands back down?" Allison asked Smoke.

"Yeah."

Allison dropped his hands then turned to leave.

"Wait a minute," Smoke called.

Allison stopped.

"Before you leave, shuck out of that gun belt. The pistol stays here," Smoke said.

"The hell it does!" Allison replied in one last attempt at bravado.

"Leave it," Smoke said coldly.

"Mister, you're crazy if you think I'm going to give up my gun."

Smoke pulled the hammer back on his pistol, and the deadly metallic click sounded loud in the room. "Oh, I think you will."

Allison paused for a moment longer, then, looking at Smoke with an expression of intense anger, unbuckled his gun belt and let it drop to the floor.

"Now you can go," Smoke said.

"When do I get it back?" he asked.

"Not until my friend and I have left the saloon."

Kennedy laughed out loud after Allison left the saloon. "Glen, drinks on the house . . . for everyone," Kennedy ordered.

"Yes, sir, Mr. Kennedy," Ethan replied.

With a happy shout, as much in relief of tension as appreciation for the drinks, all the patrons rushed to the bar with their orders.

"You son of a bitch!" Allison shouted, stepping back into the barroom, holding a rifle to his shoulder.

Many were now in Allison's line of fire. Shouts of surprise and fear erupted as everyone tried to get out of the way. The room filled with the sound of a gunshot . . . and Allison stood there for a moment with a look of shock on his face. "You? You shot me?"

He dropped the rifle and slapped his hand over a bleeding hole in his chest, standing there only long enough for people to see the blood streaming between his fingers before he pitched forward and landed facedown on the floor.

Not until then did everyone realize where the shot had come from. They all turned to see Warren Kennedy standing with a smoking pistol in his hand.

"That's the second time you've saved my life," Smoke said.

"Yes, it is, isn't it?" Kennedy replied with a self-assured smile.

CHAPTER TWENTY-TWO

New York City

Officer Muldoon stepped up to the front desk at the Fifth Avenue Hotel.

"Yes, Officer, what can I do for you?" the desk clerk asked.

"Would you be for tellin' me please in what room I might find a Mr. Cal Wood?"

The desk clerk ran his fingers down the open pages of the registration book until he found the name. "He is in room four-oh-three. Officer, there is nothing wrong, is there? What I mean is only the most select people stay here, and I wouldn't want any kind of confrontation that would disturb our guests."

"There is nothing wrong, and the lad is in no trouble," Muldoon said. "All I'll be doing is talking with him."

"You may take the elevator," the clerk said.

A few moments later, the elevator operator opened the door onto the fourth floor. "You'll find four-oh-three that way, Officer. Just down the hall and on the left," the operator said.

"Thank you."

Cal was lying on his bed with his hands laced behind his head. He had not yet sent a telegram to Smoke, and he was wondering whether or not he should. He knew there was nothing Smoke could do, and he felt that there was no sense in worrying him. If the situation turned worse, he would tell him, but for now, Cal was absorbing all the worry himself. And he was literally sick with it, primarily because he wasn't doing anything about it.

A knock on the door jarred him from his melancholy, and remembering that the police lieutenant had promised to inform him of anything they might learn, he leaped up from the bed and hurried to open the door. "Officer Muldoon! Have you any news?"

"Nothing about your lady yet, but I've some news that might be to your liking."

"What is it?"

"Your friends . . . the famous actors?"

"Yes? What about them?"

"They've gone to see His Honor, the mayor. Would you be for believin' that Mayor Grace has made you a New York City deputy? You'll be workin' on the case with me."

"Oh!" Cal said as a huge smile spread across his face. "Oh, Officer Muldoon, that is great!"

"Come along. We'll walk my beat together."

"Wait for me in the lobby," Cal said. "I need to change clothes."

Cal went down to the lobby a few minutes later dressed as he would be if he had been back in Colorado. He was wearing boots, but no spurs, blue denim trousers, a yellow shirt, and a Stetson hat with a turquoise-studded hatband. He was also wearing a pistol belt, complete with filled bullet loops. His Colt .45 rode conspicuously on his hip.

"I don't know about the pistol, lad," Officer Muldoon said.

"Remember, I'm a deputy sheriff for Eagle County, Colorado," Cal said. "And you said yourself that the mayor issued me a special license to act as a deputy here in New York."

Muldoon chuckled. "That's right, he did. Tell me, Deputy Wood, are you any good with that pistol?"

"I haven't shot myself in the leg yet," Cal replied.

Muldoon laughed. "Good enough. Come with me. I don't mind saying that, considerin' some o' the brigands we'll be seein', 'twill be good to have you along."

The first place they visited was Donovan's Pub, an Irish bar that was just across the street from where Cal and Sally were attacked. It was obvious Muldoon was a frequent visitor. Everyone in the pub gave him a hearty greeting.

"Who's the cowboy with you, Muldoon?" one of the customers asked.

"He is a deputy sheriff from Colorado," Muldoon said, using the information Cal had provided him, but withholding the fact that he was also a New York deputy. "Deputy Wood, he is."

"What's a deputy from Colorado doin' here in New York?" another asked.

"I'm looking for a woman that was taken last night," Cal said.

"Taken? Taken where?"

"That's what we're trying to find out . . . where she was taken."

"It happened right across the street, sometime between ten o'clock and eleven o'clock it was. 'Tis wondering, the deputy and I are, whether any of you might have seen somethin'," Muldoon said.

"Hey, cowboy," one of the patrons called out to Cal. "What are you doin' comin' into a man's drinkin' bar with cow shit on your shoes?"

"Damn, are you telling me I've got cow shit on my boots?" Cal replied, holding one of them up to examine. "And here they are brand new, too."

"Ha! Darby, I think the lad has got you," the bartender said to the man who had challenged Cal.

"Aye," one of the other patrons said. "Sure 'n the only shit now is on Darby's face 'n not on the lad's shoes."

"Think you're smart, do you, cowboy?" Darby had been leaning against the bar, but when he stepped away from it, Cal saw how large he was—at least six-foot-three, with broad shoulders and powerful arms. He bent both arms at the elbow and made a beckoning sign with his curled fingers. "Here now, 'n why don't you show us just how smart you be."

"Easy enough to show you how smart I am," Cal replied with an easy smile. "I'm too smart to fight with a giant like you."

"Well now lad, this has done gone too far. You've

got m' dander up, you have, 'n the only way I'm goin' to be pacified is if I teach you a little lesson."

"Leave the lad be, Darby," Muldoon said. "You touch 'im 'n you'll be windin' up in the Tombs."

"Won't be the first time I've been in jail. 'Twill be worth it to teach the cowboy a lesson," Darby said with a broad smile.

Cal knew that Darby was about to rush him, and he came up on his toes ready to deal with it.

With a yell that could almost be a growl, Darby bent over at the waist with his arms stretched out in front of him and charged Cal. Cal deftly stepped aside, drew his pistol, and brought it down as hard as he could on Darby's head. He put the gun back in its holster so quickly that no more than one or two of the witnesses even knew that a gun was used.

"Blimey now, 'n did you see that?" someone shouted.

Darby lay very still and for a moment Cal was afraid that he might have killed him.

He knelt quickly to check on him and was relieved to find that he was still alive. "Bartender, do you have a pitcher of water?"

"Aye." The bartender drew a pitcher of water and handed it to Cal, who poured it over Darby, standing ready in case any fight remained in the Irishman.

Darby came to, spitting and coughing. He got up on his hands and knees. "Begorra. Would someone be for tellin' me what I'm doin' on the floor?"

"Why, you tripped over yer own feet, you big galoot," the bartender said.

"I did?"

"Aye." The bartender drew a mug of beer. "Here,

have a mug on the house. I can't be for havin' m' customers fall all over the place in the pub now, can I? How would that look for business?"

"I'll have a drink with you, Darby," one of the others said.

Soon several others made the same offer.

"What about you, lad?" Darby asked Cal. "Would you be for havin' a drink with ol' Darby?"

"Yes, thank you. I'd like that," Cal said.

The bartender drew a mug for Cal, who blew off the foam, then held his beer out toward the others as they all drank.

"You done well in there, Cal," Muldoon said when they left the pub a short while later. "I was wonderin' how you would handle it. If you backed away, you woulda lost face that you could never recover. But 'twas for sure 'n certain that you'd be no match for him."

"Thanks," Cal said, feeling good about the policeman's compliments.

Five Points, New York City

The buildings on Baxter Street were festooned with awnings stretched out over the sidewalks and clothes hanging to dry from the windows of the upper floors. Even though night had fallen, the street was well illuminated by corner lamps and the ambient light streaming from the windows of the buildings.

"I sure wish I had a picture of her," Cal said. "I think that would help."

"No, lad. If they snatched her in the middle of the night, 'tis not likely anyone saw her . . . so a picture would do you no good. 'Tis if someone has heard somethin' that we're hopin' for."

"Mickey, if something has happened to her, I'll not be able to face Smoke."

"Smoke?"

"Smoke is her husband."

"His name is Smoke?"

"His real name is Kirby, but I've never actually heard him called that. I've never seen two people who cared more about each other than those two. I've come close to gettin' married m'self, but it wasn't meant to be. If I ever do get married though, I would sure hope to have something like those two have."

"Aye, the missus 'n I were like that," Officer Muldoon said.

"Were?"

"Aye. She took the new-monia 'n died last year."

"Oh, I'm sorry," Cal said.

"Sure now, lad. 'Twas not yer fault. You don't have nothin' to be sorry for. 'Tis just hopin', I am, that we can find your friend."

"Yeah," Cal said. "I'm hoping that, too."

"We've a few more pubs to look into. Maybe something will turn up."

"Maybe," Cal said, but his response was weak.

The next pub they went into was called Cara.

"A woman owns this place?" Cal asked.

"What? No, 'n why would you be for sayin' such a thing?"

"It's got a woman's name. Cara."

Muldoon chuckled. "Here now, 'n that's nothin' o' the sort. The word *cara* is Gaelic for *friends*. You might say the place is called Friends."

"Friends. Yes, that would be a good name, I think."

Muldoon had decided that he might have better results if he spoke to the patrons individually, rather than making a public inquiry. He reasoned that some might be more open to tell what they knew in private, rather than to speak before everyone.

The individual questioning wasn't producing any more results, until Cal saw someone in the back of the room who looked familiar. He thought back to the few quick glances he had of the three men who had been following Sally and him and he was almost sure it was one of them.

"Mickey, that man in the back, the one in the brown jacket," Cal said. "I think he might have been one of the three men who were following Miz Sally and me."

"The one in in the brown jacket, you say?"

"Yes. I'm certain he was one of them."

Muldoon smiled. "Well, now, could be that our luck is about to change. His name is O'Leary, 'n he's of the sort to do such a blackhearted thing.

"You, O'Leary. I'd like to talk to you," Cal called out, pointing to the man who had caught his attention.

"We ain't got nothin' to talk about," O'Leary said.

"I think I've seen you before."

"I told you', I've got no wish to be for talkin' to you."

"It's just a friendly question, is all," Cal said.

"No it ain't. There ain't nothin' friendly about it," O'Leary replied. He turned away for just a moment, and when he turned back he had a gun in his hand.

"Look out, lad. He's got a gun!" Muldoon said as he unsnapped the cover to his own holster in an effort to get to his pistol.

O'Leary fired toward Cal and Muldoon.

Cal's mentor in the art of the fast draw was Smoke Jensen, the master, and Cal had his own gun out so quickly there was barely a separation between the two shots. The difference was the first shooter missed and Cal did not.

Holding the smoking gun in his hand for a moment longer, he ascertained no other imminent threat and put the pistol back in his holster.

"Damn!" someone said in awe. "Did you see that?"

"Yeah, Murphy, we all seen it," another bar patron replied.

Muldoon had not even gotten his holster open in the time it took for Cal and the shooter to exchange shots. He pulled his hand away sheepishly. "Here now, 'tis damn good with that gun that you be, lad. If I had to guess, I'd say you've had to do that before."

"A few times," Cal said. "Am I in trouble?"

"No trouble. For sure 'n certain O'Leary would have killed you. Aye, 'n me, too, I'm thinkin' . . . if you hadn't shot him. 'Tis my own life you saved. No, lad, 'tis a medal you deserve, not a charge."

"You said you know him."

"Aye, Ian Patrick O'Leary. He's been a trouble-maker ever since I started walkin' this beat."

"I am absolutely positive he was one of the three men that followed Miz Sally and me."

"I think you be right. Otherwise O'Leary would not have tried to shoot you as he done. This'll give us an idea where to go next," Muldoon said. "We'll be for visitin' some o' the Irish Assembly now."

"What is the Irish Assembly?"

"At one time 'twas a gang o' Irish brigands who did nothin' but give Ireland a bad name. They got into a gun battle with the Five Points gang, 'n 'tis said they broke up soon after that. Broke up they may be, but many o' the same group o' hoodlums are still hangin' around 'n still gettin' into the same mischief they was gettin' into when they was a gang."

"Was O'Leary one of them?" Cal asked.

"Aye, O'Leary was one of them. I know a lot more who once wore the Assembly's shamrock, but since it is no more, a lot of 'em are tryin' to straighten their lives up 'n make a go of it. 'Tis them we'll be startin' with, and I'll be for askin' them what they know about Mrs. Jensen being taken like she was. I got a feelin' there'll be a lot o' folk who have heard about it, but are not for wantin' to have anything to do with it. I know a few boys who just might be able to help us out."

CHAPTER TWENTY-THREE

Sally could tell by the lengthening shadows as well as the dimmer light in her room that it was getting late in the afternoon. The man she now knew as Kelly came into her room.

"I brought you some supper," Kelly said.

"Thank you."

"I'll be for untyin' you now so you can eat, if you'll give me yer promise not to try and escape."

"Mr. Kelly, how would I be able to do that? You appear to be a very strong man. There is no way I can overpower you. I can't jump out of the window. I'm quite certain that I'm not on the ground floor."

Kelly chuckled. "No ma'am, I don't reckon you can overpower me, and you ain't on a ground floor." He loosened the ties, and again, Sally began to rub her wrists.

"When can I see Mr. Gallagher again?" she asked.

"Why would you be wantin' ter see him?"

"You said that he is the one who gave you the instructions to capture me. I want to know why he did that. What is to be gained by holding me prisoner?"

"Yes ma'am, I reckon I can see as ter how you might be some considerable plexed by it. I'd tell you if I knew, but I don't have no idee a' tall."

"Is Mr. Gallagher here right now?"

"No, ma'am, he ain't."

"You mean, you are the only one watching me?"

"Aye."

"Let me go, Mr. Kelly."

Kelly shook his head. "I can't do that."

"Sure you can. You can simply tell Mr. Gallagher that I escaped."

"And how did you escape, would you be for tellin' me that? Sure 'n you've already pointed out how that ain't possible, bein' as you can't get by me."

"My husband is a very wealthy man. You could turn me over to the police, and I would see to it that you got quite a nice reward for it."

"'Tis tempted I am, Miz Jensen, but I'll not be goin' up against the likes o' Ian Gallagher. You've no idea how evil he is."

"Evil to the degree that I have to fear harm coming to me while I am your prisoner?"

"No, ma'am. I done asked him that, 'n he promised me you wouldn't be hurt none whilst we are keepin' you."

"Thank you, Mr. Kelly." As Sally ate her supper, potato soup, she thought about Kelly. His concern for her seemed genuine, and she couldn't help but think there may be some way to exploit that.

"Is your husband a famous man, Mrs. Jensen?" he asked.

"Famous? Oh, I don't know that I would say that . . .

though he has certainly acquired quite a reputation in Colorado, as well as a few other western states. Why do you ask?"

"After we found out who you was, Brockway said that they was some books wrote about your husband. He said he read some of 'em while he was in prison."

"Oh, heavens, you must be talking about those dreadful dime novels written by Mr. Judson."

"Judson? No, I don't think that was the name."

"His real name is Edward Judson, but he writes many of his novels as Ned Buntline."

"Yeah!" Kelly said, smiling broadly. "That's it. Ned Buntline. Has he really wrote books about your husband?"

"He has."

"Wow, havin' them books wrote about him must've made your husband rich."

"My husband was not compensated in any way for the use of his name in any of Mr. Judson's books. They are, at best, the unauthorized appropriation of his name, and at worst, outright piracy."

"That don't seem fair," Kelly said.

Sally laughed.

"What are you laughin' at?"

"I am laughing at the ludicrousness of a situation in which you are concerned about whether my husband has been fairly treated for the appropriation of his name, while at the same time holding me in this place against my will."

"Aye," Kelly said sheepishly. "'Tis a foul deed I be doin', 'n I take no pride in it."

Mule Gap

The morning sun was streaming in through the window of her office, and Delilah was counting the take for the week, which had come to two hundred and fifty-five dollars, including the money paid in advance for the "visit" her girls had made the night before. She looked up to see Fancy standing at the door.

"Fancy, dear, come in, come in," Delilah invited. "How was your visit last night?"

"It was . . . all right," Fancy replied with a short hesitation before she said the words *all right*.

"What is it? What is wrong?" Delilah asked, concern chasing the smile from her face. "Fancy, did any of those men hurt any of you?"

"No, ma'am, it isn't that. It's just that there's something going on out there, something to do with the children, that I've been thinking about."

"Children? What children?"

"There are a bunch of children out there."

"Good gracious. Are you telling me those men allowed children to be present while . . . uh, while you were . . . ?"

"No, ma'am, nothing like that. They are staying in a separate cabin, all by themselves. They said that the children's parents have sent them out there so they can spend some time on the creek . . . but if they were doing that, wouldn't they be running around outside, playing and such? I kept glancing through the window, and except for the two young girls I saw at the privy, the children never once left their cabin. And from the expression on the two girls' faces, it sure didn't seem like they were having fun. I just feel like something's not quite right there."

"Two little girls? How many children are there? Oh, wait. You wouldn't know, would you?"

"Yes ma'am, I do know. One of the men told me there are six children out there."

"Six, you say?"

"Yes, ma'am. Of course I can't vouch for that myself. Like I said, I only seen the two little girls. And I don't know if the remaining children are boys or girls. When I started asking about them, Keefer didn't want to talk about them anymore, and I sort of got the idea that he was upset with Sanders for telling me about them in the first place."

"How very odd," Delilah said.

"Yes, ma'am, that's what I thought, too. Do you think, maybe, it might be the children who have been kidnapped?"

"I don't know. I am aware of only five kidnapped children, but there could be more, I suppose."

"I hope I didn't do the wrong thing by coming in here to tell you this. I mean, if it really is just kids there on a vacation, I surely wouldn't want to get anyone in trouble."

"No, don't worry about it," Delilah said with a reassuring smile. "You did the right thing."

The worried expression on Fancy's face was replaced by a wide smile. "Good, I was hoping I was."

Delilah Dupree stepped into Marshal Bodine's office a few minutes later. The man called The Professor was sitting at his desk, reading *The Death of Ivan Ilyich* by Leo Tolstoy.

"That's a very good book," Delilah said.

Putting a bookmark to keep his page, Bodine set the book down. "Really? And how would you know? Are you just saying that as a matter of conversation, Miss Dupree? Or do you actually have any idea what this book is about?"

"No, I'm not just saying that, and yes, I have read the book. It's about a man facing his own death. But then, from what I have heard about you, facing death is something you do frequently."

"It is part of my chosen profession," Bodine replied.

"You mean your secondary profession . . . after you left teaching."

"What is it, Miss Dupree? What brings you here?"

"You are aware, are you not, Marshal, that there have been several children kidnapped?"

"Yes, of course I'm aware of that. Who, around here, isn't aware of it?"

"Have you been able to do anything about it?"

"I'm . . . working on a few leads," Bodine replied. "Why do the kidnappings concern you? Do you know any of the children involved?"

"No, but three of my girls spent last night in a house on French Creek. This morning one of my young ladies reported that there are several children in a cabin adjacent to the house where my young ladies were taken. When she asked about them, she was told their parents knew they were there, and had paid for their children to be there as a vacation on the lake."

"Do you have any reason to doubt that, Miss Dupree?" Bodine asked.

"Are you asking me if I doubt the story told me by Jill? No, I don't doubt it for a moment."

"Jill?"

"Fancy Bliss is her working name. Her real name is Jill Peterson. And no I have no reason to doubt her story."

"What I was asking is do you have any reason to doubt the story that was told to Miss"—Bodine paused for a long moment before he said the name—"Peterson."

"That story was told to her by Fred Keefer, and yes, I very much doubt it. I know Mr. Keefer, and he is not a very nice man. It would not surprise me one bit if he was involved in the kidnapping."

"That's quite an accusation you are making, Miss Dupree. And about someone you know, too. How well do you know him?"

"Keefer is a frequent guest at my house, and I have had many opportunities to observe him. He is a mean-spirited man, and he is no gentleman."

Bodine smiled. "Why, Miss Dupree. I thought everyone who came to your establishment was a gentleman. That is how you advertise yourself, isn't it?"

"Surely, Marshal, as a professor, you know the subtleties of advertising. If I suggest that only gentlemen are welcome at my house, then those who do come are more likely to *act* as gentlemen."

"You have a good point," Bodine said.

"What about Keefer?"

"What about him?"

"Well, aren't you going to arrest him?"

"How can I arrest him? I have no evidence that he has committed any sort of crime."

"But I told you what Fancy told me."

"Miss Dupree, why don't you just continue to run

your house, which you obviously do very well, since I've never had any trouble with you, and leave the law enforcement up to me?"

"Do you mean to tell me that you aren't even going to look into it?" Delilah asked.

"Of course I'm going to look into it. I intend to follow every lead, but I don't intend to engage in precipitous action that would not only set my investigation back, it could also result in a lawsuit for unlawful arrest."

"But—"

"Good day, Miss Dupree," Bodine said. By way of dismissal he picked up his book and reopened it to the place of the marker.

Leaving the marshal's office, Delilah felt a sense of frustration. She had not gotten the reaction from the marshal that she had expected. How could he turn his back on information that had the potential to lead to the rescue of the kidnapped children?

Not content with being so summarily dismissed, she decided to go over the marshal's head and seek out Warren Kennedy. He was the mayor, which meant he had authority over the marshal. Delilah smiled. She should have gone to him in the first place. After all, she and the mayor had a rather special relationship.

As she walked toward the bank, she encountered two women coming toward her. When the two women recognized her, a sour expression crossed their faces.

"Come, Matilda," one of them said. "Let's cross the street so we don't have to share the walk with that woman."

"Hello, ladies. What a beautiful day it is, don't you think?" Delilah called out to them.

"Humph," one of them uttered in disgust.

Stepping into the bank, Delilah got the same reaction. A woman put her hands on her husband's arm and led him away as if she were frightened that he might succumb to Delilah's sex appeal, right there in the bank.

"Yes, Miss Dupree?" the bank teller asked as she approached the teller's cage.

"I would like to deposit last night's receipts."

"Very well," the teller said, taking the proffered bills from her.

"And I would like to speak to Mr. Kennedy," Delilah said.

"I'm afraid that isn't possible."

"Why isn't it possible?"

"Because Mr. Kennedy is busy right now."

"That's all right. I'll wait until he isn't busy."

"Do you mean . . . in the bank?" the teller asked, aghast.

"Of course in the bank. Where else would I wait to see the president of the bank? In the stable?"

"Very well. I'll see if he has time to visit with you," the teller said in a self-righteous huff.

"Thank you."

"I thought I told you never to come here," Kennedy said a moment later when Delilah was let into his office. "I thought you understood the whole idea of my being a silent partner is keeping secret any relation between us."

Delilah smiled. "Now, Warren, really. Mule Gap is a

small town. Do you think there is anyone who doesn't know of our . . . relationship?"

"Still, it's nothing I want to flaunt. Now, what is it? What do you need?"

"I want to talk to you about the children who have been kidnapped," Delilah said.

"Kidnapped children? Why, what does that have to do with me? Or you, for that matter?"

"I think I know where they are. In a cabin on French Creek."

"What?" Kennedy replied in surprise. "Now, how on earth would you know that?"

"A few of my girls went out there yesterday and they saw them."

Kennedy drummed his fingers on his desk for a moment as he considered what Delilah had just said. "Have you told this to anybody?"

"Yes, I told Marshal Bodine."

"You haven't said anything to Mrs. Condon?"

"Mrs. Condon? No. Who is she, and why should I say anything to her?"

"She is in town now, staying at the hotel. And her son is one of the kidnap victims."

"That would be the sixth child," Delilah said.

"What?"

"I was aware of only five, but there are six children out there. Don't you see, Warren? There are six children who are kidnapped, and there are six children out there in a cabin on the lake. This isn't a mere coincidence. I'm convinced the children out there are the same ones that have been captured."

"Yes, you may be right. The evidence is too strong to be a mere coincidence. What did Marshal Bodine say when you told him?"

"He said he would look into it, but really, Warren, he didn't seem all that interested. He said something about being concerned over a possible lawsuit."

Kennedy smiled. "It's good to see that he's looking out for the town. I wouldn't want us to be facing a lawsuit. If there is anything to this, I'm sure he will get to the bottom of it. Why don't you just let him do his job?"

"All right," Delilah said. "I'll leave it up to him. It's just that I thought that, as you are the mayor, you might like to know."

"You were right to come to me, Delilah. Yes, I do want to know, and I will follow up on this with The Professor." He put his hand on her cheek. "And what I said earlier about you not coming here? I'm sorry if I sounded harsh. I didn't mean to."

"I know. You're the mayor of this town. You have an image to maintain. And believe me, I don't want to do anything that would jeopardize that position. It wouldn't be good for either of us."

"I'm glad that you understand. Let me walk you to the door. That is a wise decision, Miss Dupree," Kennedy said rather loudly as he and Delilah left his office and walked through the main lobby of the bank. "Transferring your funds into the savings account will assure that the money is working for you by earning interest."

"Thank you for your help," Delilah replied, going along with the game.

CHAPTER TWENTY-FOUR

When Delilah approached the front desk of the Del Rey Hotel a few minutes later, the clerk frowned when he saw her.

"Miss Dupree, you know that the hotel owners have banned you from doing any business in here."

"I am not here to do any business," Delilah replied.

"That may be so, but you aren't welcome in the hotel for any reason, so I'm going to have to ask you to leave. I'm sure you understand."

"No, Mr. Hodge, I don't understand. I told you I'm not here to conduct any business. I'm here to see one of the hotel residents."

Hodge shook his head. "I don't care why you are here. You're going to have to leave, now."

"If you force me to leave this hotel before I am able to visit with the person I'm looking for, then I will go directly to the *Mule Gap Ledger* and give Mr. Blanton a list of names of everyone who has been a guest at the House of Pleasure. Now that I think of it, Mr. Hodge, your name and the names of both sanctimonious owners of this hotel will be on that list."

"You wouldn't dare do a thing like that," Hodge said. "It would ruin you. You would have to close your business."

"My particular business is always in demand, and I have enough money to go somewhere else and start all over again," Delilah said. "Do you?"

Hodge was silent for a moment. "Who do you want to see?"

"Mrs. Condon."

"It is room two-oh-seven."

Delilah flashed a smile then reached across the desk to put her fingers on his cheek. "Thank you so much, Mr. Hodge. You've been a great help. Come around sometime and I'll have one of my girls express just how appreciative I am."

"If you are going to up to her room, please do so quickly. I wouldn't want someone to see you and get word back to the wrong people that you were here."

"Oh? Tell me, Sylvester, and just who would you say are the wrong people?"

"Please, go. Just go on up the stairs," a very agitated Hodge said.

With a little chuckle, Delilah strolled confidently across the lobby.

When Sara Sue heard the knock on her door, she grew tense. Was it the kidnappers getting in touch with her again or was it Smoke Jensen? "Who is it?" she called.

"Mrs. Condon, please, I'd like to speak to you. It's important." The voice was that of a woman.

Curious, Sara Sue walked over to open the door.

The woman standing in the hall was a very attractive woman, but also a woman who wore more face paint than anyone Sara Sue had ever seen. Even the dress she wore seemed to be . . . the only word Sara Sue could think of was *provocative.*

"What do you want to talk about?" Sara Sue asked.

"I want to talk about the kidnapped children. And please, let me in. It isn't safe for me to be seen talking to you. I'm in great danger, standing here just outside your door." The expression on her face and the tone in her voice as she made the declaration of personal danger convinced Sara Sue that the woman was telling the truth.

"Yes, do come in," Sara Sue said, stepping aside to allow the woman to enter. She shut the door behind her visitor.

The woman smiled. "It's better for you as well. I'm not the kind of woman a good lady like you would want to be seen with."

"Oh?"

"My name is Delilah Dupree, Mrs. Condon. I am what they call a madam. I manage a house of ill repute."

"You said something about the kidnapped children," Sara Sue said.

"Thank you for not reacting to my, uh, profession."

"The children?" Sara Sue repeated.

"Yes. Last night three of my girls paid a . . . uh, professional visit to a house that is about eight miles west of here on French Creek. While they were there, they discovered that six children were there. The men my girls were visiting told them that the children's parents knew the children were there, that they were there on a vacation, and the men were just looking out for them."

"Six children?" Sara Sue frowned. Jim Harris had told Smoke the number of kidnapped children still unaccounted for would be six, counting Thad, and Smoke had shared that information with her. It was too close to be a mere coincidence. "That's how many are missing."

"I wasn't aware of the exact number until a short time ago," Delilah said. "But I knew there was something a little fishy about their story of six kids being on vacation."

"And you say they are in a cabin?"

"Yes, according to my girls there are two buildings there—a small house and an even smaller cabin."

"Have you told the sheriff?" Sara Sue asked.

Delilah's chuckle was derisive. "Mrs. Condon, our sheriff never leaves Rawlins. You may as well shout it into the wind as tell him. I did tell Marshal Bodine, but he seemed almost dismissive about it. I'm telling you. Seeing as one of the kidnapped children is yours, you have a bona fide reason to know. Though, to be truthful, I have no idea what you can do about it."

Sara Sue smiled at Delilah. "Thank you, Miss Dupree. I very much appreciate your telling me this."

"Oh, you don't have to thank me, ma'am," Delilah said. "Lord knows, I'm a sinful woman, but even I know that what these men have done—taking kids from their mamas and papas—is wrong. I hope you are able to get your boy back all right."

"I pray that I will," Sara Sue said. "Miss Dupree, there is a gentleman in town, a neighbor. His name is Smoke Jensen, and I would like to see him, but, under the circumstances, it would be ill-advised for me to be seen with him. I wonder if I could prevail upon you to find him and ask him to call on me."

"I'll be happy to do it," Delilah said. "But now, I wonder if you would do me a favor and look out into the hallway? I don't want anyone to see me leaving your room."

"Of course," Sara Sue said. Opening the door, she looked both ways down the hallway and saw that it was empty. "There's nobody here."

Delilah stuck out her hand, but Sara Sue ignored the proffered handshake and impulsively embraced her instead. "Thank you," she said again.

Delilah stepped out into the hallway, moving quickly because she didn't want Mrs. Condon to see the tears that had formed in her eyes.

Arnold Fenton had been sent to follow Delilah, and he was standing just behind the turn in the wall at the top of the stairs when he saw the door open, and Mrs. Condon stick her head out. She glanced toward the other end of the hall first, which gave him a chance to pull his head back without being seen.

A moment later the door to her room opened again, and the woman who ran the whorehouse stepped out into the hallway. His information was accurate. She had met with the Condon woman.

Fenton pulled back and hurried down the stairs so he wouldn't be seen. The person who'd sent him would want to know.

* * *

When Delilah stepped into the Silver Dollar Saloon a few minutes later, she was met by one of the bar girls who worked there. "What are you doing here, Delilah? I hope you aren't here to steal any of the girls for your house."

"Hello, Belle," Delilah replied. "No, nothing like that. I'm looking for a man."

"Aren't we all?" Belle replied with a teasing smile.

Delilah smiled with her. "No, this is a particular man. His name is Smoke Jensen."

"Honey, you won't get nowhere with him," Belle said. "Believe me, because I have tried. All the girls have tried, but nobody has been able to get him to do nothin'. They say he's married, 'n if he is, his wife is one lucky woman 'cause he is as straight as an arrow."

"I want to try, anyway," Delilah said. "Is he in here?"

"Oh, he's here all right." Belle pointed to a table near the piano, where two men sat, drinking beer.

"Thanks," Delilah said as, with a toss of her head, she started toward the table.

"Here comes a new girl." Pearlie smiled. "I have to admit, she's prettier than the others."

"Don't let me hold you back," Smoke said.

"Mr. Jensen?" the girl said as she approached him.

Smoke was surprised that she had addressed him by name. Also, he noticed, her demeanor was different from that of the other girls. Hers was a direct business-like approach without the "come on" smile the others employed.

"Yes, I'm Smoke Jensen. What can I do for you?"

"My name is Delilah Dupree. Do you know a lady named Mrs. Condon?"

"Yes, I know her," Smoke said. "Has something happened to her?"

"No," Delilah replied quickly. "I'm sorry if I gave you a start." She looked around to make certain she could talk to him without being overheard. "I just came from a visit with her, and she asked me to ask you to come see her."

"Is she still in the hotel?" Smoke asked.

"Yes, room . . ."

"Two-oh-seven," Smoke said before she could get the number out,

"Yes, that's the room number."

"Thank you," Smoke said. "I . . . was going to offer to buy you a drink, but I have an idea that you don't work here."

"No, I don't. I have my own place of business, the Delilah House. You and your gentleman friend are welcome at any time, though Belle tells me that you are married and are very loyal to your wife."

"That's true," Smoke said.

"I'm not married," Pearlie said with a broad smile.

Delilah returned the smile. "Of course the invitation is for you as well."

"Come on, Pearlie," Smoke said, standing. "Mrs. Condon wouldn't be sending for us unless it was very important."

"You say she spent some time in the room with the Condon woman, then went from there directly to meet with Smoke Jensen?"

"Yeah," Fenton said, "that's exactly what she done."

"I'm afraid Miss Dupree has become a liability."

"What does that mean?"

"It means I'm going to have get someone to take care of her."

"How much will you pay?"

"One hundred dollars."

"Not good enough," Fenton said. "I don't like killin' women. I was thinking more along the lines of five hunnert dollars."

The two men settled on two hundred and fifty dollars, a sum that satisfied both.

Smoke knocked on the door. "Did you ask for fresh towels, ma'am?" he called.

The door opened quickly, and Smoke stepped inside, Pearlie having remained downstairs in the hotel lobby.

"What is it?" Smoke asked.

"I think I know where they are keeping Thad and the other children," Sara Sue said.

"Where?"

"In a cabin on French Creek, about eight miles west of here. Do you know where French Creek is?"

"I not only know where it is, the place I'm thinking about has two buildings there. They were abandoned the last time I saw them."

"Yes! That's it!" Sara Sue said excitedly. "Delilah said there was a small house and an even smaller cabin."

"Only one way to find out, and that is for me to go out there," he said.

"Oh, Smoke, do be careful," she said. "I want Thad back, safe and sound, but I do feel responsible for

Pearlie getting shot and for that dear horse of yours getting killed. I wouldn't want to be responsible for anything else like that happening."

"Don't worry. We'll get Thad back, safe and sound. And the other children, as well," he promised.

CHAPTER TWENTY-FIVE

"What are you doing in my office?" Delilah asked. "Can't you read the signs? There are no gentlemen callers allowed in this part of the house. You have the parlor . . . and the upstairs rooms when you are invited by one of the ladies."

"You've been opening your big mouth, haven't you?"

"Opening my mouth? Opening my mouth about what? Arnold Fenton, what are you talking about?"

"I seen you goin' into the Condon woman's room. Then I seen you goin' down to the Silver Dollar to talk to Smoke Jensen. What did you tell 'em?"

"What did I tell them about what?"

"You know about what. What did you tell them about them kids that's bein' held out at French Creek?"

"It's true, isn't it?" Delilah replied. "The children who are being held out there are the kidnap victims! My God, Arnold, are you one of the kidnappers?"

Fenton took his gun out. "It's not that you know too much, Delilah. It's that you know too much and don't know enough to keep your mouth shut."

"Arnold! No!"

Delilah's office echoed with the sound of a gun being fired. Delilah's head flopped back in her chair, blood coming from the bullet hole in her forehead.

"Delilah!" Joy Love shouted, rushing into the office. When she saw her friend and employer dead in her chair, she turned to Arnold Fenton, who was standing there, the smoking six-gun still in his hand. "Arnold! What did you do?"

Arnold turned his gun on Joy and pulled the trigger.

Jasmine was upstairs asleep. Fancy and Candy were in the kitchen when they heard the shots fired. As they rushed out of the kitchen they saw Fenton leaving by the front door. They hurried into Delilah's office and saw her with her head tossed back and her face covered with blood, and Joy lying dead on the floor.

"Delilah!" Candy shouted.

Fancy looked at both of them for a moment. "They're dead. Both of them are dead."

"What will we do?"

"That was Arnold Fenton, wasn't it? The man we saw running out the front door

"Yes, that was Fenton."

"He has to be the one who killed them."

"But why?" Candy asked. "Why would he kill them? Joy said he has always been nice to her."

"I don't know, but we need to tell the marshal about it.

The two women hurried down to the marshal's office.

"He killed them!" Fancy said breathlessly.

"He killed both of them!" Candy added.

The words were shouted simultaneously by both

women so that they tumbled over each other in a way that neither could be understood.

"Here now, here!" Marshal Bodine said. "How do you expect me to hear anything or understand what you're saying if both of you are talking at once?"

"He killed Delilah," Fancy said.

"And Joy," Candy added.

"Who killed them?"

"Arnold Fenton," Candy said.

"We think," Fancy said.

"Do you think he killed them or do you know he killed them?"

"We know," Candy said.

"How do you know? Did you actually see him shooting them?"

"We think it was him, but it has to be. We saw him running out the front door," Fancy said.

"But you didn't actually see him shooting."

"No, but who else could it have been?"

"Perhaps Fenton heard the shot and ran away because he was frightened."

"Why was he in the house in the first place?" Fancy asked.

"Well, you tell me, Miss Bliss. Why would anyone visit the Delilah House? They certainly don't go there to have a photograph taken." Bodine chuckled.

"I can't believe this. We came here to tell you that Delilah and Joy have been killed, and you make a joke about it?" Candy said.

"You are right, and I apologize if my reaction seemed inappropriate. I meant no disrespect. But you must also see my point of view. Unless you actually saw Fenton in the act of shooting the two ladies, any connection between him and the murder is circumstantial at best."

"Let's go, Candy," Fancy said bitterly. "It's clear that the law doesn't care about women like us."

Bodine made no response as the two left his office.

By early morning of the next day, news of the double murder had spread quickly through the town, by word, and by the article in the *Mule Gap Ledger*.

TERRIBLE MURDER!

Two Women Shot Dead

Yesterday, Miss Delilah Dupree and Miss Suzie Fugate were both shot dead. Miss Dupree was the manager of the Delilah House, a business of ill repute, and Miss Fugate, a soiled dove in Miss Dupree's employ. Miss Fugate was better known to the clients of the house as Joy Love.

Motive for the shooting isn't known, but Marshal Bodine has suggested that the killing might be the result of a jilted client who wanted exclusive access to one of the two women.

As of this writing, the identity of the killer or killers is unknown, though it is believed that someone was seen running from the house immediately after the shots were fired. The identity of that person is being withheld as part of the ongoing investigation.

Although Miss Dupree was engaged in a business that is best practiced in the shadows, she was said to be a woman of education and mannerly bearing.

"I'm not surprised," a citizen of the town said. "The only thing that surprises me is that someone hasn't been murdered in that place before now."

"I've seen Miss Dupree around. She always seemed nice," another citizen replied.

"Nice or not, she was a whore, and when you run a whorehouse, you can expect things like that to happen."

"Oh, Smoke, do you think Miss Dupree's murder may have something to do with her visiting me?" Sara Sue asked.

She, Smoke, and Pearlie were sharing a table at breakfast in the hotel dining room. Pearlie ate heartily as he listened to the conversation.

"I don't know," Smoke replied. "But I won't lie to you. It could have been connected."

"I feel so guilty."

"There's nothing for you to feel guilty about. She came to you, you didn't go to her."

"That's true. But still, it would be very upsetting to me if I thought I'd had anything to do with her death."

"Even if her getting killed had something to do with her visiting you, the blame and the guilt belong to the person who actually killed her. Besides, two were killed. Both of them didn't come to see you."

"I suppose you're right," Sara Sue said, relieved by the thought.

"On the other hand, if her getting killed does have something to do with her visiting you, that means her story about the kids is true and someone is getting a little concerned about it."

"Yes, that's true, isn't it?"

"If that is true, they will also realize that you now know where the children are," Smoke said. "So I want you to leave."

"Smoke, I can't leave! Not until I get Thad back."

"You don't have to leave town. I just want you to leave the hotel. Too many people know you are here. I don't want you exposed to that danger."

"But this is the only hotel in town," Sara Sue said. "If I leave here, where will I go?"

"You'll be staying with Mrs. Coy."

"Who?"

"Sandra Coy. She has three rooms at Welsh's Boarding House. We'll sneak you over there, and you can stay out of sight until we bring the children back."

"And Mrs. Coy approves of this plan?"

"Yes."

Sandra Coy was about the same age as Sara Sue. She had dark hair and emerald eyes, and the lithe form of the ballet dancer she once was.

"Mrs. Coy, this is the lady I told you about," Smoke said.

"How nice to meet you," Mrs. Coy said.

"I think it is wonderful of you to put me up like this," Sara Sue said. "I hope I am not too big of a burden."

"You aren't a burden at all," Mrs. Coy said. "This way, we can wait for our children together."

"Our children? You mean you have a child among the kidnapped children?"

"Yes, my daughter, Lorena." Mrs. Coy chuckled self-deprecatingly. "I know you are probably wondering why someone would kidnap a child from a widow who lives in a boardinghouse. Lorena had been hired by the Blackwells to sit with their son Eddie while they were running their place of business. Their son was the target of the kidnappers, and she was with him when he was taken, so they took her, as well."

"I'll tell you what I told Mrs. Condon," Smoke said. "We will get the children back . . . all of them . . . and we will get them back safely."

"Mrs. Coy—"

"Please, if we are going to live together for a while, can't we use first names? I'm Sandra."

Sara Sue smiled. "And I'm Sara Sue. Sandra, has Smoke told you why I need to stay with you rather than in the hotel?"

"Yes. He told me that your life may be in danger."

"And you do realize, don't you, that by my staying here with you, it also puts your life in danger?"

"Yes, I know. Do you like tea or coffee?"

For just a moment, Sara Sue was confused by the question, wondering what it had to do with her life being in danger. Then she smiled as she knew exactly what Sandra was telling her. She was making her feel welcome, despite any inherent danger in sharing her quarters.

Sara Sue smiled. "Coffee."

Sandra smiled as well. "Oh, that's wonderful. I was afraid you might be one of those tea drinkers."

Sara Sue laughed. "Sandra, I think you and I will get along quite well."

"So do I, Sara Sue."

Delilah Dupree was well-known in Mule Gap, and though her public persona was unsavory, many knew the better side of her. Father Than Pyron of St. Paul's Episcopal Church knew that side of her. Delilah didn't attend service on Sunday, giving the reason, "I'm afraid my presence would make the others uncomfortable." She took private communion shortly after the others left.

Delilah's church attendance was secret and so were her contributions, or so she thought. Whenever she gave money through the church to help out people in need, Father Pyron always made sure the recipients of her assistance knew from whence the money came.

As a result of Delilah's beneficence, a surprisingly large number of people turned out to attend her funeral. The same church that she feared would be offended by her presence was filled with mourners.

Sara Sue Condon, who believed that Delilah was murdered because she had come to see her, was there. So too were Smoke and Pearlie. Neither Frank Bodine nor Warren Kennedy attended.

Fancy Bliss and Candy Sweet, whose real names were Jill Peterson and Ann Bailey, were there as well, dressed in black with their faces covered by black veils. Jasmine Delight, whose real name was Lin Kwan, was also dressed in black. She sat beside her two friends—sisters in sin as they had called themselves in happier times.

Two coffins—one for Delilah and one for Suzie Fugate, which was Joy Love's real name—stood at the front of the church. The organist played a funereal fugue by Bach.

When the music was over, Father Pyron stepped up to the ambo. "Was Mary Magdalene a prostitute? She has the reputation in Western Christianity as being a repentant prostitute or loose woman, though some theologians believe that that the identity of Mary Magdalene may have been merged with the identity of the unnamed sinner who anoints Jesus' feet with her hair. Regardless of whether Mary Magdalene was a prostitute or not, we know that she found redemption in her love of the Lord and, indeed, was the first of His followers to see the risen Christ.

"Because Jesus found room in His heart and His kingdom for her, we know, too, that He has welcomed our sisters, Delilah and Suzie. I call them our sisters because many in here have benefited from Delilah's kind heart and her generous willingness to help others. And yes, I count myself in that number."

From the church, the mourners followed the hearse carrying both coffins to Boot Hill, where the two graves had already been opened. The canopy, which was normally reserved for the immediate family of the deceased, had been erected and Fancy, Candy, and Jasmine sat on the chairs provided, joined by all the bar girls of the Silver Dollar and Kennedy's Saloon.

It had been Fancy who'd invited them. "Girls like us have only each other. That makes us family."

"You dumb son of a bitch! You killed both of them! Why the hell did you kill both of them?"

"The other one came in while I was with Delilah. I didn't have no choice," Fenton said.

"Yes, you had a choice. You could have planned it better. Have you seen how many people have turned out for the funeral? Half the town is over in the cemetery right now. You think the town is going to just let this go?"

"Who would've thought there would be that many people for a whore's funeral?" Fenton asked.

"Here, take this money and go. Get out of town and don't come back."

"This . . . this is only a hunnert dollars. You said I would get two hunnert and fifty."

"That was for killing one person. You didn't do the job as contracted. You killed two."

"No, now, I ain't goin' to take that. You need to pay me what you told me you would."

"Or what? You will undo your job? How are you going to bring her back alive?"

"But this ain't right." Fenton heard the click of a hammer being drawn back as a pistol was cocked.

"I said go away."

Fenton stared at the pistol pointed toward him, then, with a shrug, he picked up the money and left.

But instead of leaving town as he had been told to do, he went up the street to the Silver Dollar Saloon. "Whiskey."

The bartender poured the drink and slid the glass across the bar.

"Can you believe all the people that turned out for that whore's funeral?" Fenton asked.

"All of our girls went," the bartender said.

"She was a whore," Fenton said. "Nothin' but a damn whore." He tossed the drink down.

"You say *she* like there was only one. There were two of them, and even if they was whores, they didn't deserve to get murdered."

Fenton held his glass out for a refill. "Whores. They were whores."

"Whores are people, too," the bartender said.

Fenton tossed the second glass down, then held out his glass for another.

"I think maybe you should buy your whiskey somewhere else," the bartender said.

"You feelin' sorry for them whores, are you?" Fenton asked.

"Yeah, I am."

With a dismissive snort, Fenton left the saloon. As soon as he stepped outside, he saw a man dressed all in black standing in the middle of the street.

"Arnold Fenton, you are under arrest for the murder of Delilah Dupree and Suzie Fugate," Marshal Bodine called out to him.

"What? What do you mean, *murder*?"

"Come along," Bodine said.

"The hell I will!" Fenton made a desperate grab for

his pistol, but before he could get the gun more than halfway out of his holster, a blazing pistol appeared in Bodine's hand.

Fenton fell facedown into the dirt and lay there without moving.

CHAPTER TWENTY-SIX

As the funeral was wrapping up, nobody in the cemetery was aware that the killer of Delilah and Suzie had just been shot down.

As Fancy dropped dirt onto Delilah's coffin and Candy dropped dirt onto Suzie's coffin, Father Pyron read the concluding prayer. "Forasmuch as it hath pleased Almighty God of His great mercy to take unto Himself the soul of our dear sister here departed: we therefore commit her body to the ground; earth to earth, ashes to ashes, dust to dust; in sure and certain hope of the Resurrection to eternal life, through our Lord Jesus Christ; who shall change our vile body, that it may be like unto His glorious body, according to the mighty working, whereby He is able to subdue all things to himself."

As everyone began leaving the cemetery, Fancy walked over to talk to Sara Sue. "You've got a boy that's one of the kidnapped kids, don't you?"

"Yes, I do."

"Did Delilah tell you what we seen?"

"You were one of the ladies she was talking about?"

Fancy nodded her head. "Yes, ma'am, 'n I thank you for callin' me a lady, seein' as I ain't nothin' o' the kind. I wish now I hadn't a-told her nothin' 'bout us seein' them kids 'cause it was her knowin' about it that got 'er killed. I know it was."

"Oh!" Sara Sue said. "In that case, maybe you shouldn't be seen talking to me, either."

"I don't care now," Fancy said. "I want Arnold Fenton to pay for what he done. And I want those little children to go back to their mamas and papas."

"They will go back to their parents," Smoke said. "And safely."

"Who are you?" Fancy asked.

"The name is Smoke Jensen, ma'am. Mrs. Condon is my neighbor. Who is Arnold Fenton?"

"He's the one who killed Delilah and Joy."

"How do you know he's the one who did it?"

"I know, because me 'n Candy seen 'im runnin' out of the house just after we heard the shots. 'N besides us 'n Jasmine who was upstairs at the time, he was the only one in the house then."

"Did you tell the marshal this?"

"Yes, me 'n Candy both told 'im, but it didn't seem to make no difference to him. Ma'am, I hope you get your boy back safe."

"Thank you," Sara Sue said.

"Do you believe her, Smoke?" Pearlie asked as Fancy hurried away.

"Yes, I don't have any reason not to believe her. Pearlie, you see to it that Sara Sue gets safely back to the boardinghouse. I'm going to have a talk with my friend the mayor. Maybe he can get The Professor to do something."

"He's already taken care of it," Kennedy said, replying to Smoke's inquiry. "If you'll go down to the undertaker's, you'll see that he has Fenton laid out on his embalming table, right now. We can thank our marshal for that."

"Bodine killed Fenton?"

"Aye, and 'tis glad I am to see that the son of a bitch paid for his brutal crime."

"I wish he hadn't killed him. I wish he had arrested him."

"Why? The brigand deserved to die."

"Oh, I don't disagree with you there," Smoke said. "But I'm sure Fenton killed Miss Dupree because she apparently had some information about the kidnapped children. And I doubt that he killed on his own. I'm sure he was paid to do it, and I would have liked to know who was really behind the killing."

"Aye, I see your point," Kennedy said. "But from what I've heard, the marshal had no choice in the matter. The brigand drew on him."

"Well, if that is the case, then, no, he didn't have any choice," Smoke said.

"What makes you think Delilah had information about the location of the children?" Kennedy asked.

"Oh, I don't know that she did have information about the location of the children, though she might have. Now that she is dead, we won't know, one way or the other." Smoke not only knew that Delilah did know where the children were, he knew that she had shared that information with Sara Sue. Even with a friend like Warren Kennedy, he thought it would be best to keep such information to himself.

"You know, I very much wanted to go to Delilah's funeral," Kennedy said. "Sure, 'n there's no way you would be for knowing this—in fact, I don't think anyone in town actually knew it—but Delilah and I"—he paused in the midst of his comment as if having difficulty continuing—"well, we had what you might call a relationship."

"No, I didn't know that," Smoke said. "If that is the case, why didn't you go to the funeral? It seemed that half the town was there."

"Aye, half the town was there 'tis exactly the reason why I couldn't go. I'm invested in businesses all over town, 'n it would not be good for business for all to know o' the feelin's Delilah 'n I had for one another. Not for me, you understand. "'Twould not bother me if people held it against me for lovin' Delilah as I did. But the people who are in business with me could have suffered, not for anything they have done, but for my own doing. 'N I couldn't be for hurting the business of others, now could I?"

"I can see how you might feel that way, Warren, but based upon the people that I saw at her funeral, I really don't think anyone in town would have thought any less of you if you had attended the funeral."

"Aye, perhaps that's right," Kennedy agreed. "But I'll be payin' my respects to her when I visit her grave."

* * *

After escorting Sara Sue safely to the boardinghouse, Pearlie hid outside for a while, just to make certain that no one showed up. Then he walked down to the Delilah House and went inside.

An elderly, white-haired woman was cleaning. "We're closed. Maybe you ain't heard nothin' about it, but Miss Dupree was kilt. I don't know if we're ever goin' to open again."

"I know," Pearlie said. "I'm real sorry about that. I was at her funeral."

"Then if you know about that, why are you here?"

"I'm here to see Miss Peterson."

The woman got a surprised look on her face. "You know Miss Fancy's real name?"

"Yes, is she here? I would like to see her."

"It won't do you no good. She's not takin' on any customers. What with Joy kilt, 'n Jasmine runnin' off after the funeral, there's only Fancy 'n Candy left. Neither one of 'em doin' that, 'n I don't know if anyone's ever goin' to do that again. Leastwise, not in this place."

Pearlie shook his head. "That's not why I want to see her. I just want to talk to her, is all. My name is Pearlie. Tell her I was with Smoke and Mrs. Condon, and we met at Miss Dupree's funeral."

"All right. Wait here," the maid said.

Fancy was sitting in Delilah's office, staring through the window. Delilah wasn't the first madam Fancy had ever worked for, but she was the first one Fancy had ever had a genuine affection for. Delilah treated everyone in the house as if they were part of her family, and though Fancy had shed tears during her funeral, she was still feeling the pain of her friend's loss.

"Miss Fancy?"

Fancy turned to the woman who had spoken.

"Yes, Rose?"

"There's a fella here who wants to see you."

"Didn't you tell him we were closed?"

"Yes, ma'am, I told him that, but he said all he wants to do is talk to you. He said you met him at the funeral."

Fancy stepped to the door and looked out into the parlor. She recognized him as one of the men she had met at the funeral. "All right. Tell him to come in."

A moment later, Pearlie knocked on the door

Almost automatically, Fancy smiled at him. "You're Pearlie, aren't you?"

"Yes, ma'am. Can I shut the door? I want to talk to you, and I don't want folks to hear."

"Well, there's no one here but Candy and Rose, but sure, shut the door if you want to."

Pearlie shut the door then, at Fancy's invitation, sat down. "Who have you told about seeing those kids?"

"Only Delilah, and then today, you, Mrs. Condon, and Smoke Jensen."

"I'm going to ask you not to tell anyone else."

"Why not? Don't you think people should know about it?"

"For one thing, Smoke and I plan to get those kids back home safely. If word gets back to the kidnappers that we know where the kids are, they may move them."

"Oh, yes. I hadn't thought of that."

"And for another thing, the more people who know

that you saw them, the more dangerous it will be for you. Who else knows about them?"

"Right now, Candy is the only other person who knows."

"Tell her not to tell anyone else."

"The men out at the cabin—Keefer, Reece, Whitman, and Sanders—know that we know, but I haven't seen any of them in town since we came back."

"Smoke and I will take care of them. Do you and Candy have anyplace you could go to hide out for a while?"

Fancy smiled. "I'll bet we could go stay with Dewey Gimlin."

"Who is that?"

"He's an old trapper who lives out of town. He would never come to the house, but from time to time Candy or I would visit him."

"Who knows this?"

"Other than the three of us, nobody but Delilah knew. Mr. Gimlin is a very private man who doesn't want anyone knowin' any of his business. Truth to tell, I doubt there are half a dozen people in town who have ever even heard of him."

"You think he would put you and Candy up for a while?"

Fancy's smile grew even broader. "Are you teasing, Pearlie? I know he would."

When Smoke stepped into the marshal's office, three of his six remaining deputies were in the office with him. Smoke had been in town long enough to learn all of the deputies by name, and he recognized Duly Plappert, Chug Slago, and Boney Walls.

"You're the fella that killed Bates, Cooper, Barnes, and Gibson, ain't you?" Plappert asked.

"I am."

"I guess you think you're pretty good with that gun."

"I'm good enough, I suppose."

"Don't you think there might be somebody out there that's better 'n you?"

"If there is, I haven't met him yet, or I wouldn't still be alive."

"Uh-huh. Tell me, Jensen, just how much longer do you think you're goin' to stay alive?" Plappert asked.

"I expect to be alive right up until the moment I'm dead."

"That might just come sooner 'n you think," Plappert said.

"That's enough, Plappert," The Professor said. "What is it, Jensen? What do you want?"

"I hear you killed Fenton," Smoke replied.

"Yes, I killed him."

"Why?"

"Because when I tried to arrest him, he tried to kill me. It was self-defense. Isn't that the way it was with you and my four deputies?"

"Something like that, yes. What I meant was when the two young ladies who worked for Delilah told you that Fenton was the one who killed Miss Dupree and Miss Fugate, you didn't pay any attention to them."

"They were whores, Jensen. I have no intention of conducting my investigations on the word of whores. To quote the great bard, 'Wisely, and slow. They stumble that run fast.'"

Smoke chuckled. "I know you were an English professor at William and Mary, but given your present reputation, I have a hard time connecting you with *Romeo and Juliet*."

"And I have an even more difficult time believing that it is even a quote that you would recognize."

"You can thank my wife for that. But to get back to the subject, you came to believe that Fenton killed Miss Dupree and Miss Fugate, or you wouldn't have attempted to arrest him. What changed your mind?"

"Nothing changed my mind. I just thought I would talk to him and give him the opportunity to deny that he was in Delilah's establishment during the time of the shooting . . . or to explain why he was there if he didn't deny it."

"But you didn't get to ask him?"

"No, I didn't. Tell me, Jensen, why are you so interested in this case?"

"I believe that Miss Dupree knew the whereabouts of the kidnapped children. And I believe that Fenton's killing her had something to do with that."

"I see. So you are suggesting that Fenton was one of the kidnappers?"

"I would say either that or he was working for the kidnappers."

"Working for them in what way?"

"I think he was paid to kill Delilah in order to keep her from telling anyone where the kidnapped children are."

"You mean like someone offered to pay Allison to kill you?"

Smoke was surprised by the comment, but he was even more surprised by the next comment.

"Or how my deputies planned to collect that same reward by killing you?"

"Who is offering the reward?" Smoke asked.

The Professor shook his head. "I don't have any idea, and that is what makes the whole thing so fatuous. If one doesn't know from whom they are to collect the reward, why accomplish the mission, especially without guarantee of payment?"

"Did Delilah tell you where the children were being kept?" Smoke asked.

"No, why would you think she would do that?"

"Well, you are the law. It seems to me like you would be the logical place for her to go with the information."

"How do you know she even knew? Did she tell you where they were?"

Smoke smiled but didn't answer The Professor's question. "I'll be seeing you, Marshal." He turned and left.

"Plappert, I think you and Slago should keep an eye on Mr. Jensen," Bodine said.

"With pleasure," Plappert replied with a broad grin.

CHAPTER TWENTY-SEVEN

New York City

Sally had still not been mistreated in any way, other than the fact that she was kept tied to the bed all the time. The only time she was untied was while she was eating or using the privy, and at this moment she was lying on the bed with her arms stretched out over her head, tied to the bedposts. Remaining in such a position for so long was very uncomfortable, and she tried, to the extent possible, to relieve the pressure on her back.

The door was open between the two rooms, and she could hear her captors talking in the other room.

"He's dead."

She had learned the identity of the three men who'd brought her to this place and recognized the speaker's voice. Gallagher was the one with the pistol, who had stepped out from the alley to confront them. The three men who had been following them, she now knew, were Kelly, Brockway, and O'Leary. One of them had hit Cal from behind, and the other had used chloroform to knock her out.

"Who's dead?" Kelly asked.

"O'Leary is dead. That damned cowboy killed him."

Cowboy? Sally thought. *Smoke?* A quick, happy thought flashed through her mind. *Is Smoke here?*

"We should have killed the son of a bitch when we had the chance," Brockway said.

Cal! They have to be talking about Cal. She realized almost instantly that her thought it might be Smoke was unreasonable. Even if he knew of her situation, he wouldn't have had time to get there yet. She was happy Cal was still alive.

"'Tis walkin' around the city he is, wearin' a pistol 'n a holster like he was ridin' the range," Brockway said.

"'N would you be for tellin' me how he can be doin' that?" Kelly asked. "Wouldn't Muldoon be for arresting him for doin' so?"

"Here's the thing," Gallagher said. "Turns out that the son of a bitch is a deputy sheriff back in Colorado, 'n now the mayor has made him a deputy in New York. He 'n Muldoon are workin' together."

"Lookin' for the woman, are they?" Brockway asked.

"Aye."

"Are we goin' to be for movin' her?" Brockway asked.

"I see no reason for doin' so," Gallagher said. "Only O'Leary knew she was here, 'n he's dead. There's two million people in this town. How are they goin' to find 'er now?"

"Aye, right you be."

"I'll be for tellin' you this, though. Our friend in Wyoming is goin' to be havin' to pay us well, seein' as this little job we're doin' for him has gotten one of us killed."

Friend in Wyoming? Who could that be? Sally wondered. *And why would someone in Wyoming want me captured and held prisoner? What possible reason could there be for that?*

Sally asked that question of Kelly when he came into her room an hour later, bringing her one of the two meals she was given each day.

"I don't know who it is," Kelly said. "Sure 'n all I know is that Gallagher got a telegram tellin' that you was comin', 'n we was to snatch you up."

"But why?" Sally asked. "Why did someone from Wyoming want me to be taken prisoner?"

"I don't know," Kelly said. "But I can tell you that it was for the money that we took you."

"What money?"

"'Tis a lot of questions you be askin', woman, when you should be usin' your mouth for eatin' now," Kelly scolded.

Sally asked no more questions, and after the meal, Kelly started to tie her to the headboard again.

"Mr. Kelly, please don't tie me to the bed again. You have done that every day, and the ropes are cutting off the circulation. I could wind up losing the use of my hands. Or losing them altogether."

Kelly looked back toward the door that opened into the other room. "Put your hands up there."

"Please?"

"I'll not be for tying you to the bed," Kelly said. "But keep yer hands there so that if Gallagher or Brockway looks in, they'll be for thinkin' that yer still tied up."

"Thank you, Mr. Kelly. Oh, thank you."

"'N if either of them happen to discover that you not be tied, I want you to tell 'im that you untied yourself."

"I will," she promised, stretching her hands up over her head toward the iron headboard.

Kelly wrapped the rope around them, but he didn't tie them.

Sally waited until Kelly left, then she got out of bed and walked over to the window. It was the first time she had been able to look outside since she was brought there, and her suspicion that she was very near an elevated railroad was confirmed. There, not fifty feet from the side of the building, was an elevated track. To her surprise, she wasn't on the second floor of the building as she had thought. She wasn't even with the elevated railroad, she was looking down on it. Gauging by the building across the street, she realized that she was on the fourth floor. She was much too high to escape through the window. With frustrated disappointment, she returned to the bed but didn't lie down with her hands over her head. She sat up on the bed and was still sitting there half an hour later when Gallagher came into the room.

"What are you doing sitting there like that?" Gallagher asked in a loud angry voice.

"My back was hurting from lying down, so . . ." Sally replied.

"You're supposed to be tied up."

"I got loose. Really, Mr. Gallagher, what is the advantage of keeping me tied up? Either you, or Mr. Kelly, or Mr. Brockway, and sometimes all of you are always in the other room. And because we are on the fourth floor, there's no way I can escape through the window. There is really no need to tie me."

Gallagher stared at her for a long moment, stroking his chin. "All right," he said with a nod. "I'll leave you untied."

"Thank you."

Gallagher turned to leave.

"Mr. Gallagher?"

He turned in acknowledgment of her call.

"What's going to happen to me?" Sally asked.

"I don't know."

"You don't know?"

"Whatever happens to you won't be for me to decide."

"Who is behind all this? Who wanted me taken like this, and for what reason?"

"Blimey, woman, you sure be one for askin' so many questions," Gallagher said.

"'N can you be for blamin' me, Mr. Gallagher? For sure, 'tis my ownself that's in danger here. 'N have I no right ter know about m' own fate?" Sally asked, affecting an Irish brogue.

"Is it Irish you be?"

"Aye, 'twas from Ireland m' own sweet mither came."

"He didn't say anything about you bein' Irish."

Sally wasn't Irish, but she had been around enough Irish in her youth to be able to perfectly mimic the brogue. She didn't know if it would do her any good, but she didn't think it would do her any harm.

"Would you be for tellin' me now, Mr. Gallagher, who is the blaggard that ordered you to cotch me so, 'n keep me like a wee bird in a cage?"

"'Tis an old friend is all I can say," Gallagher replied.

"'N how is it that an Irishman like you has a friend in Wyoming? Have you traveled in the West?"

"I've never been out of New York. 'Tis a friend I know from here."

"'N is he still a friend, seein' as one of yer own was killed?"

"I'll be for confessin' to you that 'twas not part o' the deal that one of us would be killed," Gallagher said. "When it comes to settlin' with the money, I'll be for askin' 'im to pay us well."

"And if he does not?"

"'Tis not for you to worry about such a thing," Gallagher replied as he turned to leave the room before Sally could ask any more questions.

Cal and Muldoon had found nothing the night before. Cal's "commission" limited him to working with a New York policeman, and Muldoon was the policeman who had been assigned to work with him. But Muldoon was available only during his watch, which had been changed from the day watch to the one from seven o'clock in the evening until three o'clock the next morning. It was Muldoon who had asked for the change. As he told Cal, most of the people they would need to see could be seen only at night. The bad thing was that Cal was too anxious to spend an entire day doing nothing while he waited for Muldoon's shift to start.

Cal wondered whether or not he should send a telegram to Smoke. He didn't want to—at least, not until he had some sort of news to report to him, hopefully positive news. It had been his hope to get Sally's kidnapping resolved quickly enough that Smoke would not have to be worried, but it was already too late for anything to be done quickly. Smoke had to be told.

Cal went to the nearest Western Union office to send the message. A little bell on the door dinged as he stepped inside, and the telegrapher looked up. Seeing a man openly wearing a pistol, the telegrapher reacted with fear.

"Oh, don't worry about the gun," Cal said, calming the telegrapher's nerves. "I'm a deputy, working with the police." He showed the telegrapher the commission paper signed by Mayor Grace.

"Indeed, sir," the telegrapher said, obviously relieved that Cal wasn't some outlaw there to do him harm. "What can I do for you, Officer?"

"I need to send a telegram to Big Rock, Colorado."

"Big Rock, Colorado? I've never heard of the place. Does Big Rock, Colorado, have a Western Union office?"

"We sure do. It's right next to the railroad depot," Cal said.

"All right. Let me look in the book and determine the routing procedures."

"Can't you just start tapping that thing to say To Big Rock?"

The telegrapher smiled. "No sir, it will have to be routed . . . I expect through Denver." He studied his book for a moment, then nodded. "Yes, just as I expected, it will go through Denver. Can you write, sir?"

"What? Yes, I can write."

The telegrapher gave him a tablet and a pencil. "Write your message for me."

Cal wrote: *When Mrs. Sally and I were walking some men came up, knocked me out, and took Sally. She is missing now, but the police don't think she has been harmed because they have received no information about a woman being harmed. I have been made a deputy in the New York Police Department, and I am working with the police to try and find her. I will continue to look for her until we find her and I will keep you informed. If you want to send me a message you can reach me at the Fifth Avenue Hotel. Cal*

When he was finished, he slid the message across the counter to the telegrapher.

"Oh, my. That is too bad about your friend, but this message is much too long. It will cost you a fortune. Suppose you let me rewrite it for you. I promise I will get the same information across."

"All right," Cal agreed.

SALLY MISSING STOP AM WORKING WITH POLICE TO FIND HER STOP POLICE BELIEVE SHE IS NOT HARMED AS THEY HAVE NO INFORMATION ANY WOMAN HURT STOP WILL CONTINUE TO LOOK FOR HER AND KEEP YOU INFORMED STOP REACH ME AT FIFTH AVENUE HOTEL STOP CAL

Cal examined the telegram just before it was sent. He saw that it said only that she was missing, rather than that she had actually been taken, and he was about to correct it when he decided that *missing* was enough.

"That will be five dollars and eighty cents," the telegrapher said.

Big Rock

A short while later the telegrapher in Big Rock took the message. "Oh," he said aloud. "Oh, dear me, this isn't good. This isn't good at all."

"What is it, Mr. Deckert?" the Western Union delivery boy asked.

"Missus Jensen is missing in New York."

"Miz Jensen? You mean Miz Smoke Jensen?"

"Yes." Quickly, Deckert printed out the message, put it in a yellow envelope, and handed it to the boy. "Here, Tommy, take this out to Sugarloaf and give it to Mr. Jensen. Ride as quickly as you can."

"Yes, sir," Tommy said.

"I'm sorry, son," Slim Taylor said when Tommy rode into Sugarloaf. In the absence of both Pearlie and Cal, Slim was acting as the foreman over the cowboys who were watching over the ranch. "Ever'one is gone right now. Mr. Jensen 'n Pearlie are up in Wyoming, and Miz Jensen 'n Cal are in New York City."

"Well, do you know how I can get ahold of Mr. Jensen?" Tommy asked. "I've got a telegram for him that's just real important."

"Well, I know he took a bull up for Mr. Condon. He said a-fore he left that if I had to get ahold of him to go see Condon."

"Where does Mr. Condon live?"

"He lives over on the Wiregrass Ranch. That's about ten miles east o' here."

"Thanks," Tommy said.

Sam Condon leaned against the post as he read the telegram. "Damn."

"Do you know how to get this telegram to Mr. Jensen?" Tommy asked.

"Yes. Send it to him in care of my wife at the Del Rey Hotel in Mule Gap, Wyoming," Sam said.

"It'll cost more to send the telegram a second time," Tommy said.

"I'll pay the fee," Sam said.

After getting his billfold, Sam gave Tommy a ten-dollar bill.

"Oh, it won't cost that much."

"You've had a long ride out here to find out how to deliver an important message," Sam said. "Young man, I admire your adherence to the pursuit of your duty. You keep the change."

"Gee, Mr. Condon, thank you!" Tommy said, smiling broadly at his good fortune.

"Get the message through, son. It's very important."

"Yes, sir, I will."

CHAPTER TWENTY-EIGHT

French Creek Canyon

"Where's Whitman?" Keefer asked.

"We was plumb out of whiskey," Reece said, "so he went into town to get some."

"Not Mule Gap, I hope. Remember, we ain't s'posed to go into Mule Gap except on business, 'n whiskey ain't business."

"Don't worry. He went to Warm Springs."

"All right," Keefer said. "We could do with some whiskey around here. I'm goin' to get the Condon boy to write the note, then I'll be takin' it in to his mama and get the money. Sanders, I want you to come with me."

"All right," Sanders said.

"Reece, that'll leave you alone with the kids until Whitman gets back. Think you can handle that?"

"Hell, yes, I can handle it. What is there to handlin' a handful of snot-nosed brats?"

"Just don't both of you get drunk when Whitman

gets back with the whiskey, is all," Keefer ordered. "Somebody needs to be sober to keep an eye on the kids."

Leaving the others in the bigger house, Keefer started toward the cabin.

"Mr. Keefer is coming," Wee said.

"I wonder what he wants," Burt said. "He don't normally come over here. It's always one of the others."

"Can you see any of the nail holes?" Thad asked anxiously.

"No, they're well covered," Lorena replied.

The six gathered in a group, looking toward the door as they heard the lock being opened.

Keefer stepped into the cabin. "What are you all standin' together like that for?"

"Because we're all real good friends," Thad replied.

"You got a smart mouth, you know that, kid?"

"I hope so. I've always considered being smart as a virtue," Thad replied.

Lorena laughed, and Keefer shot her an angry glance.

"Here," he said, handing a paper and pencil to Thad. "I need you to write a note to your mama so she'll know you are alive 'n well."

"No," Thad said.

"What do you mean, you won't do it?" Keefer asked. "Your mama is the one who asked for the note."

"I have a feeling you'll be using the note for more than just to let her know I'm alive."

"Write the note, boy," Keefer demanded,

"No."

"Thad, don't you think your mother might want to know that you are all right?" Lorena asked.

"Listen to the girl," Keefer said. "Remember, your mama is the one who asked for the note in the first place."

"All right. I'll do it," Thad said after a moment of consideration. "I guess you are right."

"Maybe you can put all our names in the note too," Lorena suggested. "That will let our parents know that we are all right, as well."

"Yeah, that would be a good idea," Thad agreed. "I'll do that."

"No, you ain't goin' to do nothin' like that," Keefer said. "Your mama said she wanted to see a note from you. She didn't say nothin' 'bout all the other kids we got here."

"If you expect a note from me, it will also have everybody else's name on it," Thad said. "Otherwise, I won't write it."

"Mr. Keefer, what will be the harm?" Lorena asked. "I'm sure that all Mrs. Condon wants is to know that Thad is alive and well. This note will tell her that. If you are expecting to collect money for the rest of us, don't you think our parents should also know that we are all right?"

"Yeah," Keefer finally agreed. "All right. You can put ever'body else's name in the note, too."

Taking the pencil and paper Keefer presented him, Thad began to write.

Ma, I am not hurt. I am worried about Pa. There are five others with me. Will you tell their parents they are all right, too? They are Lorena Coy and Marilyn Grant, those are the girls. The boys are

Travis Calhoun, Burt Rowe, and Eddie Blackwell.
I love you, Ma.

> *Sincerely,*
> *Your son,*
> *Thaddeus R. Condon*

Thad showed the note to Lorena, who read it, then giggled.

"Why are you laughing?"

"Why did you sign your entire name to the note? Don't you think your mother knows your name?"

"When we learned how to write letters in school, the teacher said we should always sign our whole name so that the person we are writing to would know who the letter came from."

Lorena smiled. "I suppose you're right." She folded the note in half then ran her finger and thumb along the crease.

"Don't do that!" Thad said, cringing.

"Don't do what?" Lorena asked, surprised by Thad's outburst.

"Don't rub your fingers on paper!" he said. "I can't stand to rub my hands on paper, and I can't stand to watch anyone else do it."

Lorena laughed. "You're the strangest boy I've ever met." She handed the note to Keefer.

With the note stuck down in his shirt pocket, Keefer returned to the house, where Sanders had already saddled their horses. Reece was out on the front porch, watching.

"Reece, you keep an eye on the kids," Keefer said

as he swung into the saddle. "I hate to leave only one person here—we've never done that before—but I'm goin' to have to. I'll be needin' Sanders with me when I go into town to get the money from the Condon woman."

"Don't you be worryin' none about me. I'll be just fine," Reece said. "Just go get the money."

"If she gives us the money, are we going to come back here and get the kid and take him to her?" Sanders asked.

"It depends on what the boss says," Keefer replied.

Reece stayed out on the front porch, watching them ride off. Once they were out of sight, he looked over toward the little cabin and unconsciously rubbed himself as he thought of the oldest girl. "Guess what, little girl," he said quietly. "Now that the others are gone, me 'n you are goin' to have us a little fun."

Mule Gap

"When are we going?" Pearlie asked.

"*We* aren't going. Only I am."

"You mean I'm not going? According to Fancy, there are four men out there watching the kids. You plan to take on all four of 'em by yourself?"

"Yes," Smoke said. "Look, Pearlie, you're still wounded. I'm afraid that if you go, you could open up the wound and start bleeding again."

"If I do, you can always stick a piece of my dirty shirt in the hole to stop the bleeding," Pearlie suggested.

Smoke chuckled. "That's true. I could do that, but I have something else I want you to do. Sara Sue is staying with Mrs. Coy. I want you to keep an eye on both of them today. They also know where the kids are located, and someone might decide that is a problem."

Pearlie nodded. "Yeah. Yeah, I can see how that might be. All right. I'll watch over them."

"Thanks. That'll make my job easier, knowing that you're looking out for them."

Astride a rented horse, Smoke started west along French Creek Road, so named because it ran parallel with French Creek, a rapid stream that made gurgling and bubbling sounds as the white water broke over the rocks and swept the smaller pebbles downstream. He was less than two miles out of town when he saw Deputy Plappert and Deputy Slago step into the middle of the road. Both deputies had already drawn their pistols from their holsters.

Plappert held up his hand. "Where do you think you're a-goin'?"

"Oh, I'm just goin' for a ride," Smoke replied.

"Do your ridin' back toward town," Plappert ordered.

"Why should I do that? I've seen town. I thought I'd just take a ride out in the country."

"Marshal Bodine don't trust you. He wants you to stay in town," Plappert said.

Slowly and unthreateningly, Smoke dismounted and glanced over toward Slago. "Can he talk?"

"Of course he can talk," Plappert replied.

Smoke was amused by the fact that it was Plappert, not Slago, who had responded.

"Are you planning on collecting that five-thousand-dollar reward that's been offered for me?"

"Could be," Plappert replied.

"Who are you planning to collect it from?"

"Seein' as how you ain't goin' to be the one collectin', that ain't none of your business," Plappert said.

Smoke chucked. "I guess you have a point there. But don't I have to be dead, first, before you can collect it?"

"Yeah, you do, don't you?" Plappert replied.

During the entire conversation, the two deputies had their guns in their hands. Though he was still holding the gun, Slago had lowered it so that it was no longer pointing at Smoke. Plappert's gun was pointed toward Smoke, but it wasn't cocked.

"What was it you said once? That you planned to live right up until the moment you died?" Plappert asked.

"That's what I said, all right."

An evil grin spread across Plappert's face. "This is that moment."

Smoke started his draw the instant he saw Plappert's thumb tighten on the hammer of his pistol. He drew and fired before Plappert could even cock his pistol.

"What the hell?" Slago shouted, bringing his pistol up and cocking it. But he was unable to get a shot off before Smoke's gun roared.

"How about that? Turns out you could speak, after all," Smoke said.

At the small cabin, Reece unlocked the door then stepped inside. "You," he said, pointing to Lorena. "Can you cook?"

"Yes, I can cook," she replied.

"We got a mess of fish. If you'll fry 'em up, you can have fish for dinner."

"Oh, goody!" Wee said. "I like fried fish."

"Why do you want me to cook, all of a sudden?" Lorena asked. "You've never asked me to cook before."

"We've never had a mess of fish before," Reece said. "Besides, ever'one else is gone. I'm the only one here, right now, 'n I don't plan on doin' the cookin'. Now, do you want some fried fish or not?"

"All right," Lorena said. "I'll go with you."

Lorena stepped onto the front porch with Reece, and waited as he, again, locked the door.

Thad stood at the window and watched as Reece led Lorena toward the house. He had a funny feeling about the man taking her over to the big house. Thad couldn't put his finger on just what was making him uneasy . . . but he didn't feel good about Lorena being alone in the house with Reece.

He stepped back to look at the boards they had been working on. Their efforts over the previous days had removed every nail from six of the floor-boards, and it was time to pull them up. "Let's get these boards pulled up."

"I thought we weren't going to do it until tonight when nobody could see us," Travis said.

"There's nobody here now but Reece, and he's in the house with Lorena," Thad said. "He won't be paying any attention to us, and he won't see what's happening."

"I don't want to go and leave Lorena behind," Wee said.

"I promise you, Wee, we won't leave her behind,"

Thad said. "As a matter of fact, as soon as we get the boards up, I'm going to go check on her."

"What if Mr. Reece sees you?" Marilyn asked.

"I'll be very careful," Thad promised.

They began working on the boards, but it wasn't as easy to pull them up as he had thought it would be. Even though they were no longer secured, the fit was so tight that they couldn't get a grip on the first one. Thad tried using a nail to get to the end of it, but that didn't work.

"Try a bunch of nails," Marilyn suggested.

Thad took her suggestion and with four nails stuck down between the end of the board and the wall, they were able to lift the end of the board up high enough to get a hand around it. Once they did that, the board came up easily.

They had no trouble with the remaining floorboards. As each board came up, the hole was widened, and it was easy to grab the next. It took but a few minutes to open the hole, and as Thad knelt down over it, he could smell the dirt beneath the cabin, and hear the sound of the flowing creek that was only a few feet away.

"All right," he said, giving the orders. "I'll go through first and check on Reece and Lorena. The rest of you wait here until I come back for you."

"I don't want to leave Lorena," Wee said again.

"I told you, Wee, aren't going to leave her," Thad promised.

"What if you are seen?" Burt asked.

"I'm just going to have to take that chance," Thad said. "Remember, wait here until I come back."

"What if you don't come back?" Travis asked.

"Then put the boards back over the hole and swear that you don't know how I got out." Thad went through the hole, dropped down onto his belly, and wriggled out from under the cabin. Staying on his stomach, he wriggled across the distance that separated the two buildings.

CHAPTER TWENTY-NINE

Inside the main house neither Lorena nor Reece were aware that Thad had escaped from the cabin and was crawling toward the house. Busy rolling the fish in cornmeal, Lorena was also unaware of what was going on behind her. Reece had taken off his boots and shirt, removed his gun belt and holster, and was stepping out of his pants. He was staring at Lorena with a wide leering grin.

"I'll need some grease," Lorena said, turning back toward Reece. "Do you know where—" Seeing him standing behind her wearing only his underwear, Lorena gasped. "Mr. Reece, what are you doing?"

"I'm goin' to make a woman out of you, girl," he said. "'N when we're through, you're goin' to thank me."

"No! Get away, get away!"

Lorena's shout alerted Thad, and standing up quickly, he looked through the window. It took only one glance for him to realize what was going on.

Running to the front door, he jerked it open and shouted, "Get away from her, you son of a bitch!"

Reece grabbed a butcher knife lying on the kitchen counter. "How the hell did you get here? I'm going to split you open like gutting a hog!"

Thad felt a surge of fear, then saw Reece's pistol belt draped over a chair. Moving quickly, he grabbed the gun and turned it toward Reece. "Drop the knife!"

"I will, after I use it on you," Reece said with a confident grin.

Thad pulled the trigger, but nothing happened. At the last minute, even as Reece was lunging toward him, he remembered to pull the hammer back. He did that and pulled the trigger. There was no danger of him missing the mark. Reece was so close to him the only way he could have missed would be to jerk the gun to one side.

The expression on Reece's face changed from one of confidence to one of total shock. With his eyes open wide, he took a couple steps back, dropped the knife, and slapped his hands over the bullet hole in his chest. "Why, you little . . ." Reece gasped. His eyes rolled up into his head, then he fell.

"Oh, Thad!" Lorena said. "He was going to . . . he was . . ."

"I know." Thad dropped down to one knee and made a closer examination of the man he had just shot. "Well, he won't bother you again. He'll never bother anyone again."

"Is he dead?"

"Yeah, he's dead." Thad stood up, then he walked over to get the pistol belt and strap it on. "We need to get out of here before the others come back."

"How did you get out of the cabin?"

"I went down through the hole. Did you see what he did with the key?"

"Yes, it's hanging on the nail next to the door."

Thad grabbed the key. "Good. This way, the others won't have to go through the floor."

When Thad unlocked the front door to the cabin a moment later, he saw the other four gathered fearfully in the corner. "What are you all doing over there?"

"We heard a shot," Travis said. "We thought Reece had killed you."

"No, I killed Reece," Thad replied, speaking as calmly as if he had just said that the sun was shining. "Come on. Let's go."

The others joined him without hesitation, and a moment later all six were below the bank of French Creek. They could stand without breaking the skyline, and even if Keefer and Sanders returned at that very moment, they would not see them.

"Which way?" Travis asked.

"When Wee and I were brought here, we were coming west," Lorena said.

"Then we'll go east," Thad said.

"It'll be faster if we go on the road," Travis suggested.

Thad shook his head. "We can't do that. We'll have to stay down here by the creek. Keefer and Sanders were going into Mule Gap to deliver my note. We don't want to run into either of those bastards."

"Oh," Wee said. "You said a bad word."

"That's all right, Wee," Lorena said. "These sons of bitches are bastards."

The others chuckled.

"I think we'd better get going," Thad suggested. "I want to be a long way from here before the others come back."

The six started following the creek bed with Thad in front, then Lorena. Then Wee, and Marilyn, while Travis brought up the rear.

"I'm scared," Wee said. "Are you scared, Marilyn?"

"Yes."

"Are you scared, Burt?"

"No, I'm just glad to be out of there."

"Are you scared, Travis?"

"No, I'm like Burt. I'm just glad to get away from there."

"Are you afraid, Lorena?"

"No, I'm not afraid."

"Why aren't you afraid?"

Lorena looked at Thad and smiled. "As long as Thad is with us, I'm not afraid."

"Thad?" Wee said.

"What?"

"I think Lorena likes you," he said with a broad smile.

Welsh's Boarding House, Mule Gap

"I hope you like apple pie, Mr. Pearlie," Sandra Coy said. "I baked it last night."

"I love apple pie," Pearlie replied with an appreciative grin. "And you can just call me Pearlie. No *mister* is needed."

"All right. Pearlie it is," Sandra said as she cut three pieces of pie while Sara Sue was pouring three cups of coffee.

"Pearlie, do you think Smoke will be able to find the kids and bring them back?" Sandra asked.

"I don't think he will, I know he will," Pearlie said as he picked up a fork to dig into the pie.

"But won't men be there guarding the children?" Sara Sue asked.

"There are four men there," Pearlie said as he took his first bite. "Mrs. Coy—"

"Sandra."

Pearlie gave a brief nod. "Sandra, this is a mighty fine pie."

"Four? There is just Smoke against four men?" Sara Sue said.

"The odds are a bit uneven, I know. I mean, there just being four of them against Smoke. But they have nobody but themselves to thank for being put into such a position."

Sandra laughed. "Are you saying that the four men are in more danger than Mr. Jensen?"

"Yes," Pearlie replied without further explanation. "Do you think I could have another cup of coffee?"

Along French Creek

Smoke draped the bodies of Plappert and Slago over their horses, gave both horses a slap on the rump, and started them back at a trot. He knew they would return to the livery. It would be quite a shock to Evans, but he would, no doubt, get them back to the marshal to be taken care of.

Smoke had a pretty good idea where the kids were being kept. On a previous trip to Mule Gap, he had seen the deserted house and cabin and had examined them out of curiosity.

* * *

"Did you hear shootin'?" Keefer asked.

"I can't hardly hear nothin', loud as that damn creek is."

"I thought I heard gunfire, but I guess not."

"Hey, how come, do you think, that there ain't none of the other kids' parents offered to give us any money yet?" Sanders asked.

"That ain't our problem," Keefer said. "Right now our only job is to collect the money for the boy."

"We goin' to let the boy go?"

"We're goin' to do exactly what the chief tells us to do." Keefer said as they rounded the bend. Then he saw him. "Son of a bitch! It's Jensen!"

Smoke had heard the two men talking, so he wasn't as surprised to see them as they were to see him. "Where are the kids?" he called out.

The answer to Smoke's query was gunfire as both kidnappers drew their guns and began shooting.

Smoke had shouted the question with no real expectation of any kind of response other than what he had gotten. His own gun was in his hand as quickly as Keefer's and Sanders's were in theirs. However, Smoke wasn't riding Seven. Seven had been a good and stable partner in any gunfight, but the rental horse was anything but. He reared up and twisted around, which had the positive effect of making Smoke a more difficult target. The negative effect was making it hard for Smoke to be effective in his own shooting.

For a few seconds, the valley echoed and reechoed with gunfire, then Smoke dismounted and was able, in but two more shots, to knock both Keefer and Sanders from their saddles. Their horses galloped away with empty saddles. Smoke's rental horse would have done the same thing if he hadn't been holding so securely on to the reins.

With his horse calmed down and his gun in hand, Smoke advanced cautiously to examine the two men he had just engaged. The man he didn't recognize was already dead, but Keefer was still breathing in labored gasps.

"Where are the kids?" Smoke asked.

"You go to hell," Keefer said.

"What a fine thing to say as you're dying," Smoke replied, but Keefer didn't hear him. He had already drawn his last breath.

Smoke saw a piece of paper sticking out of Keefer's pocket, and removing it, saw that it was the note Sara Sue had demanded. "All right. We know the kids are all alive and well." Having spoken the words aloud, however, he felt foolish for talking to himself. It had never seemed as if he had been talking to himself when he carried on such conversations with Seven. Then they were conversations, not soliloquies. Seven, invariably, had responded to Smoke's words by whickers, whinnies, or understanding shakes of his head.

Although he didn't like to leave the two men where they'd fallen, he didn't really have much choice in the matter as both their horses had run off. So, leaving the two men, Smoke remounted and continued to follow the creek road. He wasn't looking for the cabin—he knew where it was—he was merely advancing toward it.

He heard the sound of voices ahead and pulled the horse to a halt in order to listen more intently. It sounded like kids' voices. Were they being brought out by their kidnappers? No, that didn't seem likely. The voices weren't coming from the road, but from below the bank on the creek itself.

Smoke headed the rental horse into a growth of trees, dismounted, then tied him there. Pulling his pistol, he moved back down closer to the creek, stood behind a tree, and waited. If the kids were being escorted against their will, he intended to take care of it.

"How much farther, Lorena?" That was definitely a very young voice.

"I don't think it's too much farther," a girl's voice said.

"Quit talking, Wee. We don't want anyone to hear us." That was definitely Thad's voice.

Smoke saw them then, six young people with Thad in the lead. There were no adults with them. They had to have had escaped.

"The only one hearing you is me, Thad," Smoke said, stepping out into the open.

"Thad!" Lorena said, her voice elevated by fright.

"It's all right, Lorena. That's my friend, Mr. Jensen!" Thad said happily.

Thad started running toward Smoke, and the others joined him. Without embarrassment, Thad embraced Smoke, then he introduced the others. "Mr. Jensen, how is my pa?"

"He's at home with bandages wrapped around him," Smoke said. "But Doctor Urban says he's going to be just fine. Come on up onto the road. It'll be easier walking up here. I'll go back to town with you."

"Where's Seven?" Thad asked, seeing the rental horse.

"Seven was killed, Thad."

"The kidnappers did it?"

"I don't think Seven's killers had anything to do with the kidnappers, but they were shooting at Pearlie and me, and they killed Seven and they shot Pearlie."

"Oh, Pearlie has been shot?"

"Yes, but like your pa, he'll be all right." Smoke smiled. "And your ma is in Mule Gap, waiting for you. I expect she's going to be one happy lady. I expect all your parents are going to be happy to see you," he added.

"I'll be glad to see my mama and papa," Wee said.

"All right, boys, I got the whiskey!" Whitman shouted, returning to the house and cabin. "I got us four bottles, that ought to hold us for a—" Whitman paused in midsentence when he noticed that the door to the cabin was standing wide open.

"What the hell? Hey! The cabin door is open," he shouted as he dismounted and hurried into the cabin. There he saw that the cabin was empty, and there was a big hole in the floor. *That's probably the way they escaped,* he thought, but then the door was standing wide open. Why would they go through a hole in the floor, if they could just go through the door?

Whitman hurried to the house to tell the others, but when he got there, he saw nothing but Reece's half-naked and fully dead body. Whitman didn't know where Keefer and Sanders were, but he figured they were probably in pursuit of the kids.

For a moment, he considered trying to catch up with them, but he figured they had too big a lead on him. The best thing to do, he decided, was to go into town and tell the boss.

Halfway to town, he came across the bodies of Keefer and Sanders.

CHAPTER THIRTY

New York City

Cal had still heard nothing back from Smoke, and that confused and worried him. Why hadn't Smoke replied? He wondered if he should send another telegram, and if so, what should he say? Should he word the telegram in such a way as to make the situation more critical? Maybe Smoke didn't get the telegram. The telegrapher said he had never heard of Big Rock. Maybe they couldn't find it.

But no, that wasn't likely. Big Rock did have a Western Union, and they got telegrams all the time. Maybe he should send another one asking Smoke to come to New York.

No, Cal didn't want to do that. He'd been with Sally when she was taken. He was responsible for her, and he was the one who should get her back. Muldoon had said just last night that they were making progress, but Cal would like to know just what kind of progress they were making. It was certainly nothing that he could measure.

He went downstairs to check the clock. He had just enough time to eat his supper then go to the police precinct for the change of watch.

"Hello, Cal," the dining room waiter said. "Any word on Mrs. Jensen yet?"

"No, Charley, not yet," Cal replied. He and the waiter had become acquainted over the last few days.

Charley had been intrigued by Cal's Western garb, and confessed that he had always wanted to go west and be a cowboy. "I hope you find her, and that she is unharmed."

"I'll find her," Cal insisted as he picked up the menu.

"Don't eat the beef tonight," Charley said, speaking so quietly that no one but Cal could hear. "It isn't a very good cut and is quite tough."

"What do you suggest?"

"The pork roast is quite good."

"Thanks."

Cal had never actually seen a big city police department before, so he had never seen a watch change, either. He found the entire thing very fascinating but was glad he was an observer rather than a participant in the event.

It began with the police lining up like soldiers in a formation, then the watch commander spoke, giving them the latest information. "The Five Points Gang is giving us trouble again. Vito Costaconti got of jail last week, and word on the street is he's gone right back to his old ways. Keep an eye out for him.

"Also, Officer Muldoon is looking for a woman—"

"Does your wife know that, Mickey?" one of the

policemen called out, and the others in the watch laughed.

"Here, now!" the watch commander said, scolding them by his tone of voice. "There will be none of that! It so happens that this is a fine lady of character, a visitor to our city when she got taken by person or persons unknown. And I'll also tell you this. Himself, His Honor, the mayor has taken an interest in this case.

"Muldoon and our new deputy, Cal Wood"—the watch commander looked toward Cal, nodded his head, and smiled—"are the two assigned to looking for the lady, but I want all of you to keep your eyes and your ears open. And if you hear anything, let us know."

"Lieutenant, it might help us in the search if you could be for tellin' us the lady's name," one of the policeman said. "That is, if it's not being kept a secret."

"That would be Jensen," the lieutenant said. "Mrs. Kirby Jensen."

"What's her first name, Lieutenant?"

The watch commander looked toward Cal.

"Miz Sally," Cal said automatically, then he clarified it. "Sally is her first name."

"All right, gentlemen, you have the watch orders, turn out now, and remember"—the lieutenant held up his finger—"it's us against them."

The watch was dismissed, and Muldoon went over to join Cal.

"I'm sorry, lad, that we've no been successful so far. 'Tis sure I am that she's still alive or we woulda heard about it. The brigands are holding her as prisoner somewhere, but the why of it escapes me. It can't be for a ransom, for who would know that her husband is a rich man? And how would they be for getting in touch with him?"

"I sent Smoke a telegram telling him about Miz Sally, but I've not heard anything from him."

Mule Gap

"I wonder why we haven't heard anything from Smoke," Sara Sue said. "I'm beginning to get a little worried."

"Don't be worried," Pearlie said. "Smoke will be back with the children, all safe and sound."

"You say that with such confidence, Pearlie. How can you be so sure?"

"I've known Smoke for a long time now. I've seen him in situations you would swear he could never escape, but he always does."

"I suppose that's why they write books about him," Sara Sue said with a smile."

"They write books about Smoke Jensen?" Sandra asked, surprised by the comment.

"Yeah, they sure do," Pearlie said, smiling. "But I tell you the truth. He's not too happy about being a character in a dime novel."

There was a knock on the door then, so loud that it made all three of them jump.

"Yes? Who is it?" Sandra called.

"Do you have Miz Condon in there?" a man called from the other side of the door.

Sandra looked over toward Pearlie.

"Who wants to know?" Pearlie replied.

"There's a man in there, Angus," a second voice said.

There was another knock. "Open the door!" The order was loud and insistent.

Pearlie took off his boots.

"What are you doing?" Sara Sue asked.

Pearlie held his finger over his lips, then signaled for Sara Sue to get under the bed.

"Open the door!" the voice was louder and more demanding. The knock was much louder, too, and so heavy it was causing the door to shake on its hinges.

"Sandra, get in the bed and pull the covers up to your chin," Pearlie said.

"What?"

"Just do it, please."

Sandra did so as the loud knocking continued.

"Open the door!"

"Just a minute, just a minute. Hold your horses. I'm coming," Pearlie said as he stripped out of his shirt, tossed it casually onto the foot of the bed, then tousled his hair. Bare from the waist up, except for the part of the bandage that could be seen sticking up from his pants, he padded barefoot across the floor, unbuttoning the top three buttons of his trousers.

He opened the door, but only partway. "What do you want?" he demanded.

Deputies Zimmerman and Delmer pushed into the room. Sandra let out a little scream of alarm.

"Here!" Pearlie demanded angrily. "What do you think you are doing?"

"We're lookin' for Miz Condon," Zimmerman said.

"Well, as you can see, she isn't in here. Why are you looking for Miz Condon here, anyway? I believe you will find her at the hotel."

"She ain't there," Delmer said.

"Then I have no idea where she is. What do you want her for, anyway?" Pearlie asked.

"The Professor wants to put her into . . . what was that he said, Boots?"

"Protective custody," Zimmerman replied.

"Yes, well, I think she would appreciate that. But go look for her somewhere else. As you can clearly see, you have interrupted a rather delicate moment here."

Delmer laughed. "Yeah, I can see that you're . . . busy."

The two men left, and Sandra started to get out of bed. Pearlie held out his right hand and held the finger of his left hand over his lips in a signal to be quiet.

Sandra looked at him confused by his action, but a few seconds later Pearlie's action was validated when the door was jerked open again.

"Now what?" Pearlie demanded angrily.

Without actually coming into the room, the two men glanced around then left again.

Pearlie walked over to the window and looked out. Not until he saw the two deputies walking away did he say anything. "All right, ladies, you can both come out now." He reached for his shirt.

"Oh, that was so frightening," Sandra said. "But I'm confused. Those were both deputies . . . why should we fear them?"

"It was deputies that shot me, remember," Pearlie said. "Smoke doesn't trust your marshal and his deputies, and neither do I."

"Oh!" Sandra said, lifting her hand to her mouth "What is it?"

"Those men! They will tell everyone that we . . . that is . . . what they saw. I'll never be able to hold my head up in this town again."

"Then come to Big Rock," Sara Sue invited. "I know that Sam and I can find something much better for you than what you are doing now. And you can stay with us until you get settled."

Smoke and the six children were walking on the road.

When they came close to where he had left the bodies of Keefer and Sanders, he held up his hand. "Wait a minute. When we get around this next bend, you kids are likely to see something you've never seen before, and I want you to be ready for it."

"You mean dead people?" Thad asked.

"Yes."

"It's Keefer and Sanders, isn't it?"

"I expect so," Smoke said. "I left them there, but if you kids don't want to see the bodies, I can go up now and move them."

"I don't want you to leave us," Marilyn said.

"Me, either," Burt added.

"I saw my grandpa when he was dead," Wee said.

"Well, your grandpa was laid out in a coffin, nice and neat," Smoke said.

"No, he wasn't. He was on the porch swing with his head hanging down."

"All right," Smoke said. "Just so you know."

The two bodies were lying just where Smoke had left them. He had been concerned that the buzzards or coyotes might have gotten to them, which would have made a rather gory picture for the children to see, but the bodies were, thus far, undisturbed.

The children looked at the bodies with hesitant curiosity, then hurried on by.

"I'm tired," Wee said a while later. "Can we stop and rest?"

"No, I want to go home," Travis said.

"I do, too," Marilyn added.

"What if I picked you up and let you ride on the horse?" Smoke asked. "Would that be all right?"

"Yes!" Wee said enthusiastically. "I would like that!"

About half an hour after Smoke and the children had passed by the bodies of Keefer and Sanders, Whitman came across them. "What the hell?" he said aloud, pulling his horse to a stop.

First Reece was dead, and now he'd found Keefer and Sanders. Clearly there had been a rescue made of the children, and it had to be several men involved in order to kill all three of them.

Frightened that there might be someone close by waiting specifically for him, Whitman dismounted and led his horse off the road and into the trees. He snaked the Winchester out of the saddle sheath, jacked a round into the chamber, then lay down behind the rock in such a way as to afford him a view of the road in both directions.

If someone was coming after him, he would be ready for them.

When Smoke and the children came into town about two hours later, Smoke was leading the horse, and Wee was sitting in the saddle, holding on to the saddle horn. All the others were walking.

Bill Lewis was sweeping the porch in front of his drugstore when he saw the entourage coming into town. Not sure what he was seeing, he held the broom for a moment and stared at them.

"Hello, Mr. Lewis!" Wee called. "Do you see me riding this horse?"

"I'll be damned! It's the children," Lewis said. At first, he spoke the words quietly, then realizing the significance of it, he shouted the news at the top of his voice. "It's the children! The kidnapped children have been returned!"

The entrance of the little entourage raised quite a commotion in town, and word spread quickly The first of the parents to react were Richard and Millicent Blackwell, whose Emporium was right next to the Lewis Apothecary. Both came running out to meet their child

"Wee!" Mrs. Blackwell shouted.

"Mama!" Wee let go of the saddle horn and stretched his arms out toward his mother. The sudden action caused him to lose his balance, and he fell.

"Wee!" Mrs. Blackwell shouted again, but in alarm.

Thad, who was standing close by, caught the boy as he tumbled from the saddle.

By the time the children reached the middle of town, Sara Sue and Thad had made a happy reunion, as had Lorena and her mother Sandra.

"Thad saved us, Mama," Lorena said proudly. "He saved all of us."

"Thad did?" Sara Sue asked in surprise.

"That's right," Smoke said. "By the time I got there,

they were already free. I found them walking along the side of a creek."

"Thad! You're wearing a pistol!" Sara Sue said, noticing it for the first time."

"Yes, ma'am," Thad replied. Taking the gun belt off, he handed it to Smoke. "I don't suppose I'll be needing this again."

Lorena noticed that her mother was standing next to Thad's mother. "Mama, do you know Thad's mother?"

"Oh, sweetheart, Sara Sue Condon and I are great friends," Sandra replied.

"Lorena likes Thad," Wee said.

"They're dead. All three of them are dead," Whitman was reporting. "First thing, I found Reece dead in the house, then I found Keefer 'n Sanders lying dead out on the creek 'bout halfway into town. 'N here's the thing . . . Reece was half-naked, he was. Half-naked with a bullet hole in his chest."

"Why weren't you there with them?"

"We was out of whiskey, 'n I went inter town to get it. It warn't my fault. I mean it was just a bunch of kids, 'n they was locked up in a cabin. Who woulda thought that three men couldn't look after six kids?"

"Half-naked you say? There's no doubt in my mind, but that Reece was going after one of the little girls and managed to lose control of the situation. The son of a bitch never could keep his pecker in his pants."

"His pecker was still in his pants," Whitman said.

"This has cost us fifty thousand dollars, fifteen thousand dollars for the boy, and another thirty-five for the rest of them. All because you went into town to get whiskey, and Reece couldn't keep his pecker in his pants."

"His pecker was in his pants," Whitman repeated.

"The kids are all back safe, now. With Keefer, Sanders, and Reece dead, there's no way to connect us to the kidnapping."

"Except for me. The kids seen me lots of times."

"That's right, isn't it? My suggestion is that you get out of town and stay out of sight."

CHAPTER THIRTY-ONE

As all the children began to reconnect with their parents, Smoke stepped into the marshal's office, where he found Bodine sitting behind his desk, playing a game of solitaire. "I'm a little surprised to see you setting in here, with all the kids returned."

"It is as you said. All the children have been returned. What purpose would it serve me to be out in the middle of it? After all, you are the White Knight himself, arriving on a prancing steed after having rescued the princess in distress," Bodine said sarcastically. "I wouldn't want to steal any of your glory."

Smoke chuckled, overlooking the sarcasm. "Wrong on both accounts, Bodine. I wasn't riding a prancing steed, I was walking. And I didn't rescue the children. They escaped by themselves."

"How did they manage that?"

"By taking advantage of the opportunity when it presented itself. I found them on the bank of French Creek, heading into town. Had I not seen them, they would have made it into town on their own."

"Apparently the kidnappers were unaware of the

courage and ingenuity of the young people in their charge," Bodine said.

"Apparently so," Smoke replied.

"Why are you here, Jensen? Did you come to tell me that the children were freed? Obviously I already know that. Everyone in town is aware of that bit of information."

"No, I came to tell you there are two bodies lying on the bank of French Creek."

"Yes, I know that as well. That would be Fred Keefer and Clyde Sanders. Did you kill them?"

"Yes."

"I thought you said you had nothing to do with the children's escape."

"I didn't."

"Then why did you kill them?"

"Because they were trying to kill me. I happened onto them as I was going to the cabin where the children were being held."

"Wait a minute. You knew where the children were being held, and you didn't tell me?"

"It was my understanding, Bodine, that you knew as well. Delilah did tell you where the children were, didn't she?"

"Did you kill Elmer Reece as well?" Bodine asked, pointedly avoiding Smoke's question.

"Reece? No. Who is Reece, and why do you ask if I killed him?"

"He was found dead in the house where the kidnapped children were being held."

Smoke thought of Thad, and remembered that he had been wearing a pistol belt when they met on the creek bank. Had Thad killed the man Bodine was talking about? If so, he had said nothing about it. And Smoke was glad Thad hadn't spoken of it. Someone with less moral fiber would have, no doubt, bragged about it.

"How did you get that information so fast?" Smoke asked. "We just got into town. And how did you know the names of the two men I killed?"

"A good citizen found all three of the bodies and made the report," Bodine said. "I've already got some of my deputies out to recover the bodies."

"What about Plappert and Slago? They were a couple of your deputies, weren't they?"

"*Were* is the operative word," The Professor said. "I sent them out on a routine scouting mission, and both of them returned draped over their horses. You wouldn't know anything about that, would you?"

"Apparently they were trying to collect on that five-thousand-dollar reward that someone, as yet unknown, has put out on me. That is, I think it is still a person unknown. Do you have any idea who it might be?"

"No idea at all," Bodine replied.

"Too bad. I would like to know what that reward is all about."

"Will there be anything else, Mr. Jensen?" Bodine asked, picking up the deck of cards, expressing his interest in continuing the game.

"No," Smoke replied. "There will be nothing else."

When Smoke stepped back out into the street, the rescued children, all now reunited with their parents, were the center of attention of a large and still growing crowd of people celebrating the return. Joining the gathering of the children, parents, and citizens, was the mayor of Mule Gap.

Kennedy held up his arms in a call for attention. "Ladies and gentleman, may I have your attention, please? I'd like to say a few words."

"Leave it to a politician to give a speech at the drop of a hat," Gil Rafferty said jokingly.

"Well, Gil, if you had been more of a speechifier, why, mayhaps you would be the mayor now," someone said. His comment was met with laughter, including that from both Rafferty and Kennedy.

"Ladies and gentlemen, in honor of our children being returned to us, I, Mayor Warren Kennedy, mayor of the great city of Mule Gap, do hereby declare this to be an official Welcome Home Day."

The crowd cheered.

"That's real good, Mayor, but what does that mean?" someone asked.

"Well, for one thing, it means that to celebrate the event I will provide one free drink to anyone who comes into Kennedy's Saloon during the next two hours."

Several cheered, but one of the women pointed out the obvious.

"Mr. Mayor, if we are celebrating the children, do you really think that giving away free drinks is the appropriate thing to do?"

"We all know that you are a prohibitionist, Miz Ragsdale," someone said. "If it was up to you, there wouldn't never be no drinks served nowhere, no time."

"No, Mr. Turner, Mrs. Ragsdale is right," Kennedy said, responding to the one who had challenged Mrs. Ragsdale. "Children have no business being in a saloon, so for the next hour there will be free candy at the Rafferty and Kennedy store for all the children."

"Is that for all the children, or just the ones that was captured?" a boy asked.

"Young man, that is for all the children," Kennedy said.

All the children present cheered.

"And Blackwell's Emporium will provide free ribbon for all the ladies," Richard Blackwell offered.

"I say we give three cheers for Smoke Jensen for bringing our children back to us," someone said.

But before the cheers could be organized, Smoke held up his hand. "No! I had nothing to do with the rescue. These children escaped of their own initiative. If cheers are to be given, they should be given to the children."

"It was Thad!" Lorena shouted. "Thad is the one who saved us!"

"Then three cheers for Thad *and* the children," someone said, and as the cheers were given, Smoke noticed that Lorena was looking with adoration toward Thad.

Wee saw it as well. "Mama, Lorena likes Thad."

"Yes, dear, I think the whole town likes Thad," Mrs. Blackwell replied.

After the celebration, Smoke and Pearlie went into Kennedy's Saloon and took their free beer to a table.

"Are you ready to go back home?" Smoke asked.

"Well, yeah, I am, but how are we goin' to get there, you bein' without a horse?" Pearlie asked. "On account of, I've got an idea how we can do it."

"You're not going to tell me that we'll go all the

way to Sugarloaf, riding double on your horse," Smoke said.

Pearlie laughed. "I wasn't thinkin' that, 'n I don't think Dandy would like it much, either. No, sir, I was thinkin' about goin' down to Sugarloaf, getting New Seven, and bringing him back up here for you."

"No, that is, for sure, too much riding for you right now. You could break that wound open again. If you did that, and started bleeding out on the trail, what would you do?"

"I'd stick a piece of dirty shirt in the bullet hole," Pearlie teased. "It worked the last time."

"You could do that, I suppose," Smoke replied. "Or I could rent a coach to take all four of us, Sara Sue, Thad, you and me, back home. You can tie your horse on behind the coach."

"Damn, a private coach, huh? Yeah, that will be nice. Will it be big enough to take Sandra and Lorena back with us?"

"Sandra and Lorena?" Smoke asked, curious about the additional people.

"Yeah, I think Sandra and her daughter would more 'n likely be more comfortable back in Big Rock than they would be if they had to stay here."

"Why is that?"

"Well, it's just something that . . . I mean, I couldn't come up with anything else that quick, and I didn't think about how it would look. Anyhow, I just think that Sandra would be more comfortable living in Big Rock than if she stayed here."

"Pearlie, why do I think there is more to this story?"

"Well, there is more to it, but Miz Condon was

there when it happened, and she can tell you that nothin' happened."

Smoke laughed. "Sara Sue was there when it happened, but she can tell me that nothing happened? Pearlie, you aren't making one lick of sense."

Pearlie told Smoke about the two deputies Boots Zimmerman and Angus Delmer coming by Sandra Coy's apartment, and how he fooled them by making them think something was going on between him and Sandra. "Talk like that could get all over town. I wouldn't feel good about leaving her here with all that."

Smoke chuckled. "All right. I see what you are talking about now. If you want my opinion, you did a good job of looking out for her and I think what you did was clever. But yes, we can take them. Finish your beer. We'll go see Sara Sue and Thad."

"Yes?" Sara Sue called, responding to the knock on her door.

"Western Union, ma'am," a voice called from the other side.

"Oh, it must be from your father," Sara Sue said to Thad as she hurried to the door. She was taking the telegram from the delivery boy, just as Smoke and Pearlie were arriving.

"Smoke, Pearlie," Sara Sue said. "Come in, come in. It looks as if I have just gotten a telegram from Sam."

"No problem, I hope," Smoke said.

"I sent him a telegram telling him that Thad was safely back. He may just be responding to it, though I don't know how he could have done so, so quickly." She gave the boy a nickel, and with a touch to the tip of his hat, the boy left.

"Let's see what he has to say." With a big smile, she pulled the telegram from the envelope. As soon as she began reading, the smile faded, and her face was twisted into an expression of great concern. "Oh, no!"

"What is it? Ma, has something happened to Pa?"

"No, dear. This telegram is for Smoke."

"The telegram is for me?" Smoke asked, his voice laced with curiosity and concern.

"Here." Sara Sue handed him the telegram. "You had better read it."

SALLY MISSING STOP AM WORKING WITH
POLICE TO FIND HER STOP POLICE
BELIEVE SHE IS NOT HARMED AS THEY
HAVE NO INFORMATION ANY WOMAN
HURT STOP WILL CONTINUE TO LOOK
FOR HER AND KEEP YOU INFORMED STOP
REACH ME AT FIFTH AVENUE HOTEL
STOP CAL

Smoke hurried from the hotel to the telegraph office. "When did you get this telegram from New York?" Smoke showed the telegrapher the telegram he had just read.

"Oh, about half an hour ago . . . but it didn't come from New York. It came from Big Rock, Colorado."

"Ah, yes, that makes sense. Cal has no way of knowing that I'm here, so of course he would have sent it to me there. Well, I want to send a telegram to him in New York."

"Yes sir, would that be in care of Ian Gallagher?"

"Ian Gallagher? No, why would it be? Who is Gallagher, and why would you think I would want to send a telegram to him?"

"Isn't Mrs. Jensen a guest of Mr. Gallagher while she is in New York?"

"Mister, what *are* you talking about?" Smoke asked.

"Just a minute, and I will show you." The telegrapher stepped back to a cabinet, opened a drawer, and shuffled through some papers until he found the one he was looking for. "Ah, here it is."

Returning to the front counter, he showed the telegram to Smoke. "I sent this message one week ago."

MRS KIRBY JENSEN ARRIVING
GRAND CENTRAL DEPOT ON BOARD
TRANSCONTINENTAL TRAIN HUMMER
TWO PM THIS DAY STOP ARRANGE
FOR HER TO BE YOUR GUEST UNTIL
FURTHER NOTICE STOP YOU WILL BE
WELL COMPENSATED FOR HER STAY
WITH YOU STOP

Smoke read the message, then shook his head. "I don't know anything about this. What does it mean? Who sent it?"

"Well, I assumed he was doing it for you, you know, making arrangements for your wife to have accommodations while she was in New York? I thought he was doing it as a favor, since the two of you seem to be such good friends."

"Who sent the message?" Smoke asked again, more forcibly than before.

"Why, it was His Honor, Mayor Kennedy, forcefully who sent the message," the telegrapher said.

"That son of a bitch!" Smoke said angrily. He turned and left the telegraph office.

His first thought was to go directly to Kennedy's office, but he returned to the hotel instead. "It was Kennedy," he told Pearlie, Sara Sue, and Thad. "He is the one who had Sally kidnapped. The question is why did he do it?"

"Are you going after him?" Pearlie asked.

"Yes. I need to find out where Sally is, and right now he's the only one who can tell me."

"I'll come with you," Pearlie offered. He smiled. "If you have to beat it out of him, I want to watch."

"Do I have a telegram?" Marshal Bodine asked the Western Union telegrapher when he stepped into the office.

"No, sir."

"Then what is it? What are you doing here?"

"Marshal, I think there's going to be trouble between Mr. Jensen and the mayor."

"Why do you say that?"

"Mr. Jensen received a telegram saying his wife is missing. Then he found out that, about a week ago, the mayor had sent a telegram to New York about his wife. I'm not sure what this is all about, Marshal, but when Mr. Jensen left to see the mayor, he was very mad. I'm afraid there might be some trouble between them."

"You were right to come to me," the marshal said.

* * *

"Wait, sir, you can't just go into the mayor's office without being announced!" the clerk out front said.

"Is that so? Well, you just watch me," Smoke said.

"Smoke? What is it? What's wrong?" Kennedy asked when Smoke stepped into his office.

"What is this about?" Smoke demanded, dropping on the desk in front of Kennedy a copy of the telegram he had sent to Gallagher.

Kennedy looked at the telegram and his face turned white. "How did you get this? It is against the law for a telegrapher to disclose the contents of a private telegram."

"This telegram concerns my wife," Smoke said. "That gives me every right to know about it. Now, who is Gallagher?"

"He's a friend back in New York," Kennedy said. "I . . . I thought I was doing you a favor, making arrangements for Mrs. Jensen's accommodations."

"She is missing," Smoke said. "The police are trying to find her. I suppose you don't know anything about that."

"I . . . uh—" Whatever Kennedy was going to say was interrupted by the sound of a gunshot from outside the window, and he went down with a bullet hole in his chest.

Smoke ran to the window, but whoever had taken the shot was gone. He returned to the mayor lying on the floor. Pearlie was squatting behind him.

"Dead?" Smoke asked.

"Not yet," Pearlie said. "But he soon will be."

"Your wife . . . won't be hurt," Kennedy said, gasping

the words out. "She was supposed to be . . . insurance to keep you . . . from going after the children until . . . the ransom was paid." Kennedy tried to laugh, but the effort brought blood bubbling from his lips. "Who would . . . have thought . . . the children would . . . escape . . . on their own?"

"Who shot you, Warren," Smoke asked. "Do you have any idea?"

Kennedy's eyes were still open, but his gasping breaths had stopped.

CHAPTER THIRTY-TWO

New York City

"How long are we goin' to keep Mrs. Jensen?" Kelly asked.

"As long as it takes," Gallagher replied.

"As long as what takes?"

"As long as it takes for Kennedy to send us the money," Gallagher replied.

"Warren Kennedy? He's the one that's behind all this?" Kelly asked, surprised to hear the name.

"Aye. 'N would you be for tellin' me who else we know who went West?"

"You shoulda tol' me it was Kennedy. I didn't like the son of a bitch when he was here. You might remember 'twas him who got us into a war with the Five Points gang 'n wound up gettin' a lot of our friends killed."

"Aye, but 'tis a sweet thing he has goin' now. He is the mayor of the town, 'n soon as he gets the money from somethin' he's workin' on, he'll be sendin' for me to come join him. You can go, too."

"No, thank you. I've no wish to leave New York. What if he don't send the money? What will we do with the woman?"

"What makes you think he won't be sendin' the money?"

"Do you know anythin' about this woman's husband?" Kelly asked.

"No."

"Well, I do. He's some kinda hero in the West. He's a gunfighter, 'n when he shoots someone, he never misses."

Gallagher laughed. "'N where would you be for getting that information?"

"From *Shootout at Sunset*," Kelly replied.

"What? What are you talkin' about?"

"I'm talkin' about Smoke Jensen, the legendary gunfighter." Kelly reached into his back pocket and pulled out the book, the title of which he had just mentioned. "You can read all about it in this book."

Gallagher looked at the book and laughed. "A dime novel? 'N am I to be worryin' 'bout some character in a book?"

"'Tis more than just a character in a book. He's a real person, 'n if he ever finds out it was Kennedy who had his wife took, there's goin' to be hell to pay," Kelly insisted.

"I'll send Kennedy a telegram 'n ask when he plans on sendin' the money," Gallagher said.

* * *

In the office of the Western Union, the telegrapher showed Gallagher the telegram he was about to send.

MRS JENSEN IS OUR GUEST AS
REQUESTED STOP WHEN WILL
MONEY BE SENT STOP GALLAGHER

"And this is to the mayor of Mule Gap?" the telegrapher asked.

"Aye."

"Very well, sir. That will be one dollar and ten cents."

Gallagher returned to the tenement building on West Third Street, just east of McDougal. From the chugging steam engine, the rumble of the cars, and the squeak and rattle of the elevated tracks, the site was loud with the sounds of a passing train. He could smell the horse manure coming from the Minetta Stable on the south side of the street. Standing out in front of St. Clement's Protestant Episcopal Church, Reverend Peabody nodded at Gallagher as he stepped down from the cab. Gallagher made no acknowledgment in response to the good pastor's greeting.

Hurrying up the stairs to the fourth-floor apartment, Gallagher saw Kelly reading a book. "Is it another book about Mrs. Jensen's husband that you're reading?"

"Aye." Kelly held up the book. "This one is called *Smoke Jensen and The Railroad Bandits*. He goes after ten railroad bandits all by his ownself, 'n he kills ever' one of 'em. It's a real excitin' story."

"Those are all made-up stories," Gallagher said.

"Aye, 'tis exactly what Mrs. Jensen said when I asked her about them. She said none of the books about her husband are true stories. But he must be like they say he is, or people wouldn't be for writin' books about him, would they?"

"Here now, Patrick Kelly, 'n 'tis beginnin' ter worry about you, I am. Would you be for tellin' me why 'tis so close to the women you are getting? The time may come when we'll have to take care of her. If you get too friendly with her, you may not be able to do what will need to be done."

"Take care of her?"

"Aye."

"What does that mean? Take care of her?"

"You know what it means."

"I thought you said Mrs. Jensen would no' be hurt."

"'Tis not my intention to do so. But if don't hear from Kennedy, and if we be cheated out o' the money, then we'll no be for keepin' 'er, 'n we won't be able to just let her go free now, will we?"

"Is it thinkin', you are, that we'll no' be getting the money?" Kelly asked.

"I don't know," Gallagher said. "I sent him a message, asking for the money, 'n I expect to be hearin' from him soon."

"What if he does send the money? What will we be doin' with the woman then? She'll still know who we are."

"Aye, 'tis a good point you have made. We'll see

what Kennedy has in mind, 'n if he has nothin' to tell us, we'll have no choice but to take care of the woman our ownselves."

"I would no' be for killin' her," Kelly said.

"Don't you be for gettin' sweet on her now," Gallagher warned. "You knew when you came in with us, that there would be times when we might have to do somethin' like that. It's all a part of the business."

Mule Gap

As soon as Smoke and Pearlie left the mayor's office, they were met by Marshal Bodine and his four remaining deputies. All five of them had their guns drawn.

"What is this?" Smoke asked.

"You are under arrest," Bodine said.

"For what?"

"For the murder of Mayor Kennedy," Bodine said.

"Well, now, that's interesting," Smoke said. "What makes you think Mayor Kennedy is dead?"

"Well, isn't he?"

"Yes, he is. But how do you know?"

"Soon, the whole town is going to know," Bodine said.

"I have no doubt but that they will," Smoke replied, "but don't you think there should be a motive?"

"Apparently, Mr. Jensen, you discovered that it was Kennedy who was behind the five-thousand-dollar reward."

"No, I didn't know that, but now that I think about it, it makes sense."

"Get their guns," Bodine ordered. "Get the guns from both of them."

"Am I under arrest, too?" Pearlie asked.

"No. But I have no intention of leaving you armed while I incarcerate your friend."

Within moments, the town learned that Mayor Kennedy had been killed, and that Smoke had been arrested for murder. Reaction was mixed. Some who didn't actually know Smoke were ready to accept that he was guilty, but many who did know Smoke were positive there must be some sort of explanation. Smoke would not have murdered Kennedy. If he did shoot him, there would have had to be a very good reason for it.

It was the telegrapher who supplied the reason when he personally visited the marshal. "I just received this telegram from New York, intended for the mayor. Apparently someone in New York is holding Mr. Jensen's wife as a prisoner and is doing so at the behest of the mayor."

"What are you talking about?" Bodine asked after he read the telegram. "There is nothing here that says Mrs. Jensen is a prisoner."

"I spoke with Mr. Jensen earlier, and I told him about a telegram that Mayor Kennedy had sent, arranging for Mrs. Jensen to be met by this man, Gallagher. Mr. Jensen was unaware of any such arrangement."

Bodine's smile was little more than a ribald smirk. "Well, now, perhaps this was merely the arrangement of a tryst. In that case, of course Jensen wouldn't know about it. Thank you, Mr. Cox, I had previously thought that Jensen killed the mayor because of his belief that the mayor had posted a reward to anyone who would kill Jensen. But now I believe you have just supplied the actual motive. It is obvious that Jensen killed the mayor in a moment of jealous rage."

"No, I don't believe that is it at all!" Cox said. "If you will but read the previous telegram, you will see that the mayor offered Gallagher money for meeting and hosting Mrs. Jensen. I believe the word *hosting* is a cover word for asking Gallagher to take her as his prisoner."

Bodine chuckled. "That's what you believe, is it? Tell me, Cox, do you actually think a court would listen to you stating something you *believe*?"

"Well, it isn't hard to figure out," Cox said.

"Thank you, Mr. Cox. If you don't mind, I'll keep this message. And if you would, bring the other one to me as well."

"I don't know whether or not that would be proper," Cox said. "Telegrams are protected by the government as privileged communication. You can't see them without proper authorization."

"With the mayor dead, I am now the highest authority," Bodine said. "And that is all the authorization I need now. Bring me the telegrams in question. That is, unless you want to wind up sharing a cell with Mr. Jensen."

"No, I'll . . . uh . . . bring you the telegrams."

That same afternoon, Bodine authorized the building of a gallows, right in the middle of First Street. A newly printed sign was placed on an easel next to the gallows under construction, explaining the purpose of the gallows.

ON THESE GALLOWS TOMORROW
SMOKE JENSEN
Will Be Hanged
for the MURDER *of*
Our Beloved Mayor
WARREN KENNEDY

"You can't hang a man without a trial!" Gil Rafferty said.

"Oh, there will be an adjudication," Bodine replied. "We will try him, find him guilty, and hang him at high noon tomorrow. And these two telegrams will be all the evidence we will need to make the case."

Smoke Jensen was already considered by many of the citizens to be a hero for his role in bringing the kidnapped children back to Mule Gap. News that he was to be hanged spread through the town like wildfire.

"How are they going to hold a trial without a judge?"

"Rufus Gordon is a judge."

"Gordon is a drunk. He hasn't heard a case in five years."

"He's still a judge, and Bodine plans to use him."

"Why, how can that be, in any way, a fair trial? Gordon will do anything Bodine asks of him, ever'body knows that."

Visiting with Sara Sue, Thad, and Sandra, Pearlie said, "I'm not going to let them hang Smoke."

"How are you going to stop it?" Sara Sue asked.

"I can testify in court that the gunshot came through the window. I know, because I was there. We left to go tell the marshal, but Bodine and all his deputies were standing right in front of the mayor's office when we stepped out into the street. He arrested Smoke for murder before either one of us could say a word."

"Wait a minute," Sara Sue said. "Are you telling me that he arrested Smoke for murder before you even told him that Kennedy was dead?"

"Yes, ma'am."

"How could he do that? What I mean is how did he even know Kennedy was dead?"

"Yes ma'am, that's what Smoke asked and . . . I'll be damned!" Pearlie said. "Bodine did it! He has to be the one who shot through the window. That's the only way he could have possibly known that Kennedy was dead. Uh, forgive me for the cussword, ma'am."

"No forgiveness is needed," Sara Sue said. "I think you are right. I believe Bodine is the one who killed Kennedy. Smoke is being falsely accused to protect Bodine."

There was a knock at the door and Pearlie waved Sara Sue and Thad to one side, then, drawing his gun, he jerked the door open.

"Oh!" the man in the hall said.

"You're the telegrapher, aren't you?"

"Yes, Lymon Cox," the man said.

"I'm sorry about this," Pearlie said, putting the gun away. "Do you have another telegram for us?"

"Yes, well, no. That is, not exactly. I've come to

show you a telegram I just received that was meant for Mayor Kennedy. I thought it might be of some interest to you." He handed it to Pearlie.

MRS JENSEN IS OUR GUEST AS
REQUESTED STOP WHEN WILL
MONEY BE SENT STOP GALLAGHER

"Look at this, Miz Condon," Pearlie said, showing the telegram to Sara Sue. "At least we know that Miz Sally is still alive."

"Oh, thank God for that. I hate that she is a prisoner, but I am very happy to hear that she is alive."

"Does Smoke know about this?" Pearlie asked.

"No, I showed the telegram to the marshal, but he took it from me. I didn't get a chance to talk to Mr. Jensen. They have him locked in the cell in the back of the building. There's a door between the front of the building and the cell, so I didn't even get to see him."

"Mrs. Condon?" a male voice called from the hall. "It's Richard Blackwell. May I come in?"

"That's Wee's pa," Thad said.

"Yes, please do," Sara Sue replied.

Blackwell nodded toward Cox.

"Don't mind me, Mr. Blackwell. I'm just on my way out," Cox said.

Blackwell waited until Cox was gone before he spoke. "If it's all right with you, Mrs. Condon, I would like to shut the door. What I have to say to you is for the ears of those in this room only."

"Yes, of course you can close the door."

Blackwell closed the door before speaking again. "I'm sure you know that Mr. Jensen's status now is quite precarious. It is my understanding that Bodine intends to hold a trial to be conducted by Judge Rufus Gordon. In addition, he will put only his deputies and others that they select on the jury."

"But the defense attorney will have voir dire, won't he?" Sara Sue asked.

"Have what?" Sandra asked.

"Before we got into the cattle business, my husband was an attorney," Sara Sue said. "Voir dire is used to determine if any juror is biased and cannot deal with the issues fairly or if there is cause not to allow a juror to serve because of possible bias."

"Believe me, Mrs. Condon, the defense attorney will also belong to Bodine," Blackwell said. "There is no way Smoke Jensen can win this trial. Why else do you think they have built the gallows?"

"I hope you didn't come to cheer us up," Pearlie said. "If you did, you sure aren't doing a very good job of it."

"Well, no, I don't suppose I am. However, I do have one thing that, if we are lucky, might work."

"What do you have?"

Blackwell held up a key as a big smile spread across his face. "I have a key to the cell."

"What? How did you get that?"

"As it so happens, sir, I own the jail."

"You own the jail?" Pearlie asked, surprised by the comment. "I've never heard of a private citizen owning a public building like a jail."

"Well, until Bodine was appointed, we didn't have

a city marshal, and thus, we had no reason to have a jail. Then we got a marshal, and I made one of my buildings that I had been using for storage available for the town to use as a jail. I hired a contractor to convert the building into a jail and leased it to the town. The contractor was working for me, so he made me a spare set of all the keys to the building, including to the cell, and gave the second set to Bodine. This is the key to the jail cell where they are keeping Mr. Jensen."

"All right!" Pearlie said, reaching happily for the key. "Now, all I've got to do is figure out how to use it."

"The best way would be to get the key to him," Sara Sue said. "But I don't know how we will be able to do it. You know he isn't going to let you see Smoke."

"I can get the key to him," Thad said. "I'm just a kid. The marshal would never suspect me of anything."

"Especially if I went with him," Lorena said.

"What would be your reason for going to see him?" Sara Sue asked.

"We're going to thank him for rescuing us," Lorena said.

"That won't work," Blackwell said. "The whole town now knows that it was Thad who managed to rescue you."

"All the more reason I think the marshal might be suspicious of you, Thad," Sara Sue said.

"That's why I should go as well," Lorena said. "He might suspect Thad if he is by himself, but not if I'm with him."

"Mrs. Condon, Mr. Blackwell, I think the girl is

right. I think the best chance Thad has of getting the key to Smoke would be if the girl is with him," Pearlie said.

"Pearlie, you do realize that you are putting my son's life in danger, don't you?" Sara Sue said.

"To say nothing of Lorena," Sandra added.

"Please, Ma, I want to do this," Thad said. "Isn't the whole reason Mr. Jensen is over here, and in trouble now, because of me?"

"Well, yes, but—"

"Please, Ma?"

"It will be all right, Mrs. Condon. I'll be with Thad, and Mr. Bodine would never suspect us if I'm with him," Lorena said.

"Lorena, your mother—"

"I trust Thad," Sandra said. "He got my daughter out of that awful place. I trust him to look after her now, as well."

"Ma?" Thad said again.

"All right, Thad, go ahead. God help me if anything goes wrong."

Thad's smile spread all across his face. "All right!" he said, reaching for the key. "Come on, Lorena. Let's do it!"

CHAPTER THIRTY-THREE

When Thad and Lorena passed by the gallows, it was nearly completed, and at least half a dozen people were standing around, staring at it.

"If you folks have enjoyed watchin' this thing bein' built, just wait till we actual use it." Boney Walls, one of the deputies, put his fist beside his neck, then, making a gagging sound, jerked his head to one side. "Sometimes their eyes bulge out so far they pop right out of their heads and roll around on the ground like little balls," he said with an insane laugh.

"Oh, Thad," Lorena said, grabbing Thad's arm. "That's awful!"

"It ain't true, neither," Thad said.

"Well, I tell you what, boy. Why don't you just bring your girlfriend by at noon tomorrow and see for yourself," the deputy challenged with another laugh.

As they walked away from the gallows and headed toward the jail, Lorena tightened her squeeze on Thad's arm. "He called me your girlfriend."

Thad smiled. "Well, I reckon that's true, isn't it?"

When they reached the jail, Thad opened the door for her as they went inside.

Bodine looked up from his desk. "What do you two want?"

"Please, Marshal, could we see Mr. Jensen?" Lorena asked.

"What? Why on earth would you two want to see that murderer?"

"He saved our lives," Thad said. "And if he is going to be hung, we'd like to tell him good-bye."

"Hanged," Bodine corrected. "He isn't going to be *hung*, he is going to be *hanged*."

"Then, please, let us talk to him this one last time," Lorena said.

"I've put out the order to my deputies not to let anyone see him," Bodine said.

"Yes, sir, and I can understand that," Thad said. "You are afraid that someone might try and help him escape or something. But you are the marshal, so you can do anything you want. You can let us see him, if you want."

Bodine drummed his fingers on the desk for a moment, then he nodded. "Very well. I'll let you see him. I can't imagine that a couple children could do anything to help him escape."

"Thank you, Marshal," Lorena said with a sweet smile.

Bodine opened the door to the back of the building then led them to the cell. Smoke was lying on the cot with his hands laced behind his head.

"Jensen, I have granted the request of these two urchins to visit you," Bodine said.

"Thad, Lorena, it's nice of you to come visit me."

"Marshal, would you please open the door so I can give Mr. Jensen a hug?" Lorena asked.

"Now, what kind of marshal would I be if I allowed a child in the cell with a murderer?"

"Alleged murderer," Thad replied. "In our system of justice, a person is innocent until proven guilty."

Bodine smiled and clapped his hands quietly. "Very good, young man. I'm impressed."

"My pa is a lawyer," Thad replied, "and if he hadn't been shot, he would be here to defend Mr. Jensen."

"Yes, too bad he isn't. However, the court will provide a lawyer for him."

"If we can't give Mr. Jensen a hug, can we at least shake hands with him?" Lorena asked.

"All right. I don't see why not. Jensen, don't try anything like grabbing one of these innocent children and holding them in some ploy to give you leverage over the situation, because it won't work."

During the exchange, Smoke had noticed that Thad had winked at him. He wasn't certain what the wink was about, but it did put him on the alert.

"Good-bye, Mr. Jensen," Lorena said, sticking her hand through the bars. "Thank you for coming to rescue us."

"And thank you for coming to visit me," Smoke said.

Thad was next. "Good-bye, Mr. Jensen. And thank you for giving me my horse, Fire."

As Smoke took Thad's hand, he felt the key. "You take good care of that horse, now."

"I will."

"Bodine, thank you for allowing them to visit," Smoke said. "I was wondering if you would allow my friend, Pearlie, to visit."

"I'm afraid not," Bodine replied. "I wouldn't put it

past the two of you to come with a bit of chicanery in an escape attempt. He can see you at your trial."

"We'll go now," Lorena said. "Thank you for letting us visit."

"I've got an idea, if you think the telegrapher will go along with it," Pearlie said.

"Mr. Cox is a good man." Blackwell had remained after Thad and Lorena left. "We have done a considerable amount of business together. I'm sure if your idea is feasible, he will be willing to do anything he can."

"Would you go see him with me?" Pearlie asked.

"Of course. I'd be glad to," Blackwell replied.

Just as Pearlie and Blackwell were about to leave Thad and Lorena returned. The smiles on their faces told of their success.

"Oh, I've been so worried about you two," Sandra said, greeting them.

"There was no problem," Thad said.

Pearlie smiled. "We don't have to worry about Smoke anymore. Now, let's take care of Miz Sally."

"How are you going to do that?" Sandra asked.

"By sending a telegram.

Cox smiled as he read the telegram. "Technically, this would be a violation, but under the circumstances, I think it is absolutely the right thing to do."

New York City

Gallagher smiled as he read the telegram. "Listen to this." He began to read the telegram aloud. "I am coming to New York with ten thousand dollars in cash. It is important that Mrs. Jensen be healthy and in good condition so that I may complete my business transaction. Wire me at Chicago Depot to tell me where we should meet. Kennedy."

"What do you think he means by business transaction?" Brockway asked.

"I think he has gone to see her husband and has made a deal to return her to him for cash," Gallagher said.

"Sure 'n it must be for a lot of money if he can bring ten thousand dollars in cash to us," Brockway said. "Just how rich is the man, Jensen, anyway?"

"I believe he is very rich," Kelly said. "It is said that he is one of the biggest ranchers in all of Colorado."

"That's what you've read in one of those books, have you?" Gallagher asked.

"Aye, but it must be true, I'm thinkin', or the books would have no' been wrote."

"Haven't you ever heard, *don't believe everything you read*?" Gallagher asked.

"He must be rich, or where is the money comin' from? 'Tis too bad O'Leary was killed before the job was done. He's missin' out on his share," Kelly said.

"Why is it too bad? If he was still here, our share would come only to twenty-five hundred dollars apiece. But without him, it's thirty-three hundred dollars apiece," Brockway added with a laugh.

"There will be no shares, for we'll not be dividin' the money up," Gallagher said.

"'N would you be for tellin' me why we're doin' this if not for the money?" Brockway asked.

"For to rebuild the Irish Assembly," Gallagher said.

"Do you think we could really do that? I mean, look what happened to us the last time."

"That was because Kennedy was in charge then. He won't be in charge this time."

"You'll be in charge?" Brockway asked.

"Aye, I'll be in charge. Tell me, Brockway, would that be a problem for you?"

"No, no, 'twould be no problem at all. Sure 'n you'd be a hell of a lot better 'n Kennedy ever was."

"Kennedy wants to know where we should meet. Are you going to bring him here?" Kelly asked.

"Aye, we'll bring him here."

"Ian, are you sure you want to bring him here?" Brockway asked.

"I don't see why not."

"It's just that I don't really trust him all that much. He's the one that led us into the fight with the Five Points gang, then he left, sort of abandoned us, you might say. 'Tis thinkin', I am, that we might want to arrange a meeting somewhere else."

"Aye, perhaps you're right." Gallagher smiled. "All right. We will meet him somewhere else, 'n I know just where it can be."

Mule Gap

Smoke stuck his hand through the bars, placed the key into the keyhole, and was rewarded with a satisfying *click* as he turned it. Going back to the bunk, he took the blankets and pillow from the other bunk in the cell and wadded them up in a way that a quick, casual glance would suggest that someone was in the bed. It would survive only the most casual glance, but that's all he would need.

"Hey!" he shouted from inside the cell so the location of his voice would not be suspicious. "Hey, Marshal, would you please come in here? I've got something to tell you!" Moving quickly, he stepped up to the room door and waited.

"What the hell do you want?" The gruff voice belonged to Boney Walls. He stepped into the cell area.

"I want out," Smoke said from behind Walls.

Walls turned, "Wha—" and was caught on the chin by a hard uppercut. The deputy went down and out.

Smoke dragged him into the cell, then shut the cell door and locked it.

With Boney Walls's pistol in hand, Smoke opened the door and looked into the outer office. No one was there, and seeing his own pistol belt hanging from a hook, he strapped it on, then stepped outside.

Bodine was standing at the foot of the scaffold with Lute Cruthis, Boots Zimmerman, and Angus Delmer. At least half a dozen others were standing nearby, one of whom, an older man, was dressed in a suit.

"I want the trial over quickly, Your Honor," Bodine was saying to the man in the suit. "I intend to hang him by noon tomorrow."

"How can you say you are going to hang him, sir, if you don't know the results of the trial?" the judge asked.

"That's a good question, Bodine. I'd like to know the answer to that myself," Smoke said.

"What the hell?" Bodine shouted, shocked to see that Smoke Jensen was not only out of jail, but armed.

"Answer the judge," Smoke said.

"Perhaps the hanging won't be necessary." A confident smile appeared as Bodine turned to face Smoke.

Realizing there was about to be a gunfight, the others moved quickly to get out of the way. Their move left Smoke standing alone, facing Cruthis, Zimmerman, and Delmer.

And of course, standing with the deputies, was The Professor himself, Frank Bodine. "It looks to me as if we may have just wasted time and money building the scaffold." His draw was considerably faster than most gunmen who had tried to kill Smoke. He was able to bring his gun up to level.

Smoke drew and fired before Bodine was able to pull the trigger. The bullet hit the marshal right in the center of his chest, and he went down.

Keeping his gun ready, Smoke hurried over to look down at him.

"I should have killed you the same time I killed Kennedy," Bodine gasped.

"Did you hear that, Judge?" one of the witnesses asked.

"I heard it," Judge Gordon said.

Zimmerman pulled his gun and pointed it at Smoke.

"Look out!" the same witness shouted.

Smoke fired, and the deputy went down with a bullet hole in his forehead.

"Don't shoot! Don't shoot!" Cruthis said, holding his hands in the air.

Delmer looked as if he might try Smoke, but when he saw Cruthis with his hands in the air, he raised his hands, as well. "I ain't drawin'," said in a desperate tone of voice. "I ain't a-goin' to draw on you."

"I would say that is a wise move," Smoke said.

The townspeople who had moved so quickly to get out of the way of the gunfight came drifting back. A few looked down with morbid curiosity at the two bodies, but many of the others, emboldened by what Smoke had just done, took some initiative and placed Cruthis and Delmer under a citizen's arrest. Within a matter of minutes they joined Boney Walls in jail.

Word of what had transpired spread quickly through the town, and Pearlie, Blackwell, and Rafferty joined Smoke and the judge in the front of the jail.

"I will admit, gentlemen, that I am an alcoholic," Judge Gordon said. "but I am not a crook. There is no way, except under threat of death, that without a fair trial, I would have found Mr. Jensen guilty."

"The point is, Judge, you *were* under threat of death," Blackwell said.

"Indeed, I believe that I may well have been," Judge Gordon replied.

"What are we going to do with these three prisoners?" Rafferty asked. "We have no law, we have no mayor, and we have no city administration at all."

"I will authorize their internment here until Sheriff Sinclair can send a few deputies down to escort them up to Rawlins for trial," Judge Gordon said. "A legitimate trial, I hasten to add."

As Smoke and Pearlie left the jail, they were met by the telegrapher.

"Apparently your idea is working," Cox said to Pearlie.

"What idea is that?" Smoke asked.

"I sent a telegram to Gallagher."

"A telegram?"

"Yes, sir," Cox said. "And I just got this one in return." He smiled. "It was sent to Mayor Kennedy, of course, since Gallagher believed the telegram he received had come from Kennedy." Cox showed Smoke the telegram he had just received.

MRS JENSENS HEALTH IS GOOD STOP
WE AWAIT YOUR VISIT AND THE
CONCLUSION OF OUR BUSINESS
STOP GALLAGHER

Smoke looked up from reading the telegram. "I have a couple telegrams I would like to send."

CHAPTER THIRTY-FOUR

The first telegram Smoke sent was to the railroad depot back in Big Rock, requesting that a private engine and car be made available to him, and that all track clearances be arranged from Big Rock to New York City. He emphasized in his telegram that it was imperative that he reach New York in the fastest time humanly possible.

Then he sent a telegram to Cal.

THE MAN BEHIND THE KIDNAPPING OF SALLY IS DEAD STOP HAVE GOOD REASON TO BELIEVE SHE WILL BE SAFE NEXT SEVERAL DAYS STOP DO NOTHING TO AGGRAVATE SITUATION UNTIL PEARLIE AND I ARRIVE STOP WILL WIRE YOU FROM CHICAGO STOP SMOKE

With that arranged, he returned to the hotel to meet with Sara Sue. Thad, Lorena, and Sandra were still in the room.

"Smoke, I have heard what has happened," Sara Sue said. "I'm so glad you are safe."

Smoke smiled at Thad and Lorena. "If it hadn't been for these two very brave young people, I would still be in jail and facing a very public hanging. Thad, I'd like to shake your hand again . . . this time without the key," he added with a chuckle.

Smiling broadly, Thad stuck his hand out to take Smoke's.

"Lorena, you asked to give me a hug, back in the jail. Does that offer still go?"

"Yes, sir," Lorena said, moving to him to give and accept an embrace.

"Sara Sue, Mrs. Coy . . ."

"Sandra," she corrected quickly.

"Sandra," Smoke said. "I hope you two ladies are aware of what fine children—no, not children—young man and young lady you have."

"We know," Sara Sue said, putting her arm around Thad. "Oh, I got a telegram from Sam while you were in . . . uh, while you were detained," Sara Sue said. "He is aware now that Thad is safe, and he also says that he is feeling well and is ready to get back to work."

"Good. I suggest that you withdraw your money from the bank now and pack your things. I've rented a private coach to take us back home."

"All right," Sara Sue replied. "By the way, Sandra and Lorena will be going back with us. I told Sandra that I was sure we could find a place for her to live and a good job."

"So I was told. The coach will easily take care of all of us."

"Mama, I want to tell Wee good-bye," Lorena said.

"I do too," Thad added.

The first person Lorena went to was Mrs. Blackwell.

"Hello, dear," Millicent said. "I want to thank you for how well you looked out for Wee when you were all in that awful place."

"Yes, ma'am, but the truth is, all of us looked out for each other. Even Wee had a job to do, and he did it well."

"I must say, he came back home no worse for wear. I was so frightened that he would be traumatized by it, but he seems just fine."

"Mrs. Blackwell, I've come to tell Wee good-bye."

"Yes, I thought as much. Your mother talked to Richard about it. We will certainly miss you, but not as much as Wee. Why don't you go see him?"

Wee was in the back of the Blackwell Emporium, sitting on the floor playing the game of pickup sticks. "Lorena, watch me get that one." He pointed to a yellow stick lying across two other sticks.

"Oh, that one will be hard."

"Not for me." With much concentration and his tongue sticking out of his mouth, Wee was able to press down on the back end of the stick and swing it around clear of the others without moving them.

"Oh, wonderful!" Lorena said, clapping her hands.

"You're going away, aren't you?" Wee said.

"Yes, honey, I am."

"Mama told me."

"I'm really going to miss you."

"Lorena, you know how I always told you that I was a big boy, and didn't want you to be hugging me?"

"Yes."

Wee stood up. "You can hug me now."

Lorena didn't do a very good job of hiding her tears as she and Thad walked back to the hotel. Thad reached out to take her hand in his.

Because there were six of them going back to Big Rock, Smoke hired a Concord coach and driver from the Northwest Stagecoach Company. Seven hours after they left Mule Gap, they stopped by Wiregrass Ranch to let Sara Sue and the others off. Sam came out to meet the coach, looking much better than he had the last time Smoke had seen him.

After a joyous embrace of his wife and son, he turned to his friend. "Smoke, there's no way I can ever thank you for rescuing my son."

"No need to thank me," Smoke said. "He did it himself."

"He rescued all of us," Lorena said proudly.

"You were kidnapped as well?"

"Yes, sir."

Sara Sue introduced Sandra and Lorena to Sam. "They will be staying with us until they can get re-settled."

"Wonderful," Sam replied. "I look forward to their company.

"It's good to see you up and about, Sam, but now Pearlie and I must go," Smoke said.

"Must you leave so quickly?"

"He has to, Sam," Sara Sue said. "I'll tell you why."

With Sara Sue making his excuses for the quick turnaround, Smoke urged the driver to get them to Sugarloaf just long enough to get some fresh clothes, then on to the depot.

By the time Smoke and Pearlie reached the depot a Baldwin 4-4-2 engine, tender, private car, and caboose were sitting on a side track. Wisps of steam drifted away from the drive cylinders.

"We didn't know when you would get here, so we kept the steam up," Clyde Drake, the station manager said. "You're stocked up with food, and I've got three crews for you. That way there will be no need to stop and rest. As you pass each major point, the track will be cleared in front of you."

"What about the regular scheduled trains?" Smoke asked.

"Ha!" Drake said. "They're all excited about being part of this. Everyone wants to see just how fast this trip can actually be made."

"How fast can the trip be made?" Smoke asked.

"I see no reason why we can't get you there in three days," Drake replied with a broad proud smile.

"Then let's go," Smoke said.

The chief engineer was Cephus Prouty, but he told Smoke to call him Doodle.

"I'm Smoke. He's Pearlie."

"Well, Smoke and Pearlie, if you'll climb aboard, we'll get underway."

New York City

Ryan, Doolin, McDougal, Keagan, and Quinn were sitting with Gallagher at a table in the back of Paddy's Pub. Like Gallagher, Kelly, and Brockway, the five men had been part of the original Irish Assembly.

"So, 'tis wantin' to put the Assembly together again, are you?" Ryan asked Gallagher.

"Aye. 'N if you five join, there'll be eight of us. That'll be a start, 'n 'tis my thinkin' that within a year we'll be back as big as we were before."

"It'll take a bit o' money to get started again," Doolin said. "'N have you thought of that, Ian Gallagher?"

Gallagher smiled. "Aye, I've thought of it. 'N would ten thousand dollars be enough, do you think?"

"Ten thousand dollars? 'N would you be for tellin' me how 'tis you'll be comin' up with ten thousand dollars?" Ryan asked.

"Warren Kennedy will be bringin' the money," Keagen said.

"Kennedy, himself who got us into a battle with the Five Pointers? M' brother was killed in that battle. 'N yer for tellin' us that we'll be workin' with Kennedy again? Thank you, no, but I've no wish to be workin' with the likes o' him."

Gallagher laughed. "I'm sayin' Kennedy is bringin' ten thousand dollars so he can take a woman that we're holdin' for him back to Wyoming." He smiled. "Only what he don't know is, there ain't neither one of 'em that'll be goin' back. Once Kennedy sees the woman 'n gives me the money, I intend to take care of both of 'em."

"Blimey," Quinn said. "You have the woman that Muldoon has been lookin' for?"

"Aye, all safe 'n secure," Gallagher said.

"Ten thousand dollars?" Doolin asked.

"Aye."

"The Assembly could be back on its feet with that much money. You can count me in," Doolin said.

"Me too," Ryan said.

"I'm in," Quinn added.

Keagan and McDougal added their assent as well.

When Gallagher returned to the fourth-floor walk-up on Third Avenue, Brockway was in the living room, and Kelly was in the small kitchen, cooking ham and potatoes.

"Did you meet with any o' the old lads?" Brockway asked.

"Aye. Ryan, Quinn, Doolin', McDougal 'n Keagan. They're in," Gallagher said. "They'll be with us when we meet Kennedy."

"Where are we goin' to meet him?" Kelly asked.

"I have the perfect place picked out," Gallagher replied.

Chicago

It was nine o'clock in the evening, thirty-two hours after leaving Big Rock, when the train rolled into Chicago's Central Depot in the middle of the city. Smoke had already been informed that it would take a couple hours to secure track clearance from

Chicago to Cleveland, so he and Pearlie left the small train, which had been pulled onto a side track.

They accompanied Doodle to the Western Union office, Doodle to arrange for track clearance, and Smoke to send a message on to Cal.

"Are you here to tell me that you left Denver yesterday?" asked the telegrapher.

"Yes, sir, one o'clock yesterday afternoon," Doodle said. "Why, there were times when we were runnin' at sixty miles to the hour."

As Doodle continued arranging for track clearance, Smoke checked to see if there was a telegram for Warren Kennedy.

"Kennedy? I thought your name was Jensen," the telegrapher replied in surprise.

"I am Kennedy," Pearlie said quickly.

"Oh. Well, yes, sir, Mr. Kennedy, we've been holding it for you," the telegrapher said. He located the telegram and handed it to Pearlie.

MEET AT ABANDONED COTTAGES
BETWEEN 10TH AND 11TH AVENUES
ON 52ND STREET STOP ADVISE WHEN
YOU WILL BE THERE STOP HAVE MONEY
WITH YOU STOP

"Doodle, when do you think we'll reach New York?" Smoke asked after he read the telegram over Pearlie's shoulder.

"We'll be there by ten o'clock tomorrow morning," Doodle promised.

Unseen by the telegrapher, Smoke penned a

telegram to Gallagher and handed it to Pearlie. He in turn took it to the telegrapher to send.

HAVE MRS JENSEN READY FOR TRAVEL AT NOON TUESDAY STOP I HAVE MONEY IN HAND STOP KENNEDY

Smoke then sent a telegram to Cal.

WILL BE AT GRAND CENTRAL DEPOT BY TEN OCLOCK TUESDAY STOP SMOKE

CHAPTER THIRTY-FIVE

New York City

Sally was aware that some other men had joined Gallagher, Brockway, and Kelly. She had not yet seen any of the new men, but she had heard enough additional voices to imagine that the small living room must be quite crowded. This morning, the voices were much more animated. As she listened to determine if she could learn anything from the conversation, her mind whirled.

"Today at noon," Gallagher said.

"And are you sure he'll be there?" Brockway asked.

"Aye, the telegram came last night," Gallagher said.

"Does he have the money?"

That was not a familiar voice, so Sally realized the question had come from one of the men she had not yet met or even seen. *They are talking about money. Are they talking about Smoke? Has he come to New York to pay the ransom?*

"Kennedy will have the money," Gallagher said. "For he knows what will happen to him if he doesn't."

"Aye," one of the men replied. "But does he know what will happen to him even if he *does* have the money?"

A great deal of laughter followed that comment.

"Will you be meeting him by yourself?" Kelly asked.

"No. For one thing, I think 'tis good that we all go so that Kennedy can't be for pulling any tricks on us. 'N for another, ''is to show each of you that I'll not be for holding out on any of the money."

They're talking about Kennedy. Would that Kennedy be Smoke's friend from Mule Gap? Sally wondered. *Why would Smoke be sending Kennedy with the money, instead of bringing it himself?*

"Ha! 'Tis betting I am, that when Kennedy asked us to snatch the woman, he had no idea we would be usin' the money to get the Irish Assembly goin' again," Kelly said.

"Aye, especially since the son of a bitch is the one to cause it to be destroyed in the first place," Gallagher said.

Kennedy is the one who arranged for me to be kidnapped? Yes, it would have to be him, Sally realized.

Kelly had told her that it was someone in Wyoming. She scolded herself for not realizing that earlier. After all, who else in Wyoming would not only know who she was, but also have a New York connection?

"Are we goin' to turn the woman over to him?" Again, the voice was from one of the men she had not yet seen.

"Oh, yeah, we'll turn her over to him, all right," Gallagher said.

"If he takes her back, and she goes back to her

husband, what's to say *he* won't come after us?" Kelly asked.

"What do you mean, 'come after us'?" another of the new voices asked.

Gallagher laughed. "Don't be for paying Kelly any mind. He's been reading dime novels about the woman's husband 'n what a hero he is."

"But 'tis like I said, they would not be writing books about him if he wasn't like they say he is. Why, he once took on a whole gang of train robbers all by himself," Kelly insisted.

"Even if he is the hero you think he is, how is it he'll be comin' for us? He has no idea where we are or even *who* we are," Gallagher said.

"I know Mrs. Jensen," Kelly said. "Do you think she won't be for tellin' him who we are and where we are?"

"How is she going to do that?" Gallagher asked.

"What do you mean?"

"Think about it, Kelly. If we aren't goin' to let Kennedy go back, how is the Jensen woman goin' to go back?"

"Well if she doesn't go back, what will we do with her?"

"What do you think we'll do with her?"

"Wait a minute. You told me the woman wouldn't be harmed."

Brockway laughed. "Do you know what I'm thinkin', Gallagher? I'm thinkin' Kelly has fallen for the Jensen woman. Tell us, Kelly, when you 'n the woman has been alone, have you been climbin' inter bed with 'er?"

"No, nothin' like that," Kelly replied resolutely. "I was just commentin' is all."

"Don't comment. Just listen," Gallagher said.

Although the special train had been granted clearance to come into Grand Central Terminal, the track that had been allocated was the most distant from the depot. As soon as the train stopped, Smoke and Pearlie stepped out of the private car, and Smoke walked up to the engine. Even at rest, it was alive with the sound of boiling water and vented steam.

Doodle was looking out of the cab window. "Sorry we're so far away, but this is the track they gave us," he called down.

"After being cooped up for so long, the walk will do us good," Smoke replied. "I want to express my thanks to you and the entire crew for getting us to New York so fast."

"It was a pleasure," Doodle said, smiling broadly. "For the entire time I've been an engineer, I've always wanted to open 'er up 'n see just how fast I could go. Why, for a little stretch there, we were running almost seventy miles to the hour. I'm the one who should be thankin' you for the opportunity."

Smoke smiled back at him, and with a final wave he and Pearlie started the long walk past all the other trains to the terminal. Once outside, they took a cab to the Fifth Avenue Hotel.

When they reached the hotel, Smoke started toward the front desk with the intention of getting Cal's room number, but even before he reached the desk, he heard a familiar voice call out to him.

"Smoke!"

He turned to see Cal coming across the lobby toward him.

While the meeting between the two men would normally elicit a smile, the expression on Cal's face was one of worry and shame. He reached out to take Smoke's extended hand. "I'm sorry, Smoke. I was supposed to look after her and I failed. To be honest, I wasn't even sure you would be willing to shake my hand."

"Nonsense," Smoke said. "It happened. Now, we're going to get her back."

Cal shook hands with Pearlie then turned and motioned toward a uniformed police officer who was standing some distance back. "Mickey, come up here. I want you to meet my two best friends in the whole world. Smoke, Pearlie, this is Officer Mickey Muldoon. We've been working together. We were on his beat when Miz Sally was taken."

Cal explained how it happened.

"Officer Muldoon," Smoke started, but he was interrupted.

"Sure now, the lad, Cal 'n I are usin' first names between us, 'n seein' as the two of you be his best friends, I'd like it if you'd be for callin' me Mickey."

"All right, Mickey. If this is your beat, I'm sure you're very familiar with it. The man who set up the kidnapping was someone I had considered to be a friend. His name was Warren Kennedy. He was from New York and—"

"Warren Kennedy is it?" Mickey said, interrupting. "I know the man. He was leader of a gang that called themselves the Irish Assembly, 'n 'twas an evil man he was, too."

"I found that out," Smoke said. "I'm ashamed to say, though, that he had me fooled for a long time."

"No shame to it, m' lad. 'Tis many a man Kennedy 'n his slick tongue had fooled."

"Apparently the man he was working with here in New York is named Gallagher," Smoke said. "Is that a name you can associate with Kennedy?"

"Aye, that would be Ian Gallagher. Some would say that the Irish Assembly is no more, 'n 'tis true, they are no longer the gang they once were. But there are still enough of them around to cause trouble, 'n Gallagher is one of them."

"Mickey, didn't you say that O'Leary was part of the Irish Assembly?" Cal asked.

"Aye, lad, that I did, 'n I was thinkin' there might be some connection. 'Tis glad I am that you brought me a name," Mickey said. "I think we can find him, 'n maybe get an idea as to where yer lady might be."

"No need to go looking for him," Smoke replied.

"What do you mean, we don't need to look for him?" Cal asked. "Have you got something else in mind?"

"If everything goes as we have it set up, he'll meet us at noon, and he'll have Sally with him."

"So, you'll be payin' the ransom, will you?" Mickey asked. "Well, I can't say as I'll be blamin' you. I would probably do the same thing if 'twas my loved one."

Smoke shook his head. "I'll not be paying the ransom."

"Askin' too much, is he?"

"Mickey, I just spent fifteen thousand dollars to rent a train to bring Pearlie and me here in record time.

There's no such thing as *too much* money as far as my wife is concerned. I don't trust him to turn her over to me, even if I have the money in hand, so I have something else in mind. That's why I sent a telegram, asking him to meet us."

"And he agreed?" Cal asked.

"Yes. Apparently there are some abandoned cottages on 52nd Avenue between 10th and 11th Streets. Do you know the address, Mickey?"

"Aye . . . there is a whole row of deserted houses there, 'n 'tis a place frequented by brigands 'n hoodlums. 'Tis not a place for a decent citizen to be."

"I thought it might be something like that."

"Do you think, maybe, Gallagher might suspect Kennedy has something set up for him?" Pearlie asked.

"That could be the case," Smoke said. "Or, perhaps Mr. Gallagher has something planned for the late Mayor Kennedy."

Back at the apartment where Sally was being held, Kelly stepped into her bedroom then held his finger across his lips, signaling her to be quiet.

"Ever'one but Gallagher has gone to meet Kennedy," Kelly said. "Gallagher is downstairs 'n he sent me to bring you down. But if you do just what I tell you to do, I'm goin' to help you escape."

"Thank you, Mr. Kelly. That is a courageous thing for you to do."

Kelly opened the door and looked outside, then he turned back to her. "There is a fire escape on the back side of the buildin' that goes down to the alley. Once we get into the alley, follow me."

Sally nodded, and Kelly held his hand out toward her, holding her back as he made one final check.

"All right. There's nobody here. Let's go," Kelly said.

The two moved quickly through the living room and into the small kitchen. He lifted the window, then stepped through it onto the fire escape deck. He turned back toward Sally. "Come on," he beckoned.

She climbed through the window, as well, then followed him down the ladder. Kelly reached the ground first, and he stepped back to wait for Sally.

"Which way now?" she asked.

"Why don't you come this way?" Gallagher stepped out from behind a large trash bin, holding a pistol.

"Gallagher!" Kelly gasped.

"I knew you couldn't be trusted," Gallagher said. The sound of the gunshot was loud in the close confines of the alley.

"Mr. Kelly!" Sally called out in despair as she saw her would-be rescuer go down with a hole in his chest. He was dead within two more gasping breaths. "You killed him."

"That I did, lass, that I did. Now, would you please be for putting these on?" Gallagher tossed her a pair of manacles.

CHAPTER THIRTY-SIX

With Mickey Muldoon leading the way, Smoke, Pearlie, and Cal rode the trolley car to within one block of where they were to meet with Gallagher. They stepped down from the car at about ten minutes to twelve.

"There you be, lads," Mickey said, pointing. "It's but one block that way, 'n we can't be for missing it. 'Tis one long building, all joined together. Two stories, they are, 'n mostly boarded up."

"You don't think Gallagher will be alone, do you, Smoke?" Muldoon asked.

"No, I don't. If he intended to meet us alone, he wouldn't have chosen the site of abandoned and boarded-up cottages."

"'Twould be my guess that he 'n whoever he has with him are already there," Muldoon said. "Come, we'll see what this is all about."

"Thanks, Mickey," Smoke said, "but this is as far as you go. We'll take it from here."

"But you will be for needin' me, seein' as I'm the only policeman."

"You would like to remain a member of the New York Police Department, wouldn't you?" Smoke asked.

"Aye, 'tis all I've ever known."

"Then trust me. You don't want to be with us."

"'N how, may I ask, will it be legal for you to arrest Gallagher and those who are with him?"

"I don't intend to arrest them," Smoke said.

"Then how will you—" Mickey started to ask, then he realized what Smoke was saying.

"Mickey, it's been good working with you," Cal said, putting his hand on the policeman's shoulder. "But you want no part of this. I'd advise you to take the next trolley out of here."

Mickey nodded, then he took Cal's hand. "Take care, m' friend. If Gallagher truly shows up, 'tis for sure 'n certain he won't be alone."

"Here comes another trolley," Pearlie said.

Cal stood with Smoke and Pearlie as Officer Mickey Muldoon, his new friend, stepped onto the car, then waved back at him as the driver snapped the reins at the horses.

"He's a good man," Cal said as the trolley moved quickly down the track.

"I've no doubt, otherwise you wouldn't have befriended him," Smoke said. "All right. What do you say we go get Sally back?"

At that very moment, less than one-quarter mile away were Gallagher and the six men who had come with him. His force had been decreased by one when he left Kelly in the alley behind his Third Street apartment.

"Brockway, you go up to the second floor of this apartment," Gallagher said, pointing to the one they were standing before. As he assigned each man, he pointed to three other apartments. "Doolin, you take that one, Quinn, that one, 'n Ryan, that one be yours." He also positioned McDougal and Keagan, leaving the bottom floor of the middle townhouse for himself.

"Why we doin' all this for one man?" Brockway asked.

"Sure now, Brockway, 'n you know Kennedy as well as any of us. Are you for thinkin' that he'll come here alone? He'll have some men with 'im, 'n it'll be his thought to kill us 'n take the woman back without payin' for her. He's not like us. He's not an honest man that can be trusted."

Despite the peril of her situation, at Gallagher's suggestion that Kennedy wasn't an honest man the way they were, Sally couldn't help but laugh out loud.

"'N would you be for tellin' me why 'tis you're laughin'?" Gallagher asked in a gruff voice.

"Never mind. I don't think you would understand," Sally said.

As the others took their positions, Gallagher kept Sally, who still had her hands manacled, close enough to him so he could keep an eye on her, or so he told the others. In truth, she was acting as his shield. If Kennedy really did want her alive, he would be careful where he shot for fear of hitting Sally.

With everyone in position, Gallagher stood with gun in hand, waiting for Kennedy to show.

"Hey, Gallagher," Brockway called down. "They's three men comin' this way from Tenth Street."

"What did I tell you? I tol' you he wouldn't be alone."

"That ain't Kennedy," Doolin called. "I don't know who they are."

"Look at that feller on the left," Brockway said. "He's the man that was with the woman the night we took 'er. He's also the one that kilt O'Leary, but I don't know who the other two are. They're not cops, I can tell you that. All three of 'em is dressed just alike 'im, 'n all of 'em is wearin' pistol belts."

"Smoke!" Sally said the name involuntarily, her excitement overcoming caution.

"Son of a bitch. I should have known Kennedy would be for tryin' somethin' like this," Gallagher said angrily. "Brockway, you 'n the others hold your fire 'till they get real close. When you're sure you can't miss, start shootin'."

Sally moved into position so she could see through the window and that it was Smoke, Pearlie, and Cal approaching. How many times since she had married Smoke had she seen this very thing—Smoke, Pearlie, and Cal facing death together? Even though she knew that their situation and hers was precarious, she couldn't help but feel confident that rescue was at hand.

She waited until just before she thought that Brockway and the others would start shooting, then she yelled. "Smoke, look out! It's a trap!"

That forced the issue, and though the three approaching men were not yet within a very easy, can't-miss range, Gallagher's men had no alternative but to start shooting. They were hampered by the fact that none of the three approaching men were close enough for a sure shot, and also because the warning had caused the three men to split apart so that none offered an easy target.

Pearlie was able to take cover behind one of the denuded and dead trees that grew in the front of the buildings, while Cal hurried to a rock pillar that anchored one end of the rusting, iron stake fence. Smoke stood in place, gun in hand, looking at the building waiting for the first shot.

The first shot came from a second-story window right in the middle of the row of connected buildings. He returned fire and saw a man tumble from the window. He didn't move when he hit the ground.

Firing broke out in general then, with several shots coming from various positions within the old abandoned buildings. The firing was answered, shot for shot, as Pearlie and Cal were well positioned.

The only one still exposed, Smoke was anything but an easy target. He moved around, snapping shots back at the wisps of gun smoke that drifted from the windows. He saw a shooter appear in one of the windows, preparatory to taking a shot. Before the shooter could get off a round, Smoke fired, saw a little mist of blood fly from the shooter's head, and knew he had made a killing shot.

At almost the same time, Pearlie killed one, and Cal another. Smoke had no idea how many they were against, but while the shooting continued, the intensity of the shooting diminished as each of the ambushers were killed until finally, the shooting stopped.

"Brockway?" a voice called. "Ryan? Doolin, McDougal, Keagan, Quinn?"

There were no answers to the call.

Since *Gallagher* had not been one of the names shouted out, Smoke realized the caller was Gallagher and shouted, "They're all dead, Gallagher. You're all alone."

"Where is Kennedy?" Gallagher shouted back from the middle apartment.

Smoke knew it was the same apartment from which Sally had called her warning. For that reason, not one of them shot through that window. "Sally?" Smoke called.

"I'm all right, Smoke," Sally answered.

"Where is Kennedy?" Gallagher asked again.

"Kennedy is dead."

"Are you the one who killed him?"

"No. I planned to, but someone else killed him first. Send my wife out."

Although Smoke had not really expected any response to his demand, the door opened, and he saw Sally standing there. "Sally, can you come toward me?"

"No."

Almost as soon as she responded, Sally did start toward him, but it was easy to see that she wasn't moving of her own volition.

Bent over behind her in such a way, Gallagher offered nothing as a target. "I have a gun pressed up against your wife's back. Put the ten thousand dollars down in front of you, then all three of you drop your guns and walk away. If you don't do that, I'll kill the woman."

"Then what?" Smoke asked.

"What do you mean, 'then what?' If I kill her, she'll be dead."

"So will you," Smoke said.

"'N are you for tellin' me, that you'd be for riskin' yer own wife's life?" Gallagher asked.

"I can get another wife. You can't get another life."

Sally laughed. "Smoke, I can't believe you would say something like that."

"You could always bow to my brilliance," Smoke said.

"I guess I could, couldn't I? Here's to you, oh brilliant one," Sally replied. Then, not in any sudden move as if trying to escape, but even as she was still laughing, she made a deep bow.

Sally's unexpected move caught Gallagher completely by surprise, but he wasn't surprised long. A bullet from Smoke's gun hit him right between the eyes.

Sugarloaf Ranch

Smoke was standing on the ground in front of a magnificent black horse with a white face and three white stockings. This was the son of the Seven who had been killed. Technically, his name was *Seven Number Four*, but Smoke called him, as he had those before him, just *Seven*.

"Where is the sugar, Seven?" he asked.

Seven put his nose first to one shirt pocket then the other, then lifting his nose, he pushed Smoke's hat back. Smoke took off his hat and removed the lump of sugar he had concealed there.

"Ha!" Thad grinned from atop his horse. "You can't fool Seven. He's almost as smart as Fire."

"Almost, huh?" Smoke replied.

"But you can't blame Seven. He's still learning."

"Fire might be smart, but he isn't as handsome as Sir Charles." Lorena leaned forward in the saddle and patted her horse on its neck.

"I can't believe you named your horse Sir Charles," Thad teased. "He's probably so embarrassed by his name that it's a wonder he can even move."

"Really? Catch me." With a quick slap of her legs against the sides of Sir Charles, the horse burst forth like a cannonball.

Thad dashed out after them, his and Lorena's laughter filling the air.

"Cute kids," Sally said as she, Smoke, Pearlie, and Cal watched the two riders grow smaller in the distance.

"I wonder if they'll remember this when they are both in their seventies?" Cal asked.

"Why not?" Smoke replied. "They'll be able to remind each other."

Keep reading for special preview of . . .

The First Mountain Man
PREACHER'S KILL

A fur trapper by trade, Preacher can smell a bad deal from any direction no matter how well it's disguised. It wasn't always that way—he's got the scars to prove it. Now he's ready to pass on his deadly survival skills to a boy named Hawk who just might be his son . . .

Preacher and Hawk ride out of the Rockies and into St. Louis loaded with furs. It's Hawk's first trip to civilization, and the moment he lays eyes on young Chessie Dayton he's lost in more ways than one. When Chessie unwisely signs on for a gold-hungry expedition into the lawless mountains, Hawk convinces Preacher to trail the outfit, because they're all headed straight to the sacred Indian grounds known as the Black Hills—a land of no return. To come out of it alive a lot of people will have to die. And Preacher's going to need a heap of bullets for this journey into hell . . .

**Coming this January,
wherever Pinnacle Books are sold!**

CHAPTER ONE

A rifle ball hummed past Preacher's head, missing him by a foot. At the same time he heard the boom of the shot from the top of a wooded hill fifty yards away. He kicked his feet free of the stirrups and dived out of the saddle.

Even before he hit the ground, he yelled to Hawk, "Get down!"

His half-Absaroka son had the same sort of hair-trigger, lightning-fast reflexes Preacher did. He leaped from his pony and landed beside the trail just a split second after the mountain man did. A second shot from the hilltop kicked up dust at Hawk's side as he rolled.

Preacher had already come up on one knee. His long-barreled flintlock rifle was in his hand when he launched off the rangy gray stallion's back. Now, as he spotted a spurt of powder smoke at the top of the hill where the ambushers lurked, he brought the rifle to his shoulder in one smooth motion, earing back the hammer as he did so.

The weapon kicked hard against his shoulder as he fired.

Instinctively, he had aimed just above the gush of dark gray smoke. Without waiting to see the result of his shot, he powered to his feet and raced toward a shallow gully ten yards away. It wouldn't offer much protection, but it was better than nothing.

As he ran, he felt as much as heard another rifle ball pass close to his ear. Those fellas up there on the hill weren't bad shots.

But anybody who had in mind ambushing him had ought to be a damned *good* shot, because trying to kill Preacher but leaving him alive was a hell of a bad mistake.

Before this ruckus was over, he intended to show those varmints just how bad a mistake it was.

From the corner of his eye, he saw Hawk sprinting into a clump of scrubby trees. That was the closest cover to the youngster. Hawk had his rifle, too, and as Preacher dived into the gully, he wasn't surprised to hear the long gun roar.

He rolled onto his side so he could get to his shot pouch and powder horn. Reloading wasn't easy without exposing himself to more gunfire from the hilltop, but this wasn't the first tight spot Preacher had been in.

When he had the flintlock loaded, primed, and ready to go, he wriggled like a snake to his left. The gully ran for twenty yards in that direction before it petered out. Preacher didn't want to stick his head up in the same place where he had gone to ground. He wanted the ambushers to have to watch for him.

That way, maybe they'd be looking somewhere else when he made his next move.

No more shots rang out while Preacher was crawling along the shallow depression in the earth. He didn't believe for a second that the men on the hill had given up, though. They were just waiting for him to show himself.

Over in the trees, Hawk fired again. A rifle blast answered him. Preacher took that as a good time to make his play. He lifted himself onto his knees and spotted a flicker of movement in the trees atop the hill. More than likely, somebody up there was trying to reload.

Preacher put a stop to that by drilling the son of a buck. A rifle flew in the air and a man rolled out of the trees, thrashing and kicking. That commotion lasted only a couple of seconds before he went still . . . the stillness of death.

That luckless fella wasn't the only one. Preacher saw a motionless leg sticking out from some brush. That was the area where he had placed his first shot, he recalled. From the looks of that leg, he had scored with that one, too.

Were there any more would-be killers up there? No one shot at Preacher as he ducked down again. The mountain man reloaded once more, then called to Hawk, "You see any more of 'em movin' around up there, boy?"

"No," Hawk replied. Preacher recalled too late that Hawk didn't much cotton to being called "boy." But he was near twenty years younger than Preacher and his son, to boot, so that was what he was going to be called from time to time.

"Well, lay low for a spell longer just in case they're playin' possum."

Now that Preacher had a chance to look around,

he saw that his horse, the latest in a series of similar animals he called only Horse, had trotted off down the trail with Hawk's mount and the pack mule they had loaded down with beaver pelts. The big wolf-like cur known as Dog was with them, standing guard, although that wasn't really necessary. If anybody other than Preacher or Hawk tried to corral him, Horse would kick them to pieces. But Horse and Dog were fast friends, and Dog wouldn't desert his trail partner unless ordered to do so.

That was what Preacher did now, whistling to get Dog's attention and then motioning for the cur to hunt. Dog took off like a gray streak, circling to get around behind the hill. He knew as well as Preacher did where the threat lay.

Preacher and Hawk stayed under cover for several minutes. Then Dog emerged from the trees on the hilltop and sat down with his pink tongue lolling out of his mouth. Preacher knew that meant no more danger lurked up there. He had bet his life on Dog's abilities too many times in the past to doubt them now.

"It's all right," he called to Hawk. "Let's go take a look at those skunks."

"Why?" Hawk asked as he stepped out of the trees. "They will not be anyone I know. I have never been in . . . what would you say? These parts? I have never been in these parts before."

"Well, they might be somebody *I* know," Preacher said. "I've made a few enemies in my time, you know."

Hawk snorted as if to say that was quite an understatement.

"What about the horses?" he asked.

"Horse ain't goin' anywhere without me and Dog, and that pony of yours will stay with him. So will the mule."

Taking his usual long-legged strides, Preacher started toward the hill.

As he walked, he looked around for any other signs of impending trouble. The landscape was wide open and apparently empty. Two hundred yards to the south, the Missouri River flowed eastward, flanked by plains and stretches of low, rolling hills. Preacher didn't see any birds or small animals moving around. The earlier gunfire had spooked them, and it would be a few more minutes before they resumed their normal routine. The animals were more wary than Preacher, probably because they didn't carry guns and couldn't fight back like the mountain man could.

"Since you ain't gonna recognize either of those carcasses, as you pointed out your own self, you keep an eye out while I check 'em."

Hawk responded with a curt nod. Preacher left him gazing around narrow-eyed and strode up the hill.

The man who had fallen down the slope and wound up in the open lay on his back. His left arm was flung straight out. His right was at his side, and the fingers of that hand were still dug into the dirt from the spasms that had shaken him as he died. He wore buckskin trousers, a rough homespun shirt, and high-topped moccasins. His hair was long and greasy, his lean cheeks and jaw covered with dark stubble. There were thousands of men on the frontier who didn't look significantly different.

What set him apart was the big, bloody hole in his

right side. Preacher could tell from the location of the wound that the ball had bored on into the man's lungs and torn them apart, so he had spent a few agonizing moments drowning in his own blood. Not as bad as being gutshot, but still a rough way to go.

Remembering how close a couple of those shots had come to his head, and how the ambushers had almost killed his son, too, Preacher wasn't inclined to feel much sympathy for the dead man. As far as he could recall, he had never seen the fellow before.

The one lying in the brush under the trees at the top of the hill was stockier and had a short, rust-colored beard. Preacher's swiftly fired shot had caught him just below that beard, shattering his breastbone and probably severing his spine, too. He was dead as could be, like his partner.

But unlike the other man, Preacher had a feeling he had seen this one before. He couldn't say where or when, nor could he put a name to the round face, but maybe it would come to him later. St. Louis was a big town, one of the biggest Preacher had ever seen, and he had been there plenty of times over the years. Chances were he had run into Redbeard there.

Now that he had confirmed the two men were dead and no longer a threat, he looked around to see if they'd had any companions. His keen eyes picked up footprints left by both men, but no others. Preacher crossed the hilltop and found two horses tied to saplings on the opposite slope. He pulled the reins loose and led the animals back over the crest. Hawk stood at the bottom of the hill, peering around alertly.

Preacher took a good look at his son as he approached the young man. Hawk That Soars. That was what his mother had named him. She was called Bird in a Tree, a beautiful young Absaroka woman Preacher had spent a winter with, two decades earlier. Hawk was the result of the time Preacher and Birdie had shared, and even though Preacher had been un-aware of the boy's existence until recently, he felt a surge of pride when he regarded his offspring.

With Preacher's own dark coloring, he hadn't passed along much to Hawk to signify that he was half-white. Most folks would take the young man for pure-blood Absaroka. He was a little taller than most warriors from that tribe, a little more leanly built. His long hair was the same raven black as his mother's had been.

One thing he *had* inherited from Preacher was fighting ability. They made a formidable pair. Months earlier, to avenge a massacre that had left Hawk and the old man called White Buffalo the only survivors from their band, father and son had gone to war against the Blackfeet—and the killing hadn't stopped until nearly all the warriors in that particular bunch were dead.

Since then, they had been trapping beaver with White Buffalo and a pair of novice frontiersmen, Charlie Todd and Aaron Buckley, they had met during the clash with the Blackfeet. During that time, Todd and Buckley had acquired the seasoning they needed to be able to survive on their own, and they had de-cided to stay in the mountains instead of returning to St. Louis with the load of pelts. Preacher, Hawk, and White Buffalo would take the furs back to sell. Todd and Buckley had shares coming from that sale, and

Preacher would see to it that they got them when he and Hawk made it back to the Rocky Mountains.

White Buffalo had surprised them by choosing to remain with a band of Crow they had befriended while they were trapping. Cousins to the Absaroka, the Crow had always gotten along well with Preacher and most white men. They had welcomed Preacher, Hawk, and White Buffalo to their village . . . and White Buffalo had felt so welcome he had married a young widow.

Preacher had warned the old-timer that the difference in age between him and his wife might cause trouble in the sleeping robes, but White Buffalo had informed him haughtily, "If she dies from exhaustion, I will find another widow to marry."

You couldn't argue with a fella like that. Preacher and Hawk had agreed to pick him up on their way back to the mountains, if he was still alive and kicking, and if he wanted to go.

That left just the two of them to transport the pelts downriver to St. Louis. Preacher figured they were now within two days' travel of that city on the big river, and so far they hadn't had any trouble.

Until today.

Hawk heard him coming and turned to watch him descend the rest of the way.

"Two men," Hawk said as he looked at the horses Preacher led. "Both dead."

"Yep."

"Old enemies of yours?"

Preacher shook his head. "Nope. One of them sort of looked familiar, like maybe I'd seen him in a tavern in the past year or two, but the other fella I didn't know from Adam."

"Then why did they try to kill us?"

Preacher pointed at the heavily laden pack mule standing with Horse and Hawk's pony and said, "Those pelts will fetch a nice price. Some men ask themselves why should they go all that way to the mountains, endure the hardships, and risk life and limb when they can wait around here and jump the fellas on their way back to St. Louis. I can't get my brain to come around to that way of thinkin'—if you want something, it's best just to go ahead and work for it, I say—but there are plenty of folks who feel different."

Hawk grunted. "Thieves. Lower than carrion."

"Well, that's all they're good for now."

Hawk nodded toward the horses and asked, "What are you going to do with them?"

"Take them with us, I reckon. We can sell them in St. Louis."

"If those men have friends, they may recognize the animals and guess that we killed the men who rode them."

Preacher blew out a contemptuous breath. "Anybody who'd be friends with the likes of those ambushers don't worry me overmuch."

"And what about the dead men themselves?"

"Buzzards got to eat, too," Preacher said, "and so do the worms."

CHAPTER TWO

Preacher's estimate was correct. Two more days on the trail found them approaching St. Louis. Above the point where the Missouri River flowed into the Mississippi, he and Hawk crossed the Big Muddy on a ferry run by a Frenchman named Louinet, a descendant of one of the trappers who had first come down the Father of Waters from Canada to this region a hundred years earlier.

Preacher saw the wiry, balding man eyeing the two extra horses and said, "Found these animals runnin' loose a couple days ago, back upstream. You have any idea who they might belong to?"

Louinet shook his head. "*Non.* Since you found them, I assume they are now yours."

"Reckon so. I just figured I'd get 'em back to whoever rightfully owned 'em, if I could."

"If those animals were running loose with saddles on them, then the men who rode them almost certainly have no further need for them."

"You're probably right about that," Preacher said with a grim smile.

He wasn't worried about who the two ambushers had been, but if Louinet had been able to give him some names, it might have helped him watch out for any friends or relatives of the dead men. But if they came after him and Hawk, so be it. They had only defended themselves and hadn't done anything wrong. Preacher was the sort who dealt with problems when they arose and didn't waste a second of time fretting about the future. It had a habit of taking care of itself.

That attitude was entirely different from being careless, though. Nobody could accuse Preacher of that, either.

Once they were on the other side of the river, Preacher and Hawk rode on, with Hawk leading the string that consisted of the pack mule and the extra mounts. They didn't reach St. Louis until dusk, and as they spotted the lights of the town, Hawk exclaimed softly in surprise and said, "They must have many campfires in this village called St. Louis."

"Those ain't campfires," Preacher said. "They're lights shinin' through windows. Lamps and lanterns and candles. You'll see when we get there."

"Windows, like in the trading posts where we stopped from time to time?"

"Sort of, but a lot of these have glass in 'em." Hawk just shook his head in bafflement, so Preacher went on, "You'll see soon enough, when we get there."

More than likely, window glass wouldn't be the only thing Preacher would have to explain to his son before this visit was over. This was Hawk's first taste of so-called civilization, which held a lot of mysteries for someone accustomed to a simpler, more elemental life.

As they rode into the settlement sprawled along the west bank of the Mississippi, Hawk gazed in wonder at the buildings looming in the gathering shadows. He wrinkled his nose and said, "Ugh. It stinks."

"You're smellin' the docks and the area along the river," Preacher said. "It's a mite aromatic, all right. There are a lot of warehouses along there full of pelts, and not everybody's as careful about cleanin' and dryin' 'em as we are. They start to rot. Then you've got spoiled food and spilled beer and lots of folks who ain't exactly as fresh as daisies. It all mixes together until you get the smell you're experiencin' now."

Hawk shook his head. "The high country is better."

"You won't get any argument from me about that, boy . . . but this is where the money is."

"This thing you call money is worthless."

"Oh, it has its uses, as long as you don't get too attached to it. Your people trade with each other, and it's sort of the same thing."

"We trade things people can *use*," Hawk said. "It is not the same thing at all."

"Just keep your eyes open," Preacher said. "You'll learn."

And the youngster probably would learn some things he'd just as soon he hadn't, the mountain man thought.

The pelts were the most important thing to deal with, so Preacher headed first for the local office of the American Fur Company. Founded by John Jacob Astor in the early part of the century, the enterprise had grown into a virtual monopoly controlling all the fur trade in the United States. In recent years, the company had declined in its influence and control, a trend not helped by Astor's departure from the company he had started. But it was still operating, led now by a man named Ramsay Crooks, and Preacher knew he wouldn't get a better price for the furs anywhere else.

Despite the fact that night was falling and some businesses were closing for the day, the office of the American Fur Company, located in a sturdy building with a sprawling warehouse behind it, was still brightly lit. Preacher reined Horse to a stop in front of it and swung down from the saddle.

"Tie up these animals and keep an eye on 'em," Preacher told Hawk. "I'll go inside and talk to Vernon Pritchard. He runs this office, unless somethin's happened to him since the last time I was here." He added, "Dog, you stay out here, too."

Preacher wasn't sure it was a good idea to leave Hawk alone on the streets of St. Louis, but the youngster had to start getting used to the place sooner or later. Besides, Dog wouldn't let anything happen to him or any of the horses. Preacher took the steps leading up to the porch on the front of the building in a couple of bounds, then glanced back at Hawk, who was peering around wide-eyed, one more time before going into the building.

A man in a dusty black coat sat on a high stool behind a desk, scratching away with a quill pen as he entered figures in a ledger book. He had a tuft of taffy-colored hair on the top of his head and matching tufts above each ear, otherwise was bald. A pair of pince-nez clung precariously to the end of his long nose. He looked over the spectacles at Preacher and grinned as he tried to straighten up. A back permanently hunched from bending over a desk made that difficult.

"Preacher!" he said. "I didn't know if we'd see you this season."

"You didn't think anything would've happened to me, did you, Henry?"

"Well, of course not," the clerk said. "You're indestructible, Preacher. I fully expect that forty or fifty years from now, you'll still be running around those mountains out there, getting into all sorts of trouble."

Preacher laughed. "I'm gonna do my best to prove you right." He jerked a thumb over his shoulder. "Right now, though, I've got a load of pelts out there. Vernon around to make me an offer on 'em?"

Henry's smile disappeared and was replaced by a look of concern. "You just left them out there?"

"Dog's guardin' 'em. And I told my boy to keep an eye on 'em, too."

"You have a partner now?"

"My son," Preacher said.

That news made the clerk look startled again. He hemmed and hawed for a moment and then evidently decided he didn't want to press Preacher for the details. Instead he said, "Mr. Pritchard is in the warehouse. You can go on around."

"Thanks." Preacher paused. "Henry, why'd you say that about me leavin' the pelts outside, like it wasn't a good idea?"

"St. Louis has gotten worse in the past year, Preacher. There are thieves and cutthroats everywhere. I hate to walk back to my house at night." Henry reached down to a shelf under the desk and picked up an ancient pistol with a barrel that flared out at the muzzle. He displayed the weapon to Preacher and went on, "That's why I carry this."

"Put that sawed-off blunderbuss away," Preacher said. "You're makin' me nervous."

"Preacher being nervous." Henry shook his head. "I'll never live to see the day."

Preacher lifted a hand in farewell and went back outside. Just as he stepped onto the porch, he heard a harsh voice say, "Damn it, Nix, Jenks, look at that. That's a redskin sittin' there with a nice big load o' pelts. Hey, Injun, where'd you steal them furs?"

Preacher paused and eased sideways, out of the light that spilled through the door. He drifted into a shadow thick and dark enough to keep him from being noticed easily. He wanted to see what was going to happen.

Hawk had dismounted long enough to tie the animals' reins to the hitch rail in front of the office, then swung back up onto his pony, which he rode with a saddle now rather than bareback or with only a blanket, the way he had when he was younger. He stared impassively at the three men who swaggered toward him but didn't say anything.

They were big and roughly dressed. Preacher could tell that much in the gloom. He didn't need to see the details to know what sort of men they were. The clerk had warned him about the ruffians now making St. Louis a dangerous place, and Preacher knew he was looking at three examples of that.

"I'm talkin' to you, redskin," continued the man who had spoken earlier. "I want to know where you stole them furs. I know good an' well a lazy, good-for-nothin' Injun like you didn't work to trap 'em."

Hawk said something in the Absaroka tongue. The three men clearly didn't understand a word of it, but Preacher did. Hawk's words were a warning: "You should go away now, before I kill you."

One of the men laughed and said, "I guess he told you, Brice—although I ain't sure just what he told you."

Brice, the one who had spoken first, stepped forward enough so that the light from the doorway revealed the scowl on his face. He said, "Don't you jabber at me, boy." He waved an arm. "Go on, get outta here! You don't need them furs. Leave them here for white men, and those horses, too." He sneered. "You can keep that damn Injun pony. It probably ain't fit to carry a real man."

After spending months with Preacher, Charlie Todd, and Aaron Buckley, Hawk spoke English quite well. Only occasionally did he stumble over a word or have to search for the right one. So Preacher knew Hawk understood everything Brice said.

He also knew that Hawk had a short temper and probably wasn't going to put up with much more of this.

Brice came closer. "Are you not listenin' to me, boy? I said git! We're takin' those pelts."

"They are . . . my furs," Hawk said in English, slowly and awkwardly as if he wasn't sure what he was saying. "Please . . . do not . . . steal them."

In the shadows on the porch, Preacher grinned. Other than that, he was motionless. Hawk was baiting those would-be thieves, and Preacher had a pretty good idea what the outcome was going to be. He wouldn't step in unless it was necessary.

"Don't you mouth off to me, redskin," Brice blustered. "Get outta here, or you're gonna get the beatin' of your life."

"Please," Hawk said. "Do not hurt me."

Brice grunted in contempt and reached up.

"You had your chance," he said. "Now I'm gonna teach you a lesson, you red ni—"

He closed his hands on Hawk's buckskin shirt to drag him off the pony.

Then, a split second later, he realized he might as well have grabbed hold of a mountain lion.

Hawk's leg shot out. The moccasin-shod heel cracked into Brice's head and jolted his head back. As Brice staggered a couple of steps away, Hawk swung his other leg over the pony's back and dived at the other two men.

They both let out startled yells when Hawk kicked their friend, and one of them clawed at a pistol stuck behind his belt. Before he could pull the weapon free, Hawk crashed into them and drove them both off their feet.

He hit the ground rolling and came upright as Brice recovered his balance from the kick and charged at Hawk with a shout of rage. The young man darted aside nimbly as Brice tried to catch him in a bear hug that would have crushed his ribs.

Hawk twisted, clubbed his hands together, and slammed them into the small of Brice's back as the man's momentum carried him past. Brice cried out in pain and arched his back, then stumbled and went down hard, face-first, plowing into the hard-packed dirt of the street.

Hawk whirled to face the other two men, who were struggling to get up. One of them he met with a straight, hard punch that landed squarely on the man's nose. Even from where Preacher stood on the porch, he heard bone and cartilage crunch. The man went back down a lot faster than he had gotten up and stayed down this time.

The third man had a chance to spring toward Hawk and managed to get his right arm around the youngster's neck from behind. He clamped down with the grip and used his heavier weight to force Hawk forward and down. His left hand grasped his right wrist to tighten the choke hold. He brought up his right knee and planted it in Hawk's back. That move proved the man was an experienced brawler, because now with one good heave, he could snap Hawk's neck.

Connect with Us

Visit us online at
KensingtonBooks.com
to read more from your favorite authors, see books
by series, view reading group guides, and more.

Join us on social media

for sneak peeks, chances to win books and prize packs,
and to share your thoughts with other readers.

facebook.com/kensingtonpublishing
twitter.com/kensingtonbooks

Tell us what you think!

To share your thoughts, submit a review,
or sign up for our eNewsletters, please visit:
KensingtonBooks.com/TellUs.